Lines of Control

A Novel

by

Robert Sperber

ISBN: 978-0-578-00811-0

To JoAnn,

my present;

Amanda and Katherine,

my future; and

Seymour and Frances,

my past

1

D ana Brentano could not believe what she saw in the dark of the medical laboratory at James Buchanan University Hospital: a body, clearly that of a man, crumpled in a corner between a lab table and a glass-enclosed bookcase.

She was alone in the lab, having come in to catch up on some work. As a third-year medical student at James Buchanan, she did everything she could to make sure she got high marks, including helping out pre-med students on lab experiments. While this was not strictly for a grade, it counted toward what the university considered extra points for work above and beyond what was required. She expected to come to the lab briefly this night, check to make sure some experiments were catalogued and stored properly, then go home.

She did not expect this. Flipping on the light switch, putting her purse and papers down on a lab table, she rushed over to the body and shook it, trying to wake the person up. Oh my God, she thought, don't tell me he's dead. Her gasp was audible when she turned the body over and instantly recognized the corpse: Scott Karakas, a fellow third-year medical student and, for the past few months, the man she had been seeing in rather intense physical encounters.

Such encounters were the last thing that anyone who knew Dana would have expected of her. Pretty and well groomed, with neat, short brown hair, clothes that seemed to be always creased in all the right places, she seemed the classic girl next door who was mainly interested in doing the right thing and playing by the rules.

Yet her relationship with Scott, only a few months old, had opened her up in a number of ways to new experiences, including unexpected rendezvous in somewhat unorthodox places, including the lab tables in this very room. She found these forbidden comings-together exciting, and while they had tried to be as discreet as circumstances would allow and she thought rather successfully, word had begun to seep out that they were a hot couple on campus, if not *the* hot couple. So the shock of finding what appeared to be a dead man in the lab was compounded by the fact that it was the man who had done so much to make her feel alive.

"Scott, Scott," she said, shaking him almost violently.

She looked around. As far as she could tell, there was no blood, no sign of violence. What had happened? Had Scott simply had a heart attack or stroke and died right then and there? How long has the body been here? The last students would have left the building by 6:00 p.m., anxious to get out on Friday for the weekend, especially given that it was late January and snow was predicted for later that evening throughout the D.C. area, including the city's northwest side, where James Buchanan was located. It was possible someone else came in after that, maybe from the cleaning crew. Of course, she herself had come in around 9 p.m., so she really couldn't rule anything out.

Stepping back from the body, she reached for her purse and, unable to take her eyes off Scott, after some fumbling, found her cell phone. She forced her eyes onto the phone and dialed 911.

"My name is Dana Brentano. I'm a third-year medical student at James Buchanan University School of Medicine, and I just found the…dead body of a fellow student in one of the science labs."

2

Charlotte Westbrook took aim and fired. The red dot on the second ring out from the bulls eye showed that she had hit her mark, maybe not exactly dead center, but close enough.

"Not bad," she mused, putting the laser gun down on her oak desktop.

"Don't let the press catch you doing that anymore," said Lewis Sullivan, a crumpled but distinguished-looking man in his early 60's, with a mane of silvery hair and glasses he wore on a metal chain around his neck, sitting on the sofa to her right. You've taken more than enough criticism from them and others about that thing."

Charlotte laughed, smoothed her shoulder length brown hair and pushed her chair back against the wall. Yes, the press had given her a drubbing, both when she first got the job as HHS Inspector General, and later, when what it called some of her "eccentricities" began coming out, like the laser pistol. Her critics liked to say that she was out of control. Charlotte made it a point not to respond to those kinds of attacks. It wasn't her style. Not to mention that, in her more private moments, she wasn't sure they were wrong.

"Better they write about your real achievements," Lewis continued.

Good old Lewis, faithful and a ferocious champion of protecting the public's money. Charlotte's successes in cracking down on Medicare fraud – she had increased recoveries of government money by 42 percent since she took office two years ago – was much owed to his relentless dedication to make sure lawbreakers were caught and punished. Together, they had stifled much of her original publicity, especially the articles that questioned her competency, saying she had been appointed to the job only because of her father.

As chief counsel in the Office of the Inspector General, Lewis made recommendations to Charlotte on which hospitals, physician practices, home health agencies or other health care organizations to pursue, and under what charges. His team of auditors investigated and his team of attorneys prosecuted. The result over the past two years had been record prosecutions and recoveries of government money from fraudulent Medicare claims and other improper practices.

That, after all, was their job. Most departments in the federal government have an inspector general. At the Department of Defense, the inspector general roots out fraud in military procurement, like hammers costing $200. At the Department of Transportation, where she met and worked with Lewis when they were both attorneys on the inspector general's staff, they investigated and, for the most part, successfully prosecuted, improper payments to highway contractors. At the Department of Health and Human Services' main offices in Washington, D.C., which oversees Medicare, Medicaid and other federal health-related programs, they were doing the same, only now it was against doctors, hospitals and other health care "providers" who ripped off the public.

As Inspector General, Charlotte was not only the public face of fraud enforcement, she also set the tone for the department and let it be known that cases would be followed to their logical conclusion, with special favors to none. It was a point she took special pride in, having seen politics play a role in other government departments. She knew, from her years watching her father in the Senate, how Washington worked. It was a game she didn't like much, but one she knew how to play.

"Alright, fun's over," she said to Lewis. "Let's review where we are."

Lewis, took some papers out of a battered brown valise.

"Of the 26 cases we now have under way, the ones that look most promising are the three involving large integrated health systems taking gifts from pharmaceutical companies in exchange for dispensing their drugs. Two of those go to trial this spring. I would expect not only several million dollars in fines, but a number of doctors being excluded from Medicare."

That seemed only just, Charlotte thought, but with some sympathy for the doctors, several of whom would now probably have to find a new way to make a living. While this made little difference to Lewis – a crime is a crime and the law is all that protects us from the mob, were two of his guiding standards – Charlotte at times found herself taking a more nuanced view, especially when she felt the health care professionals she and Lewis investigated and then prosecuted were people who simply made bad choices. And the punishments could be severe.

Exclusion from Medicare – meaning a doctor could no longer bill the government for treating senior citizens – was for a minimum of five years and, in more cases than not, meant the end of a doctor's business. After all, in some localities with large senior populations, such as Florida, almost all of a physician's business was with Medicare patients. Take that away and you might as well shut the doctor down. And even in areas with smaller populations of seniors, Medicare might account for 40% of business. That's a big dent for any practice to handle, she knew.

But from the government's point of view, including Lewis, his staff of attorneys and often Charlotte herself, that was fitting. After all, was it good medicine for doctors to accept junkets, thinly disguised as educational trips, from major drug companies in exchange for prescribing a brand-name drug to elderly patients, then turning around and billing Medicare for it?

Or should the government pay for referrals doctors make to send patients to costly MRI centers or physical therapy, when the establishments they send them to are partly owned by those very same doctors, or by family members?

Was it right for doctors and hospitals to "upcode" various medical procedures because those higher codes got more reimbursement from Medicare? Or to "unbundle" procedures into separate codes because they got paid more that way?

Was it right for hospitals to hire chief administrators from various physician practices, with the implicit understanding that those practices would then refer patients to that hospital for Medicare-reimbursable operations? Was it right for doctors at teaching hospitals – where residents are trained while working on real patients – to bill Medicare for supervising those students, when in fact they were not supervising them, in some cases not even in the building?

Lewis ran through a number of these cases, letting Charlotte know the office's progress on each. In some cases, there were setbacks, but in many, settlements rather than trials were in the making. The government and the health care providers often preferred reaching a settlement. It was better than a lengthy and expensive trial that would sap time and money from all, with the health care provider reaping bad publicity in the process.

Lewis put the papers down. Fond as he was of his meetings with Charlotte, the afternoon was drawing on, and he had to return to his office.

Charlotte, however, appeared to be in a mood to talk. "How's the remodeling going?"

"The upstairs library is almost done, but we still have months of work ahead. James sometimes loses his patience with all the workmen and says we should just move into the Watergate until the work is finished. But I don't have a problem with it. I like staying in familiar surroundings."

James, a public relations specialist with his own firm in northwest Washington, was Lewis' life partner, and their squabbles over the renovation of their Capitol Hill townhouse had become part of the daily talk in the office. It seemed every day they had a disagreement about how one room should be done, or the professionalism of the renovators. But, Charlotte knew, they had been together 13 years. For whatever reason, it seemed to work.

Not that I'm any kind of judge, she thought, looking at her ringless left hand.

Lewis saw where she was looking and laughed. "You do need to get out there a bit. Strongly as I feel about what we do here, there is more to life than one's career."

Charlotte raised her hand. "Let's not have that conversation again."

"I do worry about you, Charlotte. You don't want to wind up alone in your apartment with 40 cats, all because no one could live up to your image of your father. Which reminds me," he said with a twinkle in his eye, letting Charlotte know that this was going to be a good one. "I haven't heard much from you about Senator Donelin recently."

"I don't see why you should. We're not scheduled for our testimony before his committee for a few weeks."

"I meant on a more personal level. After all, the two of you did play house in your prepubescent years."

Charlotte laughed. But she wasn't going to bite. "Yes, well, Mack is a friend of long standing. Funny. When we were kids, we used to wonder if one day we'd both be powerful people like my dad, and now he's the chairman of the Senate Appropriations committee and I'm the HHS Inspector General."

"His rise had a lot to do with your father taking him under his wing. Your dad must be very proud of his star pupil. And, of course, there has been this ambiguous are-they-or-aren't-they relationship between the two of you."

"I'm actually going to see the Senator this weekend," Charlotte said, referring to her father, who was always referred to in her office as the Senator, even though he was retired and her office dealt with a number of other senators, including Donelin. But in Charlotte Westbrook's office, David Westbrook would always be *the Senator*. In mentioning him now, Charlotte was hoping that at least changing the subject from her love life – or rather, the lack of one – would get Lewis off the subject.

"How's he doing without the trappings of power?"

"Seems to miss it a bit, but he just loves it in St. Michael's," referring to the small touristy village on Maryland's Eastern Shore. "I think whenever he thinks of returning to the Senate, he looks out at his boat and the life he has now, and decides that retirement is the best thing after all." She paused. "And it's been better for our relationship, too."

"My father mellowed in his retiring years as well, although not quite enough to accept…my lifestyle."

"Yes, well…you're doing well now, Lewis, and your mom is still alive."

"And still the queen of gin rummy at the assisted living center. She is a blessing. My one connection to the past. I don't know what I'd do without her."

A knock at the door interrupted them.

"Excuse me," said an aide, poking his head in. "But I thought you'd like to see this. From the *Washington Post's* web page." He handed Charlotte the paper, then left. Charlotte read the article, then arched her eyebrows.

"Medical student found dead last night in the lab at James Buchanan."

"Not connected to our fraud investigation there in any way? I don't see how…"

"No, wouldn't make sense. Students are not the ones who commit fraud, including at James Buchanan. Why would they? The problems always end up resting with the administrators, the doctors or the staff. The article just says that the student, Scott Karakas, was found dead in the lab by another student. Cause of death yet to be determined, but there were no signs of foul play or anything like that."

"I would think not. Those students work incredible hours, you know. When you get only three hours of sleep many nights each week, that has to take an incredible toll on your body, even if you're only 24 or 25. And when you finish medical school and start your residency, it gets even worse."

Charlotte nodded. "Leaving lots of room to cut corners, for everyone involved, although this may have been nothing more than simple exhaustion. Sometimes a body cannot hold out."

3

Dana Brentano felt uncomfortable under Detective Alphonse Petrelli, Jr.'s stare. She didn't know how to answer.

"C'mon, Dana, it's not that big of a deal. Lots of students have relationships. I just need to know about yours and Scott's."

"I think what she's objecting to is your going into all the details of it," suggested Nick Rosen. Dana cast Nick a quick, that's-not-the-best-thing-to-say glance.

Petrelli sighed and pushed his large frame back in his wheeled chair behind his metal desk, covered with papers, newspaper clipping, folders and a few personal items, including a signed baseball. A green desk lamp sat on the desk across from where he was sitting, and Dana and Nick were seated in separate chairs facing him at the third district headquarters of the Washington's metropolitan police, at 1620 V Street, NW. Around them, detectives and uniformed police were conducting the business of the day, chasing down leads, interviewing suspects, calming grieving relatives, or just doing paperwork. If it weren't for the concentration Petrelli was forcing to the subject at hand – Scott's death three days before – this place might have the atmosphere of a train station, Nick thought.

"Can't help it, that's the kind of thing we need to find out. It's adding up the little pieces like this that allow us to rule out anything other than natural death."

"Do you really think someone actually…killed…Scott?" Dana asked. Quiet for most of the interview – she had never been to a police station before and asked Nick to go along with her, if only to bolster her confidence – she spoke up now, bothered by the thought that anyone would have wanted to do her boyfriend serious harm.

"Not really." Petrelli studied their faces, and the two students studied his, all three of them seemingly less than satisfied with what this revealed. "But a case is a case. Look, people die every day, the overwhelming majority from natural causes. Most of those, however, are older people, or people with a history of some kind of illness, whether it's their own history or a family history. But when a 25-year-old young man, in apparently excellent health, suddenly drops dead on you without explanation, it just makes one check other possibilities."

"I thought the medical examiner ruled it a heart attack."

"Yes, yes, he did, and ordinarily that would be enough." He paused. "I just want to rule out anything else." He paused again, then said kindly, "Look, Dana, I know you've been through a lot and I don't want to make things worse for you…or for you, Nick, I understand the three of you hung out a lot together. Just help an old detective – well, old by the standards of you kids, I suppose, since I'm 55 – sort out a few details. Okay? And then we'll be done."

"Dana, tell him what he wants to know. You know, it's not like this is an episode of 'Law and Order'," said Nick, referring to the long-running police and courtroom drama.

Dana gave a tight smile. Nick's rather sardonic sense of humor was not always appropriate. Still, he was probably right.

"Alright, yes, to answer your question, Detective, the relationship with Scott was strongly physical. That doesn't mean we didn't really care about each other, though."

"I understand," Petrelli said. "Would you meet for the, uh, physical part of your relationship in unusual places?"

"What do you mean?"

"Like the lab tables in the hospital in evening, when everyone else was gone? Or in the hospital broom closets, even when the corridors were quite busy during the daytime?"

Dana felt the blood rush to her cheeks, unsure whether it was blushing from embarrassment or flushing from this intrusion into her privacy. She could sense Nick trying to hide a smirk. Best be done with it.

"Both," she said quietly.

"I see. And how long did this go on?"

"Scott and I were involved on and off for about five months," she said, choking up suddenly, as the words brought home to her the reality that there would be no additional months. Tears welled up, and Petrelli offered her a box of tissues. She took one.

"Scott and I were very different people, maybe that was the attraction," she continued. "He had a lot of flair, a style about him, dashing really. He came by that through his family and all that breeding, having gone to Princeton, I guess."

"Not your story, though, was it?"

"No. I started out here on a loan. My parents, if you want to know, detective, especially my father, didn't want me to go to medical school. They're quite a bit older than most parents of students my age. Almost a generation older, and they tend to think that way, too. Plus they have a limited amount of money – my dad is a retired real estate broker and my mom worked in customer service at a magazine publishing company – and I have two younger brothers, so they—"

"—thought it better to spend the college money on the boys."

Dana nodded. "I've had to make a special case with them for every advancement I've taken. They're very old-fashioned like that. Scott seemed, well, he seemed so different from that world. Everything came easy to him, he had two sisters, one of whom is also at Princeton and the other who already has a successful career, and he had no problem with anybody doing whatever they wanted to. And why shouldn't he have felt that way? Money was never a problem with him."

"Did you resent him for that?"

"No, not at all, Detective. It was just different, that's all." She paused. "He died from a heart attack! Why are you prolonging this?"

Detective Petrelli turned his attention to Nick.

"And how about you?"

Nick took the question the way it was meant: *Why are you even here?*

"I came down to give Dana support."

Petrelli smiled. "I see."

Nick shifted his small, wiry frame uncomfortably in his chair, nervously touched his dark curly hair and adjusted his glasses. "Scott, Dana and I were good friends. Like you said yourself a moment ago, we spent a lot of time together. Movies, hung out at the student union, just talked. Why shouldn't I want to help her out?"

"You were the third wheel in the relationship. That's a classic story."

Dana jumped in. "Detective, you keep trying to find motives for something that didn't happen. First, you still haven't told us why you think

Scott died from anything other than natural causes. And second, even if he did, which I extremely doubt, now you are implying that Nick was somehow jealous of Scott's relationship with me."

Petrelli nodded calmly. "That's exactly right. So, Nick, were you?"

Nick had had enough of Petrelli's insinuations. He had never been the first choice of girls, going back to high school. At five foot six and somewhat geeky looking, he played the role that so many Jewish boys of his age played: smart, funny, but not the romantic choice for most girls. So he settled in as the best friend.

"It may be difficult for someone of your generation to understand, Detective, but it is not uncommon these days for men and women to be just friends. That's the way it is with me and Dana, and Scott had no problem with that. So why should you?"

"Oh, I see," said Petrelli, mock enlightenment on his face. "So what, then, do you do for female companionship, Nick?"

"Is that really any of your business?"

"Hasn't it really been more than frustrating for you, the lack of romantic relationships? There was that incident at the Improper Fraction last year. Almost got charged with assault, I believe."

What has this detective done, investigated us before we arrived? "Now, that was a totally different thing."

Petrelli picked up one of the files from his desk and read. "'Rosen, a first-year medical student at James Buchanan University, apparently attacked Byron Kilgore, a fellow student, with a beer bottle.'"

"My, my," Petrelli said, pausing in his reading to look at Nick – "'swinging it wildly at his head but missing, according to three eyewitnesses. The incident was apparently the result of his being upset that Kilgore was at a local college bar, the Improper Fraction, with a female student he had dated a few times, Susan Donat. Kilgore then apparently knocked the bottle from Rosen's hand, and hit Rosen in the face, knocking him down. Other patrons then held both men back, with two police officers from this squad arriving shortly thereafter."

Petrelli put the file down. "My, my," he said again, looking at Nick. "It can be frustrating, can't it?"

"That was one time, it happened over a year ago. You can't think that—"

"Nick, relax, I understand. Look at me. I'm married now, but that's only been for the past seven years. Before that, I was a single, overweight Italian-American police detective, who spent most of my time on the job, and without much of a social life. And I knew I wasn't the first choice of most of the ladies, that is, until my wife came along, bless her heart. And there were times I was the third wheel, just like you, going along with couples, maybe because I liked them and was their friend, but maybe, maybe, if I was really honest with myself, maybe because I was lonely and, sure, wanted a sympathetic voice from a pretty girl, even if that voice came from my best friend's girl."

Nick and Dana almost spoke up simultaneously, "But it wasn't like that, Detective."

Petrelli smiled understandingly. "Well, you're both young and like all young people, you think that human nature has changed with your generation. But, like you said, Dana, there's really no crime here, at least not that we know of."

The phone rang on Petrelli's desk. He picked it up, identified himself, listened without showing much emotion, then hung up.

"Unfortunately, Dana and Nick, it seems like my instincts were right. Scott Karakas' death was not from natural causes."

Nick and Dana sat bolt upright in their chairs.

"He was murdered?" Dana asked, her voice very quiet.

"I'm afraid so." He paused a second. "You're both medical students. Have you ever heard of succinylcholine?"

"It's used before general anesthesia when doctors operate on a patient in intensive care," Dana said. "It gets the muscles to relax, which facilitates the anesthesia and makes other things easier, like endotracheal intubation." Dana paused, realizing that Petrelli might not be familiar with medical terms. "Placing a tube down your throat." Petrelli nodded as she continued. "It's popular with doctors, especially in emergency rooms, because it acts fast, but lasts the shortest amount of time. It's readily available in most hospitals, but can also be bought in many pharmacies"

"I'd say you have a bright future in medicine, Dana," Petrelli said, "but I don't know about you, Nick."

Nick felt his face flush. "It's also been used, in rare cases, to kill people. That's the point you're driving at, isn't it, detective?"

"Tell me more about that, Nick."

"This isn't a secret, a lot of doctors and others involved with medicine know it. In fact, detective, any substance taken in extreme quantities can kill you, even something like table salt, did you know that?"

Petrelli looked at the report. "Nothing in here about table salt."

Nick sat in his chair, silently fuming. Petrelli leaned forward, looking at both of them.

"Nick is correct. Any substance can kill you, or at least induce great harm, if taken in excess amounts. But many of those substances will readily make themselves apparent when a medical examiner does the inspection. And as you know, there are other substances that do not make themselves readily apparent. At least not unless you are looking for them specifically. Succinylcholine is one of those."

"What are you saying, detective, that someone injected Scott with a lethal dose and then disguised it to look like he had a heart attack?" Dana asked.

"That's almost right, Dana. Once our lab used mass spectrometry and found traces of succinylcholine in his tissues, it began looking for injection marks and, sure enough, found one at the back of his neck. Fairly recent, too, so it most likely was the entry point. But I wouldn't say the killer disguised things to look like a heart attack. That would have just happened. Whether it was his intent to disguise it, or whether he simply didn't care, I just don't know. As you probably know, succinylcholine in proper doses" – he looked at his report – "intravenously, that would be about 1.0 to 1.5 milligrams per kilogram of body weight, does not normally do any harm. But in much larger doses, it not only causes your muscles to relax. It paralyzes them. This causes an individual to stop breathing. It may also cause a heart to stop working, hence Scott's apparently 'natural' heart attack.

"There's one other thing, too, that hasn't been mentioned in the press reports. Mr. Karakas had faint, very faint, ligature marks around his throat."

"Like someone choked him to death?" Nick asked.

Petrelli shook his head. "No, it was the succinylcholine that killed him, no doubt about that. But there may have been some kind of a struggle beforehand, or maybe not. The marks were too faint to be recent. Could have been caused by a lot of things, maybe a fight he had been in some time ago; some people bruise easily – he could have accidentally caused them himself if he had reason to grab hold of his own throat. That's what made me want to investigate this further, to answer your original question. But it turns out that they were not related to the cause of death. He was killed by the succinylcholine."

Dana felt herself in shock. *Scott was murdered.*

Petrelli tossed the report on his desk. "Not something a medical examiner would have looked for, unless he had reason to look for it."

He looked at them both.

"As my wife tells me, I have a suspicious mind."

4

"Now gently put your thumb and forefinger into the chest cavity and see if you can feel the tumor."

Dr. Peter Kenyon knew there was nothing unusual about this instruction – he had given it to residents innumerable times over the past 15 years – but there was nonetheless the shared sense of anticipation as he watched a resident, for the first time, actually get his hands inside a patient during an operation.

They were in one of several operating rooms at James Buchanan University Hospital, where he was supervising the work of a first year resident. He had been working with this young man, Bernie Rubin, for some weeks now, and found his medical knowledge impressive, but his confidence in the actual operation room less than it should be. Right now, in fact, Bernie was nervously reaching into the chest cavity of the unconscious patient, looking for what imaging had shown to be a tumor the size of a handball.

"Some caution is of course necessary, Dr. Rubin," Peter said, "but not so much that you need to take a bus to get to the desired location."

Bernie grimaced. Dr. Kenyon, in his early '40s, tall and just short of handsome with a full head of black hair, was popular among the students, if only because of his knowledge and teaching style, which was a combination of firm direction with gentle humor. But there were times when a little bit of quiet might be just as effective, Bernie thought.

He paused. "I've got it."

"Okay. Now let's get a visual." Peter motioned for a nurse to adjust the light so it showed the area where Bernie was working.

"Get a feel for its dimensions," Peter continued. "Then take your scalpel and gently but firmly cut around the area and remove it."

His gloved hands covered with blood, Bernie did what he was told, cutting through the tissue holding the tumor in place. It came loose rather quickly, somewhat surprising him. He removed it, then set it in the dish located nearby for just that purpose.

"Now let's look for any other problems, other blockages, any parts of the tumor you may have missed."

"I don't see any," Bernie said, looking some more. "No, it looks clean."

"Alright, then let's close up. You've done that before."

Bernie nodded, relieved that the worst was over. Peter continued to watch as Bernie finished the work, finally closing the chest cavity with sutures.

"Where's that sponge?" Peter asked suddenly. "Bernie, you didn't—?"

"It's right here, Doctor," said the nurse, pointing to a yellow sponge on the table. "Honestly, Doctor," she said, shaking her head as a much relieved Bernie relaxed. "He does that to new residents every now and then. First time for you?"

Bernie nodded.

The nurse gave Peter a look, shook her head, then headed for the scrub room.

Peter looked at Bernie, chuckled at the resident's slightly bothered expression, then headed for the scrub room himself.

"Overall, nice job, Dr. Rubin," he said to Bernie as he left. "I wouldn't tell the patient about the sponge joke when he awakens."

Peter raised his glass to make a toast. His wife and their guests looked at him expectantly.

"And here's to our meeting on Monday with Arun and with Paul Holden, without whom we might be in even more trouble than we probably are already actually in."

There were some groans, notably from Dr. Lyle Steadman, who was there with his wife, Angela, a somewhat mousy woman who looked about 10 years older than the 45 years her Maryland driver's license showed.

She and Lyle were among the dozen or so people at the home of Peter and his wife, Marjorie, an attractive redhead who, everyone knew, was a key player in one of the more prominent architectural firms in the District. She had had a hand in designing the plans for the new baseball stadium for the city's blighted Southeast, overlooking the Anacostia River. The area could use the economic development badly, and it was hoped by almost everyone in the city that the stadium, despite its huge cost, would be a spur to further development, just as construction of the Verizon Center years before had made a difference near the Chinatown area.

"Peter," Marjorie now said, somewhat disapprovingly. "You would all be a lot worse off without Paul as the university hospital's compliance officer…and probably a lot less anxious than you are now if you had listened to him earlier. And you know that Arun, as James Buchanan's chief administrator, has to keep Paul fixed on the compliance ball. This meeting on Monday will probably save you all a lot of grief later on."

"That's why I'm toasting them," Peter said, his arm with the glass of red wine still extended as he stood by his seat in their large dining room at their home on Saturday evening in one of the wealthier sections of the District's northwest side. The other guests raised their glasses, some clinked them together, then downed them. Peter sat down.

"Honestly," Marjorie said to him quietly. "If you weren't known to be such a cutup, I would have taken you seriously."

"Truth is, I couldn't decide how much I really meant seriously."

"If you really think about it, all of it," put in Dr. Jennifer Capaldi, in her early 40s, short and brown-haired in a way that could just pass for pretty, who was there with her husband, Dr. Michael Capaldi, a slightly overweight otolaryngologist with a small physician practice, "we really should be glad that Arun hired Paul."

"That's the advantage of working in a six-doctor practice," Michael said. "You don't have to worry about this kind of thing. We're too small of a target for OIG to go after."

"Don't be so sure," Lyle said. The eyes on his narrow face, which often gave the impression of someone whose head had been squeezed into its current form by a wine press, squinted up even more than usual behind his metal frame glasses, making his sunken cheeks and high cheekbones look even more pronounced. His receding and graying hairline, complete with fraying widow's peak in the front, only accentuated the impression. "I've read that the government goes after physician practices, and not just the 300-doctor ones. These guys are bloodsuckers. If you have any kind of a medical degree, they figure you're fair game."

"Yes, but they can't collect much from a practice like mine. What are they going to get, a couple of hundred thousand dollars in fines and restitution? Don't take me wrong, that would probably wipe us out, but they can make the same effort and get a multi-million settlement by going after a large hospital like James Buchanan. And, c'mon, OIG and the Justice Department have to go back to Congress and justify their existence when they request more funding each year. What's going to play better when you're before a Congressional committee: that you drove a six-doctor practice out of business and collected $200,000, or that you reached a settlement with a major hospital or health care chain that brought in $350 million?"

"I'm just saying that they do go after some small practices. It's a fact."

"They do it so they can say they're even-handed. It's not where their attention is."

"Gentlemen," said Jennifer. "Let's just agree that anyone the government goes after is in for some rough sledding."

There were murmurs of agreement around the table.

"And hence my toast. I'm sure Paul is going to read us the riot act for not doing some compliance thing we should have been doing and maybe he is right. But that doesn't mean we have to enjoy it," said Peter, as a caterer brought in a large roast on stoneware platter.

"And now there's a student death, on top of everything else," put in Jennifer. It had been three days since Scott's body was found. "I knew Scott Karakas a bit. He was a nice young man and I thought he had a good future ahead of him. What a shame."

"He was seeing Dana Brentano, wasn't he?" Peter asked.

Jennifer nodded. "On and off." She paused, then added, with a sly smile, "I understand they made good use of the broom closets."

"She's pretty shook up, and I can't say I blame her," Peter said. "Imagine finding the body of someone you're close to like that."

"Anything definite on the cause of death?" asked Lyle.

"Not that I've heard. Whether he had a weak heart or a brain aneurysm…"

"I'm surprised, given the stress of this place, that more students, not to mention staff, aren't found that way."

"Now, Lyle…" Jennifer often found herself thinking that Lyle would himself be found dead one day of a peptic ulcer, the amount of stress he put himself through being the chief culprit.

"C'mon, the two of you know it. For Christ's sake, we're in the business of saving lives. We spend years in medical school, in residency, and more, and now some attorneys in the government are going to tell us how to do our jobs?"

"Shall I carve?" Peter asked Marjorie in what she took as a welcome attempt to get the conversation back on a more pleasant note.

"You know you love to," his wife said. "You are, after all, a surgeon. Ever since we met when we were both on vacation in Vienna twelve years ago, he's been like this. He loves to be the host."

"And why not?" Peter asked, looking around the room. "A lovely dinner with a lovely wife – given me the best twelve years of my life" – he could see Marjorie blush and loved that they still were so enamored of each other after so many years – " in a lovely house, with great and true colleagues and friends. If this isn't the good life, I don't know what is."

"I have to let him carve when he says things like that!" Everyone laughed appreciably as she looked up at Peter. "Of course, darling, what you didn't tell them was that when we met in Vienna, we spent a lot of our time not at beautiful, romantic restaurants – we went to some, that's where I noticed this desire of his to be the host – but at medical seminars."

"And back then it didn't matter if your trip was paid for by a medical equipment manufacturer or drug maker," said Lyle, to sighs from almost everyone else at the table as they realized that there was no stopping him. "What does it matter, after all, who pays for it if you increase your knowledge and the networking with other doctors helps everyone?"

"I don't know," another of the guests put in. "If a pharmaceutical company paid for your trip, would you recommend more of its drugs to your patients?"

"I would never do such a thing. My recommendations are always based on what's best for the patient."

"Yes, but what if it wasn't that simple? Suppose you have two pharmaceutical companies, each with a competing drug that does basically the same thing, let's say to treat heart arrhythmia, and they are both good. One offers you an all-expense-paid educational junket to Hawaii, and the other doesn't. Again, each drug is equally effective with the patient. Which one are you going to take?"

"Well, in that case, probably the one with the trip," said Lyle, to some laughter. "But what is wrong with that? The patient is not being hurt in any way if the drugs have the same efficacy and one does not carry more risks than the other. Even more so if they are the same price, so the patient is not out of pocket for any more either way. At that point, why shouldn't I make a business decision?"

He picked up his wine glass and took a deep swig, confident he had made a point.

"Because, Lyle, not every doctor is as ethical as you," Marjorie said. "And when you consider the number of doctors and the number of pharmaceutical sales reps – many of them very attractive young women, there was an article in *The New York Times* the other day about how drug companies intentionally seek out former cheerleaders for these jobs, knowing the effect on male doctors – in the country, you are going to have some doctors being less ethical than you, and prescribing drugs for the wrong reasons."

"Granted," said Lyle. "I'm sure that does happen, unfortunately. But since when are the innocent punished for the sins of the guilty? I'm sure there are doctors who cheat on their taxes, too, but that doesn't mean every doctor gets audited."

"And OIG doesn't investigate every hospital and doctor."

"No, but they do put a lot of innocent health care providers through the wringer, in many cases for innocent mistakes. Some coder or biller makes a series of errors, the doctor doesn't know better and signs off on them, and next thing you know, they are excluded from doing business with Medicare, and have to close up shop." Lyle was indignant.

"The thing is," Peter said, quite thoughtfully in comparison to the heated exchange that Lyle and Marjorie had just had, "that what we are seeing in society is a loss of trust in individual decisionmaking."

"Uh oh. Here we go," Marjorie said.

"Now bear with me," Peter said, patting his Marjorie's hand. "Back in the old days, say the 1970s, when a doctor made a decision, whether it was about a drug or about how much supervision to give a resident, it was assumed he or she brought his or her best judgment to bear. Of course, as with any profession, there were bad players, and there were good players who made mistakes. But the medical community was generally trusted and highly respected. If a doctor prescribed a drug, no one though it was because he got some financial benefit from it.

"But what's happened ever since the government has begun investigating the medical community," he continued, "is that the presumption of trust is gone, and not just in doctors themselves, but in the individual decisionmaking. Now, every time a doctor prescribes a drug, or decides that some residents need less supervision than others, they have to second guess themselves and ask, 'Can I get into trouble over this?' Some might think that kind of questioning is a good thing. But there's something sad and disturbing about it. What does it say about our society when no one trusts anyone anymore, that you don't even trust the doctor who is there to make you better or even save you life?"

There was a silence in the room, as Peter's words were absorbed.

"Darling," said Marjorie. "One thing you'll never lose, and that's your ability to bring a lively conversation to a dead stop."

5

The *Washington Post* newsroom didn't look all that different from the way it did in the movie, "All the President's Men." Gone were the typewriters and the pre-numbered writing paper, all replaced by computers. But the rest of the newsroom – the wide open space, bright lights and the sense of news in the making as reporters, editors and others walked rapidly from one part of the room to another as if on some urgent mission, remained. And while this activity consumed the room's ambiance, individual reporters sat at their desks, either typing into computer keyboards, searching the Internet, or on the phone with sources, seemingly able to blot out all the noise and activity around them.

Eileen Ashburton was at one of these desks. Tall, thin and about 25 with long brown hair and long legs, she was reading a document on line when a thick hairy hand rapped on the side of her monitor. Looking up startled, she saw the round, middle-aged face of the assistant managing editor, Michael Epstein.

"What are you working on?" he asked.

"I'm looking to see if Congress plans to make any retroactive changes to the physician fee schedule cuts that Medicare issued in November."

Epstein shook his head. Every year, it seemed, this ritual occurred. Each October or November, Medicare comes out with the new rates it will pay physicians in the coming calendar year for all the procedures it reimburses – about 7,500 in all, each identified by a code. In recent years, these fees had been cut for many physicians, tightening the economic noose around their necks, as running a physician practice became less profitable. Congress would then step in and sometimes restore part or all of those cuts. But with the new year already a month over, Congress was particularly late in reviewing what action it would take this time. Eileen, bulldog reporter as always, wasn't taking any chances, checking up on various Congressional and Medicare web sites and elsewhere every day, waiting to see if any further changes were in the offing.

"They're going to do it," Eileen said, "release something at the end of the week so it won't get much attention. That's my guess."

"I wanted to show you this." He handed her two sheets of paper. She could see they were copies of a police report and, reading further, that they concerned the murder of a medical student at James Buchanan University Hospital. Apparently, it was first thought that the student had died of natural causes, but an autopsy showed that he had been injected with succinylcholine.

"Interesting," she said, handing the sheets back to Epstein. "Are Daniels and Costigan on this?" she asked, referring to two of the paper's better police reporters.

"Yeah, but I thought *you* might be interested. Didn't you say that a source told you that James Buchanan was being investigated for Medicare fraud?"

"I haven't confirmed that yet. OIG keeps very quiet about who they're investigating, just like the Justice Department So it may or may not be true. Anyway, this poor guy could have been killed for any number of reasons. And, besides, he wouldn't be involved in any Medicare fraud. He's a student, not part of the university hospital management."

"I know. All true. It just seems like an odd coincidence, and as an old time journalist, I don't believe in coincidences."

Eileen laughed. Lumbering through the newsroom on his 260-pound frame and sloppy clothes, Epstein was hard to picture as the go-get-'em reporter he was supposed to have been 25 years before, when he broke major stories involving defense contractors, corruption in past administrations, construction of various city buildings and more. His reputation was that of a take-no-prisoners journalist, but age and experience had mellowed him to look at things in what he now called a "greater context." He still got fired up when something caught his journalistic instincts, but at age 60, he was just as happy to pass the story on to a young reporter, like Eileen, that he respected, rather than do it himself. Good reporting, he liked to say, Eileen's gender aside, was a young man's game.

"Coincidences happen all the time, Mike," Eileen said. "Like that time we were all at the pub across the street roasting you and you just happened to walk in and hear half the comments before speaking up." She paused. "Or *was* that a coincidence?"

"Exactly my point."

"My beat is health care, not crime. This is something I would let Daniels and Costigan run with."

"Okay, just wanted to make you aware of it," he said, his attention now turning to another reporter, probably with a lead for him.

Then she went to the next web site to see what she could find out if and when Congress was going to restore the fee cuts.

6

The Improper Fraction was one of several college bars just off the university campus, but it was Nick Rosen's favorite. He liked the combination of polished wood and leaded glass with the informality of peanut shells thrown on the floor by patrons munching away while they waited for their beer or food to arrive.

A large bar in the pub tradition, in that it served food as well as spirits, the Improper Fraction had opened only three years before, but quickly found a customer base that included not only undergraduates and medical students like Nick, but residents and even some professors. Occasionally, entire families, including children, came in for a meal. It was the kind of place that seemed to have something for everyone. On Friday and Saturday evenings, though, it was turned over completely to the college scene, with fun-loving young men and women out for a good time.

This was a Tuesday, however, and Nick did not want a good time. He wanted to be by himself, and the Fraction, at three in the afternoon, provided a good opportunity. With the pub mostly empty except for a few conversations among patrons at corner tables, Nick was seated at the bar, nursing a beer with a plastic bowl of peanuts nearby. Sunlight came in through the leaded windows, highlighting the bar's lacquered surface, while one bartender checked out some inventory under the mirror that Nick now sat opposite from.

Nick was not looking at the mirror. Head down, he was having trouble absorbing the events of three weeks before. His good friend Scott found dead. He and Scott had been talking only the day before his death about things they might do together over the summer months, once this grueling year was behind them. More grueling for me than it was for Scott, Nick thought. Scott, after all, was the brilliant one, the one with a sense of flair and imagination in how he approached each medical challenge. I, on the other hand, thought Nick, am a solid, capable technician. A good doctor, yes, one day I will be that, but what Scott could have achieved….Well, that won't be happening now.

Then the shock of being practically accused by Detective Petrelli of having killed Scott. The sheer audacity of the man! And in front of Dana. Alright, Nick thought, maybe I do have some feelings for Dana. Always have. But I've also kept them well hidden, so as not to make either Dana or Scott uncomfortable.

That's always been my role, the third wheel, he thought. Petrelli was right about that. And Nick knew that it was a role he was comfortable with. Nick was always the one the girls wanted to be friends with. Yet how he so *wanted* to be more than friends with them, especially the ones with the pretty faces that could just melt his heart. What must it be like to have a girl like that on your arm every day? I'll probably never know, he realized, not with the real pretty ones. A guy like Scott never had a problem with girls like these. What must it be like to be Scott, to be that good looking and that brilliant, with a pretty girl like Dana on your arm every night, with a girl like Dana to take home and be with all night long, and to wake up to? It didn't seem fair.

He slammed down his beer a little too hard, causing the peanuts in the bowl to jump and the bartender to turn his way.

"Everything okay, Nick?" the bartender asked.

"It's nothing, Don," said Nick. "Just a lot of stress, what with work and with, well you know, with Scott gone."

Don, an affable large man in his late 20's, who could be as friendly and sympathetic as he could tough when necessary – which everyone said was what made him such a great bartender – nodded his head. "Scott was a good guy. I'm going to miss the three of you coming in together."

Yep, Nick thought, the three of us. Scott, Dana and me, the leftover one, the pet, their mascot. Well, now maybe he would have a chance with Dana. Maybe Detective Petrelli was right about that, at least. Dana needs a sympathetic shoulder. Maybe friendship can turn into something more. He grew hopeful.

"You've got to move forward," he said to Don. "You know, that's what I hear all the time from my parents and relatives whenever someone in the family dies. 'Don't grieve too long. Remember: Life goes on.'"

"Good advice."

"Yeah. Good advice. But you have to allow *some* time for grieving."

"That too. I guess the trick is to strike the right balance. Not always easy."

"You ever have anyone close to you die, Don?"

"Sure. My father died two years ago, but that was not unexpected. He'd been sick for a while. What I haven't had happen, and I can't imagine what this is like, is what you, Dana and everyone else who knew Scott have to go through now. That is, having someone close to you murdered." He paused. "Hard to believe. Why anyone would want to murder Scott Karakas, or any student, is beyond me. It's not like you students have a lot of money."

Nick gave a quick laugh.

"It's got everyone talking," Don continued. "Since that story on the front page of the metro section in the *Post* right after it happened, everyone who comes in here and orders a beer wants to talk about it. How's everyone on campus doing?"

"Pretty shaken up. A little on edge. Medical students, residents, faculty, undergraduates. Some undergraduates say their parents are asking them if the campus is still safe. I guess it's still too recent. Maybe as the months and years go by, people will forget. But for now, something like this affects all kinds of other things, even the number of applications for admission coming in for next year. People are afraid to walk in the hospital when it's empty, like at night, when Scott was there."

"Can't say I blame them for that. I don't know that I'd want to go in there. I guess that's just going to continue until the police solve the case."

"That's right."

Another customer sidled up to the bar and sat on a stool. Don went over to tend to him.

I can't believe that Detective Petrelli thinks I may have killed Scott, Nick thought. Scott was my closest friend. Why would he think that, just because he could see I care about Dana? That's not a reason. Lots of guys have crushes on their friend's girlfriends and don't do anything about it. That's no reason for the police to look their way when their friend is found murdered.

Or is it? Nick had to acknowledge to himself that, actually, from Detective Petrelli's point of view, he had a motive, although a thin one. And he knew that Petrelli had to track down every lead. He's probably working on others, Nick thought. And probably questioning people involved in those leads even more.

Still, as long as Petrelli thinks I may have killed Scott because I was secretly in love with Dana, the longer I will be a suspect, Nick knew. What I have to do is convince him in some way that it wasn't me. That's the key. Then the attention would go where it belonged, away from him.

Nick downed what remained of his beer, put a few bills on the bar, thanked Don, then walked a little unsteadily out the door.

7

N ot what I expected, thought Chamroeun Arun, looking around the room. Conference rooms at private law firms are much more impressive, usually with huge polished wood tables, glass walls and high-tech gadgets, like remote-control speaker phones that sit on the center of the table. All meant to convey power and competence. And to intimidate.

This OIG meeting room, by contrast, was almost quaint in its appearance. Instead of the sleek, modern look of a corporate law office, it was small, with an oak-veneer table that could accommodate maybe ten people if the chairs were squeezed together. The table stood in front of a wall lined with a couple of bookcases, occupied not only by books, but with stacks of newspapers. The beige carpet seemed worn and in need of replacement. A few pictures of current administration figures, including the current president, hung on the walls.

This mid-February meeting was Arun's first visit to OIG since becoming chief administrator of James Buchanan University Hospital several years ago, and one he made with some reluctance, seeing it as "entering the lion's den," as he put it before he and Paul Holden left the comfortable and familiar confines of the James Buchanan campus. He had been involved in OIG investigations at previous institutions he had worked at before, but nothing on this scale, and nothing that had caused him to visit OIG itself.

"I've learned to be very careful at meetings such as these," the diminutive and well-dressed Arun said in his slightly French accent. From an aristocratic Khmer family, had been educated in some of the finest schools in France before he and his family emigrated to the United States about thirty years ago. He carried with him the traditions of his family in his expensive Brooks Brothers suits, silk ties and top-of-the-line shoes. Although his hair was thinning on his 5 foot 7-inch frame, there was never a strand out of place. He shifted uncomfortably in his chair and looked over at Paul, the university hospital's chief compliance officer, who had accompanied him on this trip. Paul, a tall sandy haired young man in his mid-30's, smiled back wanly.

"It's just a preliminary meeting, to acquaint us with various aspects of the investigations," Paul said, trying to get him to relax. As a professional compliance officer, he had been to OIG several times in his career, both when representing past employers and for professional educational meetings that the government put on, sometimes in cooperation with outside associations, to build communication with the medical community. "If anything, this will give us a chance to see for ourselves where they are and what they may be targeting."

Arun nodded. Paul was right, and he was glad he didn't have to be here alone. Still, he couldn't help but look forward to being home this evening for dinner in his house, complete with all the fine art he had collected over the years, with his grown daughter and son-in-law, his wife having passed away some years earlier. These are the times when both being with his family and appreciating the timeless beauty that great art brings give life meaning. Not meetings like these, he told himself, at the same time reminding himself that he mustn't get caught up in negative emotions.

The door opened and a tall, thin, angular woman, dressed in a beige two-piece suit, stepped in. Arun immediately recognized her as HHS Inspector General Charlotte Westbrook. Following behind her was a man he had never met before, but recognized from his photo: Lewis Sullivan, the OIG's chief counsel and, by all reports, the "killer shark" behind the current crackdown on so many health care providers.

You wouldn't it guess it by his appearance, Arun thought. Hardly a lean barracuda type, Sullivan appeared almost a fuddy-duddy, less-than-average height and a bit portly, with a thick mane of gray hair somewhat disheveled, his tie at an awkward angle hanging outside his jacket, and a pair of glasses hanging by a chain around his neck. Quite the contrast to Arun's own immaculate appearance. But then Arun maintained a formal style even for his daily work. Today, for instance, he had prepared for this meeting by wearing a dark brown, pin-striped suite, silk chocolate tie over a beige shirt complete with brass collar stays, a monogrammed handkerchief in his jacket pocket, and brown leather wing tip shoes. He reached a manicured hand over to Charlotte and introduced himself.

"Pleasure," Charlotte said, admiring his attire. She and Lewis also shook hands with Paul, then all four sat down to an awkward moment of silence.

"Gentlemen," Charlotte began, using her most official voice. "This is what we call a courtesy meeting. It's not something we have to do, but we have found that communication and openness often result in these matters, which can sometimes become uncomfortable, being handled with greater ease. So please, let's look at this as an opportunity to try and work together and help James Buchanan University get in compliance with all laws and regulations."

"I am still not aware that James Buchanan is in violation of any laws or regulations," responded Arun, trying to maintain a civil tone.

"Quite a few, I'm afraid," Lewis said, "and several indicating a long pattern, not just one-shot errors, which could be dismissed as mistakes." He tapped on a two-inch-thick manila folder next to him. *Is he suppressing a smile?* Arun asked himself.

"Your investigators have been reviewing our claims for some weeks now, so I guess it's not that surprising that you found something," Arun said. "You can spend that much time in the most immaculate of institutions and still find…"

"Actually not true, Mr. Chamroeun. We have investigated many institutions and found little to prosecute. Unfortunately, that is not the case at James Buchanan."

Paul touched Arun's arm before he could respond further. "Why not just tell us the areas where you say we are not compliant?" he asked. "We appreciate the meeting and the chance to informally find out, before anything…formal…is done."

Charlotte nodded her head, indicating to Lewis that he should begin.

"There are four areas where we found what appears to be an ongoing pattern of fraud," Lewis began, as Arun tensed up next to Paul. This would cost the university a fortune, Arun knew, not to mention the damage to the university's and his own reputation.

"Specifically, they are:

"First, ongoing instances over the past three years of unbundling, where claims to Medicare for reimbursement of medical procedures were divided into several parts so they would result in more reimbursement." Continuing before Arun could respond, he added, looking at them over the rims of his half-moon glasses, "despite repeated claims denials from fiscal intermediaries telling you that these claims should *not* be unbundled."

That could be explained, Arun knew. Sometimes coding and billing staffs might be too aggressive. Changes in personnel sometimes leave a gap in training, and he would agree that needed to be fixed. But that didn't mean they were guilty of fraud. With Paul's cautionary hand on his arm, though, he bit his tongue as Lewis continued.

"Second, what can only be described as massive amounts of upcoding, particularly for procedures where there might be more than one code for a particular ailment, such as pneumonia. Without going into each case," he continued before Arun or Paul could respond, "it simply doesn't make sense that 75% of your pneumonia cases, for instance, are classified as bacterial pneumonia, which pays higher reimbursement, than viral pneumonia, which pays lower. Especially when the national average from all other hospitals is that a much lower percentage of pneumonia cases are bacterial. And pneumonia is just one example, by the way. There are dozens of claims we audited for procedures where James Buchanan claimed the higher reimbursement code for percentages well above the national average."

"You audited every claim we filed?" Arun asked in amazement.

"That's not how it works, Mr. Chamroeun," Charlotte said, trying to explain. *Was that sympathy Paul saw in her face?* "Obviously, we do not have the time or the staff to go through the thousands of claims a large institution like James Buchanan does over the course of a year. We use a probe audit."

"A probe...?"

Paul jumped in. "They take a sample of our claims, maybe three or four percent, then find the error rate. They then extrapolate that to the entire body of claims."

Arun was flabbergasted. Could such a methodology be accurate? "That seems a pretty thin reed to hang your statements on," he said. "You may have just gotten a few bad claims that are not typical of the rest."

Lewis looked at him patiently. This was not the first time he had heard this argument. People found it hard to accept that a representative sample was always true to the whole, the merits of modern polling aside. But the fact is, in every case he had been involved in, including those where an appeal led to a larger sample being audited, the results were the same. "I understand your skepticism, Mr. Chamroeun, but I assure you, the use of probe audits has not only been proven valid, but has been held up in court."

Arun turned up his hands and shook his head. "Let's continue. What else?"

Lewis cleared his throat. "More serious," he said, "are the final two areas."

Good God, thought Paul, looking at him. What did he do, save the best for last?

"I don't have to tell you, of course, that James Buchanan is considered one of the finest teaching hospitals in the country," Lewis continued

"Certainly not, and I appreciate your being aware of that fact. We would like to *continue* being one of the finest teaching hospitals," Arun said.

"Then you need to make sure that your residents are more properly supervised by your medical staff, and that you bill for supervision only when it is truly provided."

"Have you found instances when it was not?" Paul asked.

Lewis nodded. "More than a few, I'm afraid. As you know, Mr. Holden, the government has strict rules on exactly what constitutes proper supervision of medical residents, and it may be that not all of your teaching physicians are aware of them."

Paul understood. What a medical professional might consider proper supervision and what the government did were definitely two different concepts. Put simply, a member of the senior medical staff supervising a resident might consider proper supervision to be spending some time with the young doctors in an operating room, then leaving the building to return to his or her office to catch up on some work, before returning later to see how the residents were doing. How often this happened, of course, would depend on the teaching physician's individual judgment as to the ability and experience of the residents being supervised. In some cases, a teaching physician might stay with one resident for an entire operation, if that was needed in the teaching physician's judgment. At other times, the resident might be so experienced and talented that the teaching physician's judgment might be that less direct supervision was needed, and he or she could leave the resident alone for a while and tend to other needed work.

Unfortunately, government rules did not allow for such individual judgments. Teaching physicians were required to be in the building at all times, preferably in the operating room, but certainly physically available, when supervising a resident. Should a medical facility file a claim with Medicare for direct supervision by a teaching physician and a later investigation showed that the doctor, even for the best of reasons, had left the building or begun an operation on another patient, that could constitute Medicare fraud. And, of course, teaching physicians who truly left the residents alone while they went out to the golf course with other doctors could not even argue they were right on medical judgment grounds. Do we have any doctors like that? Paul wondered.

"Finally, there is the question of the accuracy of your cost reports," Lewis said, taking some satisfaction at the barely disguised look of shock that crossed Paul's face. "As you know, all providers are required to keep accurate records of their costs on capital improvements, such as construction of a new wing or building. These would include the cost of paying contractors, the cost of materials, the schedule for those payments, and more. These rarely get looked at by us, unless, of course, in cases like this, when we are involved in an audit."

Paul and Arun looked on as he continued. "What we have found are reports where the costs for new construction do not match industry norms, with your costs inflated by a factor of at least 15%. In short, gentleman, James

Buchanan has, on average, been billing the government for new construction and related expenses with a 15% surcharge added on, at least when compared against industry norms. A review of the actual bills will show the actual amount of surcharge, or if there was one at all. Perhaps, gentlemen," and here Lewis found it difficult not to smirk at his hidden sarcasm, "since we do want to go into this without preconceptions, a review of the bills from your various contractors will have things turn up in your favor and show that you actually *undercharged* the government."

Lewis liked to study the faces of health care administrators when he confronted them with findings like these. Some sat there stone-faced, while others had difficulty showing their reactions. A few put on what he thought were feigned looks of shock, when, he believed, they knew full well what was going on. It was interesting to meet with Charlotte after these meetings and compare their thoughts on these reactions. But this one wouldn't be so easy, he could see. Paul Holden, the professional compliance officer, sat there with a poker face. Lewis suspected that Paul was profoundly shocked, but too much of a professional to let it show. Chamroeun Arun, on the other hand, seemed to be fighting back emotion.

"You…can't have found that out. This would not happen on my watch."

"We've seen the books, Mr. Chamroeun. Now I know you don't put them together yourself, but you do sign off on them."

"And that's how I know this can't be true. Our accounting staff is highly professional, something like that couldn't get through."

"It has been getting through, though, I'm afraid."

Charlotte touched Lewis' arm. "Mr. Chamroeun, I can see you are upset by this revelation. But I assure you that if you just take the time to match what your cost reports show to what the actual bills are, you will see this yourself. Unless, of course, your contractors are the ones inflating the prices, or if we find out that someone at the university hospital colluded with the contractors to charge higher prices, with a kickback then going to the contractor for doing so. Have you ever made this comparison?"

Arun stopped. "No, that is not my practice. Please understand, I hire the best people. And when you hire the best, you expect them to do their jobs in the most professional manner."

"Apparently not in this case," Lewis said, "at least based on industry standards. If this turns out to be true, gentlemen, as we believe it will, what this means is that somewhere there is probably another set of cost reports showing the true, lower costs that you should have billed the government for, but did not. That's so the administrators behind this can keep a handle on how much profit they really made." He paused. "We need to see those books."

"I don't know where they would be," Arun said. "I don't even know if they exist, because I don't know if what you are saying is true. I find it hard to believe that anyone at James Buchanan would do such a thing."

"You signed off on the reports."

"Yes, I did. As I told you, I am not an accountant myself. I do not second guess the work of my professionals. Frankly, if I looked at an individual charge, I would have no idea if the charge was correct, inflated, or understated. And as for the other areas you are investigating, I am not a professional coder. That's not why I chose to become a university hospital administrator. I chose my job because it could make a difference, both in saving lives and in teaching new doctors."

"All very commendable, Mr. Chamroeun. But don't you think that should not include Medicare fraud? We have a mission, too, and that is to make sure that the public's money is not taken fraudulently. You talk about helping people? Medicare is not a limitless pool of cash. Just read the papers, the system is in trouble. If any of that can be abated by reining in fraud, intentional or not, that is our mission. Every Medicare dollar we save allows more money to be spent on senior patients. There is just as much nobility in that, Mr. Chamroeun, as there is in your profession."

Charlotte touched Lewis' arm again. He could get so worked up when health care providers pushed his 'I'm-doing-good-deeds-so-leave-me-alone' button. But she could see that this was all getting too much for Arun, and she wanted to keep the relationship cordial to the degree possible. Clearly, she saw, this man holds honor high, whatever may be happening at his hospital. The best course right now, she knew, is to bring this meeting to a close, preferably on a note of agreement.

"It sounds to me," she said, "that we all want the best medicine practiced for the greatest number of seniors, would that be correct?"

Arun could see where this was leading. He could only say, "Of course."

"So," Charlotte continued, "you and Mr. Holden would therefore be as interested as we are in finding out where these problems are and putting a stop to them, would you not?"

"To the degree they are problems," Paul said.

"Of course," Charlotte said. "If we are making any mistakes, believe me, gentlemen, we want to know. And if you can point these out, please do. We are not trying to put the medical community out of business, far from it. We are just guardians of the public's money."

"We understand," Paul said.

"Excellent. So, we can count on your cooperation as the investigation continues?"

"Yes. Certainly." Paul and Arun spoke up almost simultaneously. They were not bad people, they knew, and did not wish to be treated as such. But they would make sure the university's point of view would be heard. The Inspector General, it seemed to Arun, at least was willing to listen, unlike her chief counsel.

Charlotte stood up and extended her hand. Lewis stood after her.

"Then, that, gentlemen, concludes this meeting."

8

Dana wasn't sure what to do. Used to catching up on work in the evening hours at the university hospital, now she, like almost every other student and faculty member on campus, was avoiding the building at night. But she did need some papers and other materials she had left there earlier in the week, and was considering making a quick trip in to get them. After all, the hospital was still open in the evening; it was just that no one was going in once night fell.

Scott was murdered. She couldn't get over it. *Actually murdered.* Who would…and why would…anyone do such a thing? Scott did evoke some jealousy because everything seemed to come so easy to him, but she had never seen anyone, even past girlfriends who he peremptorily dropped, get so mad at him that they would have murdered him.

She choked back a sob. It hit her every now and then and the passage of three weeks hadn't made it any easier. She had cared about Scott, more than she wanted to admit, more than she wanted to when she first got involved with him, given his history of female conquests. Scott was so typical of the men she was drawn to: successful, a bit flashy, more into sex than emotional sharing, and commitment-avoidant. Why do I go for these types? Of course, she knew, this was a question she had been continually asking herself since her sophomore year as an undergraduate, and was only somewhat closer to an answer. The thing was, with Scott, she felt she had been making some headway in building a relationship in the weeks before his murder. Now it was all for nothing.

Thank you, Dad, she said somewhat bitterly to herself. Maybe a bit unfair, since she knew that ultimately her decisions are up to her and she has to take responsibility for them. She nonetheless felt its truth. Roger Brentano, her father, was also a somewhat distant, as well as demanding, man, but with a peculiar double standard when it came to women, even his own daughter. Throughout school, she had found the best way to please him was by being a good student and bringing home high grades. A straight-A student throughout high school, she glowed when her father would nod in approval each time she brought home a report card.

But that was as far as her father's expression of approval would go. Her father loved her, she knew, loved her mother and two younger brothers, but was withdrawn emotionally, reticent even about saying, "I love you" or giving out hugs. Maybe it was his generation. Unlike the parents of most of her fellow students, Dana's parents were a generation older, both in their late 70s. They had married late in life and had children later than most. The result was that Dana found herself raised by parents of the World War II generation.

Roger Brentano was raised in a time when men did not easily express their emotions and when most people, men and women, did not talk about intimate matters, even with family. He seemed more at ease at work than with his family, sometimes going into his old real estate brokerage, from which he had officially retired years before. To his co-workers, he was handsome and charming, even at his advanced age, ready with a quick quip and smile. But to his family, after the initial greetings when he came home each day, he would vanish to watch television after dinner, and not emerge until close to bedtime.

Dana's mother, Barbara, seemed to accept this, as far back as Dana could remember. She filled her time with traditional women's activities, staying home to tend the house and raise the children, with an occasional temp job as a secretary, typist or clerk. For the past few years she had worked customer service at a magazine publishing company. And she seemed quite content with that. If she had any other career plans, Dana never knew, and her mother was not one to engage easily in conversation about such topics. In fact, Dana thought now, communication…real communication about important issues, rather than day-to-day activities…was not something she ever saw. If it existed, would it have made her parents marriage richer, or would it have exposed fault lines that both, deep down, knew existed but chose to deny?

Dana got a shock when she told her parents, in her senior year of high school, that she wanted to take pre-med courses at college. She expected they would enthusiastically approve. After all, good grades and academic excellence were the ticket that had always worked for her, especially with her father.

"Pre-med? What on earth for?" her father asked.

After Dana explained that she wanted to become a doctor, she got a second shock. Her mother actually gave out a short laugh, and her father shook his head. "That is no job for a young woman."

Dana couldn't believe it. There were already plenty of female doctors out there. This battle had been fought back in the 1970s, hadn't it? But yet, here were her parents, showing that not that much had changed, at least not in her own family.

"Maybe you'd like to be a nurse," her mother suggested.

The matter rested there through her undergraduate years. She took her pre-med courses and graduated summa cum laude with a degree in biology. When she told her parents that she was determined to go on to medical school, they tried to discourage her again, and she ended up financing her entire first year on her own through a loan. That was fine with her, if that was the way it had to be. Fortunately, it didn't. In one of her most cherished memories, if only because it told her of the depth of feeling her father must have held for her deep down, after she did well her first year, he agreed to pay for it, as well as the rest of medical school. And was that a bit of a smile of approval she detected on his face when he told her?

Seeking approval from distant yet successful men had carried over into her choice of boyfriends, and Scott fit the bill nicely. He was, in many ways, just like her father: a winner in his field, but not one to open up in his personal life. Scott never had a problem finding a woman, just staying with one. And that seemed to be fine with him. In many ways, he seemed to meet the male stereotype that unhappy women have of men, that he was just interested in one thing.

And was Scott ever interested in that one thing. In closets, on lab desks, even once in a faculty office, Dana found his desires to be almost insatiable and, she had to admit, creating a more-than-willing response from her. The more risky the location, the more Scott wanted to do it. Did he want us to get caught?

Yet apparently it was all an open secret. Scott had a reputation and, Dana knew, she was just one in a line of women with whom he had had similar relationships. She had tried to get him to open up more than once, but he always managed to turn the conversation back to day-to-day topics, whether it was gossip about others or the daily grind of being a medical student.

Unfortunately for her, along the way she began to develop strong feelings for Scott. And that was the trap, wasn't it, she asked herself now. Find an emotionally distant man, give everything to him, fall in love with him, and then be upset when he does what she always knew, deep inside, he would do: not return her feelings.

Nick understood. She could talk to Nick about almost anything. He had been, and remained, a great friend, a confidant who would not only listen to her, but also give her the male point of view on things, as she tried to figure out what she could do to get more emotional commitment from Scott. That Nick might secretly have feelings for her was something she thought possible, but since he never mentioned it, she chose to keep it quiet. She liked Nick a lot, but clearly, he did not fit the pattern of men she was drawn to.

The surprising and sad thing was that in the weeks before his murder, she seemed to be making some headway with Scott. They had found a way of relating that seemed to open him up more, and increase his emotional involvement with her. She had taken a certain satisfaction in that, which only increased her own emotional commitment to him. Maybe there is a future for us after all, she had begun to think.

Such were the thoughts going through Dana's mind as she walked down the asphalt path leading to the front door of the university hospital. Not a modern building at all, its huge granite stones, some covered with the traditional ivy, recalled an earlier day when medicine was practiced only by a learned few.

Should she go in? Now that she was here, she couldn't decide. Going through the front door would mean walking through the large lobby and down a side corridor, where she would take the elevator up to the second floor, then down two corridors to the room where her materials were in a cabinet. Then she would have to go back. That promised to be a long walk though a largely deserted building, one that had already seen one murder, and it made her nervous.

She turned off the path and walked on the grass around the right hand side of the building. The rear entrance, which was sometimes unlocked in the evening, opened immediately onto a second set of elevators. Once on the second floor, the room she needed was half a corridor away. Quicker this way, she thought.

She turned her head at the sound of someone on the grass.

"Oh, hi," she said, relieved. "I was just—"

The vision of a gun pointed at her face, the blast from its barrel, and the shock of who fired it were the last things Dana saw and felt as she left consciousness. She was dead before she hit the ground.

9

The sound of the gunshot rang through the university hospital section of the James Buchanan campus, grabbing the attention of anyone there that night. Students sitting and talking on benches, professors working late in their offices, people simply taking a stroll through the university hospital quadrangle, suddenly had their attention diverted by the noise.

No one was sure at first just where it came from, but after a few seconds of what seemed like frozen time, figures could be seen in the dark and under the lights that shone down on the paths from light posts and from the buildings, running and searching, as if expecting to find a body somewhere. If true, everyone knew, this would be the second murder on campus in less than a month. The implications of that fact, and that the university might be facing what would be a serial killer, were beginning to dawn.

"Oh my God! Over here!" one female voice suddenly called out, piercing the darkness. "At the side of the hospital!"

A group quickly gathered around where the young woman was standing and, beside her, the body of another young woman, face down in the grass.

"Excuse me, excuse me, let me pass." Everyone recognized the distinctive French accent, as Arun made his way through the crowd and stared down at the body. "Alright, everyone, back off a bit, let's see just what happened and if," he paused, "she's still alive." He bent down to turn the body over.

"Maybe we should wait until campus security or the police get here before touching anything," someone said.

Arun looked up. "We don't know if this young woman is alive or dead. We have doctors here, they may be able to help. Is there one here? If not, please find one, somebody."

He turned the body over. Everyone gasped.

The killer had found his mark. A good part of Dana's face was damaged by the impact of the bullet, with her left eye and cheek ripped out. But not so much that Arun couldn't recognize her. And, he knew instantly from the head wound, she was dead. He lowered her body back to the ground sadly.

"It's Dana Brentano. She's dead."

There was gasps from those who knew her in the group of 40 or so that now surrounded the scene, and a few muffled sobs, perhaps from close friends, or perhaps from some just overwhelmed by the horror of it all. *What was happening on this campus?*

The siren and rotating lights of two police cars broke the shock. A number of officers, with campus security personnel in tow, quickly secured the scene, while a large middle-aged man, wearing an inexpensive plaid sports coat over a shirt and tie, approached Arun and Dana's lifeless form.

"Detective Alphonse Petrelli," he said, holding out his badge. Arun nodded.

"You a doctor?" he asked. Arun shook his head, introducing himself as the chief administrator of the university hospital.

"You always work this late, Mr. Arun?" Petrelli asked. Arun was taken a bit aback by the directness of the question.

"Mr. *Chamroeun*, not Arun, detective," Arun said, correcting Petrelli. "In Cambodia and other Asian countries, the surname comes before the Christian one."

"Umhmm. So, Mr. Chamroeun, you always work this late?"

"Yes, well not always, but it's not uncommon. I have a lot of work to do," he said, motioning expansively at the hospital building. "You can imagine."

"Well, yes, I suppose I can." Petrelli turned his attention toward the body. "Any idea who this is?"

"Dana Brentano. She is, I mean, she was, a medical student here. We all just heard a gunshot and came running out. I was working up in my office…"

"Which is where?"

"Third floor."

"Umhmm."

"I took the elevator down, then joined everyone else here."

"So there were already people here when you got to the body."

"That's right. But I turned her over. I realize that one is not supposed to touch anything at a crime scene, detective, but at that point I didn't know if the victim – I didn't even know it was Dana, at that point – was still alive. Maybe I could have found a doctor who could have saved her. But when I turned her over and I saw.." He motioned to Dana's face and wound. "There was no way she wasn't already dead."

Petrelli looked at the body. "Yep, you were right about that. No way." He paused. "Then you put her back face down in the grass?"

Arun nodded. "Just the way I found her."

Petrelli turned and looked at the crowd of students and others, all seemingly riveted on his every word and deed. "Who here found the body first?"

A young woman with red hair raised her hand and stepped forward a bit nervously. "I did. Mary Savoy. I'm a sophomore, pre-med."

"Umhmmm," Petrelli said. "And what did you do when you found it?"

"I, um, I'm not sure, but I think I screamed."

"Understandable." He looked at the rest of the crowd. "And that's when all of you," he looked at Arun, "including you, gathered round?" There was a general murmur of assent from the group, including Arun.

"Did anyone, anyone, see someone leaving the scene here, going the other way? The perpetrator of this crime may not have been running or even had a gun in his or her hand. The murderer may have been casually strolling. In fact, if thinking properly, that's what the smart move would have been."

No one said anything.

"Detective?" someone asked from the crowd. "Do you think this murder is linked to the other one, you know, the murder of Scott Karakas? Two medical students in three weeks, that seems like it's not a coincidence?"

"Yeah," someone else said. "And you know what, detective? They used to go out together. That can't be a coincidence."

Petrelli held up his hand. "We will check into all leads." He motioned to one of the uniformed police officers who were standing by. "Call the crime scene unit and get them over here. Meanwhile, keep all these people here until you question each one. Get their contact information. Then you can let them go home. Then take the body in for an autopsy." He looked at Arun. "Of course, we'll notify family members."

"What do you need to do an autopsy for?" Arun asked. "It seems pretty obvious how she died."

"Please, Mr. Chamroeun, I already went through the question of doing an autopsy with the first victim, who everyone, including Miss Brentano here, I might add, thought died of a heart attack. I am nothing if not thorough."

Arun nodded.

"When you get a chance, Mr. Chamroeun, I would appreciate it if you would stop by my office for a little more discussion. What you knew about the victims, both of them, as well as the atmosphere on campus. Helps me paint a portrait of the scene, you understand?"

Arun, now deep in thought, nodded again.

10

"Now maybe you'll be interested."

Eileen took the sheets that Mike Epstein was offering her, read them for a few minutes, her eyebrows raised.

"A *second* murder, in less than a month?"

Epstein nodded, lowering his pot-bellied body into a nearby chair. "There's something here, Eileen. I'm not sure what, but my instincts tell me this is more than a police story."

"But wait, Mike. See, here it says that the two victims – Scott Karakas and Dana Brentano – knew each other, apparently they were romantically involved. So this could all be part of the same thing. Some jealous boyfriend or girlfriend. It's not like they're isolated cases."

"Yeah, but it's also happening at the same time that James Buchanan is being investigated for fraud by the government."

"Which I have confirmed, off the record. But that is a far cry from linking these two murders which, again, are related to each other, with that investigation. Sounds like some kind of personal dispute. What are Daniels and Corrigan doing with it?"

Mike shrugged. "As far as I know, they're just reporting it like any other police story, maybe giving a little bigger play because it's two on the same campus in a short time frame. Might make the front page of the Metro section. After all, this could, you know, be something else. This could be a Son of Sam-type serial killer."

"Yeah, but the victims of serial killers don't typically know each other. Son of Sam's didn't, and neither did the victims of the Hillside Strangler, or even Jeffrey Dahmer's creepy crimes."

"So why not look into it?"

Eileen gave it some thought. Mike typically didn't come to a reporter with a lead like this unless he believed something was there. And this was the second time he had come to her. Add to that the fact that Mike was rarely wrong, his instincts were that good, even though he had no real evidence, just a feeling.

"Just what is it exactly that makes you think these murders are linked to the HHS investigation?"

"Hard to say. I don't know. Maybe nothing. But when has James Buchanan had a murder before? As far as I remember, never. And are we to believe that these two were the first romantic couple to have difficulties? That there was some jealous third person involved? Yet never was there a murder, let alone a double murder. But it just so happens that this time, the university is being investigated, also for the first time, I believe, for fraud, something that could severely hurt it. I don't know, Eileen. There's no obvious connection, yeah. But I also don't believe in coincidences."

Eileen nodded. "Okay, I'll look into it. I'll start right away."

Mike smiled. "That's what I wanted to hear."

"You'll square this with the metro desk? I don't want any problems with Corrigan and Daniels, if I can avoid them."

"I will, if we get to that point. But right now, we're not talking about writing anything. Just see what you can find out, then let me know. Then we'll decide if we are going to do anything."

Mike heaved his frame out of the chair. Eileen noticed some stains on his white shirt, probably from lunch. Some woman would have one hell of a time with a guy like him, she thought Then she fired up the Internet, called up Google, and entered "Scott Karakas" for a search.

11

The meeting with Arun and Paul Holden was only slightly less harsh than what Lyle and the other doctors anticipated.

"It is essential that each of you complete four hours of compliance training a month," Arun told his 12 colleagues around the large, lacquered oak mahogany table in one of the university's board rooms about a week later. "And that's every month for a year."

The groans were audible, and no one even tried to say anything. Jennifer almost choked on her morning latte, while Lyle threw down his pen in disgust. Peter, like several of the other doctors from the university's medical staff who were at this board meeting, just stared down at his writing pad.

"I'm sorry, I don't like it any more than you," Arun continued, "but with the ongoing medical supervision investigation and who knows what else the OIG investigators are looking at, we must make sure we are in the clear." He cast a look at a Paul, who sitting next to him.

"If anything, we are late in doing this." Paul, wearing a navy blue suit and matching tie, rose from his chair and walked toward the front of the room, a thick loose leaf manual in his hand.

"How many of you know what this is?"

Several hands went up. "I assume it's the university's compliance plan that you want us to follow," one of the doctors said.

"That is right." Paul walked back to the table and stood the book up on it. "You'll excuse me for being a bit concerned, my friends, but much, if not all, of this investigation could have been avoided if we had just paid more attention to this book. It was, after all, put together with your help."

Peter grimaced. Only if you call "help" having to answer Paul's questions as you raced from one medical appointment to another, or dealing with the man when he approached you late in your office as you struggled to complete mountains of paperwork that your medical duties left little time to complete. If that was help, then okay, then the doctors had helped Paul.

"The only thing worse than not having a compliance program," Paul continued, working up into a fine lather of hardly muted indignation, "is having one and then not following it. Because that, my friends, is like telling the government you *knew* what to do, but *chose* not to do it."

This perception was, in many ways, more important than the reality of the actual compliance work. Any health care provider without a compliance plan was similar to a combatant on a battle field waving a flag to show the enemy where to concentrate its fire.

So in many ways, as Arun well knew, Paul was correct: creating the compliance plan but then not following it – if that were indeed the case, and neither he nor the doctors were convinced it was – was indeed the worst thing to do. Because if true, it told the federal government that the perception of compliance, as opposed to the reality, was indeed all the university hospital cared about.

And as far as Lyle and some of the other doctors were concerned, that was fine with them. For reasons that Arun found himself sharing, they were insulted by the federal intrusion into how they conducted medicine, and regarded the compliance manual, Paul, his staff, and now this new training requirement, as simply nuisances that had to be put up with in today's world. But the difference for Arun was that, as chief administrator of the university hospital, he had to make sure the plan was followed, whatever his own feelings about it. The reputation and financial future not only of the hospital, but of the doctors in the room, not to mention his own, depended on it.

"My colleagues," he said now, reluctant acceptance in his voice, "Paul is correct. The surest way for us to be able to conduct medicine unencumbered is follow the government's rules. We already have auditors and investigators looking over our claims and more, looking to find some wrongdoing that they can pin us down with and collect lots of fines, plus, I might add, pin some scalps on the wall and ruin some careers. And I can tell you from the meeting Paul and I had at the OIG offices the other day, that this entire situation, unfortunately, is only going to get worse." He made eye contact with several of the doctors with that one. "That's why we have a compliance officer, so we don't have to go through all that. Alright, maybe we are a little late, but better late than never. We need to show OIG that we are taking compliance very seriously."

"So what do you want us to do?" asked Jennifer. "No one wants to get James Buchanan in trouble."

"First, I need each of you to schedule compliance training with Rebecca Croft on my staff," Paul said. "I might add that it's not just the doctors. The administrative staff, the coders and billers who file your claims with Medicare – they have even more time they will have to schedule."

"Yes, but they are not taking it away from someone who needs a heart transplant," said Lyle.

"You want to be able to continue performing heart transplants at James Buchanan, or perform them at all, Dr. Steadman?" Paul shot back, as Lyle shrunk back in his seat. "I am sorry, doctors, truly I am, for speaking to you like this, but believe it or not, I have come, in my three years here, to love this institution, too. And I also have a career. And I do not want to see either the institution hurt, nor my own reputation damaged."

There were nods in the room at this. Yes, in some ways, Paul was also a prisoner of the system.

"Alright," Paul continued, "I also want to meet with each of you individually, review your documentation, talk about your supervision practices for those of you who supervise residents, how you code your evaluation and management procedures, and more. I would allow a couple of hours for each meeting. We will try and get these scheduled before any of you get any interview requests from OIG investigators. If any of you do, I want you to be as cooperative and friendly with them as you can, but tell them that, on the advice of counsel – me – you need to speak with me first, and that I will schedule all of your interviews with them. Since most of them are attorneys themselves, they should understand that."

"Paul," Arun said now, reaching out and grabbing Paul's hand in a two-handed grip, "I know this isn't easy for you and it is important that we not blame the messenger." He looked at the medical staff assembled in the room. "Paul is here to help us. He is not the one we need to be concerned about. OIG is."

As Paul left the room and the door closed behind him, Arun put his hands to his head, a gesture several of the doctors had seen him do before when stressed.

"I have to tell you." he said, "We may be in for some real trouble."

12

"You're getting to be a regular here, Nick."

Nick looked up from his beer into the smiling face of the Improper Fraction bartender. It was his fourth beer, and it was keeping his mind occupied. But that was its purpose, he told himself.

"Yeah, well, you know, I think bars like this are underappreciated in society. They serve a definite purpose, in this case, to get me rip-roaring zonkered, so I don't have to think about…"

"I know," said Don sympathetically. "You and I were just talking about her the other day, after Scott's death, um, murder. Dana was a great girl. I really liked her."

Nick winced at the mention of her name. He was doing all he could not to think of her. But he couldn't quite seem to get it out of his mind. Dana. *Murdered.* He had loved her, and now she was gone. And right after Scott. The three of them had been a team, a flawed but welcome group of friends, and now he was the only one left – in the space of less than a month! Was this some kind of cosmic joke?

"Maybe I'm next," he said out loud, without realizing it.

"Hey, Nick, don't talk that way. That's not good."

"I don't know, Don, maybe if Dana had thought that way, she'd still be here. Anyway, doesn't it seem odd to you that a little over a month ago all three of us were alive and kicking, and now I'm the only one left? Maybe someone is out to get us. Maybe I *will* be next."

"I told you, there's no good in talking like that." He paused, looking toward the pub's entrance. "Isn't that the detective I've seen on TV, you know, the one who's investigating the case?"

Nick groaned. "A large man, middle aged, bad dresser? That would be Detective Alphonse Petrelli, Jr., here to question me, I bet, about what happened to Dana." He turned to look at him, then raised his hand to wave. "Detective Petrelli! I'm over here," he called out with false bonhomie.

Petrelli came over as Don moved on to another customer. He looked Nick over a couple of times, obviously taking stock of his current condition.

"Drowning your sorrows, Nick?"

Nick took another drink from his glass. "You could say that. Can I buy you a drink, detective?"

"No, thank you. I heard you've been spending some time here, so I thought I would check the place out, maybe find you, and it looks like I did."

"Right you are again, detective. I suppose you want to ask me how I did it. And why I did it."

"Are you confessing, Nick?"

"Might as well. I am obviously your first suspect. Let me see, how does your theory go? Something like this: First, Nick Rosen, third wheel to Scott Karakas and Dana Brentano, and secretly in love with Dana, who happens to be Scott's girlfriend, kills Scott out of jealousy. Then, let me guess, when he tries to comfort Dana as more than a friend, as you suspect, she rejects his advances, he kills her too. Then he comes here to drown his sorrows and wait for your arrival."

"Well, you have to admit, you do have a motive, and you are the last of the three left alive."

"And it has a good beat and you can dance to it."

Petrelli paused. "A confession while you are under the influence of alcohol does not carry much weight, Nick, so it really doesn't count. Nonetheless, maybe it would make you feel better to unload a bit. Why not just tell me how it all happened? Get it off your chest. Then you can sleep all this off downtown and in the morning, we can go over it again when you're sober."

"Not a chance! I hear those jail cells are damn uncomfortable!"

"Here's an alternative, then. Tell me what happened now and then I'll make sure you get home okay. You can sleep in your own bed tonight, and then tomorrow, after you wake up, I'll take you downtown and we can talk further."

"Aren't you afraid that I'll 'skip town'?"

"Not really. I'll have officers posted at all the entrances to your building."

"Ah. Very thorough, detective. I guess that kind of thinking is how you made detective."

"So, do we have a deal, Nick?" He offered his hand, which Nick took.

"We have a deal, detective."

"Then let's hear it."

Nick took another gulp of his beer. "Okay, here it is. The truth is that I did love Dana, and maybe I was a little jealous of Scott. But he was still my friend, and I was his. The envy I just buried. Wasn't the first time I was in this kind of situation, anyway. I was used to it, maybe too used to it. I don't know. Anyway, detective, what the truth is, and what you don't want to hear, but which is nonetheless the truth, is that despite these feelings, I didn't kill either of them. Wouldn't have done it. Couldn't have done it. Don't even own a gun."

Petrelli was disappointed. He hadn't come to the bar expecting a confession, but his hopes had risen given Nick's drunken state. Now he was back to square one.

"Then, if that's the truth, Nick, let me ask you: Who did kill them?"

"Damned if I know. Let me know if you find out, okay?"

"I should tell you right now that as we are talking, some of my men are searching your apartment." Nick looked up at this, as Petrelli continued, "We've gotten a search warrant, it's all legal. If we find the gun, Nick, or anything incriminating, it won't go well for you. I don't have to tell you about the mood on campus right now. Students and faculty are torn between fear for their own lives and the lives of their friends, and anger over the loss of Scott and Dana. If it turns out to be you, Nick, and you didn't cooperate – had several chances to confess, but didn't take advantage of them – there will be no pressure on me to allow for any extenuating circumstances. On the other hand," he paused for dramatic effect, "if you confess now, I can accurately say that you were filled with remorse, and the whole thing will be looked at more as a tragedy. A lesser charge may be possible."

"Let me ask you something, detective. When Dana and I were down at the police station and you first questioned us a few weeks ago, you also thought she might have done it, right? I mean, you questioned her about being jealous about Scott's relationships with other girls, right? That might have given her a motive."

"I was looking at all the possibilities."

"But now she's dead."

"And your point…"

"My point, detective, is that you were wrong about Dana. If she were still alive, she'd still be a suspect, just like I am. But you would be wrong about her. The only way she stopped being a suspect was that she was smart enough to get herself killed. That seems to be the only way to get off your suspect list. Well, did it ever occur to you that maybe the same thing is true of me?"

"Maybe, Nick, maybe. But," he leaned over close to Nick's ear, "between you and me, I don't think so."

With that, Detective Petrelli walked toward the door.

13

Charlotte felt comfortable on Senator Mack Donelin's arm as they walked the path to the Capitol Hill townhouse shared by Lewis and James. Capitol Hill was now such a desirable location to live, so different from twenty years before, when it was a haven of low lifes and crime. But regentrification was already underway then, with entrepreneurial "yuppies" moving in, taking advantage of tax breaks and restoring many of the beautiful brownstones that lined the streets.

"And here we are," she said to her oldest friend as they approached the red painted door with the large brass knocker.

"Here we are," agreed Mack, who, at age 43, had grown only better looking. Tall and dark, with a strong face that easily broke into a smile, blue eyes that crinkled when he laughed, Charlotte saw him on the borderline between "cute" and "handsome." Since their summers growing up together in St. Michael's when they were eight years old through their respective rises to Washington positions of influence, they had always been there for each other, even now, when it was a bit awkward and even politically dangerous. Mack, after all, was chairman of the Senate Appropriations Committee, which among its other duties oversaw OIG's budget.

And that wasn't their only connection. Mack had risen to his position as a protégé of Charlotte's dad, the powerful Senator David Westbrook, who, at the height of his influence, had been chairman of the Senate Armed Services committee. A real power in his day, David Westbrook saw something early on in Charlotte's young friend, and advised and guided him through law school and into politics, using his influence when and where appropriate to help him out. The two men remained close to this day, although with David Westbrook now retired and living in St. Michael's, Mack, like Charlotte, saw him less often.

Charlotte and Mack had never crossed the line from close friends to romantic partners and, from a career perspective, avoided a lot of complications, especially given their current jobs. They provided emotional support for each other during crises in past relationships, including Mack's divorce four years ago and Charlotte's series of relationships that never seemed to pan out.

Despite this, those who knew them would not infrequently comment on how well-suited they seemed to each other, and how there was an obvious chemistry between them. Did Charlotte and Mack feel it too? Mack once tried to make an advance, when they were both at law school – he at Georgetown and she at American University – but it was awkward. Charlotte hadn't known how to respond, or even what her own feelings were. She called off any further steps in that direction the next day, and they decided to stay friends. After a while, they settled into a comfortable pattern. They talked regularly, saw movies and had dinner together, and were usually available to go somewhere when neither had another companion.

Mack banged the knocker against the door three times. There was a pause, and then Lewis' face appeared in the open door. Not the determined face of the crusader that Charlotte saw at their recent meeting with Arun and Paul Holden, but a happy, even jovial face, a face Charlotte saw only rarely. It was a face that Lewis allowed to show only in situations when his instincts told him that he would not have to be on his guard about either his work or his personal life, when he was with people he regarded as true friends. Charlotte, through her long years working with Lewis, always felt honored that he considered her in that category.

"Welcome, welcome," Lewis said, ushering them in. Wearing a natty plaid vest with a pocket watch under his corduroy jacket, Lewis was in his hosting element. He and James loved to entertain, and these small dinner parties, usually with a dozen or so people, some very influential like Mack, others not influential at all, were among their favorite activities.

James walked over as Lewis took their coats to lay on the bed in one of the spare bedrooms. A tall, thin man in his mid-50s, he seemed the perfectly cast urban professional. His usual pipe in hand with its familiar scent of cherry tobacco, James beamed as he recognized the two arrivals. Wearing a small gray mustache under a prominent nose and high forehead with receding gray hair, James grasped Mack's hand with a hearty handshake and gave Charlotte a kiss on the cheek.

"Here they are!" he said. "Now the evening is complete."

"Such a charmer, James," Charlotte said.

"You know, Charlotte, that I don't say things I don't mean," he replied with a twinkle, "at least when I'm not working." A senior executive with a public relations firm, James spent a great deal of his work day coming up with statements for clients that neither he nor they actually meant.

Lewis rejoined them in the foyer as the four walked into the living room of the townhouse. Classic and beautiful, with dark hardwood floors and terracotta walls abutted by colonial molding and cornices, the townhouse was in the middle of an expensive renovation that Lewis and James were directing. Most of the downstairs was complete, with an elaborate gourmet kitchen, complete with island countertop and wall-to-ceiling ash cabinets. The upstairs was reported to be a mess, with the master bathroom undergoing the primary renovation.

Lewis and James made an odd yet comfortable couple, Charlotte thought, almost like a Mutt and Jeff of the old comic strips or, as someone else once commented, like Laurel and Hardy. Lewis, shorter and somewhat heavier, was more the anchor of the two, more methodical in style and just taking up more visual weight in a room. James, taller and more active, seemed to be on the go all the time, pacing when he spoke, at times a fountain of nervous energy. Yet they seemed to complement each other and, in their six years together, seemed quite happy. Both middle-aged, they cared less what others thought about their lifestyles than they might have when they were younger, and had made peace with who they were and what they expected from the world. James did have a former life with a wife and daughter, who he kept in touch with and provided financial support for, but it was clear that was in his past.

"You know most of the people here, I think," he said now, after delivering a white zinfandel to Charlotte and a Tanqueray and tonic to Mack, motioning to the eight or so others chatting in various clusters throughout the room. "Make yourselves at home. Lewis and I need to check on the arrangements," which Charlotte knew meant that something special was being prepared for dinner.

"There's Milt Swarzniak," said Mack, motioning to a young brown-haired man of about 30 talking with two other men that neither she nor Mack recognized. "He's on Senator Owens' staff and, if you will excuse me, I need to talk with him." Senator Barbara Owens of Texas was the ranking minority member on the appropriations committee and, while she and Mack did not always see eye to eye, they made an effort to keep each other informed and get along. Mack undoubtedly had some Senate business to talk about with the young staffer. With a nod from Charlotte, he headed over like a bee and was quickly engaged in conversation.

Charlotte eyed the rest of the room. She recognized a few officials from her and Lewis' days at the Department of Transportation, acknowledging some looks with a nod. But the person who really caught her eye was a rather unconventionally dressed woman in her mid-40s with dark hair, oversized glasses and lips several shades too red, who was just concluding a conversation with another woman as Charlotte approached.

"Ah, Charlotte," Dr. Penelope Langrishe said, grabbing Charlotte's arms in her surprisingly strong hands. Shorter than Charlotte by a few inches, Penelope was wearing her usual bohemian assortment of clothing: a long wool skirt over Western boots, topped by a silk blouse and a men's brown sports jacket. A gold necklace and matching hanging earrings completed the ensemble, and her face, so dominated by the brown glasses and red lips, hid the piercing blue eyes, which could jump out at someone unexpectedly during conversation.

"Penelope, I am so glad to see you. It's been, what, two months since we last spoke?"

"Bring me some more cases and then we can see each other more," Penelope said with a laugh. "Helping law enforcement with psychiatric profiles is one of the more interesting parts of what I do."

Charlotte was surprised that Penelope would find any part of her job *un*interesting. It was not generally known that OIG, like the Justice Department, the FBI and many law enforcement organizations throughout the country, sometimes consulted a psychiatrist in regards to illegal behavior. OIG would, on occasion, contract with her to help profile the behaviors of individuals and organizations who might, or who were suspected of, committing fraud. Her insights, which could be penetrating at times, had helped the agency on numerous occasions, not only in terms of fraud investigations but, if truth be known, in settlement negotiations.

"You've been a great help to me, personally as well as professionally, you know that," Charlotte said, feeling her eyes moisten, such was her affection for the woman. "There are times when I have felt quite grateful to you. And I appreciate the fact that you have kept those personal conversations private."

"Not a problem, my dear, you know how fond I am of you. And you are not the first government official with whom I have worked who I have also helped in their personal lives. That said, though, I am really not sure how much help I have been to you."

"What do you mean?" asked Charlotte. "You've been a tremendous help on all sorts of things, from handling my job to, well, you know…"

Penelope motioned to a nearby sofa, where they sat down.

"I'm glad to hear that, my dear, and it's up to you whether you take my advice or not, of course, but…"

Charlotte nodded. "You mean the laser gun."

"Yes, that totally useless, trouble-causing laser gun of yours. Why you persist in firing that thing in your office, given all the trouble it has cost you, is quite beyond me. Or, excuse me for being falsely modest. It is not beyond me. We both know why you feel a need to do it, but that doesn't mean you have to do it. The trouble it has caused you with the press, with your reputation among your legal staff, not to mention the Administration, is just not worth it, Charlotte."

Charlotte thought a moment. There was no doubt Penelope was right. Ever since she took the OIG job and decided to show her seriousness about cracking down on fraud by firing the laser pistol at the bullseye on her wall, she had been in for it. The press, which already had run skeptical articles about her appointment three years ago, saying she got the job only because of her father, had jumped on this as an example of her not being the right person for the position. Two senior staff attorneys who, like their colleagues, prided themselves on showing the public that their prosecutions were based on sober and fair-minded analysis of medical providers, resigned their positions when she refused to stop, saying she was trivializing the agency's image and purpose. Many of the attorneys still on staff agreed. Even Lewis had told her more than once that this "affectation" of hers was causing her problems. And HHS Secretary Balcom was not happy about it. He had told her so himself. And he was not a man who would say something without being sure that his boss – at the White House – agreed.

And yet Charlotte persisted, taking out the laser gun almost with a relish at defying conventional wisdom. She knew her own intent as to combating Medicare fraud and felt she didn't need to prove it to anyone. But she also know that, as an official in the public eye, that wasn't the case. Public officials constantly have to prove and re-prove their worth. The irony was that her original intent was that the laser gun would be a symbol of her dedication to the cause. That it wasn't taken that way, and that it was instead perceived as some kind of flakiness on her part, irritated her, but it also did something else. It triggered that rebellious side that she had had since growing up as a Senator's daughter, as if to say, "No, I am going to do this my way." And so she took an almost fiendish delight in pulling out the gun and firing at the wall. Was she overcompensating? she asked herself. Penelope had suggested as much, noting that many professional women felt a need to do, to create a "tough" image, but sometimes went too far. In Charlotte's case, Penelope had suggested, the need to overcompensate was even greater, given that she also felt a need to overcome the perception the she got her position because she was her father's daughter. In the end, Charlotte believed, it wouldn't matter. She would be judged on the cases she successfully concluded and the Medicare money she returned to the public coffers.

"I know," she told Penelope.

Penelope sighed and shrugged. "Among your many wonderful and not-so-wonderful qualities, my dear, I am going to have to add a dose of stubbornness."

Both women laughed. Such was their relationship that they could be completely candid with each other. After all, Penelope had been a sounding board to Charlotte not only on numerous cases, but on many aspects of her personal life, including her relationship with her father and Charlotte's own ambiguous feelings about reaching age 42 and having never been married, with no prospects in sight, although Penelope, like her other friends, had noticed the bond between her and Mack.

"I'll keep working through it with you, if that's alright."

"Always, my dear," Penelope said. "Now, what do you think about this?" She took a folded newspaper article out from her purse. It was that morning's *Washington Post* article about Dana's murder the night before.

"There's been a *second* murder?" Charlotte said, scanning the article. "I didn't have time to read the paper this morning."

"This is beginning to get interesting to me," Penelope said. "The coincidences here, you know. The two victims apparently knew each other, were romantically involved. They were both medical students. And, of course, the murders happened just as James Buchanan is being investigated for fraud." Her blue eyes stared out at Charlotte from under the glasses.

"Penelope, are you suggesting that the murders are linked to the fraud investigations we're doing?"

Penelope shrugged. "I tend not to believe in coincidences."

James gave a loud clap with his hands as he stood in the middle of the room.

"Dinner is ready, everyone," he said, with a gleam of pride in his eye. "And may I just say: crown roast of lamb a la Tobias." Off to the side, Lewis looked at his partner with a mixture of humor and affection, as Charlotte, Penelope, Mack and the other guests made appropriate noises to show they were impressed.

They then all rose from their seats and hurried into the dining room for what they knew would be a delicious meal and a delightful evening.

14

Charlotte was reading the *Washington Post* the next morning with what seemed like unusual interest, or so Lewis thought as he walked in for their daily meeting. She hardly looked up as he entered, her pants-clad long legs and high-heeled feet up on her desk, her body reclining against the wall in her office chair.

"Something of interest?" Lewis lifted his glasses to his face and settled himself into his usual place on the couch nearby.

"Second murder at James Buchanan, did you hear about it?"

Lewis nodded. "Yes, I read about it yesterday. Seems like the university will have their hands full with the killer and the police investigation." He chuckled. "Not to mention our investigation. I actually sometimes feel bad for Chamroeun."

Charlotte put the paper down and leaned forward. "I do feel bad for him." Before Lewis could protest, she continued. "I know, I know, if someone there is ripping off government money, they do not deserve our sympathy. Still, he seems like a kind man."

"Many people do," Lewis said. "And many of them will argue that they are not misusing government money. In their eyes, they aren't. But we cannot allow any one group of citizens to define the law and how it applies to them.

What would society be like in that event? The law applies to *everyone*." He said the last line with particular force.

Charlotte smiled. Good old Lewis. A victim of so much persecution by his peers when he was younger, the equal application of the law was a passion with him. And she had to agree.

"Anyway, old friend, here's what crossed my mind: What if these two crimes – the murders on the one hand and our fraud and abuse investigation on the other – are not isolated, but linked? What if the murders are tied into the fraud?"

"What makes you think so? Do you know something?" He leaned forward, waiting expectantly to hear about some inside tip that Charlotte may have received, perhaps from an anonymous university official or maybe someone in the police department.

"Just something Penelope said last night. It just seems to be an odd coincidence, that's all, that these murders would occur just as the fraud cases are heating up."

"Maybe, but what would the motive be in killing two medical students? No one is suggesting they were involved in the fraud."

"Who knows, Lewis? I'm just thinking out loud. Maybe they knew something, or maybe one of them did, was killed to protect the person really committing the fraud, and then the other was killed because they found out about it."

"Or maybe they were both spies for Al Qaeda, and had a falling out with their Taliban supervisor."

Charlotte took the point. "Okay, we have no proof. But I'm going to look into this a bit."

"What? How…? Your authority doesn't extend to criminal police work. Besides, you have more than enough to keep yourself busy here."

"True, but…" Charlotte took her laser gun out of its drawer and aimed it at the bullseye across the room. Lewis shrunk back in his seat. "Penelope is rarely wrong, you know, and this sparks my interest. Who knows, Lewis, we may actually find a connection."

The red laser hit the target, several inches away from the bulls eye. Lewis could imagine the reaction if OIG's employees, deep in work on their computers or reviewing testimony or other legal papers, could see what was going.

"Whoa, let's slow down. I don't even know where to begin. First, have you done this kind of work before? Won't the police object to your being involved? Where would you start? What do you intend to do, walk down to the crime scene yourself with a big magnifying glass and a deerstalker cap, like Sherlock Holmes? How do you plan to coordinate with the police? Aren't you concerned that you will be acting outside your mandate as HHS Inspector General? What if the press, or the TV, God forbid, catch you and put you on the evening news? How about Congress and Mack's committee? There's probably more, but I thought I would stop there."

"Okay." Charlotte put down the gun, noticing Lewis's body language relax a bit as she did so. "I don't intend to be very obvious, give me a little credit, so I don't expect the media or Congress to hear about this. There are lots of reasons for you and I to visit the campus that fit in well with our fraud investigation – and in fact I do not want that fraud investigation to slow down, not one bit – so I could argue that I would have to be in many of these places anyway. If I run into the police, into" she looked at the newspaper for a name, "Detective Petrelli, I will simply ask him some questions about the case as a professional courtesy. That is not unusual between law enforcement officials. He can ask me questions about the fraud case. And, finally, Lewis, I am hoping that I will not be doing this alone, that you will help me, so I won't have to be around the campus that much."

"Me? This is a little out of my line. What would you have me do?"

"I don't know yet. You're getting way ahead of things. All I suggest is that, for a start, when we speak with university officials and others in the course of the fraud investigation, we also ask how progress is going on the murders. That's only natural, right?"

Lewis nodded, a bit weakly.

"And you know what? Let's say they do turn out to be linked. Then I think we can make a case that we should be involved, because it involves Medicare fraud."

"Of course," Lewis noted, "the reverse would also be true."
Charlotte looked at him, puzzled.

"If the two are connected, there's nothing stopping the D.C. police from getting involved in our fraud investigation."

"Hmmm…" Charlotte thought about this a moment, then took out the laser gun and fired it at the wall again. Lewis didn't even look to see if she had hit her mark.

15

The sobs were audible.

Mostly they came from Dana's mother, standing with her husband at her daughter's graveside as the minister concluded his eulogy.

"And when one so young and talented as Dana is taken from us, we have to ask God, 'Why?' Yet too often the answer is not forthcoming. In such moments we have really two choices: to give up, wallow in despair at life's unforgiving nature, which I do not think is what Dana would have wanted us to do; or to accept what has always been true, and what is stated in the Bible: that the ways of the Lord are not always clear to us, but there is a purpose nonetheless."

It was not the best day for a funeral. The sky was overcast and a light drizzle had begun falling at the cemetery in nearby Gaithersburg, the Maryland suburb where Dana grew up and where her family still lived. At the funeral, in addition to her parents and the minister, were her two younger brothers. From the university were many friends and faculty, including Arun, Peter and Marjorie, Lyle and Angela, and Jennifer and Michael. Also there was Detective Petrelli, who kept one eye on the funeral and the other mostly on Nick, who hung back from the others, seemingly not wanting to get too close. Another mourner who no one seemed to know also hung back, but leaned her head forward so as not to miss any of the minister's words. A tall, slim woman in her mid-20s with long brown hair, she was doing something that others thought incongruous: she was taking notes into what looked like a long, thin reporter's notebook.

The minister finished his remarks and the casket was lowered slowly into the open grave by an electronic platform. Then workmen covered the casket with dirt, patting the earth dry with the backs of their shovels as they were done.

Arun walked up to Dana's parents and introduced himself.

"I cannot express to you how sorry I am that this happened," he said, visibly affected. "I know that nothing I can do will really make a difference, but I just wanted to let you know that if there is anything that I, personally, or any faculty member, or the university hospital itself can do, please let us know."

"Thank you, Doctor." Roger Brentano, whom Arun noticed was elderly compared to the parents of most college students, was a tall, reedy man with a nasal voice and a reticent manner. "I suppose every parent says this, because they, like we, had some issues with their children. Usually most get resolved as the children get older. One of the things that hurts me the most is that Dana and I will never have a chance to put all of our issues to rest."

Arun nodded sympathetically. "Yes, my own father and I had several issues, but before he died, we had, I believe, successfully reached an understanding on most of them."

Dana's mother's eyes welled with tears and she leaned into husband's chest.

"I…I'm sorry," Barbara Brentano said, as the two men sought to comfort her. "I just miss her, and I don't know how I'm going to get through this."

Her husband said nothing as he held her. "Excuse us, Doctor." He guided her away from the crowd.

"How awful." Arun turned to see Jennifer beside him, along with Michael. Peter and Marjorie joined them, followed by Lyle and Angela.

"Yes, there's no going back for them. They will hopefully be able to go on, but their life will never be the same," Arun said.

Peter let out a deep sigh. All turned to look at him.

"Darling?" Marjorie asked.

"I knew both of them fairly well, you know. They were in my classes. They were both good people. This is harder on me than I would have expected, especially now that it seems we may have some kind of serial killer on the loose. Who knows – "

"Peter, don't," said Marjorie.

"The police don't really know yet it if it is a serial killer," said Lyle, motioning to Petrelli standing nearby. "From what I understand, that's one possibility, but it could just as easily have been a personal quarrel. After all, Scott and Dana were involved with each other. If a serial killer was randomly picking victims, it seems unlikely he would pick both of them by chance. More likely it was someone who had some issue with them, either with Scott or Dana separately, or with them as a couple."

All eyes turned toward Nick, who was now at Dana's grave, staring down at the dirt mound.

"I'm sorry, I just can't believe it," said Jennifer. "I've had Nick in some of my classes, just as the rest of you have. He is not some kind of psychopathic killer." She shook her head in emphasis.

"Maybe not, I grant you it is hard to believe in Nick's case," said Lyle. "But on the other hand, if we accept the theory that the killer is someone who knew Scott and Dana, then we also have to accept that it may be someone we know. And I don't believe any of us think that someone who we know is the murderer, and yet someone we know probably is."

Lyle's remark hit home. Any of them, or anyone they worked with or who saw Scott and Dana regularly, could be the killer. Maybe it was another student, but even then there was a good chance they knew the person.

"But there's another possibility" said Marjorie. "Not someone we know, yet not a stranger to Scott and Dana, either. We've all read about individuals who get obsessed with people or things. It could be that some guy, maybe a vendor who makes deliveries to the university or a part time student who audits courses, or anyone at all, became enamored of, say, Dana, jealous of Scott, and in his sick fantasy, killed them both. Or the other way around. A psychopathic woman became enamored of Scott and—"

"This may not be the best place for this kind of discussion," Arun interrupted.

"He's right, Marjorie," said Peter.

"I am so sorry, I just…" Marjorie looked at each of them apologetically.

"It's alright, Marj," Arun said. "We've all been caught up by this, unfortunately."

"That is right," said Peter, "which is why Marj and I are going to take some time off and maybe go on a vacation."

All heads turned toward Peter.

"A vacation? Now?" Marj asked.

"Especially now," Peter replied. "I have just had it." He walked away from the group for a second, then came back.

"This is not what I bargained for in my career, you know? And I don't think it's what any of us bargained for."

The others looked at him, waiting for him to go on. Sure, no one planned for students to be murdered.

"Scott and Dana. Then there's the OIG investigation. The stress is, well, the stress is unbelievable. I think some time off, for all of us frankly – I would urge each of you to do the same thing and go off somewhere for at least a couple of weeks. We should work out a schedule, Arun. We have to restore some sort of mental health, some balance to life. It's just not good to live in this kind of pressure-cooker environment. You know, with all this stuff going on, there's still the pressure that we *want* to have: saving lives, teaching young minds. That's why we're here."

Arun nodded. "Actually, not a bad idea. But I don't think I can leave anytime soon, not with the OIG investigation. They want me around, since I'm the chief administrator."

The others understood. Arun, after all, was the man in charge. But that didn't mean that any of them couldn't take some time off. They could always answer OIG questions when they returned. And the murders, well, the sad truth is, Lyle thought, if there are going to be more, they will happen whether they were there or not. Not much we can do to help.

"Any place in mind?" he asked Peter.

Peter smiled. "This is the first I've mentioned it. I haven't even had a chance to discuss this with Marjorie yet."

"I'll say," Marjorie put in. "When did you plan to go? I would need to work it out with my office. And there's the whole question of where."

"I was thinking of Vienna," Peter said. Marjorie lit up at the name, and the others repeated the city's name.

"It's the perfect place to get away," Arun said, "if you're not the type to want an island resort. I've been there several times. Wonderful city."

"It also has special meaning for Marj and me. That's where we met."

Marjorie looked up at Peter. "That is a great idea, darling. What's it been, twelve years?"

"Anyway, just a thought. I don't want to build up hopes too much. But then again," Peter said, looking at the others. "Look at how just the mention of something positive has brightened up the group. A few seconds ago, we were all glum, pressured. Now we mention a trip to Vienna, and there's something positive on the horizon."

Lyle looked over at Roger and Barbara Brentano, now sitting on a bench near the grave site, with Dana's dad continuing to comfort his wife. "Positive for us, you mean," he said.

16

Charlotte found Arun's office at the university hospital to be much like the man himself: impeccably appointed, with beautiful dark wood, book-lined shelves, Persian rugs on a polished hard-wood floor. On one wall near the door was a glass display case with what she took to be various family memorabilia. Arun, she understood, came from an aristocratic Khmer family and that his father was very high in government service before they fled Cambodia after the Khmer Rouge took over.

Arun himself, wearing a gray suit with silk matching tie, rose from behind his large mahogany desk to greet her, shaking her hand and then motioning her to a comfortable upholstered hard wood chair across from him. She noticed the expensive, amethyst pinky ring on his outstretched hand.

If only the government spent like this on its offices, Charlotte couldn't help thinking, recalling the spare conference room where she and Lewis had met Arun and Paul Holden. She was glad to receive Arun's invitation, however unorthodox it was, because it also gave her a chance to get more involved in the murder investigation. She would not only be able to visit his office, but look over the campus, talk to some people, and get a sense of how things worked, maybe gain some insights Killing two birds with one stone was not a bad thing, she mused.

Looking around the office, she saw that Arun had a number of photographs of himself on various trips with family members, as well as with some notables: in one, he stood beside a famous software manufacturer, each holding up a salmon they had caught, presumably near the magnate's home in the Pacific Northwest. In another, he and Bill Clinton relaxed at Hilton Head, probably during one of the "idea weekends" where the rich and powerful retreated every few years, and which the former President was known to enjoy; and in a third, at what looked like the inside a famous restaurant, apparently in New York, if only because the picture showed the mayor and his wife seated a few chairs away from Arun.

Also on the walls was some of the original art that Charlotte had heard Arun collected in abundance at his home. Some were surprisingly American, including a William Dean Harnett and a Winslow Homer. But the majority looked like the works of European masters from the seventeenth through nineteenth centuries. Each painting had its own light fixture and was mounted in a large, beautiful, gold-lacquered frame. The Persian rugs were, she had no doubt, original, as were some of the small Asian sculptures in the room's far corners.

"Do you like the artwork?" he asked her.

Arun had been making his own study of Charlotte. Clearly well-educated, he knew that she too came from a background of some privilege. Her father, after all, was Senator David Westbrook of Maryland, now retired, but who in his prime ruled the Senate Armed Services Committee as its chairman for a generation. Charlotte, he had heard, had grown up in her parents' two homes: a refurbished Dupont Circle townhouse, and an estate on the water near St. Michael's, on Maryland's eastern shore. Her mother reputedly was content to preside proudly over her domiciles as the senator's wife. Priding himself as a keen judge of human nature, Arun guessed that Charlotte, given her career choices, was more influenced by her father than by her mother and, like many women, was motivated largely by a need to win her father's approval. He understood, in fact, that Charlotte turned to her father for advice from time to time, frequently visiting him in his retirement at the St. Michael's estate. Charlotte herself had taken over the Dupont Circle home.

But what struck Arun at this moment was what he did not yet know about Charlotte. Was she an attack dog, like her colleague, Lewis Sullivan, had showed himself to be at the OIG meeting? He had sensed then, and continued to sense, that there was more to Charlotte than simply investigating and prosecuting OIG cases. She had expressed some sympathy for the university's predicament when they met earlier. He hoped to now see how deep that side of her went.

"Always get the true measure of the person on the other side of the table before deciding if he is a true enemy," said his father, affectionately known by intimates as the Old Soldier, *le Vieux Soldat*. It was advice he had found useful through the years.

Charlotte settled herself in the chair. Her first question took Arun by surprise.

"So, who do you think the murderer is?"

"Somewhat away from the main course of your investigation, isn't that?" he asked.

Charlotte shrugged. "Everyone seems to have an opinion, and it's in the paper and on TV, so I was curious what you thought."

This is an icebreaker she is using to find out something else. Smart woman. "I really have no idea," he said. "And I've spoken to a number of people here on the campus, no one does. But it is a very disturbing thing, to think that someone out there..."

"Yes, I can imagine it is. You don't think, do you, Mr. Chamroeun, that there might be some link between these murders and our investigation?"

Where was this woman going with this line of questioning?

"I must admit, Inspector General, that you have taken me a bit by surprise here. I asked you here, and was glad you accepted, to see what we might be able to do to speed up the investigation your office is conducting."

"Is there a problem with how it's being conducted? All the reports I receive indicate that everything is going apace."

"Yes, but at what pace, Inspector General? Please don't misunderstand me, I am not suggesting that OIG do less than a thorough job. But you must understand, an investigation like this has a devastating effect on the work that gets done here, on morale, on the credibility of the university hospital, the university itself, and more. I was hoping you might be able to give me some sense of how long this would take. Are we talking weeks, months, not much longer, I hope?"

So this was the reason for the invitation. Charlotte knew from experience that this feeling was not atypical. A health care provider gets into trouble, gets investigated for alleged wrongdoing that in almost every case turns out to have at least something behind it, and then complains about the length of the investigation and the effect on the university's business. The truth, of course, was that if the university had not gotten itself into trouble to begin with, there would be no investigation at all.

"No charge has been proven to date," Arun continued. "It would be ironic, would it not, Inspector General, if all charges ultimately were dropped, but the university hospital, the university, and all the fine doctors who work here had their reputations damaged and business affected, all for nothing?"

So you're the one who is truly innocent. Charlotte had yet to see one in her three years on the job. Sure, a small physician practice might have legitimate explanations for filing some bad claims, but in a major investigation like this, there always turned out to be something. And Lewis was convinced that this was a significant case.

"I appreciate your concerns, Mr. Chamroeun, but I am really as much a prisoner of our auditors and investigators as you are. We tell them to do a thorough job. Now we have to let them do it. Just how long this takes depends on what they find out. I don't have to tell you, I am sure, that in some past investigations at other institutions, they began by looking into one set of allegations, but along the way, discovered other irregularities. So there was a cascade of separate investigations, each handled individually. We told you the main areas we were looking into when we met at OIG. It would be a mistake to think they will necessarily all be handled as one case. For some of those areas, we might be able to wrap things up quickly, then decide if charges need to be brought or not, which of course can be handled through either a settlement or going to court. But for other areas, the investigations could continue for months. And if my staff finds additional problems along the way, I won't lie to you. This could take years. It really depends on what they find."

"How do you expect a major health care institution to operate under those conditions?" Arun asked, showing some exasperation. "Staff are constantly looking over their shoulders to see if someone is watching, doctors second guess their every move, the reputation of the institution is besmirched, which affects admissions…"

"The alternative, then, would be for us *not* to investigate major institutions where we have good reason to suspect wrongdoing?" Charlotte countered. "Are you saying that institutions like James Buchanan should be exempt from the rule of law?"

Arun leaned back in his chair, ratcheting down the tension. "Well, no, of course not. I would never suggest that. All I am asking is that, since we are all innocent until proven guilty, that the effect of the investigation on the institutions you are investigating be taken into account."

Charlotte mirrored his body language, leaning back in her chair and crossing her legs. "Of course. I do understand. We are aware of this, and try to balance our investigations with some sensitivity for the operations of who we are investigating. We are, of course, aware that you provide health care for thousands of patients. We don't want to get in the way of that. Nor do we prosecute innocent mistakes."

"I am glad to hear that."

An awkward silence punctuated the tension. Arun looked at the brass clock on his desk, which read 12:55.

"May I show you something, Inspector General?" he asked, rising from his seat and motioning Charlotte to follow him toward the window. Charlotte, curious, walked over with him. The window overlooked a large university quadrangle, the same one that Dana had walked through just before she was murdered. It was a bright, pleasant day in the third week of February, and students and faculty could be seen hurrying along, doubtless on their way to class, Charlotte assumed. She remembered her own college days with some fondness.

"Ah, there," said Arun, pointing to a group of faculty, five men and women – doctors, Charlotte assumed, since she could see that, under their winter coats, they were wearing long white coats over their shirts and blouses – heading toward the university hospital. She didn't know any of them by sight.

"Those five people represent some of the finest medical minds on any university campus in the country," Arun said. "And they find themselves under incredible stress. Stress because of this investigation. And stress because of the murders. Two of them have spoken to me of seeking employment at another university. Another is planning a vacation to Vienna, just to get away from it all. And another is thinking of taking an early retirement."

Charlotte looked at him blankly. "I am not sure of the point you are making."

Arun was clearly agitated. "Inspector General, can we take a bigger view than simply whether this university committed any irregularities?"

"That's an interesting way of putting it. We are investigating suspected crimes that may have involved millions of dollars in taxpayer money."

"Alright, crimes. But look at those doctors. Do they look like criminals to you?"

"I don't know that they are. I don't even know if we are investigating them."

"Do I look like a thief to you, Inspector General?"

This was beginning to get out of hand. "Mr. Chamroeun, I am starting to feel a bit uncomfortable in this meeting. I've explained to you what we are doing and why. If you don't want to accept —"

Arun held up his hand and took a deep breath. "My apologies, Inspector General, I behaved badly." His father's warnings about grace under pressure took hold. "The point I wanted to make, and made badly, is that there is a larger good here. Again, please don't misunderstand me. If there was a crime, it should be investigated, and it should be punished. Fine, do that. But if the price of that investigation is that medical institution after medical institution in this country — I am not talking just about James Buchanan here — is less able to provide effective health care, that some guilty people are caught but in the process the reputations of good people are ruined, that this country's position as a leader in medical education is undercut. ... Doesn't some discretion have to apply?"

"We've already —"

"Individual judgment, Inspector General. That's what is at stake. Doctors' careers, as many others, are based on their individual professional judgments. Most of the time, given their education, make correct decisions. But sometimes those decisions are wrong, and they make a mistake, whether it is not supervising correctly or assigning a wrong code to a procedure. Great medical institutions, like James Buchanan, are built on the decisions of those doctors, and the professional administrators that run them, people like me, and the staffing decisions we make. Some mistakes will be made, no doubt. But great institutions rise up.

"What would be the societal cost, Inspector General, if professionals like those doctors I just showed you, or people like me – all of us trained for years in our fields – suddenly felt that society no longer allowed us the freedom to exercise our individual judgments? What would be the affect on patients, even those at small physician practices, since you investigate them, too, and at large practices, at hospitals across the country, and at medical centers, if professionals trained in the craft felt they could no longer rely on their own individual judgments? The effects would be devastating: They would no longer be trusted to make judgments, because they might make mistakes, both medical mistakes and administrative mistakes, and those mistakes could lead to government investigations like yours, and financial and career ruin.

"You know what would happen, Inspector General? I do. Some would leave the field entirely, their incentive to do good dried up by fear of a government not accepting their value to society and second-guessing their every move. Others would stay. But those who stay would become bureaucratic. There would be little room for following a hunch, or cutting a corner for a greater good. There would be fewer breakthroughs in medicine and in new equipment, and in lesser matters, all because the government no longer trusted them.

"You know, Inspector General, you can look at any profession and the people in it, and it you put it under the microscope long enough, you will find problems. Do you think Marie Curie or Louis Pasteur worried about procedures and rules when they did their work? No, because they were concerned with the work itself. That's what they went to school for, that's what they trained for. But today! If they lived and worked today on a medical university campus, maybe they would be too busy making sure they were not accidentally misspending government money, or too afraid of having their reputations tarnished, to achieve what they did."

Charlotte took it all in. She could see the passion and sincerity in Arun's statement. And he had a point. But they all had a role to play in society. And someone had to watch out for the public's money. That was OIG's role, and she was the inspector general. And then, of course, this case did have that one additional wrinkle.

"Or perhaps these doctors want to leave because they just don't want to get caught."

17

Whistleblower: Qui tam (Latin): One who acts in the name of the king.

W histleblowers are as old as human history. Whether one calls them informers, rat finks, stool pigeons, or high-minded public citizens, they have been with us since people began living together in communities. More recent incarnations have included Linda Tripp, who recorded her conversations with Monica Lewinsky, the one-time intern of President Bill Clinton; and those officials who came forth after 9/11 to say the government had warning of the plot to hijack domestic airliners and fly them into key buildings, but that the government did not do enough to stop it.

It is not unusual for law enforcement authorities to rely on whistleblowers to find out about crime. In the United States, the federal government and some states have what are known as *qui tam* laws, which allow whistleblowers in certain areas, including health care, to come forward and bring charges against a wrongdoer. The *qui tam* relator, as the whistleblower is called, is, in fact, acting in the name of the state (or in ancient parlance, the king). Most of these cases come to nothing, unless the government joins in. Then the odds of a settlement or conviction ratchet up sharply, with current law allowing whistleblowers to collect as much as 25% of any settlement or award. When settlements with major medical institutions reach hundreds of millions of dollars, suddenly a bookkeeper, coder or even a compliance officer who turns on his her employer is looking at a huge increase in income.

"To catch a rogue, set a rogue," is how the practice is justified. Government attorneys, after all, do not have to actually like the whistleblowers they work with. They just have to be convinced that the information is accurate. And, in fact, many of the government's best health care convictions, with the largest settlements, have been brought forward by whistleblowers, many of whom received substantial dollars for their efforts.

Whether a whistleblower is a virtuous person or simply a greedy one is, of course, one of those subjects that is never settled, perhaps in part because both kinds of individuals come forth. In some cases, both motivations are simultaneously in play. Certainly it is true that few, if any, whistleblowers become rich quickly. Once charges are brought, it may take years of investigations, negotiations, trial and more before a settlement is reached. During that time the whistleblower – despite increasingly strict anti-retaliatory provisions written into law – is, in effect, blacklisted at work. He or she may be able to stay employed because the law forbids being fired, but the whistleblower is ostracized in many other ways, and feels it, socially and more. If you wanted to get rich and were considering becoming a whistleblower, you had better first be informed of what you were going to go through and whether you were prepared to pay the price. Unfortunately for them, many would-be whistleblowers sometimes do not take this into account, motivated either by frustration with institutions that do not work well, or simply by dollar signs flashing in their eyes.

"We have a *qui tam* relator in the James Buchanan case," Lewis informed Charlotte a couple of days after her meeting with Arun.

Charlotte recalled her conversation with Arun two days before. It was increasingly looking like his fears might prove to be true and that this investigation could go on for months. *Am I beginning to feel bad for him?*

"What, exactly, is the relator alleging?"

"Personal witnessing of improper supervision, followed by claims to Medicare for full supervision."

Charlotte nodded. "How widespread?"

"Not sure yet. But more than one. She's going to come in later for a deposition."

"All we have is her word on it? How do we know she's not just looking to cash in and is making something up that can be successfully challenged?"

"We don't, at this point. It's just her word against what will be those of the doctors and the residents they worked with. But it's a starting point. We interview the doctors, the residents, check various logs, etc. You know, there have been several instances at other hospitals of doctors getting caught because they left supervision early to play golf. And we found out, after they denied it, by checking with their tee up times at the golf course."

Lewis seemed very pleased with himself as he recalled these instances.

"Let's just make sure we have our facts straight before we go about wrecking anyone's reputation," she said.

"I thought you'd be excited at the news."

Charlotte sighed. "We work in an advocacy system, Lewis. The prosecutors push for one side and the defense for the other. I just wonder sometimes if that system works best for everyone."

"It's worked for over 200 years."

"It's worked, but sometimes I wonder how well. I've always wondered about that, since law school. Actually, it seems very macho, this whole advocacy system. Like a boxing match. But the best result is not always that one guy gets pummeled and ruined, and the other victorious. Sometimes the truth is more complicated."

Where was Charlotte going with this? "Aren't you the one firing the laser gun at the wall?"

"Because I believe we are working for the public good, and take satisfaction whenever we make progress. But let me ask you this, Lewis. If a doctor, or an institution, generally does good, then it turns out it did some things bad, should the punishment be so bad that the good is not taken into the picture? Should the community lose all the good that gets done? And should we take such glee in convicting or settling for huge sums of money with otherwise good people, ruining their reputations in the process?"

"There is some discretion in punishment."

"Not as much as many people think. You know that if a doctor gets excluded from Medicare, for instance, the minimum is five years. That's not negotiable. You can't exclude someone for, say, six months, arguing they just needed to get their hand slapped. And for many physician practices today that get so much of their income from Medicare, that means they go out of business. And the community loses a valuable service."

"You sound like a defense attorney," Lewis said angrily. "Are you thinking of changing sides?"

Lewis caught himself. Even for someone with as close a relationship with the Inspector General as he had, that may have been overstepping the line. "I'm sorry, Charlotte. I shouldn't have said that."

Charlotte shook her head. "Don't worry about it. No, I am not arguing that we should be any less vigilant in going after Medicare fraud. It is the public's money that is being misused and it is our job to safeguard that money. But I just wonder…"

"What?"

"If the number of casualties in these cases have to be so high."

18

Peter liked supervising residents during surgery. Well, most of the time. The ones who showed special skill were a pleasure to watch. He admired their confidence and ease of motion when reaching into the chest cavity or leg of a patient and making repairs, something that more mediocre residents did with much more caution. Did I have that much confidence when I was a resident? he wondered. He wasn't sure.

Today he was overseeing two residents in the operating room. One, Cathy Arliss, was performing an appendectomy on a 68-year-old woman. Peter had seen her work before and thought her fairly talented. Truth was, he knew, she probably did the job better than some of the staff who supervised her. The other, Gretchen Wyle, lacked the talent that Cathy showed. She was preparing another patient, a 72-year-old man, already unconscious, so she could fix a hernia before it became strangulated.

Operating rooms could be intimidating for those not familiar with them. Aside from the pressure of doing the operation itself, there were the bright lights and the presence of other personnel: an anesthesiologist, two nurses, and Peter himself. Being an effective surgeon under such circumstances took the same concentration that Tiger Woods needed during a golf tournament when, surrounded by television cameras and crowds, he had to give his full attention to the shot.

"Alright, I'm in," Gretchen said. She had found the tear in the abdominal wall where part of the intestine had poked through.

"And you know what to do," Peter said.

"I'm going to stitch the wall back together."

"Making sure you put the protruding part of the intestine back in first, of course," Peter said from behind his surgical mask.

"Yes, doctor, of course."

"Just kidding, Gretchen. You're doing fine. Carry on. I have to see how our other resident is doing."

He walked over to Cathy, where the patient lay unconscious on the table. Seeing him nod to give her the go-ahead, Cathy, using a sure but light touch, expertly cut a 2.5 inch incision in the lower right section of the patient's abdomen. Like she's been doing it for years, Peter thought.

The appendix was red in its enflamed state.

"Now that's a cry for removal," Cathy said.

"Go to it," Peter said, leaving her and the nurses around her to the operation. The best help I can give her is to not get in her way, he knew. Gretchen, on the other hand, seemed to steady whenever Peter returned.

"Dr. Kenyon, would you mind signing this?"

Peter turned to find Carla Calloway, one of the reimbursement staff, offering him a clipboard and pen. Administrative staff, particularly coders and billers, did not typically come into the operating room – and, in fact, given that they had to wash up, put on a gown and mask, few wanted to bother – but there were times when an important signature was needed and time was pressing. This was apparently one of those times.

"Been seeing a lot of you in here, Carla. What is this, the third time in the past two weeks? I'm beginning to think you want to go to med school."

Carla, a plump woman in her early 50s with auburn hair and glasses, laughed behind her mask. "No way, doctor. I'm glad you can all do this work, but not me," she said, looking around, "I'd probably pass out first."

Peter chuckled, initialed the form where she indicated, then handed the clipboard back

19

The knock on Nick's apartment door woke him up with a start. He buried his head in the pillow, praying it was one of those vivid dreams when you couldn't tell if it was really happening or not. But a second knock, louder and more insistent, told him that, unfortunately, this was not a vivid dream.

His head hurt from too much drink the night before. He turned to look at the display on his clock: 8:30 a.m. Who would be knocking at this hour of a Saturday morning?

Forcing himself to sit up, he found his slippers and began to put on his bathrobe, when the answer came through with the third knock.

"Nick, are you in there?" the all-too-familiar voice said. "It's Detective Al Petrelli."

The last person on earth I want to see. Nick reluctantly stumbled to the door and opened it, surprised to find another man with Petrelli.

"This is Detective Michael Civoletti, a member of my team," said Petrelli, wearing a typical ill-fitting sports jacket, shirt and tie. Nick noticed that one of the collar ends on Petrelli's shirts was sticking up.

The two men walked into the apartment.

"Hey, don't you have to ask me —"

"Nicholas Rosen, you are under arrest for the murder of Scott Karakas. Detective Civoletti will read you your rights."

"Wha--?" Nick said as Civoletti, a man as thin as Petrelli was heavy, but sharing the same taste in clothes, began Mirandizing him.

"Do you understand your rights?" Civoletti asked when he was done.

"Yes, I understand them," Nick said, turning to Petrelli.

"Better throw on some clothes, Nick, unless you want to go to jail like that."

"Detective Petrelli, look, I know maybe I wasn't as cooperative as I could have been and maybe a little rude, but you have to understand, Scott was my best friend. I swear to you, I did not kill him."

"I'd like to believe you, Nick, but the evidence we found here provides you with the murder weapon, and we both know that you have the motive."

"Murder weapon?"

"Succinylcholine. We found it in one of your cabinets when we were reviewing the items we seized in the search of your apartment earlier."

"Hold on, Detective, that substance can be found in any almost university laboratory. In fact, you can buy it at the drug store."

"But it's not typically found in the home of a medical student. Can you tell me why you would have that in your home? It's primary use is as a muscle relaxer before surgery. C'mon, Nick, get some clothes on. I've seen a naked man before. Let's get going."

Nick took off his bathrobe and began changing.

"No, I can't tell you why you found that here, at least not off the top of my head. But sometimes I put things in my bag without thinking and take them home, then realize I should have left them at the university and take them back the next day. When you put in 16-hour days, your brain can get pretty fogged."

"That's pretty weak, Nick, don't you think? I will bet you that I could search the apartments of five other medical students, picked at random, and none of them would have this in their possession."

"Well, I don't know. ... But you might find they brought home other things, things I didn't."

Petrelli grunted. "Maybe. It is not my job to convict you of this crime, Nick. But I have enough in the way of evidence and motive to arrest you. You can tell the rest to your attorney, the judge and a jury."

"But I didn't do it!" Nick protested, as he put on his shoes.

"Well, Nick, if it turns out you didn't, you can tell the newspapers how I was wrong to suspect you from the start," said Petrelli, as he and Civoletti escorted Nick out of his apartment, making sure he locked the door behind them.

20

Nick again heard the sound of knocking on his door, but this was Sunday morning. He didn't answer it, convincing himself that he was simply reliving the events of the day before: the knock, opening the door to find Petrelli and Civoletti there, the arrest, the trip to police headquarters, the fingerprinting and mug shot, and finally the jail cell. How much worse can this nightmare get, he had asked himself as he sat in his jail cell. Actually, from what he had heard about what could happen to young men like him who were sent to prison, he knew that, in fact, it could get a lot worse. And he was scared to death.

Scared because it was beginning to look like the system might just convict an innocent man. He didn't kill Scott or Dana. Sure, he was a little jealous of Scott and he did love Dana, but they were also his friends. And the fact was, he simply wasn't a murderer. It wasn't in his character to do that. And he wouldn't know how to do it if it was. But he missed his friends horribly.

Now to be arrested for their murder. It was beyond belief. *Petrelli is an idiot.* But, he also knew that being an idiot would not stop Petrelli from sending him to prison.

His first problem had been making bail and getting home. He did what he had to do, but hated to do: he called his parents in New York and explained what had happened. After he calmed them down, they promised to hire an attorney for him, while they electronically forwarded the $50,000 in bail money to the D.C. authorities. How they got it so quickly, given their incomes, was a mystery to him. Maybe they cashed in some insurance policies. If so, that made him feel worse.

Then cell door opened and Petrelli had stepped through.

"You've made bail, Nick. Your parents came through. More than you deserve, in my opinion."

"You are going to be so sorry when you find out you are wrong."

"If I am, I will be. But I don't think so."

"Yeah, right."

Nick took the Metro home, then tried to relax, which proved impossible. He went for a walk outside and tried to enjoy the early March weather, watched TV, nothing worked. It all seemed so surreal. Wasn't this the same apartment he had spent every day in this year, coming back late in the day from the university, making himself a late dinner, then falling asleep on David Letterman? And now, he had no one to talk to. His friends were dead. That was one of the worst things about being arrested and charged with Scott's murder: It robbed him of his ability to grieve for them.

So he laid down on his bed, fully clothed, and fell asleep.

Now it was Sunday morning and there was another knock on the door. And, he realized, it again wasn't a dream.

This is some kind of surrealistic play. Was he caught in some kind of time loop, doomed to repeat the same experience with Petrelli over and over again? Like the horror version of the movie, "Groundhog Day." Even the clock had the same time as yesterday: 8:30 a.m.

He went to the front door and opened it. But it wasn't Petrelli.

"Oh. What are you doing here?" he asked, not meaning to sound as if the visitor was unwelcome. "I mean, you've never…"

"I heard you were arrested," the murderer said. "And then I heard you made bail. So I wanted to come over and see how you were doing. I hope I'm not too early."

"No, not at all. I'm actually grateful for the company," Nick said. "Come on in. Can I get you anything? I think I have some orange juice in the refrigerator."

The murderer entered the apartment and closed the door.

"No thanks. So, how are you doing, Nick? It's been rough, I suppose."

"You have no idea. And I didn't do it, I hope you believe that. I mean, one of the worst things about this is that as soon as you are accused, everyone assumes you must be guilty. Even if they give you the benefit of the doubt, they're not sure, you know?"

"And now it's in the papers," the murderer said, showing him a copy of the *Washington Post* with a below-the-fold front page story by Eileen Ashburton on his arrest. Nick grabbed the paper.

"Oh my God," he said. "This is, this is just all so wrong. You believe me, don't you? I would never have killed either one of them. They were my friends."

"I do believe you, Nick," the murderer said. "And I know they were your friends. And I was very sorry to see them go, too. But I guess there was just no choice."

"What do you mean?" Nick asked, then gasped as he turned around to see the murderer holding a gun on him. "Wha—? You? You're the one? I don't believe it."

"I am truly sorry, Nick. I never intended for any of this to happen. But now it's all too late. And, I'm afraid I can't do much to help you, either."

"You, you're going to kill me?"

The murderer sighed, almost choked back a sob, it seemed to Nick, then motioned to one of the chairs at Nick's kitchen table. "Sit there."

Nick sat. The murderer walked up behind him.

"Please understand me, Nick, if there were any other way." Nick heard him rustling in his pants pocket for something.

"But wait," Nick said. "Why kill me? They've got me pegged for Scott and Dana. If they find me guilty, you're off the hook."

"Can't chance it, Nick. The odds are something will turn up to show that you were not the one who did it, and they might eventually come to me. I can't risk that. That's why I'm here. Anyway, you know it was me, now."

"I don't get it. So you kill me. They're just as likely to find you."

"Not if they think you killed yourself out of guilt for killing Scott and Dana."

"You can't make me kill myself. You can threaten me with that gun, but I will be dead either way. So I'm not going to do it for you."

"I figured you might say that. I was hoping I might scare you into cooperating enough so you would kill yourself, but my hunch was that you wouldn't."

"Wait, wait, wait! Just wait a second! Why are you doing all this to begin with? This doesn't make sense. Why would you have killed Scott, and then Dana? After all, you're a very successful man. It doesn't make sense."

"I would like to explain that," the murderer said. "I would like to talk about that very much. But, unfortunately, we do not have the time, Nick, and now I must say goodbye to you."

Nick thought he heard another sob. But that was quickly superseded a sharp jab, like a needle, in the back of his neck. He felt himself losing consciousness.

The murderer put the gun on the kitchen table and dragged Nick's lifeless body to the bathroom where, as in many of the older D.C. apartments, pipes were visible near the 10 foot ceiling. He produced a rope from his coat and, while still wearing his gloves, tied one end around a pipe above the bathtub, the dragged Nick's body into the tub and, after checking the rope for length, cut the other end, then tied it around Nick's neck. He then held Nick's body up and let go. Much to his relief, the pipe did not break, but held Nick in place, his legs dangling in mid-air. He then brought a stool from the other room into the tub, stood on it, then pulled Nick's body up and let it fall hard, just as it would if Nick had done this himself. He left the stool in the tub, as Nick would have needed it to tie the rope.

The job done, the murderer picked up the excess rope, the knife he used to cut it, retrieved the gun he had left on the kitchen table and, with his hands still gloved, shut off the lights and left the apartment, leaving Nicholas Rosen's dangling body behind him.

21

H eadline, subhead and story in the next day's *Washington Post:*

Third death of James Buchanan student

Medical student found hanged;

Police won't confirm suicide or murder

by Eileen Ashburton

"March 2, Washington, D.C. – Nicholas Rosen, a third-year medical student at James Buchanan University Hospital and the man arrested two days ago for the murder of two other students, was found dead yesterday, hanging by his neck from a rope tied to a pipe in his bathroom, police reported.

"Rosen, 25, is the third medical student found dead at the hospital in the past six weeks. While police would not confirm whether his death was linked either to his arrest or to the murders of the other two students, Scott Karakas and Dana Brentano, the logic of the incidents seems to point in that direction. Whether Rosen did, in fact, murder them, the three are linked, if only because the three of them were considered to be close friends and were frequently seen socializing together, sources said.

"Certainly the way Rosen was found by police yesterday afternoon, hanging by his neck over his bathtub, would lead one to consider suicide a possibility. Police found the body after responding to an anonymous tip, a police spokesperson says. But this case has consistently proven to not be what it seems.

"Karakas, 25, who was found dead in a corridor of the hospital on Jan. 23, was originally thought to have died from natural causes. The death was later ruled a murder after D.C. police found traces of succinylcholine in his system. On the other hand, there was no doubt that Brentano, 24. who had been romantically linked with Karakas, 25, was murdered, after she was found shot to death about three weeks later outside the hospital building.

"As of press time, police were carefully avoiding stating a cause of death in the Rosen case. But clearly the possibilities were suicide, possibly because he had murdered or in some other way caused the deaths of his friends, or because he had been wrongfully charged with the crime and feared for his future; or murder. If Rosen himself was murdered, then the question becomes whether police suspect the same perpetrator as in the Karakas and Brentano killings and the police have not yet officially linked even those two events, according to sources.

"But if the deaths are linked – which seems to be the point of view of many District students – then the question becomes why. The question has clearly frustrated the D.C. police, who are increasingly getting heat from the mayor's office, City Council members, university officials and others to identify and apprehend the killer. Detective Alphonse Petrelli, Jr., a 20-year veteran who has worked many murder investigations, was reportedly meeting with his team yesterday, and could not be reached for comment.

"The case is now drawing nationwide attention, as…

Petrelli sat at his desk at the department's third district headquarters, the newspaper in his hands, his head down. Around him the usual sights, sounds and motions of the office continued, but he seemed oblivious to them. His large frame seemed to weigh his chair down even more heavily than usual as he stared at the ground, then sighed and put the newspaper, with the story about Nick's death, on his desk.

He was waiting for the report, but he knew what it would say. Knew deep in his gut. Then, he thought, I will have to live with myself.

"Autopsy report's in, detective," someone said. "It's on the network."

Petrelli grunted his acknowledgement and turned toward his computer, calling up the file that contained this year's autopsies. Despite what he expected to find, he prayed that he was wrong, that it would turn out Nick had indeed committed suicide, which would probably confirm Petrelli's original suspicions about him. Because otherwise it would mean that Nick was murdered. Petrelli was not sure he could live with himself if that was the case.

He found the key line on the report: "Cause of death: Succinylcholine, injected in the back of the neck. Ruling: Homicide."

Petrelli's moan was loud enough that others in the office stopped what they were doing and looked at him, then somewhat awkwardly went back to work.

He knew it. Knew it when the first report of Nick's hanging had reached him. It was too neat, too tidy, the timing a little too precious after his own visit to Nick the day before. That poor kid, Petrelli thought. What a living hell he must have made of Nick's life. First he loses his best friend, then the girl he secretly loves, and then he's accused of murder by some know-it-all detective and has to ask his parents for bail money. Now he's dead too.

But why? Why would the killer murder Nick, who was the chief suspect? The killer should have figured that if Nick was found guilty, he could have gotten away with it. The perfect crime helped with the creation of the very-imperfect detective, Petrelli thought: me.

Clearly, there was something else going on…and I need to find out what it is, before some other innocent is killed, Petrelli told himself. No sense feeling sorry for myself. That won't help Nick now. The best thing I can do is redouble my efforts. With the mayor, the media, the university and everyone else breathing down my neck, that won't be hard to do.

First, though, Petrelli had to do something he dreaded. He had to call Nick's parents, already mad at him for his mistaken arrest of Nick, and tell them how sorry he was. Truth was, they had no idea how sorry.

He reached for the phone.

22

Lewis had been to the James Buchanan campus before, but this time, standing with Charlotte at the front gates, he found himself a bit nervous.

Usually Lewis entered a university hospital campus feeling supremely confident. He thoroughly believed in the rightness of his cause, and knew from experience where to look and who to speak to. There was little that would surprise him.

But today was different. They were there under the rubric of the fraud investigation, but their real reason was to find a link between the fraud and murder cases. And Lewis was no police detective. The thought of him and Charlotte putting their personal prestige on the line, not to mention the prestige of OIG, to investigate these murders, did not sit well with him. He still thought Charlotte was way off base, but his loyalty and friendship with her were such that he couldn't say no.

Charlotte, he saw by looking up at her face, had a look that he could describe only as something akin to rapture. Her eyes glowed with anticipation of the coming quest, her jaw thrust forward, and he could swear there almost appeared to be a new radiance to her skin. She seemed to possess an enthusiasm that would sweep all obstacles out of her way.

"Relax," she told him, when he expressed his concerns. "Use the fraud investigation as a wedge – you may even find something along the way that will help the fraud case – to get information about the three deaths. But remember, what we want to prove is that there is a link between your fraud investigation and the murders. That, more than anything, will legitimate our getting involved."

Lewis nodded. This he understood. "Okay, then, I'm off to the reimbursement office. I want to get a first hand look at those cost reports."

"And I am going to speak with some of the medical staff. I want to see how they feel about the possibility of a connection." She looked at her watch. "It's 10 a.m. now. How about if we meet up in the university cafeteria for a late lunch about 1:00?"

The reimbursement specialist's eyes opened wide when Lewis showed her his identification. While not all visits from the government were announced, it was almost unheard of for the OIG chief counsel to visit. Even the OIG attorneys working for Lewis did not typically do so, unless it was to discuss a legal matter. The usual pattern was for the lead government attorney working on a case to send an investigative team, which might include specialists in reading various financial documents and others, skilled in computer technology, to take hard drives out of computers and bring them back to the office, or sometimes take the computers themselves.

In fact, defense attorneys gave their clients strict instructions on how to act when government investigators arrived: Always be cooperative, but don't volunteer more than what the investigators ask for. If your employee doesn't want to talk, you cannot force him or her. But by the same token, you must never, under any conditions, tell employees that they should *not* talk. If investigators want to remove original documents, ask if copies will do, pointing out that taking the originals would disrupt the business flow of the office.

There were some physician practices where so much was taken out of the office by seemingly uncaring investigators – entire computers or their hard drives, entire file cabinets, papers and more – that the practice simply had to shut down, as it was unable to do business. That meant loss of income for the practice, the doctors, and the employees, not to mention loss of medical services for the patients.

In a large facility like James Buchanan, with its own compliance officer and legal staff, this was usually able to be avoided, as employees were well-versed in how to cooperate with government investigators without being too cooperative, and what suggestions to make to investigators so they could get what they needed without disrupting the business flow and medical operations of the institution.

And, finally, the government knew that large institutions had both far more patients and medical responsibility in their community, as well as far greater legal resources to bring forth, than a small practice, so they tended to have their investigators act more sensitively.

So the front-office person who greeted Lewis knew who he was when she saw his badge. Excusing herself somewhat nervously, she left the window and brought another woman, more formally dressed in a dark blue business suit, back with her.

"This is Brenda Morehouse, the reimbursement office manager, Mr. Sullivan," she said, leaving the two of them alone. Brenda, a self-possessed woman of middle-aged years who bore the air of running the show in what Lewis could see was an office of about 10 billers and coders, held out her hand.

"How can I help you, Mr. Sullivan?"

"I'm just doing a little follow-up on the cost reports our investigators have been looking at. I'd like to review the reports for the past three years, beginning with the last calendar year."

"Well, of course. We have them here. Your auditors looked over them pretty thoroughly already, you know."

Lewis gave a tight smile. "I would just like to see them again, if you don't mind."

"Certainly. Would you like a table to sit at so you can review them without interruption?"

"That would be helpful, thank you."

Brenda led him through the central office, where the various coders and billers tried not very successfully to hide their interest in his visit, and down a corridor to a small meeting room with a round table inside and four chairs around it.

"This will be fine," Lewis said, as Brenda left, then returned a few minutes later with three sets of reports, each about two inches thick. They were basically stacks of spreadsheets, held together with a binder by metal clips. Each one was labeled, "James Buchanan University Hospital Cost Reports," with the year immediately after the name.

Opening the reports, Lewis saw columns of figures and rows of items. Cost reports did not cover the regular claims that hospitals sent in to Medicare. What they covered were large ticket items – what other businesses might call capital costs – that were also Medicare-reimbursed. These might include items like the construction of a new wing on a campus medical building, or the purchase of an imaging system.

Lewis knew what to look for, as he had brought the summary findings from his staff with him. James Buchanan was believed to have overstated the costs for a variety of projects under way on the campus or at facilities it owned off-campus. He spot-checked the summary findings against what the reports showed and found that his investigators had correctly stated the figures, not that he expected anything less. To determine if costs were inflated for building new facilities, the government used a system called "fair market value" to determine proper costs for construction, supplies, labor and more. OIG investigators had found that James Buchanan should have been paying a lot less for these than it said it was paying in its cost reports. *This is where the real ripoff of the public occurs, Lewis thought.* You can say all you want about the stress these investigations put on doctors and medical institutions, but why is this going on? The real crime would be to allow it to continue.

What many institutions that ran into cost report problems were hiding, as both Charlotte and Lewis knew from experience, was that the additional money that came in was used for other expenses, such as making up for shortfalls in Medicare reimbursement elsewhere, to hire additional staff or, in the worst cases, just for profit. In some cases, however, that extra money made the difference between an institution like James Buchanan being in the red and being in the black. Without it, the institution might have to go out of business.

Which is no excuse to steal.

Lewis closed the last report. There had been no surprises here, nor was he really there to check his staff's work, although he was pleased to find it quite thorough, something he reminded himself that he would have to compliment them on upon his return to the office later that day. The question was whether he could draw a connection between these reports, or other problems for which James Buchanan was being investigated, with the murders of Scott Karakas, Dana Brentano and Nick Rosen.

He stuck his head out the door and saw Brenda, indicating he wanted to see her. She quickly ended her conversation with on the coders and came down the hall.

"Yes, Mr. Sullivan?"

"Mrs. Morehouse, who has access to these cost reports? I mean, not now, but as they are put together during the course of the year?"

"Just about everyone. The entire staff here."

"I see. Who else?"

"Well, the CFO, Mr. Proctor, reviews them from time to time. Just part of the due diligence of his job. Whether he shows them to anyone else, I don't know. His door is always locked, sometimes even when he's working in there, so no one else can get in. But that's about it."

"Do any of the medical staff, the doctors, review them?"

A smile crossed Brenda's face, which she quickly suppressed. "Doctors are the last people who want to see these, Mr. Lewis. We can't get them to take enough interest in things like even giving us the right codes or doing their paperwork, as I'm sure you've run into elsewhere."

"Yes, indeed." She was right, Lewis knew. Physicians were notorious among administrative staff for taking almost no interest in the administrative – or the compliance – side of health care. "This is not what I went to medical school for," "I'm in the business of saving lives," and "That's what we have an administrative staff for," were just some of the more common reasons given. And those were the nice ones. Many cardiologists, for instance, were so arrogant they wouldn't even respond when the topic of doing anything outside of what they considered to be medical was broached.

Simon Proctor, the James Buchanan University Hospital chief financial officer, held out a manicured hand for Lewis to shake as Lewis entered his comfortable office. Well-tailored in an expensive suit, complete with handkerchief in jacket pocket, well-shined shoes, and carrying an air of precision about him, Lewis immediately cataloged Simon as what might be called a "dandy," a man who takes undue pride in the correctness of his dress, as well as the expense of the clothes he buys. And Simon's office was also a study in anal retentiveness, with everything on his desk seemingly in neat piles at right angles. Other than a current paper he had apparently been reading – Lewis noticed an old-fashioned fountain pen nearby, another affectation – his desk was spotless, and antique, judging by the border design that ran around the mahogany desktop.

Lewis could also see a wedding ring on Simon's finger. Funny, he thought, many would think Simon gay and myself straight, yet here the reverse is true. Lewis was always surprised at the shock shown by the few people who he informed about his lifestyle and relationship with James. Apparently, maybe because of his somewhat careless style of dress and the fact that he did not come across as effeminate, most people he met did not think he was gay. Yet here was a man who, while not exactly sounding effeminate, seemed so precise in detail and took so much care in his dress and surroundings, that some might think he was, in fact, gay, while if the wedding ring and the photo of his wife on the credenza behind his desk were to judge, he wasn't. Well, Lewis had made his piece with human nature and people's perceptions long before. He moved on to the subject at hand.

"Thanks for seeing me, Mr. Proctor."

"Always pleased to help the government, Chief Counsel." Lewis noted the formal use of his title as a form of address, something most people didn't bother with. Charlotte was frequently called "Inspector General," but for some reason, chief counsels were more frequently called by their last names, as the woman at the reimbursement office had done with him. "How can I help you?"

"I was reviewing the James Buchanan cost reports for the past three years, and the thought crossed my mind: Who has access to these reports, Mr.

Proctor?"

"Why, anyone with a need to, and that would include a great many people. Anyone in the reimbursement office might need to refer to one, although they are not allowed to make or change entries. The director of the office, Mrs. Morehouse, can make or change entries upon my direction or with my permission. Other than that, I, of course, have access to them, as does the chief administrator, Mr. Chamroeun. Oh, and of course, our legal counsel and tax accountants. I think that's all. Is there a problem?"

"I see," said Lewis. The question is, he knew, who made those changes to the reports? Who authorized inflating the costs in the various line items? Experience had showed him and has staff that it was rarely anyone working in the administrative office, unless they were ordered to. In fact, most coders and billers take their careers quite seriously, taking classes, earning certification with nationally recognized organizations, and, if anything, grow frustrated when they find irregularities or outright mistakes in the reports and bring them to doctors or senior staff for corrections, only some of which are made.

No, Lewis knew, these changes usually come from higher up, if only for the reason that no one below wanted to take responsibility or lose their job. Someone like Simon Proctor might be involved, but more likely the directive came from the very top, in this case from Chamroeun Arun. Legal counsel would not know the day-to-day operations of the university hospital, as they are involved only in ongoing legal matters, and tax accountants are typically concerned only about correctly paying the IRS. It was almost inconceivable, however, that the top administrator and the CFO would *not* know about it.

"How often has Mr. Chamroeun borrowed these reports?"

"That's hard to say, Chief Counsel. He could, of course, go down to the reimbursement office at any time and see them, and I wouldn't even know."

"But were there times when he asked you to provide them to him, for whatever reason?"

Simon thought a moment, then answered, somewhat slowly, "I'm certain there were, although just when and for what, I don't recall. You see, Chief Counsel," – Lewis was beginning to find the use of his title annoying – "we are so concerned here with the day-to-day business of running the university hospital, that if someone senior, certainly like the chief administrator, asks to see the cost reports, we think nothing of it. There are so many reasons why he may want to, from simply looking at some costs to refresh his memory, to check on our work, and more, that it's not unusual at all. The reports are not logged out every time they go from one office to another."

"But as you know, Mr. Proctor, there are inflated costs in those reports."

"I know that OIG is suggesting that, Chief Counsel, but that has yet to be proven. Every cost in there has been thoroughly vetted by myself, the staff, and it may be that Mr. Chamroeun also reviewed them."

This is going nowhere, Lewis thought. What am I looking for, anyway? If Arun were responsible for the inflated costs, wouldn't he keep a record of his changes somewhere? Or if Simon Proctor or someone else were the party that made the changes, wouldn't that person keep a record? *A second set of books,* showing the correct costs, so the university hospital could keep track of how much additional reimbursement was received. That would be the smoking gun. But finding such a second set was difficult, although in some cases at other institutions that had been investigated, such books had turned up. They could even be kept at someone's home.

And even if a second set of books was found, that would certainly put the last nail in part of the fraud case, but he was not sure how, if at all, it would link to the murders of Karakas, Brentano and Rosen.

23

Charlotte, unlike a number of Washington, D.C. residents, was no stranger to driving a car. Her trips to her father's Eastern Shore home, plus her own inclination to travel and visit historic sites in Maryland, Virginia, West Virginia, Pennsylvania and other nearby states made her comfortable behind the wheel. Many District residents, like some citizens of other major American cities, rarely chose to leave their urban areas, and took a perverse pride in not having to drive, or even not having a car. Walking was not only healthier, but it allowed you to learn about a city, its people, restaurants and more. And Charlotte, a long devotee of walks throughout Northwest Washington, agreed. But that didn't mean one shouldn't learn to drive as well.

A mid-March heavy downpour on the way to Pennsylvania was not what she had in mind, however, and as she drove up Interstate 81 on her way to Wilkes-Barre, she found herself wishing for the usually unwelcome presence of the Washington Metro, despite its long waits, delayed schedules and crowded trains.

But Scott Karakas' parents had agreed to see her today, somewhat reluctantly, she sensed during the phone call, and she didn't want to risk losing the opportunity and calling back to reschedule. Although the forecast had called for rain, she hadn't expected the wind whipping it up to such intensity that, even with her headlights on, her visibility would be affected. If it weren't for the red tail lights of cars ahead on the road, she probably would have driven her maroon BMW into a guard rail by now, she knew.

Her visit to the university hospital with Lewis the week before had proved uneventful and unhelpful. The three or four students she spoke with were shook up about the killings, and one who knew all three brought herself to tears whenever she spoke about it. Charlotte sighed. This was not something they would never forget, and it would become part of who they are in the years ahead. College was supposed to impress young minds, but not like this. Nonetheless, the murders were a fact of life, and the students who knew Scott, Dana and Nick would have to learn to live with them, rationalize them and bury them, then move on. The killings would color their lives, in ways both subtle and deliberate, in their years ahead.

Most of the students she spoke with had focused on Scott, the golden boy of the group: promise snuffed out so early, how success seemed to come so easily to him, what he could have achieved had he lived, and so forth. These accounts mirrored those she had read in the newspapers.

Dana, on the other hand, was seen by her fellow female students simply as one of them, someone who had, quite understandably, fallen under Scott's charismatic spell. Whatever the motive for killing her, one girl said, it had to tie into her relationship with Scott, because Scott was killed first, and her relationship with Scott was her only connection to that first crime. Another student, who knew Dana fairly well, said she had trouble not blaming Scott for whatever he must have got Dana involved with, but since Scott was dead, she tried not to think bad thoughts about him.

As for Nick, there was almost universal anger at the police, Detective Petrelli in particular, for making Nick's life what one called "a living hell" before he too was murdered. Any idiot could see that Nick may have had a crush on Dana and been a little envious of Scott, but that he would never have committed murder because of those feelings. He was a loyal friend to Scott and kept his feelings for Dana on the inside.

All to be expected, Charlotte thought, as she moved her car closer to a pair of tail lights up ahead on the road, so as not to lose sight of them if the other car went around a bend. Yet the key, if one was to believe there was a link between the fraud investigations and the murders, had to be some connection between one of the students, most likely Scott, since he was the first victim, and at least one of the types of fraud, or one of the people committing fraud, at James Buchanan. That meant she needed to find out everything she could about the students and their backgrounds, hence the call to Scott's parents for a visit. It was a fishing expedition, she knew, but that was where she had to start.

Richard and Amy Karakas were somewhat confused about Charlotte's call, but they too wanted to find out who killed their son and why, so they reluctantly agreed to see her. Dwelling on and going over the details of their son's death, as well as his life and the promise it held, was not something they relished doing. But, as Amy Karakas told Charlotte on the phone, "We can't help doing it all the time anyway, so you might as well come up."

Charlotte reviewed again the kinds of fraud OIG was investigating at James Buchanan, trying to find some way that a medical student might be tied into any one of them.

Upcoding – There was no way a student could be involved with this. Not only did students not have access to the Medicare claims forms, but they lacked the knowledge of coding. And why would a student be interested in raising a medical procedure's code to a higher level in order for the university to get more reimbursement?

Unbundling – Same thing, just a different activity. Students lacked the knowledge of coding and the interest to care about helping the university get more reimbursement by separating procedures into different components so that, collectively, they would bring in more money.

Supervision of residents – Medical students aren't even involved in this, Charlotte thought. A resident might care if a senior staff member were improperly supervising his or her work, but why would a student? Students are not allowed to perform operations, so they are not part of the program.

Cost reports – Students don't have access to these, and if they did, unless they were accounting majors, wouldn't know how to read them.

Charlotte was flummoxed. There was no way and no motive for any of the three victims to have been involved in Medicare fraud. Maybe Lewis is right, she thought, maybe these two situations are just coincidental. Maybe there is no connection. But then she would hear Penelope's voice: *I don't believe in coincidences.*

She had been on the interstate almost three hours now when she saw her exit sign. She followed the directions that Richard Karakas had given her, and watched as the Wilkes-Barre streets changed from retail to residential to wealthy residential. Finally, she turned onto the street that Scott's father had identified. I wouldn't call this a neighborhood at all, she thought. It was more like a group of estates, each on several acres of property. The estates themselves varied in style from Tudor to Victorian to Normandy. One even had what looked like a corral for horses. This was the world Scott Karakas grew up in, she realized. Her own background was also one of wealth and privilege, plus, given her father's position in the Senate, some power. But it was different from Scott's. Dana's background was in the world of Washington, D.C., and it revolved around the movers and shakers of the nation's capitol. She went to the same kind of private schools as Scott probably did, but the context was different. This was settled money, old money, she saw, looking around. These people are doctors, lawyers, owners of companies. Not the kind to pass laws. *The kind to pay others to pass laws.*

Charlotte found the house, a large Tudor with lots of stone and wood. She pulled into the long driveway and took it down to a circular parking area in front of a large garage. She parked her BMW next to a Mercedes convertible and a beautiful chocolate brown Jaguar, wishing that OIG culture didn't frown on flashy cars. But when you're investigating corruption, you don't want to be seen driving a Jaguar. A BMW was about the most she could get away with.

Amy Karakas greeted her at the door, apologizing for the fact that she had to answer it herself. Since it was a Saturday, she had given their domestics the day off, she explained. A short, petite, impeccably-dressed woman in casual, at-home Town-and-Country-style clothes with carefully coiffured blonde hair and expensive-but-sensible gold earrings, she walked Charlotte through the foyer, a large living room dominated by a huge stone fireplace, an even larger dining room with a table that could quite comfortably sit 16, with a large well-appointed kitchen off to the side, and into a back enclosed porch, where Richard Karakas rose from a wicker sofa to greet her.

Charlotte took the outstretched hand and had her first look at Scott's father. An unmistakable air of breeding and entitlement emanated from every middle-aged inch of Richard Karakas, from the short-sleeved cotton pullover shirt and creased trousers, to the casual loafers worn over white socks. His face, handsome with blue eyes, had skin that had clearly been the subject of some treatment, Charlotte thought, noticing its even tone. Hair she imagined was once jet-black now had some gray in it, and it looked to be receding a bit.

"Have a seat, won't you, Miss Westbrook? Can we get you something? Iced tea, perhaps?" he asked, motioning toward a pitcher and glasses on a tray on a matching wicker table. The entire porch bespoke country estate, with a flagstone floor, mesh screening with slatted windows that were opened and closed with a hand crank, and flowers throughout.

"Yes, that would be nice, thank you." Charlotte accepted the tea that Amy offered her.

Here the facade of civility that had led them to this point began to crumble, as Amy began to speak, with a quaver in her voice.

"I'll be candid with you, Miss Westbrook, if I may," she said, with Charlotte nodding. "I really did not want this meeting. It's not going to…bring Scott back. I, we, have to live with this every day, and that is something that is never going to change." Nor," she paused, "should it."

"We want to always keep Scott in our hearts and minds," said her husband, explaining. "The day we start forgetting, or putting him in the past, is the day he really starts disappearing."

Yet they would eventually have to, Charlotte knew, if life were to go on. "I am so sorry about your loss," she said. She glanced at a picture on a nearby wicker display shelf that showed Scott with two young women, about the same age. "I'm sure it is a comfort to have your two daughters."

"Yes, a great comfort," said Amy, looking at the photograph Charlotte had been studying. "Deborah is in her third undergraduate year at Princeton, and Lilly is out of school now, working at an investment bank."

"She should do well there," Karakas put in. "I used some connections to help her get her job – something I'm sure you're familiar with, Miss Westbrook," he said, emphasizing her last name. Charlotte caught the veiled reference to her father immediately. Another assumption she got her job through her father's influence. And, in fact, it had been a big help. But Charlotte also knew that her achievements on this job and her past jobs were due totally to her hard work and success. Her father's help stopped at the hiring room door.

"I have made it my business that all our children do well," Karakas continued.

"We want them to be happy, as well, dear," said Amy.

"Yes, of course. Neither Amy nor I insisted on any particular career for them. They could do whatever they wanted. My only insistence, and this was true from grade school forward, was that once that decided what they wanted to do, they do it well, and they take whatever steps are needed to succeed. I was very firm with Scott on that point, and I think the progress he was making at medical school and the feedback I received from his teachers bore out that philosophy."

"I think Richard took it a little easier on the girls," Amy said, her husband shaking his head in disagreement, "even though he doesn't think so. You know how fathers and daughters are. Well, I'm sure you do, Miss Westbrook, with such a prominent father as your own."

Charlotte nodded. "Yes, my dad and I are still very close to this day."

"Retired to his St. Michael's house, is he?" Karakas asked. "That is a beautiful area. We don't get down there enough."

Conversations tend to have their own natural rhythms, their ebbs and flows, and this one, a bit more uncomfortable than most, was no exception. They had reached one of those pauses, with dead air seeming to fill the time.

"As I said to you on the phone, Miss Westbrook, and as my wife just mentioned, we agreed to this meeting because, on reflection, it can't make us feel any worse and if it may help catch the perpetrator, well, we certainly want to be of help there. If we don't seem drenched in tears, it's just that, well, speaking for myself, we're used to having Scott away. You know, he's been gone for almost six years now, first getting his undergraduate degree at Princeton, just like his sister is doing now, then on to James Buchanan. So it's easy for us to think that…"

"He's still going to walk in the door on some weekend or Thanksgiving, whatever," said Amy. "Seeing you here, though, Miss Westbrook, and I hope you won't think this rude, but seeing you here reminds us, that, well…" She couldn't continue. Charlotte reached out a hand to hers for comfort. "That's why I was perhaps a bit more reluctant than Richard to have this meeting. But," she said, straightening herself up a bit, "now that you're here, what can we do for you?"

"As you may know, my office is in charge of investigating Medicare fraud and, as such, we audit and prosecute a number of health care providers each year…" Charlotte began.

"…and James Buchanan University is currently under such an investigation, for, I believe, upcoding, unbundling, supervision of students and possibly more," put in Karakas.

"You're well-informed, Mr. Karakas. That's more than has been in the press."

"In my line of work – I run the family investment firm, Karakas and Castille, in case you didn't know, Miss Westbrook – it's always a good idea to find out what you can before a meeting. So I hope you don't mind that I had my staff do some checking before this meeting into just what the relationship is between OIG and James Buchanan."

Charlotte was taken a bit aback, but also impressed. This was the kind of entrepreneurial spirit she liked to see from her own staff.

"The question you are hoping we can answer is whether there might be some connection between Scott's death, and the death of the two other students – that girl he was seeing and that Rosen character – and your investigation."

Charlotte was again impressed, but not as favorably this time. Although Richard Karakas was clearly thorough and someone who took the initiative, it was also clear that he wanted her to know it. But why? And from his reference to Nick, it seemed that he was also someone who formed quick judgments, sometimes harsh judgments, about people. Charlotte couldn't help but wonder what opinions he had made of her in their brief encounter today, as well as what it was like to grow up under such a father.

Karakas chuckled. "Relax, Miss Westbrook. I use this tactic – I suppose you might call it intimidation by homework – with a lot of people I sit across from. It was not my intention to intimidate you. After all, you are here to help discover our son's killer."

"Yes," said Charlotte, "although, and I suspect you already know this, Mr. Karakas, I am not in any way authorized to do so by the D.C. police. Rather, I am approaching this from the angle of what we might learn about the Medicare fraud at the university from these three deaths."

"Miss Westbrook, I can assure you, Scott was not involved in any Medicare fraud," said Amy. "Why would he?"

"No," her husband said, "but he may have some knowledge of it that led to his murder. Am I correct, Miss Westbrook?"

Like a barracuda, Charlotte thought. "That's what I was hoping to find out from you."

Karakas shook his head. "If he did become aware of something, he didn't tell us. He might have told his two friends, and maybe you are right, that got them all killed, but I know nothing of it."

Charlotte tried a different tack. "Scott was always very successful, I understand. He was a straight A student in high school and college, excelled in several sports, good looking, the kind of person who someone marks for success, am I correct?"

Karakas beamed at the description. "Exactly right. We groomed him that way. Same thing with his sisters."

"What do you mean, you 'groomed' him that way?"

"Like any parent, you set standards and goals for your children. Amy and I provided a good home and a good education for them, but I always made a point of implanting something more: the desire to excel, to rise to the top. Scott felt the pressure sometimes, but I believe it helped him. Had not this incident happened, there's no telling how high he may have risen."

Amy opened her mouth as if to speak, but then closed it.

"Go ahead, Mrs. Karakas," Charlotte urged, as Karakas looked over at his wife.

"Sometimes I think we put on a little bit too much pressure," she said, more to her husband than to Charlotte. "There's more to life than getting ahead, you know."

Her husband sighed, then looked at Charlotte. "You'll have to excuse us, we've had this conversation before." Turning to his wife, he said, "Did we ever see a time when Scott was not a happy child? I mean other than normal teenage shenanigans. Didn't he take pride in his achievements? Do you remember how proud he was when he became a National Merit Scholarship finalist? Or when his team won the Model U.N. competition?"

"Yes, I know, that's all true, Richard. I just wish we gave him more time to smell the roses, as they say," she said.

"He had plenty of time to smell the roses! Look at the girlfriends he had, his friends in high school. You would think," he said, turning his attention back to Charlotte, "from my wife's description that Scott was some kind of miserable child forced to work on his schoolwork for unconscionable hours. Nothing could be further from the truth."

"That's not what I'm saying," Amy said. "Just that you take such pride in giving our children this 'drive to succeed,' as if it were everything in life. But it's not."

"I don't see you complaining," Karakas said, making a point at looking around the house. His wife flinched at the comment.

This was beginning to get uncomfortable for Charlotte.

"You wouldn't happen to have anything of Scott's, maybe from his high school years, that I could see? Perhaps one of his high school yearbooks?"

"I'll get his senior year one," Amy said, rising and leaving the room for a few seconds.

"I am so sorry to intrude on your grief," she said to Richard Karakas after his wife left the room. "I'm sure that all parents who lose a child retrace all the steps they took in raising him or her and wonder if they did the right thing. I didn't mean to cause any problems between you and Mrs. Karakas."

Karakas gave her a small smile. "Nothing you saw that hasn't been between us a long time, Miss Westbrook," he said. "And it doesn't change the final truth: Scott is gone." For a second, he shuddered, and Charlotte thought he was on the verge of breaking down, but he didn't. A blow like this to a man like Richard Karakas must be hard, and despite his protestations to his wife, she was sure he would spent the rest of his life second-guessing every move he made with his son.

Amy returned with a green-covered high school yearbook. She gave it to Charlotte. "I suppose you want to study this, looking for some insight into Scott. I don't know what you might find. It's just filled with the usual high school comments from friends and teachers, that sort of thing. But if you promise to return it – as you can imagine, these kinds of memories are precious to us now, and if you think it may do some good in finding out what happened to Scott – you can borrow it for a while."

Charlotte nodded, taking the book. "I will return it to you, don't worry," she said. "I understand."

Karakas looked at his wife, then at Charlotte. There was mix of sadness and frustration in his face, she thought. He held out his hand.

"Is there anything else we can do for you, Miss Westbrook? I'm sorry you had to see us in such a state. But we do appreciate your efforts. Please give us a call if we can be of any further help."

24

Arun was beside himself, and the medical staff knew it. Between the student murders and what felt like the ever-tightening noose of the OIG investigation around the university hospital's neck, the staff realized, just by looking at him, that the pressure was taking its toll. The smooth, urbane bearing that Arun brought to so many meetings was replaced by something that seemed almost like paranoia.

Watching Arun, the doctors could only nod in sympathy. Peter, Lyle, Jennifer and several others felt the pressure themselves. But they could take solace in the actual vocational nature of their work, be it surgery, treating patients, or simply teaching. Arun, on the other hand, was the chief administrator, a position that left no time for almost anything else. There was no professional activity he could turn to, as they could, for some mental balance. *I hope he saves stamps*, Lyle found himself thinking.

Arun had been speaking almost non-stop for 20 minutes now, in something close to a rant. As he did, his French accent, so minor in most conversations, became increasingly prominent, forcing the doctors to listen more attentively so they could understand each word, as he ran down all the university hospital had been through in just a few short months: the toll of the investigation on the university hospital's reputation and the reputations of himself and the doctors who worked there; his meetings with the Inspector

General (who, some noticed with surprise, he seemed to almost like) and with the OIG Chief Counsel (who he clearly did not like); the murders of Scott Karakas and Dana Brentano, now followed by the murder of Nicholas Rosen; meeting with Detective Alphonse Petrelli about those murders and his leading questions; meeting with Chancellor Wilmotte about what he planned to do to get the university past all this when, in fact, he had no answers; meetings with Paul Holden to make sure that everything the university did was on the up and up as far as compliance was concerned; and more.

"And now, the latest. Believe it or not, the Inspector General and the Chief Counsel have begun to take a direct hand in the investigation. Mr. Sullivan spent a good part of the day here last week with the cost reports and Simon, while Miss Westbrook, as I understand it, actually interviewed students in the hallways."

"What? That's not the usual way OIG acts, as I understand it," Jennifer said. "She conducted interviews *in the hallway*?"

"I know something about OIG," put in Peter, "and this definitely is not normal. They have a staff, and a fairly large one at that. This is really odd. Do you know what she was asking them?"

"Even odder," said Arun. "She was asking about the murders."

Stunned silence filled the room.

"But that's a police matter, isn't it?" one of the doctors asked.

"Apparently OIG is exploring the possibility of some kind of link between the allegations of fraud here and the murders," Arun said. "And apparently that possibility has, shall we say, fired up the Inspector General's imagination. Hence her interest, and the interest of her lackey, Mr. Sullivan."

"This is absurd. They are targeting us, and going out of their way to make some kind of example of us," said Lyle. He snorted. "Impartial prosecution of justice! You'd think there was no fraud going on elsewhere in the country, if they can afford to spend their time here. Linking the murders and the fraud. Hey, here's an idea. Maybe the Inspector General murdered the students."

"Lyle, that's not —" began Jennifer.

"Why not? She's supposedly always firing that laser gun of hers. Maybe she practices for a reason."

A few snickers filled the room.

"Alright, enough, that's in bad taste," Arun said. "Although I can certainly understand the sentiment behind it. On the larger point, Lyle, I have to agree with you. For the inspector general and the chief counsel to both take an active part in the investigation seems outrageous. They must have dozens of other cases. I can only hope that the Senate committee grills her thoroughly about this when she next appears before them, and that the HHS Secretary reins her in, as well. Not that that will do us much good, though."

Peter sighed. "All this proves my point."

All heads turned toward him.

"The answer is just to get away. Work helps, but you can't do work all the time. Take a vacation, like Marjorie and I are doing. We're leaving in a week."

"Make sure you have the Hungarian goulash at the Café Leopold in the university section," one of the doctors put in. "It's a great city. And don't forget to have a Sacher torte."

"I'm taking notes," Peter said. "See, the mood here is lighter already."

"Peter is on to something," said Jennifer. "Michael and I are following suit. We're going to Ireland the month after Peter gets back."

Arun laughed and relaxed a bit for the first time. "I just wish I could do the same. But I cannot afford to be gone during this period. Can you imagine what the board would say? You'll both have to send me some postcards, and bring back some of the cuisine!"

"I'm in the same boat as you, Arun," Lyle said. "We'd love to get away but, frankly, with the second house we're building by the lake, this is not the best time, cash flow wise."

"We all have great sympathy for you, Lyle," Peter said in mock sincerity. "You suffer so."

"You all laugh," he said, "but you also all know that working here right now is like being in a pressure cooker. And without some kind of release, like the vacations you and Jennifer have planned, Peter, something is going to blow."

"Yes," said Arun. "But what?"

25

What was next for Arun came a week later, when both Charlotte and Lewis paid him an unscheduled visit. Gracious as always, he ushered them into his office, motioning them to seats at a round conference table he kept in the opposite corner from his desk, offering them tea, coffee or water, which both declined. He noticed they seemed even more serious than before, if that was possible.

Normally, Arun would have had Paul Holden or someone from the hospital's compliance staff to sit in on the meeting, and any attorney would have agreed that would be the smart thing to do. But Arun was not sure just what good that would do at this point. It was clear the investigation would continue and he had no doubt the university would pay the price. He was weary of meetings, including those with Paul, and simply wanted to be done with the whole thing. Aside from that, he felt he had taken his measure of both Charlotte and Lewis at their previous meeting and could handle them on his own.

"I suppose you are here to tell me about some new avenue of investigation you are opening," he said.

Charlotte couldn't help but notice that Arun seemed almost resigned to whatever fate awaited the hospital. How would she handle a situation like this, if her professional life and that of her university were collapsing around her, her reputation likely to be affected, and at the same time, there were three unsolved murders on campus? The truth, she told herself, was that she might not handle it as well.

Lewis, on the other hand, had wanted this meeting ever since he met with Simon, when the CFO had confirmed that, of the upper management at the hospital, only he and Arun would have reason to view the cost reports. That there was fraud at James Buchanan was already a given, and there was no doubt in Lewis' mind that it was so pervasive, in so many areas, that only a dunce of a chief administrator could not know about it. And Arun was not a dunce. Then there was that little surprise that Lewis wanted to spring on him.

"I have to tell you, Mr. Chamroeun, that a *qui tam* relator from your staff has come forward." Lewis watched as Arun tried to take this in without showing any reaction. But he could see that he had delivered another body blow to the man, one that he felt was more than deserved. *You lie with dogs, and you get fleas.*

"A whistleblower," Arun said, as if mulling it over. "Well, I don't know why I should be surprised. How much are you offering to pay this person in exchange for turning us all in? What's the blood money?"

"That is set by law, Arun, as you know," Charlotte said, realizing she had unintentionally used his first name. Occupational hazard. Sometimes prosecutors work so long with those they are investigating that, even though it's an adversarial relationship, they unintentionally bond with the person. They feel some sympathy, and wonder if the situation had been reversed, if they might have done the same thing, just as Charlotte found herself doing now. Some called it a kind of 'Stockholm Syndrome,' based on the theory that kidnappers and their victims bond from the experience. But Charlotte thought that a little too glib. Arun was clearly a man to whom principle and honor meant a lot, not unlike both their fathers. The truth, she told herself, is that I rather like this man. But the greater truth was that she also had a job to do.

"Yes, Charlotte, I know it is," Arun said, using her first name in return. Perhaps he senses my sympathy, Charlotte thought, or realizes I see things in more than black and white. But he must also realize that, when the time came to negotiate a settlement against overwhelming evidence, which she had no doubt would come, she could cut him some slack for being cooperative, but she still had to enforce the law.

"What do they currently get, up to 25% of your take?" Arun continued. "When you're talking about multimillions of dollars in settlement money, that's a pretty good incentive for anyone to come forward and make something up."

"Are you beginning settlement negotiations now, Mr. Chamroeun?" asked Lewis.

"Not at all, I was simply speaking to the subject of *qui tam* relators, in general. Nice little law you have there."

"Passed by Congress, not by us," said Lewis. "Would you like to know what the relator is alleging?"

Arun leaned back, his face seemingly resigned. "Proceed, please."

Lewis took a sheet of paper from the portfolio he was carrying. "Specifically, as you know, we are looking at the possibility that a number of your teaching physicians are submitting claims for medical supervision of residents when, in fact, no such supervision took place. Our relator was there to personally witness this lack of supervision in several instances."

Arun was stunned. Not because of the charge, but because someone was saying he or she had actually witnessed it. Is it possible to witness something *not* happening? He supposed it was, if a resident were operating on a patient, for instance, and there was no teaching physician on hand. But he was not aware of any such practice. Most of the doctors at the hospital supervised residents from time to time, and he was not aware of any that did not take part.

"I don't see how that can be. I suppose you cannot tell me the name of this person, but can you give me some idea of what he or she does here? I'd like to be able to defend this institution against the charges."

Charlotte leaned forward. "No formal charges against James Buchanan have yet been filed, Arun, and may never be, if this goes into settlement negotiations and they reach a satisfactory conclusion." She noticed the somewhat ironic smile on Arun's face when she said "satisfactory conclusion." Not satisfactory to him or James Buchanan, of course. But still better than going to trial and the huge disruptions and publicity that would bring, not to mention potentially much more severe monetary penalties.

"I still think it is right, it is the American way, is it not," Arun asked, "for a person to face his or her accuser and respond to any allegations – whether legally filed or not?"

"And there will be a time for that," Lewis said.

"But not now, while the charges have not yet been decided upon, and you are gathering evidence."

"That is correct. As you know, we are looking at several areas in regard to James Buchanan. The medical supervision issue is just one, and it is perhaps the most difficult to prove, given that it involves proof of where doctors were at particular times. That's why a witness is so valuable here. The other areas, however, the upcoding, the unbundling, the cost reports, can be traced through financial records, bank deposits, and more. There is usually a long paper trail, when one begins looking into these things."

Arun rose from the table and walked to the window, the same one that he and Charlotte had looked out earlier.

"And how is that side of your investigation going?" he asked.

"Fairly well, I must say," Lewis said. "As you know, I met with your CFO, Simon Proctor, the other day, and I also reviewed your cost reports.

Surely, Mr. Chamroeun, you had to be aware that those reports contain grossly inflated charges for certain university capital expenses, such as improvements to buildings."

"I don't really spend a lot of time on those reports, Mr. Sullivan. I hire professionals and trust them to do their jobs."

"So you are laying the blame on Simon Proctor?"

Arun turned, angry. "I am not laying the blame on anyone, because I don't know that there is blame. Simon is a fine CFO, as far as I am concerned."

"But," Lewis persisted, "someone had to know those charges were inflated. They can't all be innocent mistakes."

"That's a presumption on your part, Mr. Sullivan, one that OIG seems to make a lot. Why can't these so-called inflated costs be, in fact, innocent mistakes? Same thing with the upcoding and unbundling. We get new coders and billers in here from time to time. Sometimes, I am sure, claims are sent out asking for the wrong amount of reimbursement."

"The sheer volume of –"

"You know, Mr. Sullivan, you know what is missing in this country, in this great country that so many other nations look up to, that I grew up looking to, and that my family migrated to? That holds itself out as a model to the world? Trust. Trust. My father, sir, was a top military aide to Prince Sihanouk himself. Did you know that? Trust was the coin of the realm where the prince was concerned. Business in those days, and these days as well among people of honor, is not done by constantly checking up on each other through investigations and computer samples and whatever else you might come up with, but on the strength of relationships, the trust those relationships entail, and a personal sense of honor. My father told me that the prince wouldn't give the time of day to a man who he sensed lacked honor. A man without honor, he told my father, is a man that cannot be trusted."

He turned to Charlotte. "I never heard my father cry, Charlotte, except on that day, years later, when Sihanouk was overthrown by those bastards, the Khmer Rouge, who destroyed the country and the people, destroyed much about the great Khmer culture. On that day, he went into his study and closed the door, but my mother and I could hear him weeping like a child. He agreed to work with the Khmer Rouge for a while, hoping to moderate its extreme course. But it proved to no avail. Honor could not be upheld. It was then he decided that we had to surreptitiously leave the country. Because, at that point, leaving was the only way the family's honor could be upheld."

Charlotte didn't know what to say. Arun was so clearly sincere in his remarks, and looked so stricken, that, simply on a human level, she had an urge to touch his arm, provide some human contact. But she was the HHS Inspector General. And her office was investigating a potential crime. So she couldn't do that.

"My father," he said to both of them now, "raised me with these principles. I was very close to my father. Do you for one minute think, Mr. Sullivan, that I would betray my father's principles, betray the very values my father instilled in me, in order to get this hospital a little more reimbursement?"

"Mr. Chamroeun, I realize this is difficult for you. But the fact is that these irregularities exist. They are not figments of my imagination. It is our job to get to the bottom of them. Now, getting back to these cost reports. Someone at a management level had to review these, had to, in my opinion, be aware of the inflated costs. More so, they would have known how much extra money all this extra reimbursement brought in, otherwise they would not be able to use it elsewhere. I have seen this pattern in hospital after hospital," Lewis continue, as Charlotte noticed his voice rising, "so don't stand there and tell me it isn't happening. You are either complicit, sir, or you are ignorant of what is going on in your own hospital. If I were you, I would choose the ignorant route. At least that way you can say your sense of honor was not…besmirched."

"Lewis," Charlotte said quietly. "That is enough." Perhaps realizing he had said too much, Lewis closed his mouth. Arun was at the window, his back to them. He spoke to them in a quiet, almost faraway, voice.

"Well, I do want to thank you both for stopping by and keeping me informed. Most kind of you. I hope you won't mind if I ask you to show yourselves out?"

"Not at all," said Charlotte, wondering if the reason Arun's back was turned was because of tears in his eyes. She motioned to Lewis to leave.

As he heard the door close, Arun turned around and sighed. There were indeed tears in his eyes. He walked over to his desk, sat down, then opened a bottom file drawer and removed one of several heavy binders, each containing printouts held together by metal clips. The one he removed was labeled, "James Buchanan Cost Report" with the current year on it. But unlike the ones in the reimbursement office, this one had a large Roman numeral II penciled on the cover.

26

Five years before, Arun found himself sitting in an even larger office than his own, that of the James Buchanan University Chancellor Michael Wilmotte. A distinguished academic in his mid-50s, Dr. Wilmotte – the "doctor" was for a Ph.D. in philosophy – had built a reputation for himself during his 10 years as chancellor by rejuvenating James Buchanan's reputation as a center of learning on the cutting edge of several disciplines, medicine among them. He had invested heavily in raising the level of faculty by luring top academics from Princeton, Yale, Harvard, George Washington University and Cornell. And he did that by promising a combination of academic freedom with top dollar salaries. Wilmotte also invested in the university's infrastructure, upgrading existing classroom buildings, labs, and dormitories. With these changes, he was able to raise the bar on what constituted an acceptable admission to James Buchanan, making the student body increasingly select. This, in turn, enhanced the reputation of the school, which assisted in drawing in more faculty. More important to his plans, it allowed him to raise tuition substantially over the years, which helped pay for these changes.

But academics were not all Wilmotte concerned himself with. Much of his success was due to his business acumen. In order for James Buchanan to succeed academically as a center for higher learning, it had to be run like a business. And if some of the university professors or department heads forgot this, that was fine, in terms of their jobs and their role at James Buchanan, it didn't matter. But he could not let the heads of the schools forget it, and that included the chief administrator of the university hospital. It was their job, together with keeping academic standards high, to make sure each school ran in the black. A year without profits was literally a day without sunshine for the head of any school, and Wilmotte made it known that more than one such year would not be tolerated. A new school head would be found.

So there was Arun at that meeting five years before, facing Wilmotte across his large glass desk. The chancellor did not look happy. His usual bonhomie had given way to a stern look, with his glasses, normally worn high up his patrician nose, pressed down to the tip as he stared at Arun over them. His distinguished gray temples and remaining head of black hair, so popular on his television show appearances where he was frequently asked to speak about the future of higher education, now seemed to highlight only the intensity of his gray eyes. The handsome face had given way to the look of a stern parent.

"I don't think I need to tell you why you are here, Arun," he began.

"I understand that the finances this year are down. Let me assure you, chancellor, that I am aware of this problem and will take all the necessary steps to alleviate it next year. I have already scheduled extra calls to alumni, and the university hospital is also bidding for some government grants on research projects, which will help us offset our expenses."

"Good first steps, Arun, but I don't have to tell you that it is your job to *ensure* that the university hospital is in the black next year. Do you know where this entire university was when I came here 10 years ago? Its academic reputation shot, its tuition barely able to keep up with expenses, and what had been an excellent faculty well on the road to becoming a mediocre one."

"Yes, chancellor, we, all the heads of the schools here, are great admirers of yours—"

Wilmotte cut him off with a wave of his hand. "I'm not after your admiration, Arun, nor the admiration of the other school heads, much as I appreciate it. My motivation is to keep this university on a sound financial footing, with a profit, so we can continue to be where I brought it – to the top level of academic institutions in this country. I will not retire one day to hear that I was the chancellor who raised the university back up only to see it come crashing down again." Wilmotte's eyes blazed at this thought as he glared at Arun. "Do we understand each other?"

"Certainly, chancellor, and I share that goal."

"Then I expect you to do what is necessary to turn things around. The fundraising calls are fine. I hope those grants come through. But I expect you to come to the board meeting next month with a failsafe plan that shows how you will make sure the university hospital is in the black, regardless of how the fundraising calls and grant applications do. We can't count on what we can't control. You know the business, man. Just look back at what kept it in the black before, and repeat it."

Wilmotte rose from his chair and extended his hand. His face was more relaxed now, his smile pleasant, like the congenial, literate academic Arun had come to know at university events.

"Thanks for coming by, old fellow. Much appreciated."

Back in his office immediately after the meeting, Arun looked over the financial sheets and tried desperately to find ways he could cut costs or bring in new dollars. None of sufficient magnitude presented themselves. Why had it worked before and why was it not working now? Studying the financials, the answer was plain for all to see. Costs of just about everything – from medical supplies to staff salaries – had risen, while reimbursement, from both the government and from private insurance companies, had fallen, as these payers sought to cut their own costs by cutting back on reimbursement. There were also some medical procedures they no longer paid for, and others with increasingly stringent conditions, making it harder to get paid.

What would the old soldier, *le Vieux Soldat*, have done? His father, Chamroeun Reit, had been in tougher spots than this and had always found an honorable solution. Arun could not let him down now by failing. His father may have been dead these past seven years, but for Arun, he was a living presence, a shining role model, a moral and intellectual guide, and a stern countenance against which to measure his own progress in life.

What was the greater good? That was the question Reit told his son to ask himself whenever he found himself in a difficult spot. When working with Prince Sihanouk, he would sometimes be in a position where disciplinary action against fellow Cambodians was called for. Some would say he was acting wrongly. But, Reit told Arun many years later, he knew that Sihanouk always had the peoples' best interests at heart, and that Sihanouk's success meant success for Cambodia holding off groups like the Khmer Rouge and the horrors that would bring. With this in mind, it was not difficult for Reit to make the decision of always publicly backing the prince, even when some incidents with fellow Cambodians might prove unpleasant. Besides, such incidents were rare and Reit always found Sihanouk, who could have a mercurial personality, fair and open to suggestions, when made in private. The fact that the two men grew close also helped. And, if in the end, the Khmer Rouge did rise to power and the genocide of the killing fields took place, Reit could hold his head high and say he had done all he could.

Of course, the Old Soldier never worked for Michael Wilmotte.

Still, a man can't choose the time or conditions of his own crisis. It must be met, head on, with the right choice. And in this case, Arun told himself, the right choice, the honorable choice, was keeping the university hospital, and by extension the university, solvent. His father would not have accepted anything less, would not have accepted his failure to do so, and his disgrace should he be drummed out of his job.

Now Arun looked at the financials again.

If only the Department of Health and Human Services hadn't cut reimbursement this past year. Arun could only laugh. Even without the cuts, which, while slight, amounted to tens of thousands of dollars in lost reimbursement for James Buchanan when multiplied by the number of patients and visits they would affect, the lack of an increase in most of the past five years had put many medical institutions in an extraordinary bind. With less money, they couldn't keep up with rising costs, meaning they would either have to reduce service, which many doctors would not do; squeeze more patients into their already busy days; or find other ways to cut costs or raise revenue.

James Buchanan University Hospital had done all these options. Arun had pressed his staff to spend no more time than necessary with each patient, cutting back on answering questions or simple conversation. The doctors complied to the extent they felt comfortable. Some doctors, in fact, really didn't like patients, especially patients who asked questions, so this was no problem. Other doctors, however, approved of patients getting more involved in their own care, so they were constantly torn between answering questions and moving on to the patient who was waiting in the next examination room. Similarly, they tried, as Arun had directed, to increase their patient visits, but there were limits to how many patients any doctor could see in a day. And as for costs, Arun had ordered all contracts with suppliers reviewed, put a freeze on administrative salaries, and more.

All this had made a difference, but not more than half of what was needed to ensure that the university hospital remained in the black that year. Even if the government grants came through and there was an extraordinarily successful alumni fund drive, the business of the university hospital would most likely still be in the red. And there was really no talking to Wilmotte. The chancellor delegated immense amounts of authority and responsibility to each school head. In many ways, the school heads enjoyed this vote of confidence and fashioned the kinds of schools they wanted, which was one reason why James Buchanan had developed such a cutting edge reputation. But when things went bad, Wilmotte did not want to hear the details or understand the reasons why. And Arun suspected that Wilmotte's eyes would have glazed over as he tried to explain the complexities of Medicare reimbursement to him. Wilmotte really didn't want to know. He wanted Arun to solve the problem. That was his job.

So what to do now? The Old Soldier had taught Arun that there was always an honorable solution to every problem, if only one looked at all the parts of the puzzle and kept in mind what was most important. Arun tried to do that now. What was most important? Maintaining the academic standards of the university hospital. How could that be achieved? Only by keeping the business of the university hospital in the black, otherwise everything else would fall by the wayside. Therefore, all other considerations must fall behind this main one.

But to what extent should I do this, Arun asked himself. Where do the borders of honor lie? Again, the voice of the Old Soldier returned to him. "More than once, I was forced to take steps that, at the time I took them, many would not have approved. But I kept my eye on the greater good: the well-being of the Khmer people. With that in mind, I took those steps, prayed they would not be found out before the public was ready to accept them. A man who finds himself in this position runs incredible risks. Yet I know that I made the honorable choices."

Arun sighed. Now he was faced with such a choice, but on a much smaller scale. Still, the consequences could be horrific for him. But, mulling over all the alternatives in his mind, it remained true that the worst option would be having the university hospital fail. That would not only hurt him, hurt the medical staff, and James Buchanan University itself, it would hurt the community.

If the university hospital failed, thousands of patients who came for treatment would be robbed of its expertise and have to seek treatment elsewhere. Some of these patients came here from across the country and even from foreign countries. That meant that, not only would a failure of the university hurt the community. It would, he realized, by extension, hurt the medical reputation of the United States itself. The country benefited from the work conducted at James Buchanan, as it did the work conducted at other medical colleges which, Arun was sure, were probably undergoing the same problems he was. It seemed likely to him, in fact, that the chief administrators at the hospitals at Harvard, Princeton, Cornell and other well-regarded schools might be going through the same soul-searching.

But what am I thinking of, he asked himself. Honor forced him to be honest with himself: *I am thinking about committing Medicare fraud.* Yet perhaps that paled beside the greater good. There are things that could be done to increase reimbursement that would run risks, but would achieve the greater good of keeping the university in the black. There would be no dishonor before the Old Soldier. The university hospital would remain a cutting-edge medical and academic institution. And he would not have to resign for failing to keep it so. Arun felt the Old Soldier, if alive, would have told him, "You are faced with a difficult situation, but you are facing it forthrightly, thinking of the broader community, of the medical community in the country. Your choice runs risks, but the risks are greater if you fail."

Arun sought out Simon Proctor for advice, because his cooperation as chief financial officer would be essential if this were to work. Arun was hopeful that Simon would see the light. He and Simon were really the only two people at the university hospital who understood the hospital's financials from a big picture perspective. The doctors didn't want to know, and Arun understood and respected this. They wanted to practice medicine. The chief counsel and the compliance officer were experts in the law, not finance. And the coding and billing staff, while experts on individual procedures, did not have the perspective nor the corporate training to see the forest for the trees.

Simon, he believed, like him, was an honorable man, so when Arun approached him, it would have to be in the right context. Surely Simon realizes the situation the university hospital is in, Arun told himself. If allowed to continue unchecked, they would all be out of work anyway. He decided to take him out to lunch at the university's Excelsior Club.

Simon met Arun at the club restaurant the next day. The restaurant, considered posh by university standards, was visited frequently by school administrators and senior faculty. Students were not allowed in, nor would they probably want to eat there. Arun and Simon sat at a table on the enclosed veranda, overlooking much of the campus. The entire room seemed created of white wicker, with the walls lined with it. White linen tablecloths covered white wicker tables with glass tops.

"I had a rather severe meeting with Wilmotte earlier this week," Arun began.

"Yes, I would expect that was in the offing," Simon said, carefully placing a linen napkin in his lap. As always, he was well dressed, today wearing an off-white suit, cream shirt and beige tie, with matching handkerchief in the breast pocket. "Did it turn out well?"

"No, it didn't. And that's what I need to talk with you about, Simon. The very future of the university hospital. Not to mention our own futures."

"Really." Simon, somewhat to Arun's surprise, did not look that alarmed. "I've actually been giving that some thought myself. You know, I spend even more time on the financials than you do. It's my entire job."

Arun laughed. "I'm sorry it's been so unpleasant recently."

Simon picked up a breadstick and played with it. "The truth is, it *is* an unpleasant prospect and it's going to get worse. Not just for us, but for every academic medical institution in the country. I talk to my peers at other universities, you know. They are facing the same thing. They don't come out and admit it, of course, as they are bound by confidentiality, just like I am. But their meaning is clear."

"Yes, I would have thought as much. No institution can survive when its reimbursement does not match its expenses."

"Certainly not if it wants to remain of service to the community."

Arun sighed in relief. Good. He was certain Simon would understand. He told Simon how he was doing all he could to raise capital through fund drives and grant applications, and how he was trying to cut costs, yet there was no guarantee this would work. And Wilmotte didn't care about the details. It was up to him, up to *them*, Arun told Simon, to find a way.

"We have to look at the greater good," Arun said.

The conversation was interrupted by the waiter bringing their lunch. He presented Arun with a club sandwich, and a cobb salad for Simon.

"If I understand where this conversation is going," Simon said, "we … and the university … could get in serious trouble."

"Let's first just take a step back and look at what we are talking about, before we make more of this than it is," Arun said. "No one is really talking about taking more money from the government than what it costs to keep this university in the black. Why, under the formula HHS used several years ago, there was no problem. Now, however, with reimbursement down, we cannot get reimbursed for the actual costs of our medical procedures. We can maybe seek to redress this imbalance through how we submit our claims. At the same time, though, there are other areas where we have more control. Specifically, the cost reports."

Simon broke into a rare smile and almost, Arun thought, laughed. "If I haven't heard of a rationalization before, that is certainly one."

Arun gave a thin smile. "We would not be doing this for personal enrichment. We would be doing it to save the university hospital. Isn't that the greater good?"

Simon was silent for a moment, then said, "I won't leave you hanging out here alone, Arun. The truth is, I've had the same thoughts myself. But I didn't know what to do with them. You, at least, had the courage to speak them to me."

"Sometimes the honorable course skirts the dishonorable. But if you keep your eye on what's important, it makes moral sense. I would never do anything that was truly dishonorable, Simon. You know me better than that. I am a man of honor. This was drilled into me by my father. I always keep my word."

Simon nodded. He liked this side of Arun.

"But sometimes choosing the honorable course is not easy, not when you are faced with two less-than-attractive alternatives. And that's where we are. But I know which is the correct course."

Simon nodded again. "I think we can do this in ways that will save the university hospital, while at the same time minimizing the chances of being detected. Yes, you are right, we have more control over the cash reports, and we can do things that will bring in more money there. And while Miss Morehouse would not approve, there are ways we can bring in more revenue on the claims, as well, which I will take care of."

27

Peter and Marjorie took the escalator up from the Vienna underground and emerged in Stephansplatz to an early April breeze. Just to their right, across the cobblestone plaza, stood the 12th century St. Stephen's Cathedral, the heart of the old city. They had already been to Stephansplatz several times, but found themselves lured back by the beauty of old Vienna.

Vienna, they found, was a city built on architecture, culture and food, and not necessarily in that order. Scores of tourists thronged the plaza and the corresponding streets, most paved with cobblestone, and took in the Baroque and Gothic architecture and quaint stores. Cafes sometimes ran two a block. St. Stephen's Cathedral itself, a massive Gothic structure with its enormous south tower and a large ornately patterned roof, was in the middle of a restoration, as the scaffolding along one of its sides attested. Open to the public, yet also in service, the cathedral drew both the curious and the devout.

They had been in Vienna a week now and were thoroughly enjoying themselves. It was just the vacation Peter wanted, a place to get away and put his thoughts in order, to concentrate on life itself, not all the political and other machinations going on back in Washington. They dined on wienerschnitzel and tafelspitz, the famous Vienna boiled beef dish, and topped it off with ample portions of Viennese apple strudel. The Viennese coffee was well-known for being strong, and shops abounded. Marjorie couldn't help but laugh, though, when she noticed that a famous Seattle-based coffee chain also had several locations there.

Now they walked, hand in hand, like they had when they met years before, down the side streets off Stephansplatz, stopping to look at one of several houses where Mozart reputedly had lived, at various museums, or just to admire the pastry and chocolates in the store windows.

"Such a beautiful city," Marjorie said.

"Yes, it was good to get away. I think every doctor, or for that matter, anyone at all, has got to travel. As a colleague of mine at work says about travel, 'It's good for the soul.'"

There was so much more of the city to see. They were staying in the famous Hotel Sacher, across from the State Opera House. The Sacher is known for many things, not the least of which is being founded in the 19th century by a former chef to Austrian-Hungarian Emperor Franz Joseph, and then taken over by his daughter, who was famous during the early decades of the 20th century for smoking cigars and walking her many dogs. Severely damaged during the Second World War, it was used as a British headquarters during the occupation, and was even filmed as such in the movie, "The Third Man." Long since rebuilt, it is now famous not only for its old-world elegance, but for the Sacher Torte, a chocolate cake that was a favorite of the late emperor's.

"What shall we see today?" Peter asked. "We've been to the districts one, two and four. Should we go to District 12? That's where the University of Vienna is. I'd like to see how campus life there compares to what we have in the States. I hear it's a dynamic part of the city, if only for all the students."

"Okay, let's do that." Marjorie found herself falling in live with Peter all over again on this trip. How could she not, in such a romantic city? And

Peter had been right. They had to get away from all the craziness in Washington.

Taking the underground to Schottentor-Universitat, they came up to the surface and immediately noticed the college students walking, as well as a few bookstores. Across the street they saw an establishment that looked to be popular, if the number of customers coming in and out was any indication. A sign said, "Café Leopold."

"Let's go in there," Peter suggested, as they headed toward the door.

The Café Leopold was full of polished dark wood, brass railings and glass. A large oval bar dominated the center of the room, with waiters/bartenders with white aprons filling orders, whether for drink or food. Like much of Europe, the functions of a bar and a restaurant in Vienna were mixed together at the popular cafes. Peter and Marjorie slid into a booth not far from the front door. A middle-aged plump waiter, looking very much like a Viennese shopkeeper from a story book, came up and asked them what they would have. Peter ordered a beer, and Marjorie a café mocha.

"They've all got to do this. Lyle, Jennifer, all the doctors and their spouses at James Buchanan," Peter said, looking around the café and outside through the window at the students passing by. "Puts it all in perspective."

Marjorie nodded, but noticed that there seemed to her something else on her husband's mind.

"What is it, Peter? Something's troubling you."

Peter sighed. "It's Arun I'm concerned about."

Marjorie nodded. "I have never seen him so stressed as before we left. Usually he's so calm, so reserved and polite. But I think the combination of the OIG investigation and the murders are taking their toll on him. He's the one who really needs to get away."

"Yes, but that's just it, Marj. I don't think he can."

"Because he's the man in charge? Come on, everyone's entitled to a vacation. I can't believe that OIG will think it a problem if he announces he is coming here, or going to some Caribbean island for a couple of weeks."

"That's not it. I'm worried about him for another reason, and I think that's the cause of his stress. I think he knows more about the so-called fraud at the university than he's letting on."

Marjorie paused as she took this in. "Are you saying that –"

"There's no way he can not have known about the finances at the school. Just no way, if he was doing his job right. And one thing we both know about Arun is that he is a very hands-on, responsible sort of guy."

"Exactly. And, okay, maybe he saw something. But he is too responsible not to fix it."

"Unless he was behind it."

"C'mon, Peter. This is Arun we are talking about. We've known him for years. He's the farthest thing from a criminal that I can imagine."

Peter sighed again. "That's just it. Most of the people who get accused of these Medicare crimes are not criminals. Not in the traditional sense. They're not holding up liquor stores or embezzling money. The bulk are good people, doctors like me, like Lyle and Jennifer, or good administrators like Arun, who are turned into so-called criminals by the government."

"I think that's stretching it a bit."

"Is it? I don't know what kind of financial shape the university hospital has been in. I've made it a point not to know, so I can concentrate on my medical duties. Arun doesn't have that luxury. Now, I agree with you that he would never, under any circumstances, steal money or do anything like that for personal gain. But what if the university hospital was in trouble? I've given this some thought, and it explains a lot of the changes we've seen in Arun these past few weeks. What if the university hospital was losing money? It would be up to Arun to find ways to turn that around. That's a big part of his job, to make sure it runs profitably."

"It's a big part of any administrator's job. But that doesn't mean he would stoop to illegalities to do it."

"Can you imagine the cost reports and other financials not being looked over by Arun? He has to sign off on them, you know? And one of the big areas the government is looking at is cost report fraud."

"So he is covering up for someone else?"

"Maybe. Or maybe… You know, we don't know what may have motivated him. It's possible that, to keep things in the black, he made changes to reports, or even directed that the billing staff charge Medicare more for services that cost less."

"He couldn't get away with that. He'd have to have someone on the staff cooperating with him."

"Yes, he would. And for all we know, he might. One thing is clear, much as I don't like it. When there's this much smoke, and OIG is investigating us for so many things, it can't all be wrong. And then we have to believe that Arun is either aware of it, or incompetent in his job. And we know he's not incompetent."

"And how about the murders? Are you going to say he's responsible for those, too?"

"I've given that a lot of thought. They may very well be totally unrelated to the fraud, and I hope they are. But, if you really think about it, it's not impossible that he's involved."

"Peter!" Marjorie could scarcely believe what her husband was saying.

"What if Scott Karakas somehow found out about the fraud and Arun's involvement in it?"

"Now how many students do you know who care about their school's finances and cost reports?"

Peter downed the rest of his beer. "Well, there you've got me. Not many. Probably none. And it is hard to picture Arun killing anyone. I agree. But I'm just speculating. Let's just leave aside the question of why Scott Karakas would want to be aware of the school's finances. Let's just say that he was and he let Arun know about it, or Arun somehow found out about it on his own. Now Arun's career, reputation and entire life, really, are on the line. Mightn't he just snap and do something to protect himself, like kill Scott?"

"No, I don't think he would."

Peter nodded, then reached for the check.

28

"You've got a visitor."

Eileen looked up from her computer into Mike's face. The expression he wore, plus the fact that he came over to her desk to tell her himself, made it clear that he considered this visitor significant. Or that he wanted to see her reaction. Either way, Eileen didn't have time for a visitor now. She was on deadline and had two separate stories needing considerable work.

Mike jerked his head in the direction of the glass-walled conference room on the other side of the newsroom. Eileen saw why he was interested. Sitting there and looking rather impatient was police Detective Alphonse Petrelli, Jr. Eileen grabbed her pad and pen and headed off in his direction.

"Thanks, Mike," she said over her shoulder. Mike watched her make like a beeline to the conference room, grunted and headed on to the next reporter he had something to say to.

Petrelli had his head down, apparently deep in thought, when Eileen opened the conference room door. He quickly looked up.

"Thanks for meeting with me, Miss Ashburton," he said, as Eileen placed herself into a conference room chair facing him. "I need your help."

"You need *my* help."

"Yes."

"On the James Buchanan murder case?"

"Yes, well, in a way. Certainly if you have anything that might prove useful."

"I'm sure you've heard the speculation that the murder case and the fraud case are tied together," Eileen said, hoping she might get some information.

Petrelli shrugged. "Heard a lot about it, but not much proof." He seemed ill at ease, as if wrestling with whether he should say something. "May we talk off the record, Miss Ashburton?"

"How much off the record are we talking about?"

"What do you mean? I thought "off the record" meant you didn't use my name."

"That is what it means, but there are degrees. For instance, in some instances, a source might want his or her name 'off the record' but doesn't mind if I write, 'a high-level police department source,' or 'a police detective'. Others want more protection, so I might say, 'a source close to the investigation'. And still others want no mention of anything related to them, no title, nothing. There are all sorts of combinations."

Petrelli listened attentively. "Interesting. I had no idea this was all so...nuanced. The truth is, Miss Ashburton, I've never had much use for the press. It can be helpful in publicizing a name if we want it, and you might not be happy to hear that there have been times when we've actually planted false leads in your paper, and in the media in general, to smoke out someone. But you all do more harm than good."

Eileen had heard this before and she loved it. The man was honest. So much easier to deal with than your typical politician who tried to spin the truth in whatever way would play the best with her. All she had to do now was get Petrelli to trust her.

"So, if that's how you feel, why are you here, detective?"

"You get right to the point. They told me, down at the station, that you were like that, knowing I'm a no-nonsense kind of guy. Guess they were right."

"You were sent down here by the station?"

"Before I go further, Miss Ashburton, are we, in fact, off the record? And I mean in the complete sense, no titles or anything else, not even 'someone closely connected to the investigation'. Nothing. Nada. This is on, how do you call it, deep background."

This was getting good and Eileen had to see where it was going. "Alright, detective. We are off the record from this point forward unless we both agree to go back on the record. And I mean, by your definition of off the record."

"And you do keep your word on these things, don't you? You would go to jail rather than reveal a source?"

"I've never had to yet, but yes, anonymous sources are respected here. You just have to make the decision to trust me. I've never burned a source yet."

Petrelli nodded, then hesitated. *God, is he nervous*, Eileen thought. What could this possibly be?

Petrelli hesitated, then said, "If I seem nervous, Miss Ashburton—"

"Eileen, please. Since you are trusting me with whatever it is you are going to tell me, we might as well be on a first-name basis."

"Eileen, it's because, well, one branch of law enforcement usually doesn't publicly complain about another, nor do they do what I am about to do, and that is, essentially, to rat on them."

"You have a problem with some other police force, or the FBI? I'm aware that intramural rivalry sometimes plays a part, but – "

"You don't understand, Eileen. I'm not talking about another police agency or government arm that investigates criminal misconduct. I'm talking about an agency that is not supposed to get involved in investigating things like murder at all. I'm talking about the Dept. of Health and Human Services' Office of the Inspector General. It's getting involved in this murder investigation, something that is, I believe, beyond its mandate. There. I've said it. You want to know how the murder case and the fraud case are connected? There's one way. They are both being investigated by the HHS Office of the Inspector General."

Eileen was thunderstruck. She could understand why Petrelli was so bothered. OIG is supposed to limit itself to health care fraud and other areas. It is not supposed to be investigating other crimes, let alone murder.

"How do you know this?"

"I know it."

"I need more."

"You need more? Okay, here's more. I have it on good authority that the Inspector General herself, Charlotte Westbrook, went up to Pennsylvania to visit Scott Karakas' parents, and that she's been nosing around the campus, asking students what they knew about Scott, Dana Brentano and Nick Rosen. And also that her chief counsel, Lewis Sullivan, has been investigating on his own, too, paying visits to the university hospital's accounting department – although since it was the accounting department, that might be okay, given that he may have been looking into the fraud."

"The inspector general and the chief counsel *themselves* are doing the investigating? Why not their staff?"

"Good question. Maybe you can find out. It is causing some headaches in my office, I can tell you. That's why I got a wink-wink, nudge-nudge from my higher-ups about the idea of coming down here to speak with you. Frankly, we'd like to have a public spotlight thrown on Miss Westbrook and Mr. Sullivan. That might get them off this, and back to what they should be investigating."

"Apparently, though, Westbrook and Sullivan think there *is* enough of a connection between the two cases for them to get involved. They could use that as a reason for OIG's getting involved in the murder investigation. But it doesn't explain why the two of them are getting *personally* involved in this."

"This is not the first time that Westbrook has drawn attention for her unusual behavior. There's her laser gun, her alienation of the career attorneys on her staff, her father's influence to help her get the job, and more."

"Yes, we covered that pretty extensively." She thought a second, Petrelli watching her as she did. "I will need some proof, eyewitnesses, statements, copies of hotel bills from Pennyslvania, anything that will prove what you are saying, detective. You understand, we can't go public on this just on your say-so. If we did, it would look like we were in cahoots with the police in an intramural dispute."

Petrelli nodded. "I can get some material together for you."

"Then I will be calling Miss Westbrook and Mr. Sullivan, giving them a chance to say why they are getting involved here. Leaving our source completely out, of course. I'll tell you what, detective. I don't know if these two cases are connected or not. I've done some stories on that possibility, but we have nothing definitive. But once your story hits, whether the two cases are, in fact, connected or not, I can assure you this: they will become connected in the public's eye."

"We just want her off the case. She can stick to the fraud side, but let us do our jobs as professionals to catch this murderer. If it turns out at some point that they are connected, then we can talk about that."

"Why haven't you tried contacting her yourself and objecting?"

Petrelli smiled. He was clearly more relaxed now. "You said it yourself, Eileen. Intramural rivalry. They wouldn't take it well if we did. Besides, having it appear in the paper first will give it more impact."

"Are you trying to use me, use the press, detective?

"We all use each other, Eileen. It's a karmic game." He began walking toward the door. "I'll get you that material."

Eileen watched him leave. This story was getting more complicated by the minute.

29

L ewis could feel the eyes of his staff on him as he got his morning coffee. He could sense their thinking as he passed them in the hallway. And he could see that they couldn't wait to question him at the weekly roundup, when he and attorneys with active fraud cases updated each other on progress.

This morning's roundup had 15 attorneys in the room with Lewis. He spoke first.

"I imagine you've all seen the morning *Post*, and you are all wondering whether this is true and, if so, what I have to say about it." He could see from their expressions that this was exactly what they were thinking. Some undoubtedly saw the story about his and Charlotte's involvement in the murder cases as another example of Charlotte's trivialization of their work, demeaning the department, and were concerned about the effect working for what a *Washington Post* editorial called a "rogue prosecutor" might have on their careers. Justice Department lawyers were nothing if not career-driven.

"I'm sorry to say that I am not going to talk about the story just now. I haven't met with the Inspector General yet, so my freedom of discussion, particularly since the story, whether it is true or not, involves me, is not complete. I would ask you all to be patient. But in the meantime, the business of this office must go forward. So let's proceed with the updates. Charles," he said, turning toward a tall, sandy-haired attorney, "why don't you go first, and let us know where matters stand with the medical director situation at Bay Ridge Health Systems in San Francisco?"

"Our careers are over!"

It was about 90 minutes since the roundup ended, and Lewis, the need to appear calm and in charge before his staff gone, now frantically paced Charlotte's office, with Charlotte watching him from behind her desk.

"I should never have let you get me involved in this," he continued. "It was none of our business to investigate. If we had some actual link between the murders and the fraud, well, then maybe you could make a case. But we don't. And it is not in our purview to go hunting for that link!"

Charlotte was, at least to Lewis' eyes, surprisingly serene. A copy of the *Post*, with the front page story, just below the fold, "HHS Investigating James Buchanan Murders," and the subhead, "Fraud-fighting inspector general finds new mission?" clearly visible.

"I received a call from the Secretary today," she said. "He's not very happy, either."

"I would think not." HHS Secretary Balcom was not a man who liked policy made or actions taken without his knowledge. He must have been incensed when he read the article, Lewis thought.

Charlotte stood up, taking the newspaper with her. She walked around her desk and leaned against the front of it, facing Lewis. There was almost a slight smile on her face as Lewis watched her. *Was she actually enjoying this?*

"Here's what I told Secretary Balcom, and it's not that different than what I told Eileen Ashburton when she called: We go where the fraud investigation takes us. And if that involves murder, then we have every right to look into it, sharing what we find with the police and any other law enforcement bodies that might be involved, of course."

"But we don't know that the investigation takes us there. It's just your hunch. And besides, even if did, it's not in our purview to investigate murders."

"A case can be made that it is, when it involves fraud."

"But we don't know that it does!" Lewis was almost beside himself.

"It's true, we have nothing concrete yet. But there is enough circumstantial evidence there to make the case that we are correct to get involved, I think."

"That's not even circumstantial evidence, you know that. It's just coincidence."

"So, let's say that's true. What's the best way out of this, Lewis?"

"What do you mean? I don't know. Apologize and pray they let us keep our jobs, I would think."

Charlotte shook her head. "No. The best way out of this is to go where our gut instinct takes us and find that link."

"We don't know if there really is one."

Charlotte gave him a long, hard look. "Leave the law aside for a moment, Lewis. What do you really think?"

Lewis didn't like this question, didn't like being told to 'leave the law aside,' and he found it especially incongruous coming from the HHS Inspector General. The law was what he had built his entire professional life around. It was there not only to catch wrongdoers, but to provide for a civil society, a society of tolerance, a society that allowed him and James to live together in peace, and to be able to defend themselves if attacked. But he also knew that not everything in life could be reduced to law. Now, faced with Charlotte's question, he knew the answer. And he didn't want to give it.

"Did you see that editorial on the op-ed page? Where they referred to me as the 'Dr. Watson' to your 'Sherlock Holmes'? The only thing missing was a picture of you in a deerstalker cap and a magnifying class. I know you don't smoke a pipe."

"Lewis."

"Alright, let's just say I wouldn't be surprised if it turned out the two are connected."

"Alright. And let's just say we find that proof. And it breaks the case. What do you think Secretary Balcom, or the Senate, or the press, will say then?"

Lewis knew the point. Everyone loves a winner. Senator Donelin, whom he gathered Charlotte had not yet heard from, would not severely criticize them, not if the case turned out as Charlotte was painting. The press would love it and would most likely turn Charlotte from a "rogue prosecutor" to a "crusading prosecutor." As for Secretary Balcom, if the story proved to be correct, he would probably still object to Charlotte's self-appointed role in all this, but the White House would probably tell him to quiet down.

"In for a penny, in for a pound, that's where we are?"

Charlotte nodded. "Unless you want to throw in the towel now and just take the abuse and disciplinary action that doubtless will be thrown our way. Wouldn't it be ironic to have our careers ruined, as you say, and then later find out that we were right, but didn't have the nerve to move forward?"

"What will you say to the Secretary, and to Senator Donelin, when he doubtless summons you before his committee?"

"That we are doing our job and that we will be extra vigilant not to step over the bounds of where our investigation takes us."

Lewis was not sure they would buy this.

"Lewis, even if they were inclined to do something to us, it would probably be weeks before they actually took action. Sure, the Secretary could fire us on the spot, but Balcom is a cautious man."

Lewis nodded. That was his assessment of the man, as well.

"So let's just redouble our efforts on finding this link. Once we do, it will probably help your fraud case, as well."

"What do I tell my staff? The same thing you are going to tell the Secretary and the Senator? They're far from thrilled with you, you know. About a third of them are ready to join the others who have quit since you took over."

Charlotte nodded. "I know. And I am sorry about that." She paused, thoughtful for a moment, then turned to Lewis. "Alright, so we are agreed. The best way out of this is to move forward, and that is what we are going to do. Now, get that glum look off your face, Lewis. The game is afoot!"

Lewis didn't appreciate the Sherlock Holmes reference. Didn't appreciate it one bit.

30

C harlotte would have considered the drive to Maryland's Eastern Shore beautiful every time she took it, were it not for two things: the large amount of traffic typical on weekends, as harried Washington and Baltimore residents rush to get away for two days of peace and quiet; and the nerve-wracking passage of each one-way span of the seemingly impossibly high and narrow Bay Bridge, which took her over the Chesapeake. Whatever architect had come up with the idea of creating what amounted to two bridges – one going East and the other going West – to accentuate the thin elegance of them, Charlotte imagined, probably never had to drive across them.

Nonetheless, she was used to the trip, having made it many times before. Her father still owned the family's St. Michael's retreat and even now, with him retired from the Senate and she busy in D.C., she made it a point to see him as often as possible. Recently, she had more and more begun to see the affects of age creep up on him, and the dawning realization that one day there would no more visits was increasingly with her.

Age was something that was occupying Charlotte's mind quite a bit recently. As her father showed his, she became more aware of her own, as well as what she had achieved with her life so far, and what she hadn't. At 42, no one could deny her success, first as a government attorney with the Department of Transportation, and now as inspector general at HHS. Whatever people and the press said about her father's help in her rise up the ladder, she knew that she worked hard in all those jobs and did them well.

What's next? she wondered as the bridge approached and she steeled herself for its passage. Life had always taken care of her and she supposed it would continue to do so. Maybe she would run for office, like her dad had. Or maybe she would go into private practice. It didn't seem likely, with recent events, that she would continue for long as the HHS Inspector General, even if her theories about the murders proved true. She had stepped outside the traditional boundaries of the job too often and she knew it.

Charlotte had, in recent years, begun wondering if she would spend the rest of her life alone, sharing that concern only with Penelope. There was no man in her life, and hadn't been for some time. She couldn't help but wonder why. The truth was, she didn't know. She had good relationships with both her parents. When her mother, Mary, was alive, before giving in to the evils of lymphoma eight years ago, they were close, exchanging confidences, going shopping, talking about family. Although Charlotte had been something of a rebel in her teen and college years, as she entered her late 20's she began finding her mother a good companion. Her mother had given up a lot to spend her life in her father's shadow. Charlotte had despised this when she was younger, but later saw it as a choice that her mother had wanted to make, was happy to make, and, although Charlotte herself had made a different choice, she learned to admire her mother for deciding what she wanted and sticking to it.

Charlotte's dad was her guidepost. As a child, she played with him constantly, and was clearly daddy's girl. Her brother, Gary, and she used to go out of their way to pull tricks on him, hiding his pipe or saying they had lost some important Senate document he had been waiting for. But, Charlotte remembered as she got off the bridge and breathed a sigh of relief, no matter how powerful and busy a senator he was, to her and Gary, he was always their dad, and that was the way he liked it. She couldn't remember a time when they weren't close, even during her rambunctious college years and some of the more offbeat boyfriends she had then, as well as later, boyfriends whom the press had had some fun with when she was nominated for the HHS Inspector General position.

There was Adam, who wanted her to move to a commune with him; Doug, whose idea of a good evening was going over a new set of computer calculations; Peter, who tried to convince her father about reincarnation over dinner one night; Michael, whose family was rumored to be connected to the mob; and her parents' least favorite, Brandon, who was 23 years older than her.

What was I really looking for? she wondered. Did any of those boys and men really interest me, or was I just rebelling? She didn't know. But what was odd was that, as her career took off in her late 30's, she found she didn't have time for men, although she did occasionally miss them. And Mack was always there for male company. But now that she was approaching middle age, she had begun wondering if her best years were behind her. Would she spend the rest of her life alone? Not a pleasant prospect. What she was really troubled by, however, was that, despite the concern about a life without companionship, she did not feel especially motivated to do anything about it. It bothered her that she felt that way, and even more so that she did not know why. She fell back on her guiding line: Life has always taken care of me. And it most likely would continue to do so.

She pulled into the gravel driveway of the old, rambling house that abutted the shore. Her father, who loved the place, liked to tinker inside, repair things and enjoyed spending time on his boat, opened the door as she approached and greeted her with his usual bear hug.

"How's my girl?" he asked. She looked up at the familiar, craggy but still handsome face. David Westbrook's famous mane of flowing white hair was there, not having receded an inch. He kept it a bit longer these days. There were more wrinkles in the face now, but his blue eyes were just as alive and penetrating as ever. His crooked smile was there, too. Charlotte was home, and she was glad to be there.

"Causing a little bit of trouble, as I am sure you know."

"Well, well, what's life without stirring up the muck a bit now and then?" he said. Charlotte had no doubt that the Senator, as she sometimes called him, was well aware of everything that had been in the press and more. He maintained his contacts on Capitol Hill and elsewhere in the government, was still good friends with Mack, who, after all, he had mentored, and, Charlotte had no doubt, kept him up to date on his daughter's progress.

They settled in the family room, where her father had installed a large pool table, something that would never have gone well with her mother. But her dad found pool relaxing and, he told her, a good way to keep his hand-eye coordination in shape. They both sat down, Charlotte on one of the deep cushion couches, and her dad in his favorite recliner, positioned perfectly to watch the large screen TV and with a remote control and a telephone nearby. *In charge of his world as ever*, Charlotte noted.

"Got a call from Gary last weekend. He's a little worried about the coming season. The grapes are so sensitive, you know."

They both laughed. Her brother, who left the area for California long ago, worked in a winery in the Napa Valley, where he hoped to one day have his own vineyard. Unlike Charlotte, he developed a wanderlust at an early age. Plus, she suspected, he had wanted to break away from his father's image and be his own man. A winery might not be what she and her dad had expected, but maybe that was the point. He seemed happy at it, and that was the important thing. Gary came back about once a year for Thanksgiving, along with his wife and two kids. *So at least Dad has grandchildren from one of his progeny.*

"How are you doing out here, Dad?"

"Fine, just fine. James Caldicott – you remember him, honey, he used to be the chief lobbyist for the teachers union – we're going to take the *Princess* out next week and see what a little fishing will do." Caldicott was one of handful of retired Washington power brokers that lived in the area. Charlotte liked to imagine them all sitting around a local pub, talking about the good old days when they ruled the nation's capital.

"Looks like I'll be seeing Mack soon, in an official capacity," she said.

Her father lit up his pipe. "I would imagine so. Especially after your most recent escapade."

"Now, Dad, it wasn't –"

" – an escapade? Running off and chasing down murder suspects? What would you call it?"

An observer unfamiliar with the two of them might think the Senator was scolding his daughter, but Charlotte knew better. Her father had some concerns, that was for sure, but they were for her career and her welfare. At the same time, she could read her father pretty well, and she knew, just from his body language, the way he held his pipe and the look on his face, that he found the whole thing somewhat entertaining. He had been one to stir up the muck himself. That, as he would often tell her as a child, was how you knew you were alive. *Is that why I do what I do?*

But she also knew that the Senator expected her to defend her actions. If you're going to break the rules, be prepared to stand up for what you do. So she was ready.

"I would call it following the leads of a Medicare investigation," she said. "There is reason to believe the murders are linked to the investigation at James Buchanan."

"Nothing concrete yet, though, is there?"

"No, nothing concrete. Not yet."

"But your instincts tell you that all this can't be a coincidence."

"That's right."

"Hmm." Her father puffed his pipe, thoughtful. "Well, you're probably right. Your instincts are good. Always have been. But you're going to need more than instincts when you go before Mack's committee next week. Can't blame him, now. He's fond of you, has been since you were a little girl. But you're not a little girl now, haven't been for a long time. And he has a job to do."

"I know, Dad," she said softly. Her father, like most fathers everywhere, remembered the times when their daughters were little girls with almost reverential fondness.

"Then there's your whole future as Inspector General. How long do you think you can keep doing this before Balcom fires you? Or he's told to do so by the President, given that Balcom doesn't do anything until he has to?"

"Not that long. Maybe a few weeks."

"Or less, depending on how much the press does with it."

"I feel bad. I've dragged Lewis into it. It's his career on the line, too."

"Yes, well, that's something you'll have to take responsibility for." This *was* a mild rebuke. Her father was old-fashioned and believed in loyalty, especially to staff members who had served him well. Loyalty went both up and down the ladder, he believed.

"I know. But once we find the link, he'll be seen as having done the right thing."

"Then you had better get to it. Don't let the grass grow under your feet."

"I know, Dad."

"I'll talk to Mack. Express sympathy for the spot you've put him in, but ask him to take it a little easy on you. The rest is up to you."

"Thanks, Dad."

He brightened up. "Alright now, enough of that. Listen, I've got a new helper here, her name is Maria, and she makes the best crab cakes. I've had her make some, just because I knew you were coming, so let's go back to the kitchen and see just where she is, alright?"

Charlotte felt her eyes misting up. "Right behind you, Dad."

31

Carla Calloway was feeling some pressure from OIG to help build its case against James Buchanan. But just *what* she should do was a problem. And she certainly couldn't do anything right now. Not with Brenda Morehouse so close by.

Carla continued her computer work, adding data into the CMS 1500 form, the standard form that the government required when providers submitted claims for Medicare reimbursement. She and the other coders in the university hospital accounting office were busy preparing claims for stacks of medical procedures performed during hundreds of patient visits that month, from simple office visits, known as evaluation and management procedures, to complex surgeries. With approximately 7,500 codes to choose from, and then any of a number of modifiers available to indicate special circumstances, each claim took some time. Then there was documentation that had to be attached. And with the government changing the rules every now and then, it was more than easy to make a mistake.

And mistakes were made. Carla had made several herself in her career, and she had seen others, in some cases more than should be tolerated, in her view. When she had brought these to the attention of Brenda, she was thanked, but nothing was done to prevent future problems, at least in her view. *They don't take me seriously*, she thought.

So she had made the decision to turn whistleblower, to become a *qui tam* relator. Since making that decision, she had told the investigators and attorneys at OIG about lots of these, in some cases secretly making copies before heading over to the OIG offices. But mistakes weren't good enough, she was told. The government wanted evidence of intentional and explicit fraud.

She found what she could, such as when she caught doctors improperly supervising residents. Those doctors knew the rules, and when they left a resident during an operation, even to go to a neighboring building to check on another resident, they were violating the rules. From the OIG perspective, it wasn't so much a quality of care issue, but a Medicare billing violation. Simply put, under the Medicare rules, the hospital and the doctors cannot file claims for supervision if they leave the building and do something else.

But OIG wanted still more. They had lapped up her eyewitness accounts of improper supervision but, after all, it was simply her own eyewitness account, meaning it could be challenged; she could be called a liar. What they really wanted, and what Carla had been unable to provide them with so far, was something on paper, something that showed hard, physical evidence of wrongdoing. She didn't know where to look for it, and she also knew that it was unlikely to be with Brenda, who while a taskmaster and not very popular among the coding and billing staff, was honest and respected.

Now it was time for Carla to visit OIG again. She had told Brenda she would be leaving early today for a doctor's appointment. Carla viewed these visits to OIG with a mixture of dread and thrill. Dread because of fear she might get caught and some morsel of guilt over what she was doing. Thrill because it was exciting, like being part of some movie, surreptitiously taking the Metro and hoping no one she knew would be on the train, then walking as quickly as possible, trying to hide her face with sunglasses and an upturned collar or a hat, as she went into the OIG offices at 330 Independence Ave., SW.

It was, after all, too late to back out now. She could not take back the visits she had already made and her statements to Lewis Sullivan and his staff, nor was she sure she wanted to. The only thing she could do was move forward, and the best way to ensure success so the case was won, and she and her family got the millions of dollars in settlement money that was, by law, their rightful share, was by collecting the best evidence she could and handing it over.

It was hard on her, though, hard on her system. She wasn't sleeping well, waking up several times a night, often in a sweat. The number of anxious dreams she had, which had always been a problem, had increased. She was more short-tempered with her husband and their children. Was it the fear of being caught or was it subconscious guilt at turning in doctors and other professionals whom she did not really regard as bad people?

She asked herself this question over and over, but could never arrive at a satisfactory answer. She was brutally honest with herself about the money. That was the biggest part of this for her and, when it was all over, if people wanted to vilify her for actions, that was their choice. But she had a family with needs, and the fact was, her actions were justified. Justified because – and here was where she felt righteous and knew that those who would vilify her would be on the wrong side of the moral equation – the fact was that Medicare dollars were indeed being ripped off. The public's money was being stolen, and that was one of the reasons why the Medicare system, which exists to provide health care to the elderly, was in trouble. Wouldn't it have been more of a crime, given that reality, to have kept her mouth shut?

So she walked into the OIG offices later that day, relieved as always that she had escaped detection, took off her sunglasses and took the elevator up.

John Stadler, the lead attorney on the James Buchanan case, was there to greet her. A tall, good-looking man in his mid-30s with wavy dark hair, he was well-dressed and suave. Carla, plump and in her early 50s, with auburn hair and glasses, looked forward to every meeting with him.

"Hello, Carla," he said with a big smile, taking her hand in two of his. "Any problems?"

Carla felt herself blush and tried to suppress it. "Not at all. I'm very careful, you know."

"I do know, and so does everyone on the staff. We really do appreciate your efforts, Carla." He motioned down the hall. "We've got a conference room reserved. Can I get you anything?"

"Maybe some water."

"Coming right up. Bottled or tap?"

"Bottled would be great. Thanks."

Carla noted how they treated her with respect here. They listened to what she had to say, unlike Brenda Morehouse and the others at the hospital. Carla would not be ignored. It had happened to her on other jobs and she wouldn't put up with it. You would think that an organization would appreciate some input from someone trying to make things better, she thought, but it is amazing how many simply did not want to hear what she had to say.

But at OIG, they treated her with respect. Maybe that's because they had seen this before, seen good people get frustrated with their employers, good people who just wanted to do the right thing, good people who, instead of being appreciated by their employers, were treated as pains-in-the-asses, even troublemakers. That hurt, and Carla wasn't about to get hurt anymore.

Stadler returned with a bottle of *Perrier*. "It's only a little cold, I'm afraid," he said. "I hope you don't mind. I can run downstairs to the cafeteria and see if I can find you one colder, if you like."

"This will be fine, John. Thank you for making the effort."

Stadler led her down the hall to the conference room. Carla was surprised to see sitting there not only two other attorneys, but Lewis Sullivan himself. She had met Lewis a couple of times before, but those were brief visits during which Lewis just told her how much the government appreciated her help and that he wanted to stop by and say hello. *The government appreciates my help.* It was amazing how much power that statement had. *She was helping her government.* How could anyone say that what she was doing was wrong?

But she quickly remembered that Lewis was taking a more active interest in this case than he had before. He had visited the accounting office that one time – she had practically froze when she saw Brenda escort him into the room – and she knew that he had met with Simon Proctor.

After pleasantries were exchanged, Lewis got right to the point.

"Carla, I know you've been trying to find us some hard evidence to back up what you've been telling us. I think we may be able to help you. Are you familiar with the university hospital's cost reports?"

"Certainly, Chief Counsel. I've reviewed items in there from time to time. But only with Mrs. Morehouse's permission, of course."

"It's Lewis, please, Carla. Since we're all on the same team here, we should be on a first-name basis, don't you think?"

Carla nodded. See how they are playing up to me, she thought. I am finally getting the respect I've been denied.

"Anyway," Lewis continued. "We know that false cost reports have been filed with us, because so many of the figures are out of touch with market conditions, too many for it to be anything but intentional. We have those reports. But what we don't have, and what we believe must exist somewhere, is a second set of cost reports, ones showing what the charges to Medicare *should have been.* How else would the hospital be able to keep track of how much extra reimbursement it got?"

That does make sense, Carla thought. "But I've never seen anything like a second set of books."

"No, that's not surprising," Lewis said. "And we don't want to ask you to do anything that would be improper or that you would feel uncomfortable with."

"Of course not, Chief— er, Lewis. I know you all well enough for that."

And the faces of Lewis, John and the other two attorneys in the room agreed with her, all smiles and nodding.

"We appreciate your faith in us, Carla. And you know how much we admire you. I tell you, " Lewis said, leaning back in his chair, "we've had conversations here among us, wondering if any of us would have the courage you've shown in doing what's right."

"Oh, Lewis, please. I'm just doing what I think is necessary."

"Exactly, Carla. And the sad truth is that there are very few citizens today who take the idea of citizenship as seriously as you do. People less moral than you vilify you and others who come forward, then they try and retaliate against you, which is why we have anti-retaliation laws. You're a great American, Carla."

Carla felt her eyes moisten. She didn't know what to say.

"So I don't know what else I can ask of you specifically. Maybe think about this question of the second set of books. Who would have something like that? Where would they be kept? If we knew, of course, we could get a search warrant and get hold of them. But we would have to know. Do you think you might give that some thought?"

"I will, Lewis."

Lewis nodded. Carla could see that he expected nothing less from her ... and she knew there was no way she was going to let him down.

32

"I take it, Inspector General, that you will not be firing your laser gun my way during this committee hearing."

Charlotte looked up from the witness table into Mack's face, the face of her longtime friend and protégé of her father's. It also happened to be the face of Senator Mack Donelin, chairman of the Senate Appropriations Committee. She saw the twinkle in his eye, but also knew, from past experience and her father's assessment, that he would be putting the nation's interest before her own today. And she also knew that he was aware that she knew it.

"Only metaphorically, if that, Senator," she said. "Can I trust that no projectiles will be hurtling my way, as well?"

Mack smiled, and Charlotte could not help but warm to the boyish charm that she knew so well. "Only questions, Miss Westbrook, only questions." He spoke to one of the aides who lined the wall behind him, then turned to Charlotte. "I understand you have an opening statement?"

"Yes, Senator, I do. It won't take long."

"Take as long as you like. You may proceed."

"Thank you, Senator." She looked at the 12 members of the committee before her, eight men and four women. She had come to know them well, as had Lewis. Part of the job for both them was testimony before this committee. After all, Congress appropriated hundreds of millions of dollars each year to OIG for the fight against Medicare fraud, and it was only understandable that it would want to know how the fight was going.

Charlotte, at this mid-April session, sat at the witness table before the full committee, with only her papers and a microphone in front of her, and one aide next to her. She had told Lewis that she would handle this one alone. No fan of testifying before Congress, Lewis readily agreed, if anything even more relieved this time, given his concerns that Charlotte might be asked about their involvement in the murder investigation. As for the aide, actually an intern on a break between college sessions, he was simply there to learn about government. But he served the dual purpose of being able to hand Charlotte notes and papers as she needed them. Right now, he handed her what looked like a report.

"Senators," Charlotte began, "I think these numbers say it all: In the fiscal year just concluded, the Office of the Inspector General reported savings and expected recoveries of $38.2 billion. In addition, we excluded 3,425 individuals and entities for fraud or abuse, 472 criminal actions against individuals or entities were undertaken, as well as 272 civil actions.

"I wish I could say, senators, that with these actions the job is now completed, but the truth is quite the opposite. As our team of investigators and attorneys builds its own sophistication and experience year after year, we find new ways in which some health care providers – and I emphasize the word some, senators, because I do believe that the overwhelming majority of medical professionals in this country are honest and do the people of this country a great service – in which some health care providers, nevertheless, are gaming the system. By that, I mean bending the Medicare rules in such a way that their actions look alright, but upon closer examination, may not be."

"Just as an example," she continued, taking another report from her intern, "and here I quote from our annual work plan, where, as you know, we list the areas we plan to investigate. As this plan indicates, there are over 300 distinct and specific areas that we plan to concentrate on this year, 25 involving hospitals, 17 involving physicians and other health professionals, six involving home health agencies, and many others. For instance, we plan to look at whether hospitals incorrectly charged Medicare for dialysis services when all that was required was patient observation. We also plan to examine the relationships between physician practices and the billing companies they use, to see if either party is encouraging the other to submit more claims to Medicare than would be proper.

"So what does all this show you? As you can see, Senators, at a minimum, it shows that the dollars you have invested in us are well-spent, returning many times their value to the government. Beyond that, of course, there is the perhaps even more important value of keeping the Medicare program sound and making sure that patients are given medical choices for the right reason, that is, their care, and not because a given choice is profitable for a particular health care provider."

She put down her report and looked up at the committee. "That concludes my testimony, Senators. I will be happy, at this point, to answer any questions you may have."

"The chair recognizes Senator Barbara Owens from the state of Texas," Mack said.

Senator Owens, the ranking minority member, was a middle-aged blonde, professional-looking woman known among her colleagues for playing to the crowd.

"Inspector General, let's go back to your point about the appropriations you receive from this Congress being well spent."

"I believe the numbers show that they are, Senator," Charlotte said.

"No question we are getting value for the money, Inspector General. I am not questioning that. My question goes to a related, but I think important, point, which is this: It's one thing to crack down on fraud and abuse. Goodness, no one wants to see perpetrators of fraud, especially against our senior citizens, get away with it, and this committee congratulates you on those cases where actual perpetrators have been caught. But there seems to be something else here. There seems to be a need to show a profit on the dollars we give you."

"I assure you, Senator, that —"

"Just let me finish, Inspector General. Time after time in these committee hearings, you come in here, as does the Chief Counsel, to tell us that the money this committee appropriates for your part of HHS is a 'good investment.' And so it has been. But that should not be the goal of your agency, Inspector General. After all, if your agency has it in its head that it had better catch some more crooks or we won't be able to come back to this committee and show how much money we made the U.S. government, then, well, the name of the game isn't catching real fraud, is it? It becomes finding fraud, or perhaps even stretching the definition of fraud so you can keep your funding for next year. That's what is causing this atmosphere of fear in the medical community, Inspector General. I'm sure you are aware of the Illinois podiatrist who was recently sentenced to death for the murder of a woman who was going to testify against him about Medicare fraud? I'm not saying that justice wasn't done in that particular case, Miss Westbrook. My concern is not that you are going after existing fraud. It's that you feel an obligation to search for it, even when it is perhaps not apparent, in order to justify the funding this committee gives you."

"Senator, nothing could be further from the truth. Believe me, nothing would make me happier than to come back to you and say, 'Senators, the fight against fraud is almost won. We won't need as much in appropriations next year.'"

Senator Owens chuckled. "Really, Inspector General? You'll excuse me if I find that a bit hard to believe. It's well known in Washington – and you should know this yourself, Miss Westbrook, given your pedigree –" Charlotte bristled at the reference to her father – "that any department's or agency's number one purpose is remaining in existence and maintaining, if not increasing, its level of funding. I'm sure you know that."

"All I am saying, senator, is that we do not make up fraud or go after innocent providers. We go where the evidence takes us."

"Such as stretching your mandate to include a murder investigation?"

Mack jumped in. He turned to look at Senator Owens. "Will the senator yield her time so I may follow this line of questioning?" Senator Owens nodded her assent. Charlotte, relieved to be done with Senator Owens, now dreaded where Mack was going to take this. Was this some kind of tag team that Mack and Owens had worked up in advance?

"Inspector General Westbrook, please tell this committee why the HHS Office of the Inspector General, charged with rooting out fraud in the Medicare and Medicaid programs, should now be investigating a set of three murders, especially when the District police already have this well in hand?"

Charlotte decided to pass on countering Mack's "well in hand" comment. She didn't see how anyone could believe that the District police have the matter "well in hand," given not only their lack of progress in solving the case, but their wrongful targeting of Nicholas Rosen.

"Senator, let me first assure you that my office does recognize that its first obligation is Medicare and Medicaid fraud, and nothing else. There is no question about that. As to the specific case you refer to, the reason we are involved, and only peripherally so, I might add, is because it might tie into an existing Medicare fraud case."

"So the newspapers have speculated," Mack said. "But do you have any evidence to support this?

"That is what we are working to get, senator. We have good reason to believe it may be forthcoming soon."

"Will the senator yield his time?" asked Senator Owens. Mack agreed.

"So, Miss Westbrook, what you are saying then is that you do not yet have any empirical, hard evidence linking the murders to the James Buchanan University fraud case."

"Not yet, senator, no. But we believe—"

"Never mind what you believe, Inspector General. If we greenlighted this…scavenger hunt…of yours, we'd have to let every inspector general in every department get involved in all sorts of investigations outside their areas, simply because they had a hunch, or at least not much more. And I do not believe this committee is going to do that."

"Senator, I assure you, no Medicare fraud case is being left untended because of this."

"No?" Senator Owens asked. "But your individual time, and that of your chief counsel, is being spent this way. If you really think about it, Mr. Chairman," she said, facing Mack, "this is really astounding. You have two grown professionals here, playing cops and robbers at the government's expense. You know, Miss Westbrook," she said, turning back to Charlotte, "given that that is the case, I wonder if maybe you aren't guilty of Medicare fraud."

There was a gasp in the room at the comment.

"After all, you are spending HHS money, if only your salary and that of your chief counsel, that is meant to be spent on Medicare fraud investigations, on a police matter instead."

"Senator, I assure you—"Charlotte began.

"Senator, I think that is going too far," Mack said, jumping in. "Every inspector general has some discretion as to what he or she investigates. We may disagree with the choices an inspector general makes in that regard, as I do in this case. But we cannot second guess their work and, if we disagree, say they are committing fraud."

"Thank you, Senator," Charlotte said. *Mack had come through for her, after all.*

"Not so fast, Inspector General," Mack said. "It may not be the function of this committee to tell you what to investigate. But it is the function of this committee to review the work, and the funding, of your office. And it would be wise to listen to our assessment, given that we do appropriate your budget, and we can call public attention to our concerns. With that in mind, I am going to ask this committee to pass a non-binding resolution recommending that you call off any investigation into the murders at James Buchanan University, immediately, and that this committee also recommend that you limit any future investigations to matters specifically concerning Medicare fraud."

"And what if it turns out that there is Medicare fraud connected to the murders?" Charlotte asked.

"If the police uncover that," Mack said, "then, at that point only, you would be free to look at it, but concentrating your efforts only on the fraud angle, not the murder. That's what the citizens of the District of Columbia have a police department for."

In the visitor's gallery, Eileen Ashburton was busy taking notes. Ever since she broke the story that the already controversial laser-shooting HHS inspector general was getting involved in a murder case, there had been a marked upturn of interest in her stories, as judged by letters to the editors, e-mails and phone calls. It seemed that the information had touched the public imagination. I need to get back to the city room right away and get this new story out, she thought. "Inspector General chastised by committee for murder investigation," she thought excitedly, picturing the headline.

Unfortunately for Charlotte, this sort of publicity would not please the members of the appropriations committee, particularly Mack, who seemed considerably more agitated with her when they met in his office alone after the hearing ended.

"I'm sorry, Mark, to cause you such trouble," Charlotte began.

Mack sat down behind his desk and looked up at Charlotte, standing before him. The expression on his face was a mixture of concern, anger and perhaps a touch of amusement.

"Honestly, Charlotte, you have gotten yourself in some fine fixes before, but this one takes the cake. Taking the HHS Office of the Inspector General into a murder case, and actually doing the sleuthing – along with Lewis, who I have trouble seeing doing this sort of thing – on your own. What's next, your own TV show?"

"It's not like that, Mack, really. Believe me, I have no desire to get in the way of the District police or any other law enforcement body."

"Try telling that to Detective Petrelli. I spent half an hour with the man on the phone earlier today. He's urging me to pull the plug on you and, I have to tell you, he has a case. He's on a campaign to get you off this, Charlotte. I take it he feels a personal stake here, from his tone. It might do you some good to talk with him directly."

"The only reason I am looking into this case is that I do believe there is a connection to the fraud cases, of which, by the way, there are several, and substantive evidence to back them up."

Mack shook his head. "Not enough, Charlotte, I'm afraid. Look, we go back a long way and you know how I feel about your dad. But I also have a job to do as the head of this committee. And we are going to go ahead and pass those resolutions recommending you get off this case. Now, I realize these are just resolutions and this committee has no direct authority over what you do. But they will be taken seriously by the Secretary and the White House, especially with the publicity they will bring. I trust you saw Miss Ashburton in the gallery?"

Charlotte nodded.

"The *Post* is starting to get some mileage out of this, and I don't mean the fraud case, or even the murders, which it has been covering all along. It's *your* involvement in this, Charlotte, that has added a whole new element to the story. I know how the press works and what they like, and you are going to put all of this on page one. If you persist in the investigation, the heat will ratchet up, and the Administration will cut you loose, despite your dad. You'll also be something of a laughing stock – the Inspector General who though she was a female Sherlock Holmes, that kind of thing. Is that what you want for your career? On the other hand, I won't deny that if you continue your investigation and turn out to be right, you'll be pretty close to untouchable," he said, smiling at the thought.

Charlotte smiled at him.

"But the odds of that happening, Charlotte, are slim. Even if you are right, and there is a connection, how are you going to prove it? You're not a trained police officer. And then there's the question of Petrelli. He is trained in this. Why not leave the murder side of this to him? If there's a connection, he'll find it, and you can still be proved right, your stature enhanced. And if nothing is found, at least your neck will no longer be on the line. What's happened so far will just be considered another of your eccentricities."

"Detective Petrelli was certain that Nick Rosen, who later turned out murdered, was the murderer himself. Do you have faith in that man?"

"Cases always have several leads. Some don't pan out."

Charlotte shrugged. There was nothing more to say. They knew each other well enough to know that neither was likely to shift course.

"You going out to see the Senator anytime soon?" she asked.

"This weekend. He's taking me out on that boat of his that he's so proud of. I suspect he'll ply me with his best liquor and then talk to me about … things."

Charlotte nodded. In other words, they would be talking about her.

"I suspect you are right."

33

The lights in Simon Proctor's office were off when Carla walked in. Fortunately, enough daylight came in through his large window overlooking the quad to let her see what she was doing.

Carla considered putting on the light, but decided not to chance it. With the mid-April spring recess under way, the university hospital was far less crowded than usual. Students, faculty and many of the administrators were all at home or with friends, leaving only doctors visiting patients, along with the administrative staff, in the building. There was a chance that someone might recognize her, but that was the chance she was taking. And even if someone did see her, she reasoned, she could probably make a case for being in Simon's office, given her own role in reimbursement.

That aside, she hoped her visit wouldn't take long. It had already taken her longer than she had expected to get into the locked office, using keys that Brenda kept near her desk. Brenda, who was on vacation, had a fairly large key ring, and Carla had to try four or five before she got in. If only Simon didn't keep his door locked all the time, she thought. If Brenda ever found out that Carla had appropriated her keys, Carla had no doubt that she could kiss her job goodbye.

Now, however, she was in the office and anxious to do what she had to do and leave as quickly as possible. She knew what a cost report looked like and all she had to do was make sure the one she hoped to find was indeed different from the "official" one. Lewis and Stadler had told her they needed that second cost report, what most people would call a "second set of books," showing what the hospital really should have charged Medicare on capital projects and other expenses. Once she found that, she was to simply leave it there. OIG would do the rest with a search warrant. But the agency needed to show a judge a reasonable belief that a second cost report existed before it could obtain a search warrant. That's what she was there for.

How did I ever get into this situation, she wondered, knowing full well the answer. She got into it all by herself, and she knew all the reasons why. It was just that now, with flashlight in her hand in the darkened CFO's office, she felt like either a burglar or a spy, she wasn't sure which. *I am here because the U.S. government wants me to be here.* The government hadn't exactly asked her to break and enter the office of the hospital CFO – it couldn't do that, of course – but she got the drift of what Lewis wanted from their most recent meeting. They want me to find this information out, just not get them in trouble. They want – what's the word she would hear on television? – "deniability." She felt a flush or excitement, but also of pride. They are trusting me to do this, they are counting on me to help the government out. She breathed deep, felt better, and continued her search.

Opening the drawers of Simon's desk, she found a variety of things: file folders, papers, staple refills, extra white lined pads, a what's what of office supplies. But not was she was looking for.

She walked to the large credenza behind Simon's chair. Simon used it, as many executives do, to place photos of his family, as well, she noted, of his prize boat. Maybe one day soon she'd be able to afford one.

On the front of the credenza were two sliding wooden doors. She tried to slide one open, but it was locked, as was the other door. She didn't have tools to open the lock, and was fairly sure that OIG would not want her breaking it open. She could try using a paper clip to open it, but she doubted she'd be able to, and further, it might leave scratch marks on the wooden veneer surface.

She turned to his large, four-drawer metal filing cabinet, opened the top drawer, and then the others. Nothing in them but files, which was what one would expect. No large, two-inch thick cost reports.

If Simon has a second set of books here, it has to be in the credenza. There was no other place in the office for it to be. Of course, that assumed he *had* a second set of books and that, if he did, he kept them in the office. There were other possibilities. One was that he kept them at his home, or in a safe deposit box somewhere else offsite. Another was that there was no second set of books at all, that OIG was wrong. Still another was that it was in someone else's office, and, if so, that would most likely be that of the chief administrator.

Carla wasn't sure of Arun's involvement. If, for instance, the fraud was being perpetrated by Arun, there would be no way that Simon, who looked over the books carefully as the CFO, would not know, so they would have to be tied up in this together. But if the fraud were being perpetrated by Simon, it was possible that Arun did not know. As the chief administrator, he had to know the main numbers that affected the university hospital. But he didn't have to know the details, such as how much the university charged the government for specific line items. Some administrators got involved in those things, and others didn't. She didn't know Arun well enough to know which type he was.

It would probably be worth a visit to Arun's office and hope that he wasn't keeping anything in a locked credenza, she thought. The idea of snooping in the chief administrator's office scared her, but she also thought it might just give her what Lewis and Stadler wanted. CEOs are sometimes more casual in their treatment of sensitive papers than are CFOs, she had noted, watching Arun and his predecessors leave documents on their desk tops or otherwise in unlocked drawers. CFOs, on the other hand, trained in fiduciary responsibility, tend to follow rigid security procedures.

Carla stood up, shut off her flashlight and looked around the room to make sure she had not left anything that might indicate her visit. If I am discovered, she knew, she would be fired immediately. Whistleblower protection laws did not protect her against charges of breaking and entering. And much as she liked her new friends at OIG, she somehow doubted they would step up to the plate and say that she was working for them. But that's the spy game, she told herself.

Satisfied that everything was where it should be, she walked carefully toward the door, looked out to find no one around, then walked out, closing the door and locking it with one of the keys from the administrative office, then headed down the hall and back downstairs.

34

Dr. Penelope Langrishe was lying on her couch in her office, seemingly studying the ceiling, when Charlotte walked in. She seemed deep in thought, her red-lipped mouth contorted into a frown with her glasses up on her forehead. She brightened immediately when Charlotte entered.

"Just the person I was thinking of!" Penelope exclaimed, jumping up and grabbing hold of Charlotte's hand. "The very person to make me feel better on a glum, overcast day like this. Would you like some tea?"

Charlotte laughed out loud. Penelope's spontaneity was always an antidote for her own let's-get-down-to-business attitude. The contrast between the two personalities in their style of dress was also still there to see: Charlotte in a gray two-piece business suit, with her hair in its usual easy-to-take-care-of business style; Penelope in a large, brown peasant skirt, colorful patterned blouse, frizzled hair and large earrings.

And, also as usual, Charlotte felt an immediate rush of affection for her.

They sat down with their tea, Charlotte on the couch which Penelope had just vacated, and Penelope in an easy chair next to it, angled so she could face Charlotte. On a white long-hair rug in front of them rested a glass coffee table, flower decoration in the middle. They rested their cups and saucers on the table, then Penelope clasped her hands in her lap and looked at Charlotte.

"So, what is it today, my dear? Personal or business?"

"Business," Charlotte said.

"Ahhh. I suspected as much. Given all the publicity you've been getting lately–" she motioned toward a nearby newspaper – "I would be surprised if it were anything else. You seem consumed with this murder case, my dear, or else you wouldn't be putting your career in such jeopardy."

Penelope always seemed to find the personal angle in the business questions, Charlotte noted. Maybe that was because Penelope really did not see much difference between the two. *Was she right?*

"What I am hoping you can help me do is establish a link between the three murders and the fraud case. I don't mean hard evidence. I mean in terms of the motivation of the killer. The assumption I've been going under is that the killer must have felt that these three people were some kind of threat, that they knew about some kind of Medicare fraud the killer was involved in and, to protect himself – or herself, it could be a woman, after all – the killer felt he had to end their lives, felt he had to take the action he did. Now, of course, whenever I say this to anybody, they all have the same response: that it's possible, but so are other explanations, such as a personal dispute, some bad business that the three may have gotten themselves into, anything at all. What, I need, Penelope, is some kind of working theory I can then investigate, showing that the killer murdered those three because of the Medicare fraud. In short," and here Charlotte faltered, "I need to know that I am right."

Penelope hesitated a second, as if considering just what to tell Charlotte.

"But, my dear, of course you are right. I've been piecing this together myself for weeks now. It must be tied to the Medicare fraud. There is just no other explanation."

Charlotte was stunned. This was not what she had expected. She thought Penelope might be sympathetic, but feared that Penelope might tell her, as the others had, that her theory was just a hunch, and that many more equally plausible explanations were available.

"Are you sure?' Charlotte asked.

"Certainly. Again, my dear, as you say, this is not hard evidence. But if you simply study what the circumstances of each murder shows about the state of mind of the murderer at the time each murder was committed, there is no other conclusion to reach. Of course, the murderer did us a favor here. If he had – and by the way, my dear, it almost certainly *is* a he, given the physicality involved in lifting Nicholas Rosen's body to the pipe over the bathtub and letting it drop – stopped with the first murder, I couldn't make a convincing argument. But it is clear, after looking at all three, that I may have to pen a new theory: "Langrishe's Theory of Subsequent Actions." The key, you see, is that each subsequent murder holds a secret to the previous one."

"I don't see how—"

"Well, it's simple really. Let's start with the first one, that of the very bright young man who everyone seems to have adored, Scott Karakas. As I understand it from reading the papers, the body was discovered by his girlfriend, Dana Brentano, correct? Alright, what strikes you as odd or singular about the body when she found it?"

"That he was murdered with succinylcholine and that meant only someone with knowledge of the substance and what it does could have killed him?"

"Certainly that is true, but there is something more basic, is there not?"

Charlotte looked at Penelope, realizing her face must be a complete blank.

"My dear, that the body was there at all!" Penelope said. "That is a most singular incidence."

"But where else would you expect to find it? That's probably where he was murdered!"

"Yes, exactly, and it was the one place the killer should not have left it. Consider this, Charlotte. Would an experienced killer, or even an experienced criminal, who had thought this through and hoped to get away with it, leave the body of his victim right there where he had killed him? Wouldn't he have carted it away somewhere, in the hope that no one would notice Mr. Karakas' disappearance for several days? Or, if that was not possible because he was afraid of being seen, wouldn't he have approached Mr. Karakas some other time, when he could have disposed of the body and therefore left no clues whatsoever for the authorities? At the very least, mightn't he have hid the body somewhere within the building, at least delaying discovery? Now, someone who wanted the body to be found, because he perhaps wanted to send a message – as in a mob hit – would have left it out in the open, but there is no indication that I know of that Mr. Karakas was tied to the mob. And given that he was a medical student with a bright future, I don't believe that anyone would seriously think so.

"No, my dear, what this tells me is that the killer was a rank amateur. Certainly he had the forethought to think of killing Mr. Karakas with succinylcholine, and to have the substance with him. This suggests that he knew the young man was in the building and went there to kill him – although it is also possible that he had the succinylcholine with him to kill him later in the day, or even the next day, but unexpectedly ran into him. Either way, it doesn't matter. What does matter is that the killer must have had some kind of emotional reaction after killing him, something akin to panic I would say, because at that point premeditation left him, and whatever he may or may not have planned for Mr. Karakas' body was not acted upon. He left the body, with the evidence of succinylcholine, right there for all to find."

"Mightn't a professional also have made a mistake and left the body?"

"Charlotte," said Penelope as if addressing a pupil, "the one thing that has distinguished *professional* criminals – as opposed to amateurs, that is – is that they know what they are doing and they survive to do the next crime or, in this case, murder. And one of the chief ways they do that is by leaving as few clues behind as possible. A professional would never have left the body there. We might still be guessing today what happened to the missing young man or about how he may have died."

Charlotte considered. There was a certain sense to this. "Okay, but then how did the second murder give us more information about the first?"

"Well, where to begin?" Penelope said, musing out loud. "Dana Brentano was the deceased's girlfriend, right, and this was not exactly a secret on campus, as I understand it? The murderer killed Mr. Karakas with succinylcholine in what was clearly a plan, yet killed Miss Brentano with a gun, a gun without a silencer, for God's sake. So that informs the first murder by providing more evidence that it is an amateur at work. And also evidence that hers was not a planned killing, otherwise he might have poisoned her, too."

"Then if he had no plans to kill her, why kill her?"

"I didn't say he had no plans to kill her. He just had no plans to kill her when he ran into her."

"You mean he planned to kill her later? How could you know that?"

"Because he did, ultimately, kill her. He didn't have to, you know. When he ran into her, he could have just said hello to her, especially if our murderer was someone with access to the university medical supply cabinet, as we agree was probably the case. Chances are he was – he is – someone known to the student body and faculty."

"Go over that again, Penelope. I am a bit confused."

Penelope smiled, clearly enjoying this chance to spin out her theory.

"The fact that he killed someone who he didn't have to kill – after all, there was no reason for him to think that this young woman suspected him of killing Mr. Karakas, as she wasn't there when he committed that first killing – can only mean that he meant to kill her all along. But the fact that he used a gun without a silencer and ran the risk of being caught right outside the hospital can only mean that he did not have a premeditated plan to kill her right then, but perhaps later, as he killed Mr. Rosen. Most likely, he was carrying that gun for protection and shot her when he did, perhaps out of a sense of panic to protect himself. My theory, you see, is that the man's entire ego structure has probably collapsed."

"I'm not a psychiatrist, Penelope."

"Alright. Ego structure. We are all the sum of the way we are brought up and our early life experiences. Genetics is in there too. Ultimately, by the time we are in our late teens, we are pretty much who we are. Some of us are risk takers, others are cautious; some of us are confident and speak up in class, others are meek and take seats in the back of the room; some of us are intimate, relationship-oriented people, while others hold people at a distance."

Charlotte wondered if this last comment was meant for her, but Penelope showed no sign of slowing down.

"That's our ego structure. It defines the way we act, the priorities we have, the choices we make. Our character and values, so to speak. Now, you take someone who acts way outside of that ego structure, in a truly radical way – such as someone who would never dream of committing a murder being driven to commit one, for instance – and you have a situation where you now have a very fragile person close to some kind of mental breakdown. He may be able to compartmentalize those feelings so he can get on with his job, and friends and colleagues notice nothing more about him than maybe he seems more on edge, but believe me, this man is dealing with some devastating actions he took, ones that he tells himself are not him, yet in fact he took them. Think, Charlotte. You are not a murderer. Other than in self-defense or to protect a loved one, would you ever plan and execute someone with succinylcholine, or any poison for that matter? I don't mean some kind of fantasy where you say, 'I wish that person were dead,' I mean, really, actually premeditatedly kill someone."

"No, I wouldn't."

"Of course not. That isn't you. It's not who you are. Yet, the truth, Charlotte, is that under extreme stress, some of us sometimes can act outside our ego structure, although not without severe psychological consequences, of course."

"What would those stresses have to be?"

"Something very threatening, enough that the killer might feel he had nothing to lose. Something so threatening that he felt his loved ones would leave him, or —"

"—his career might be affect by a fraud investigation and prosecution?"

"It would have to be more than just a job. After all, we are not all as wrapped up in our careers as the next person. This person's identity *would have to have been his career.* He was his job. It defined him, made him who he was. And he might have felt that losing that identity would in some very fundamental way diminish him, or rob him of that identity. Affect his relationships. He simply wouldn't be who he was. If your Medicare fraud investigation at the university hospital would have done that to anyone, then yes, that person may well have felt himself forced to take actions that he would never otherwise have dreamed of taking."

Charlotte considered. A name was coming to mind, and it all made sense. But still, there may well have been others at the hospital affected the same way. What a shame for whoever it was, she found herself thinking. *Is this guilt that I'm feeling? Did my office's fraud investigation cause these murders?* She know better than that, she told herself, reminding herself that OIG was safeguarding public money.

"So," Penelope continued, "now let's go back to the run-in between Miss Brentano and our killer outside the university hospital that night. You now have a killer with a gun in his pocket, quite possibly for the first time. He bought it because, inside, he is literally freaking out, my dear, if I may use a non-professional term. He has become paranoid and he wants protection. He has no plans to use it as his next weapon. He probably plans to use the same succinylcholine.

"But then he runs into Miss Brentano. In his paranoid state, he asks himself, 'Why is she here? Does she know something? Does she suspect that I killed her boyfriend?' It may also well be, and I think this likely, that he saw her before she saw him."

"How would you know that?" asked Charlotte, more than confident that Penelope had an answer ready.

"Because, my dear, the building lights that would be on would be those closest to the building, and that means they would be on Miss Brentano, while our killer was approaching from a distance. Now, he sees her. Perhaps she does not yet see him. He panics. He gets ready the gun. Maybe he is thinking that someone will hear the gun. But he looks around and sees no one else in the immediate vicinity, the closest people are some distance away. He figures he can take his shot, dispose of the gun, then get away in time. Maybe he can even dispose of the gun later. After all, if he is a normal face on campus, then he is just one of many, and if he gets far enough away, then there is no more reason to question him than anyone else. Why would anyone suspect he had a gun, or that he was the killer?"

"Or," said Charlotte, remembering that Arun was the first on the scene, "people might think it perfectly normal to find him there if, for instance, he sometimes worked in the building."

"Precisely. But also remember, he didn't have to kill her at all. He could have chanced that she didn't know he was her boyfriend's killer – which she probably didn't – and just said hello to her. He didn't kill her just because he was paranoid. If that were the case, he would be killing other students too. He had planned to kill her anyway, because of whatever connecting threat between her and Mr. Karakas that he perceived they shared. He was just panicked into doing it *when* he did."

"So let's go back to your theory. What does this murder tell us about the previous one?"

"Well, aside from reinforcing the likelihood that the murderer is an amateur, it means there was something that Mr. Karakas and Miss Brentano shared – it could be knowledge, or it, at least at this point – before we get to Mr. Rosen's murder – it could still be that their relationship was the motivation for the killing. But knowledge of Medicare fraud has to at least be considered a possibility now. Consider this, Charlotte. If Mr. Karakas had been murdered alone, and there was no subsequent murder, would there have been any reason to link it to Medicare fraud? At best, it would have been one of dozens of theories and probably not the one people thought of first, am I correct?"

Charlotte nodded.

"But when you add in Miss Brentano's murder, then the two are linked, because the two of them were lovers. And more than that, they talked to each other."

"But it could just as easily have been some personal matter involving them as a couple."

"Such as the police theory that Nicholas Rosen killed them because he was jealous of their relationship?"

"Well, that turned out to be wrong, but there still might be a personal relationship behind the killings."

"But not when you factor in the circumstances of Mr. Rosen's murder, and here was where the killer really tipped his hand."

Charlotte could see that Penelope was clearly enjoying herself.

"Yes, you're right," Penelope continued. "Up until Mr. Rosen was killed, there was reason to suspect that it was the personal relationship between the first two victims that led to their deaths. There might have been other reasons, but certainly, that would come first to people's minds, as it did to Detective Petrelli. And poor Mr. Rosen, the 'third wheel' in their friendship, paid the price for that."

"I think I know where you're going here," Charlotte said. "There was no reason for the killer to kill Nicholas Rosen. In fact, it was in his interest *not* to kill him."

"Precisely. Mr. Rosen was the perfect foil for the theory of the murder that rested on someone having a personal problem with Mr. Karakas' and Miss Brentano's relationship. Mr. Rosen, the poor fellow who always wanted a girlfriend like Dana Brentano but couldn't get her. And who always wanted to be brilliant and popular like Scott Karakas, but wasn't. So he did the next best thing. He became their best friend. He spent time with them, shared intimacies with them, but secretly, he was jealous of Scott, wanted Dana, and hated them for being and having everything which he was not. That was the theory. He even got arrested for the murders. So why kill him? The killer, if he had any brains at all – and both his use of succinylcholine and the likely fact that he is someone on campus indicate that he does – should have just let him take the rap for him."

"Unless," Charlotte said, "unless he had *some other reason* to kill him. Which would most likely mean that *his reasons for killing Scott and Dana were not about their relationship.* It could only be because they had something else on the killer, some knowledge, something."

Penelope rapidly nodded. "Yes, clearly, the killer could not take the chance of letting Mr. Rosen take the rap and reveal something later that might incriminate the real culprit. Now, what could that be? It's unlikely, given the relatively modest financial means that most students have, that they would on their own recognize any financial misdoings, even if they ran across them, or that they would be interested. What's left?"

"Knowledge of wrongdoing. Knowledge, very likely, of something that would turn up in our investigation."

"There's not much else left. I suppose it could be some other kind of wrongdoing, but given that the university was being investigated at the same time as the killings and the general fear this was causing among administrators and faculty on the campus, it seems likely that fear of being exposed for some kind of Medicare fraud – and possibly having your career, your entire identity and sense of who you are – ruined in the process, was the catalyst that drove our killer to his actions."

Charlotte considered. "Okay, I buy it. But exactly what was it that these three knew—"

"—or that the killer suspected they knew," Penelope said. "Remember, we don't know for a fact that all three did indeed share the knowledge. Given that Mr. Karakas was murdered first, it seems likely that he had the original knowledge. But it was only the killer's assumption that he shared that with his two friends. Scott may have, or, in fact, he may not have. In which case, and this would be really sad, Dana Brentano and Nicholas Rosen were killed for nothing."

"So the key is, what did Scott Karakas know? And also, and here's an interesting question, why would Scott care about Medicare fraud? After all, he had no stake in Medicare. And how would the killer have found out that he knew?"

"Now you are getting beyond my pay grade, Charlotte. I can only comment on the psychological state of the killer. But as for what Scott Karakas knew and what he may or may not have done with that knowledge, that is up to the police and, if you continue on the course you are on, up to you."

"I went up to Pennsylvania to see his parents, you know," Charlotte said.

"And what did you learn?"

"Not much. His father pushed him very hard to excel, that was clear, as he does his other children. But that's true of a lot of parents."

Penelope looked directly at her. "Sometimes the parents don't know everything. Or tell you everything."

35

D etective Petrelli was in his office later that week, head down in a sea of reports, when he heard the knock on the door. He looked up to see the HHS Inspector General, whom he recognized immediately, standing there.

"I believe, detective, that we have something to talk about," said Charlotte. "May I come in?"

"Sure." Petrelli was somewhat taken aback by the visit. *Does she know that I was the source of the leak to the press about her investigation? Did Eileen Ashburton break her word?*

He motioned her toward a chair in front of his desk. Charlotte took the seat, then the two looked at each other awkwardly for a moment before Charlotte spoke.

"I am under the impression that you are bothered by my involvement in the murder investigation."

"What makes you think that, Inspector General? Have you heard that somewhere?"

"Let's drop the boxing gloves, alright, detective? I am not here to give you a hard time. But there does seem to be an intersection between our two investigations and I think it would be in both our interests to share notes, maybe work together a bit, don't you?"

Petrelli sighed. Charlotte was different than he had expected. Less the tough-as-nails federal enforcement officer. More open and reaching out. Or was this all a tactic?

"I'm an old dog, Inspector General, so please forgive me if I ask a few questions before I immediately give my trust."

"Ask anything you want," Charlotte said, leaning back in her chair and crossing her legs. "I will tell you everything I know."

Really? I will put her to the test, maybe find something out.

"Alright," he said. "Tell me where the fraud investigation is so far." *Might as well learn what I can. If there is a link, maybe she'll reveal it.*

"There are several areas. Now what I share with you, detective, is totally confidential between us. I can trust you on that, right?"

"Er, sure." *She knows what she's doing. She's building a connection between us. Well, let's see what she has to say.*

Charlotte proceeded to tell Petrelli about all the elements of the investigation, including upcoding, unbundling, direct supervision issues and the matter of the cost reports. She did not share with him, however, any news about Carla Calloway and OIG's plans to get their hands on a second set of books.

Petrelli listened, impressed. It certainly sounded like OIG had the hospital dead to rights, but was she telling him everything?

"Alright, thank you for sharing that, and I wish you luck in your investigation. But what does it have to do with the murder cases?" he asked, his voice showing just the slightest hint of irritation, which he saw Charlotte pick up on.

"Maybe nothing, but more likely everything," Charlotte said, sharing with him the psychological analysis that Penelope had done, and why the murders most likely were connected to the fraud case.

"Hmmph," Petrelli said, digesting it all. "Interesting theory. We have psychiatrists on staff, too, Inspector General—"

"Charlotte, please, detective. After all, we are exchanging confidences now."

Damn this woman! He could see she was playing him. And now she had shared real information with him, and he felt some sense of obligation to help her. Besides, he was beginning to think she had a point. There might be a connection. And maybe they *could* help each other out.

"—Charlotte, as I was saying, we have psychiatrists on staff too, and they could probably come up with entirely different motivations."

"Tell you what, detective – may I call you Al? – why don't you run it by them and find out? I'd love to hear what they have to say."

Might be an interesting idea at that, Petrelli thought. Dr. Langrishe's theory made a lot of sense.

"Let me ask you this, Charlotte. Where did you get the idea that I had a problem with your investigation?"

"I read the paper, Al. It was clear from that article that the police department feels I am stepping onto its turf. And it was also clear from the tone of the senators on the House Appropriation committee, when I testified before them, that they had maybe heard something from the police. They would rather I stuck to Medicare fraud."

"Doesn't sound like an unreasonable proposition, Charlotte. After all, even if the cases are linked, you are not seeing me or my people investigating fraud at the university hospital. Maybe I should." *Let's see what she says to that.*

"Maybe you should, Al. Maybe you should. Maybe, we should simply meet and compare notes from time to time. I am not against you getting involved, as long as it does not disrupt our fraud investigation. I hope you feel the same. But I honestly believe these cases are connected – directly. And I think we can get to the bottom of both of them if we work together."

"I thought the Senate committee ordered you to stick to your own knitting."

Charlotte smiled. Was "knitting" a reference to the fact that she was a woman?

"The committee has no direct authority over my office. They can pass resolutions and make life difficult for me, even pressure the HHS Secretary or the White House to fire me. But unless ordered by the Secretary, I am not obligated to follow their advice."

"Aren't you concerned that the Secretary will order you to do so? Or that your job will be on the line?"

"Yes, I am. I am indeed, Al. But, on the other hand, I also believe, and I have come to believe this down to the depths of my soul, that I know what went on here. I don't know all the particulars, but I can tell you as sure as we are sitting here, that these poor three students were murdered…and murdered because of my investigation." Charlotte felt her eyes misting up, more than she expected.

For the first time, Petrelli felt some sympathy. *She thinks she's responsible. That's what's driving her.* He was no stranger to deep feelings himself. His suspicions about Nicholas Rosen may have cost the young man his life, a thought he had to constantly chase from his head just to get his work done. And the truth was, his investigation was going nowhere. Maybe some cooperation was warranted.

"Alright, Charlotte, maybe you have a point. If we can get to the bottom of all this quicker by joining forces, at least to some degree, I say let's do it."

"I am so glad to hear you say that, Al," Charlotte said. "Now, I do have just one favor to ask."

Here it comes.

"Let's not publicize this, okay? Because as you just mentioned, I have enough headaches with the Senate committee and the press. And the longer I am free to investigate all this, the better the chance for a solution."

She extended her hand. Petrelli took it.

"Not a problem, Charlotte. I don't even like the press."

"Well, not most of the time, I gather."

Damn, she does know! Well, she seems willing to move on, Petrelli thought, so I will, too.

"Let's also agree to keep anything we share between us confidential, unless we both agree otherwise," he said.

"That suits me fine. In fact, it has direct bearing on something that I wasn't sure I was going to share with you, but now that we have our agreement, I will," Charlotte said, and proceeded to tell him about the whistleblower – without revealing her name – and the cost reports. "If we find that second set of books, you may also have your suspect."

Petrelli listened, then nodded.

36

Back in her office, Charlotte sat down at her desk and took from a nearby bookcase the high school yearbook that Scott Karakas' parents had lent her. A large green volume with "Panthers" and the class year on the cover, it was a little over an inch thick and still looked relatively new. After all, it was only six years ago that Scott had graduated high school. *So young to lose his life.*

Looking up from the volume, Charlotte surveyed her office and then looked out a window. With the last week of April here, the cherry blossoms that were so ubiquitous in Washington a few weeks earlier were gone, but the weather was warming considerably. In a few weeks it would become hot and humid, the annual reminder that the nation's capital was indeed built on a swamp.

Her own high school years had been years of rebellion against her parents, her upbringing and what she assumed was expected of her, rebellion she now regretted, especially with her mother gone. The parade of inappropriate boyfriends she went out with, her clothing, the late hours she kept, one could consider them all normal teenage cries of independence, but how many high school students had a national political figure as their father?

What does my high school yearbook say about me back then? Charlotte wondered. She wasn't even sure she knew where it was. Probably buried in a box at her townhouse, or possibly even at the St. Michael's estate. *Would I even want to look at it today and see what I was then?*

She opened Scott's yearbook and began flipping through the pages. There were the students in their caps and gowns in group pictures, and there were the sections in the front of the yearbook showing various student activities, such as putting together the school newspaper or taking part in the sports teams or cheerleading. She chuckled at a few of them. *I would never have been a cheerleader.*

The bulk of the book was composed, of course, of individual head shots of each students graduating that year, in alphabetical order by last name. She turned to Karakas and found the smiling face of the murder victim she felt she had come to know so well, staring out at her. There he was, the success-to-be, good looking, the charm apparent in his expression, and his rank as class valedictorian listed just below his picture.

Near his picture on this page, and on many of the other pages, were signed wishes from fellow students, many of them from girls. "You are such a great person," "I wish we got know each other better," and "Best of luck in college," were just some of the many listed. Some of those from girls were signed, "Luv you," and had little hearts next to them. The ones from boys mainly remembered sporting events with lines like, "I'll never forget how we creamed the Wildcats last year," or "To the best teammate anyone could want." Yes, Charlotte thought, popular indeed.

But one signed picture caught her eye that seemed different from the rest. And she realized, before she even read it, that what made it stand out was the impression of the ink into the page, as though it was written by someone pressing his pen down with great intensity and, after she read it, she thought, perhaps with great anger.

The student was Gregory Betorin, also a good-looking young man, not unlike Scott in appearance, with dark hair and somewhat intense eyes. The smile on his face seemed to belie the words he wrote over his photo.

"To my 'best friend' –

"You made your choice and I made mine, but you can go on with your life. How much more hurt will you leave behind: Del Phinney, Carrie, who else? Look again at your morals. See you in purgatory, if you get that far."

She sat back in her chair and took a breath. The intensity in the comment was overwhelming, especially coming from a high school student. Purgatory? What was he referring to? Probably just two friends who fell out during high school but, given the current circumstances, Charlotte wanted to find out.

She picked up the phone and dialed, pleased that Amy Karakas, and not her husband Richard, answered the phone.

"Mrs. Karakas, I am sorry to bother you again after your kindness in seeing me the other day, but I have found something in Scott's yearbook that I thought you might be able to clear up for me."

She could almost hear the sigh on the other end of the telephone as Scott's mother paused and then said, "Of course, Miss Westbrook. What is it?"

"There's a note written here from a young man named Gregory Betorin that is less than friendly. I was wondering if you had any insight into that, or into his relationship with your son?"

A long pause ensued and it seemed to Charlotte that Scott's mother had put her hand over the mouthpiece and was talking to someone.

"Miss Westbrook?" The voice on the phone was now that of Richard Karakas. "You are barking up the wrong tree here. Gregory Betorin was a friend of Scott's since elementary school. If they had some teenage falling out,

I'm sure neither I nor my wife know what it was about. Now, I don't mean to be rude, but this is a trying time for us." The click on the other end of the line told Charlotte that the phone call had ended.

37

Charlotte sped up Interstate 81 in Pennsylvania, doing her best to stay within the 65 mile per hour speed limit, but not always succeeding. Most of the vehicles were doing well over 70, but the last thing she needed now, she thought, was to be caught getting a ticket. At least there was no rain this time.

In fact, it was the kind of day she loved: clear and bright with the temperature in the mid-50s, only a few white clouds and a gentle breeze, the kind of day on which anyone might like to take a casual drive in the last week of April. But this was hardly a pleasure trip.

Charlotte had been somewhat taken aback by Richard Karakas' brusque treatment of her on the phone. But she reminded herself that the man and his wife had just lost a son. It was sad, Charlotte thought, to see people reduced to such a state, having raised a child into a fine young man seemingly liked and respected by just about everyone, and then see him killed. "There's nothing worse than losing a child," was a common expression. Charlotte could see the truth in it.

However, whether Scott Karakas was, in fact, liked and respected by everyone was the reason for her trip to see Gregory Betorin. She had called Gregory a few days before, using a phone number she got from directory assistance, and left a message on his answer machine. The next day he replied and they spoke for about three minutes, during which she explained who she was and why she wanted to see him. The call ended with him agreeing to see her, somewhat ambivalently, she thought.

She pulled her BMW into the driveway of a small, ranch-style house in a rural suburb of Wilkes-Barre, and looked around at the threadbare condition of the place. The house was clearly in need of repair, with pieces of blue aluminum siding hanging off one cornice near the driveway, probably the result of a car hitting the house. The lawn needed mowing; there were weeds in the flower bed. A tire suspended by a rope, clearly used as a swing, hung from a large tree in the front yard. Children's toys lay near the doorstep.

I might be a bit overdressed, Charlotte realized, looking at her well-tailored dark blue pantsuit and heels. Given the affluence of the Karakas family and their house, she had expected something of the same upon visiting Scott's friends.

The front door was opened by a young man who she knew to be about age 25, but who seemed to carry considerably more weight on his shoulders than one would expect from someone his age. He was wearing a pullover shirt and jeans, and had a day's worth of stubble on his face. But the face was friendly, under sandy hair, blue eyes and a ready smile that greeted Charlotte.

"Miss Westbrook? How do you do? I'm Gregory Betorin. C'mon in."

Charlotte stepped in, to see the house was more than occupied. Two young boys, each no more than two years apart, were running around the floor, which was scattered with toys. The television was on, tuned to a football game. In the adjoining kitchen, a pretty young woman in jeans and a tee shirt was preparing lunch.

"Hi, Charlotte. I'm Helen Betorin. Welcome. Sorry about the mess. Can I offer you some lunch?"

"Thank you, but no," Charlotte said. "A glass of water would be nice, though."

"Coming right up."

"C'mon, we can talk in here," Gregory said, after Helen handed Charlotte some water in a glass with cartoon figures on it. He led her to a small room, apparently used as an office, down a hallway off the living room. He motioned to a chair, then closed the door and sat down himself. Charlotte noticed that he seemed to brighten up with the door closed.

"All that noise, it would drive anyone crazy," he said. "If I didn't have this room to escape to, I don't know what I would do."

Charlotte smiled, unsure of where to begin.

"You're the inspector general of the Department of Health and Human Services?" Gregory asked.

"That's right."

"So you are in charge of investigating…what? Excuse me for asking, Miss Westbrook, but it was once expected that I would go to law school, so I am in the habit of interrogating my guests, something Helen chews me out for a lot."

"It's no problem. My office investigates fraud against the Medicare and Medicaid programs, as well as some other programs."

Gregory nodded. "But you said on the phone that you wanted to speak with me about Scott's murder."

"I have reason to believe it may be connected to a Medicare fraud case."

"No kidding." He thought a second. "Well, you were the one who wanted to see me, Miss Westbrook. How can I help you? Ask away."

Charlotte noted Gregory's directness and found that she liked it. Such a change from the people in Washington.

"Well, I understand you knew Scott since elementary school."

"That's right. We were close in those days. Always did things together, along with several other friends. Pretty much we all remained friends until the later years of high school."

"What happened then?"

"Most of it was just normal growing up stuff. You know, as you get older, even in high school, you start getting more discriminating about who you choose to hang out with." He paused, then added, "I understand this happens even more so in college. What's the saying? 'You spend your sophomore year shedding the friends you made in your freshman year.' Well, I wouldn't know."

"You say that with what seems like some bitterness."

Gregory nodded. "I won't deny it, Miss Westbrook, there is some. I try to stay positive. But Scott and I made different choices. I guess our families did too. I'm supposed to have made the right choice, but it certainly doesn't seem that way, at least in terms of the consequences," he said, looking around the room. "Scott supposedly made the wrong choice, but – at least until his murder – I couldn't help but think he was profiting from it. Life is funny like that."

Gregory seemed to be referring to something that Scott's parents knew but hadn't even hinted at. Penelope had said that maybe there are some things that parents don't know. Undoubtedly she was right, Charlotte thought. But Penelope also said that maybe there are things that parents know, but don't want to share, either to protect their children, or maybe out of their own guilt.

"I'm sorry, Gregory. I don't understand."

"Well, I don't know that this is really relevant to your murder investigation, so I probably shouldn't have said anything."

"No, please do. Anything about Scott's background, that tells me what kind of person he was, could be relevant in terms of what he might have been involved in, who he spent time with, or something else entirely, that might lead us to his murderer."

Gregory hesitated, then shrugged. "He's dead now, and I've carried his water long enough. Scott and I, Meredith – that was one of his girlfriends at the time, we both had a lot – Franklin, Webster, there was a whole group – we were the knights of Whitman. We went to Walt Whitman High School, not far from where Scott's parents live now."

"So you grew up in that neighborhood?"

"Oh yes, Miss Westbrook. My background is not like what you see here. I grew up to a relative life of privilege, just like Scott. And maybe if I had made the same choices he had, I would still be having that life. But my conscience wouldn't let me."

He leaned forward. "We were all so freaking popular. Scott, Franklin and I were on the sports teams, Scott had charm up the yin-yang, more than any of us, but we both had our share of girls. Maybe that was where the trouble started.

"In our junior year, Scott had been dating Meredith about three years, going back to middle school. Meredith was, still is, I guess, although I don't see her anymore, great. Not only pretty, but smart, and with lots of character. She's going to law school now, you know, right here in town, and is already married to an older guy who is a practicing attorney. Guess what their kids will be?" He laughed, it seemed to Charlotte, almost cynically.

"To make a long story short, Scott was cheating on her. And a lot more than once. In fairness, it wasn't always that he was seeking it out, although it wouldn't surprise me if that happened too. A lot of girls just hit on him. They found him magnetic. Plus they thought he was a success at everything he did.

"Scott was serious about Meredith, though. He planned to marry her at some point, at least he thought he did. Who knows what happens to high school romances? But as far as where his head was at, she was it.

"So when Carrie Pankow, one of the girls he had on the side, got pregnant – I don't know why, whether he or she was careless about birth control, I'm not sure – Scott was knocked for a loop. We were still great friends then, and he shared a lot of this with me. Carrie, it seems, wanted to keep the kid, despite the risks to her reputation. I think she was hoping Scott would do the right thing and marry her. But Scott didn't want Carrie for anything more than sex. Carrie was not from our part of town, at least the part I lived in then. She was what we called a 'rung-upper'."

"A 'rung-upper'?"

"Not really a nice expression, but hey, what were we, 17 years old? It means someone from the lower classes who is always looking to climb up to the next rung on the social and economic ladder. Carrie was like that. And now that I've dropped a few rungs, I can't say I blame her."

"So she saw Scott as her ticket to a better life."

"You could say that. But there was no way Scott was going to marry her. The trouble was, Carrie really wanted to have the baby. I think she would have wanted to whether Scott married her or not."

"*Would have* wanted to? You mean she had an abortion? Or she lost it?"

"She had an abortion, but it was hardly of her own choosing. Listen, Miss Westbrook, I think it's ultimately up to a woman whether she wants to have a child or not. And lots of women choose abortion in a situation like this.

But that works both ways, doesn't it? I mean, in this case, Carrie wanted to have the child, and she certainly had that right, even if Scott didn't want her to."

"Are you saying that Scott made her have an abortion?"

Gregory shook his head. "No, Scott didn't have the means to do that and, even if he did, I don't think he had the guts. Underneath it all, Miss Westbrook, underneath the sports teams and the honors student, the charm and the smile and the looks, underneath that whole story of success, Scott was basically a wimp, at least with his father."

"How do you mean?"

"Under his father's thumb. Have you met Scott's father?"

Charlotte nodded.

"Successful man. Strong man. Scott would do anything to win his approval. And yet, Scott hated him, too. Hated his father for how he dominated him and his sisters, how he dominated his mother, although he told me more than once that he thought his mother actually liked being in that role. I guess she was what you might call an enabler, not that Richard Karakas ever needed any enabling. He told Scott what was expected, Miss Westbrook, whether it was his grades or sports, then left it to Scott to figure out how to do it, and it wasn't always by Marquis of Queensbury rules."

"How did he not play fair?"

Gregory paused. "Maybe this will make the point. Then we'll get back to Carrie and the baby."

God, Charlotte thought, he's got *a lot* of pent-up frustration. She reminded herself to take whatever Gregory said with a grain of salt. People with axes to grind often have their own versions of the truth.

"Scott was smart, that was true enough. He got his share of A's in high school. But every now and then, he had a course that caused him trouble.

Once, when he did get a B and his report card reached home, I saw him the next day. He was shaken badly. I don't know what his father said to him, but he had put the fear of God into him. I don't think Scott ever got a B again."

"Are you saying that his father beat him?"

"I don't really know one way or the other. But, honestly, I doubt it. Richard Karakas didn't need to beat anybody. He just has a way about him. If you met him, Miss Westbrook, you must have seen some of it, although like Scott, he hides it behind a lot of charm. But he can be the most intimidating and controlling man you ever met. I would never want to get in a fight with Richard Karakas.

"Anyway, of course, despite what his father said, the next year there was a course that gave Scott some trouble. He was worried sick about getting another "B," that was clear. But then, about three-quarters through the year, he brightened up. Said an "A" was guaranteed. Okay, but how? I didn't find out until a few months later, when he told me how he put the squeeze on Mr. Del Phinney."

"His teacher?"

"Political science, 11th grade. Del Phinney was a funny sort. Overweight, and one of those male teachers in high school, where most of the teachers are women, let's face it, who was probably wondering what he was doing there instead of teaching at some college. He wasn't married. Had a decent sense of humor and wasn't a bad lecturer. In fact, some of his presentations could be quite compelling. He liked to pound his fist against the blackboard or the desk for dramatic effect. Or he would rapidly pace the front of the room as he got excited. I suppose, to some of the girls in the class, he was sort of a dramatic authority figure, despite his looks."

"What are you saying, that he was seeing a student?"

"Scott saw him making out with an 11th grader on the bleachers after hours one day, he told me. Really kind of careless to do that out in the open, even when not too many people were around. Not a bad looking girl, either, and I guess he saw it as a chance to get some attention from the kind of girl who never gave him any when he was in high school. Underage, yes, but I wouldn't say he was a pedophile. These things aren't all one way, Miss Westbrook. Some of the girls in high school would flirt with a male teacher. And if you are the kind of guy who never got the girl when you were younger, it can be hard to resist, especially if they are very pretty and look to be over 18."

"He took advantage of her age."

"Whether he went all the way with her and had sex, I don't know. In all honesty, Miss Westbrook, I don't know much about Mr. Del Phinney, and it may have stopped at making out. He may have had a conscience, felt guilty, whatever. Or he may have gone all the way. I just don't now. In terms of Scott, it didn't matter. Scott had him. And, from what he told me, he used it to make sure he got an A."

"Scott blackmailed him."

"That's what he told me. He said he cornered Mr. Del Phinney one day after class and told him that he knew about him and the girl, about making out on the bleachers. Del Phinney got very nervous, Scott said, and asked him what he wanted. The interesting thing, Miss Westbrook, is that as Scott was telling me this, I could see he was reliving the event again, and enjoying – no, a better word is 'savoring' – every moment. Maybe he liked controlling someone like his father controlled him. Anyway, Scott told him to make sure he got an A, or his career would be through and his reputation shot. Scott got the A. I also noticed that, even in our senior year, when all this was over, Del Phinney would go out of his way to avoid Scott when they were about to pass in the hall. Sometimes he would duck down a stairwell. Other times, when he had to pass, he would get over to the far wall, to be as far away from Scott as possible. Scott would just smirk. I think he loved having this kind of power over another human being.

"It was around this time that I decided that Scott had turned into someone I wasn't sure I wanted to hang out with anymore. I began cutting back on our activities together, just making excuses. Scott got the message, I think. And maybe he agreed with it, because he didn't ask me why we weren't as good friends as we used to be."

"You were going to finish telling me about Carrie Pankow," Charlotte said.

"Right. I don't know why Carrie ultimately got the abortion, Miss Westbrook, but I can tell you that Richard Karakas had something to do with it. He put a lot of pressure on Scott to persuade her. Scott tried, but there is only so much you can do with a girl in that situation. I think he threatened to never see her again, then went the opposite way and said that if they ever had any chance of being together long term, she could not have a child. That probably had some effect, since she did want to marry him. But she wanted the child more.

"Then, I think, Karakas met with the Pankows. Maybe Richard Karakas offered Carrie's parents a lot money, maybe he threatened them in some way, but whatever happened, a few weeks later, Carrie was no longer pregnant. Of course, no one knew, she had never got that far along. But Scott told me about the meeting between the parents. Said his father put the fear of God in Carrie's father."

Charlotte thought back to her meeting with Richard and Amy Karakas. She had sensed that Richard Karakas was a man who was used to getting his way, but not to this extent. Had the charming veneer affected her, too? And Scott, with his reputation on campus as the most popular and successful student, how much of that was the result of simple charm, looks and reputation?

260

Suddenly, in the course of one conversation, her entire image of Scott Karakas was altered. She still had some sympathy for him, having to grow up with a father like that. But he hadn't turned out that different from his father, it seemed, and now he was the one doing the bullying. Did he blackmail doctors or administrators at James Buchanan to give him the grades he got? Did he do that because he had some knowledge of their engaging in Medicare fraud? Yes, that could be it. Those doctors or administrators would have been scared to death to have their reputations ruined if they were found it. They might have to leave teaching or the practice of medicine altogether and find jobs as consultants, or go into a new field. Giving Scott an A for a course would have seemed a small price to pay.

So then why kill him? Did Scott have something he held over the killer's head that was just too onerous? Or was it a collective series of blackmails, forcing the killer to end it by terminating Scott's life? Or did the killer just not like being blackmailed? Whatever the reason, what Gregory had told her, if true – she reminded herself that Gregory seemed bitter and she needed to check elements of his story out – showed that Scott may not have been some innocent victim, but may have been the cause of his own death. But, if so, why did the killer then murder Dana and Nick? Maybe, Charlotte realized, because he feared that Scott had told them the secret. The revelation unnerved her. Did Scott tell anyone else and, if so, does the killer know about it? *Might another murder be in the offing?*

"One last question, Gregory. You've made a number of references to choices being made, saying that the choice you made was the right one and the choice Scott made was the wrong one, yet you seem to have been punished while Scott seemed to have prospered. What's that about?"

"That's the crux of it for me, Miss Westbrook. Scott made the choice, maybe pushed on him by his father, but he still made the choice of forcing Carrie Pankow to have an abortion. However you feel about abortion, Miss

Westbrook, I think you will agree that no one should put such pressure on a woman that she feels forced to have one. Yet what was the result of this? Carrie Pankow disappeared after high school, moved to some other city. And Scott went on to an illustrious career, first as an undergraduate at Princeton, then as a medical student at James Buchanan. If it weren't for his death, I would think there was no justice."

"That's a pretty strong statement."

Gregory nodded. "Yeah, I know. But the thing is, Miss Westbrook, is that I should have had the same career, but I made a different choice. Scott wasn't the only one to get a girl pregnant. I was stupid that way, too. I got Helen pregnant."

"Your wife."

"Yes, my wife. But she wasn't my wife then. She wanted to keep the baby. I like to think it was because she really loved me and really wanted to have a family together. Maybe it was. Or maybe it was because she wanted to climb up some rungs, like Carrie did. They were friends, Carrie and Helen. Both grew up in the same area of town. Only I guess Helen was luckier in her choice of a boyfriend.

"My parents wanted her to have an abortion, too. They were furious with me, and even more furious when I said I wouldn't force her too. My dad is not like Richard Karakas. It was not his style or in his makeup to go over and threaten Helen's parents and I don't know if they would have caved the way Carrie's parents did, anyway. But my mom and dad were both hurt, pretty bad. They told me that if Helen and I persisted in having this child and dragging the family name through the muck, that I could forget about their financing college. They haven't exactly cut me off, but look around, Miss Westbrook, look around. I am not exactly the heir to the estate any more, am I? I tried not to let this stop me. I went to community college for a year, hoping I could then get an associate degree and maybe win at least a partial scholarship to a four-year

262

school, but my heart wasn't in it. I'm in charge of operations at a mail-order company now."

Gregory paused, as if absorbing the impact of his position in life for the umpteenth time. "All my life, I had my future ahead of me. A good school, then maybe law school. Instead, I did the right thing, which was to let Helen make her own choice. And she did what she thought was the right thing. And, as you probably saw, after we got married, we had a second child."

"Helen seems like a loving wife and mother," Charlotte said.

Gregory smiled. "Funny thing is, Miss Westbrook, she is. And you know what, I do love her. And I love my kids. But," he said, motioning with his hand to the door, where the noise from the kids and the television set was coming from the small living room outside through the door, "I didn't bargain for this."

38

Brenda Morehouse had been working in the reimbursement office for almost 20 years, but she was not prepared for this: the front door to the university hospital swung open as seven men, all in suits, ties and overcoats, burst into the foyer, rapidly climbed the entryway stairs into the lobby and headed toward the reimbursement office. Several of them were carrying a large number of broken down cardboard boxes. Brenda was returning from an errand in another part of the building when she saw them.

"May I help you?" she asked. The men stopped dead in their tracks and their leader, somewhat shorter than the others, most of whom were large and well built, approached her, a piece of paper in his left hand.

"Would you please tell us where the reimbursement office is?"

"I'm Brenda Morehouse, the director of reimbursement. Just how may I help you?" Brenda tried her best to put on a brave front, but she was beginning to suspect what this was, and it was every director of every health care reimbursement's worst nightmare.

The man flashed an identification card. "Ma'am, I am Investigator Charles Dutton with the HHS Office of the Inspector General. I have here" – he held up the paper he was clutching in his other hand – "a warrant to search and, if necessary, seize, materials relating to ongoing Medicare fraud investigations at James Buchanan University Hospital. If you would take us to the reimbursement office, we will begin our work."

Brenda, like many others in her office, had been trained by Paul Holden in how to respond in the event they were ever investigated. She took them to the reimbursement office, where members of her staff, including Carla Calloway, were working on claims and other paperwork.

"I need to call our compliance officer," she said to Dutton. "Please wait one minute."

Brenda picked up the phone and dialed Paul's extension, only to find that he was in a meeting. "Interrupt the meeting," she told his administrative assistant, "and tell him that investigators from OIG are down here." She then turned her attention back to Dutton.

"Paul Holden, our compliance officer, will be down shortly. Would you care to wait until he arrives?" She motioned to some chairs. "I can get you and your men some coffee, tea or soft drinks, if you like."

"No thank you, ma'am," Dutton said. "We need to begin our investigation now. We are not required to wait for the compliance officer to arrive."

"I see," Brenda said. "Well, alright." She stood at the front of the room and raised her hand. The staff, already quiet and waiting to hear what was going on, listened raptly. "Attention everybody," she said. "These men are with the HHS Office of the Inspector General. Please cooperate with them."

"Thank you, Miss Morehouse," Dutton said. He turned to his men and nodded.

Like a hurricane with Dutton as its eye, the six men fanned across the office, asking the coders and billers to remove themselves from their desks so they could sit at their stations. They then proceeded to take files from every desk drawer, as well as many in the file cabinets, and placed them in the cardboard boxes, which they had quickly assembled.

"Mr. Dutton," Brenda, now trembling with a combination of fear and outrage, said, "It might be easier for you and your men if you tell me what you want. We could make copies for you."

"I appreciate that, Miss Morehouse, but we are authorized to remove anything that might relate to the nature of our investigation."

"And what is that?"

"You'll need to contact the attorneys on the OIG staff for that, ma'am," Dutton said. "I'm sure Mr. Holden is familiar with it. You might ask him."

If he shows up, Brenda thought. She watched in something close to horror as Dutton's men began taking the hard drives out of the office computers. There would be no way for her staff to do its work. How would the hospital even begin to function? The patient financial records were stored in this office.

Paul came into the office, looking concerned, but trying to be friendly. He quickly assessed the situation, looked at Brenda's face, then spoke to Dutton.

"I'm Paul Holden, the compliance officer here, sir. I take it you have a search warrant?"

Dutton introduced himself and showed Paul the warrant. Paul studied it closely.

"Well, it does seem to grant you some wide latitude. Is there any way we can help you that would also allow the business of the university hospital to continue?"

"The best way you can help us, sir, would be to direct us to the office of the chief financial officer, Mr. Simon Proctor, and the chief administrator, Mr. Chamroeun Arun. As you can see, we are authorized to conduct a search in whatever areas of the building we believe there may be evidence."

Paul swallowed hard and looked at Brenda.

The investigators then split into three teams, with two of the men staying in the now somewhat disheveled reimbursement office – what a horror this must be to Brenda, who is so fastidious and neat as a pin, Paul thought – and the other four, plus Dutton, forming two teams to ostensibly do the same to Simon's and Arun's office. This put Paul in something of a quandary, as it was his intention to monitor the investigators' work. He quickly put in a call to the compliance office, directing two colleagues to come down. That way, there would be someone from the compliance office with each of the investigative teams. Paul himself would accompany the men leaving to search Arun's office.

Simon was in his office with the door locked, as usual, when he answered a knock to find two investigators and Rebecca Croft, a pretty compliance associate in her early 30's from Paul Holden's department. Impeccably dressed as always, this day in a cream-colored blazer over matching pants, with an off-white shirt and silk-patterned tie, he stood up to greet them.

"Gentlemen," he said to the OIG investigators, "I understand you need to rifle through my office."

Rebecca gave him a stern look.

"We need the keys to all your file cabinets, drawers and any other place you may keep material here," one of the investigators said.

"Certainly," Simon said, reaching into his top desk drawer and handing the man two small keys.

They started work immediately, unlocking the file cabinets and taking literally every file out of each drawer, placing them all in the boxes. At one point one of the men had to go back outside, then returned with more boxes.

"Since you are going to be taking everything," Simon asked, "why not simply wheel the entire file cabinet out on a dolly? Then you wouldn't have to unload it."

"Sir, our instructions are to take what we need, no more, so as to minimize disruption to the hospital business."

"I see." Simon could barely contain contempt. "Well, the empty file cabinet may prove useful." He received another stare from Rebecca that seemed to say, "You should know better."

"The keys do not work this door, sir," one of the investigators said. He was kneeling by the credenza behind Simon's desk, trying to unlock one the sliding doors. It was the same door that Carla Calloway had been unable to open during her surreptitious visit.

"There's just some personal material in there, nothing more," said Simon, now appearing a little shaken.

"I will need the key, sir, or I will have to force it open," the investigator on the floor said.

Simon, all signs of condescension now gone from his face, looked in his top drawer, seemingly trying to find the key. Then he tried some other drawers. He shook his head. "The truth is, gentlemen, I haven't unlocked that door in so long, I don't know where the key is. If you want to come back later, I am sure I will find it."

The investigator in front of the credenza looked up at the head of his team, who nodded. Taking a screwdriver from a toolkit, he put the blade between the credenza door and its right side, and began prying it open. Simon watched intently.

The door snapped open. The investigator, looking inside, was not entirely successful in suppressing a smile. Simon was silent.

"Is this your pornography collection, sir?"

Simon could feel all eyes on him, especially Rebecca's.

"Yes," he said quietly. "I wish you had not opened that. As I told you, there is nothing financial in it. Now you have embarrassed me." He tried to brazen it out with the men, but didn't dare look at Rebecca.

"Should we take these?" the investigator at the credenza asked his colleague, who thought it over.

"Yes." He turned to Simon. "These will be returned to you in due time, sir."

"Now, come on. What do you need to take that material for?"

"To be honest," the senior investigator said, "there probably is nothing there, sir. But on the other hand, there might be financial notes or other material hidden inside the pages, under the theory that no one would look there, since they would assume it is just pornography. That might explain why a well-dressed fellow like you keeps his collection here, instead of having it at home."

"I assure you," Simon said, "there is nothing financial in those magazines, nothing about the university hospital's business at all."

Simon realized what his statement meant. It meant he was admitting to all in the room, as well as to doubtless others who would hear about this encounter or read it in court papers, that the only other explanation for the pornography magazines being there was for his own personal enjoyment. He could already hear the jokes about why he kept his door locked. And he felt Rebecca's stare.

"Go ahead and take them," he said.

Arun had, of course, been immediately notified by Paul Holden as soon as Paul received word of the raid. Paul told him there was a good chance the agents would not limit their search to the reimbursement office, but might also search other offices, including his own. In a calm voice, Arun thanked him and prepared himself for the visit.

Of course, he knew what they would find. The second sets of cost reports were where they usually were, in the bottom left hand file drawer of his desk. But he felt no great rush to hide them. Which was odd, he knew, but somehow he just didn't care any more. Yes, he told himself, I could move them out of the office and hide them in any one of a dozen places, from the copy room to someone else's desk. He could have done that all along, and probably most administrators would have. *But that is not who I am.*

He was brought up by an honorable man to do honorable things, to further the family name and certainly not to dishonor it. The steps he had taken to keep this institution in the black, while distasteful, were done for a higher cause, for honorable reasons, namely, to keep a great medical learning institution alive and healthy, not only for students and doctors, but for patients. Certainly pressure was brought on him by the chancellor to get the finances in the black, but that was beside the point. What he did, and what Simon did, he believed, was to simply restore to the university hospital the reimbursement that the government had no right keeping from it in the first place. The government, he reminded himself, with little medical knowledge of its known, cuts the reimbursement it gives medical institutions and sets all kinds of arbitrary rules, for who knows what reasons. But they are not doctors, as the dedicated professionals he works with are. He was certain, he repeated to himself, that he had done the right thing. To believe otherwise would be to dishonor not only all he believed in, but the memory of the Old Soldier, his guidepost in all things.

Still, the deception and subterfuge the system had forced him to engage him had taken their toll. Lost nights of sleep, irritability, worry, anxiety, self-doubt and more constantly plagued him. He wished there had been more forthright ways to restore financial balance to the university hospital, but in fact, there were none. And now, with agents about to raid his office, he had just had enough. *I am clear in my conscience and my actions. Let them find what they will.*

Dutton and his two investigators, along with Paul, arrived a short time later to find Arun sitting behind his desk, seemingly lost in some paperwork. He seemed as calm as ever, Paul thought. How does he do it?

"Ah gentlemen," Arun said, extending his hand to Dutton, who, somewhat awkwardly, took it. "I understand you have a job to do. We have nothing to hide. Please proceed."

"You understand, Mr. Chamroeun, that we have a search warrant that includes the right to seize anything that may help the various investigations the HHS Office of the Inspector General has under way."

"I do indeed, Mr.....Dutton, is it? By all means. And please, let myself or Mr. Holden know if you have any questions or run into any problems. And I hope you have found other personnel equally helpful."

"No major problems. And we appreciate your cooperation, sir." He turned to his men. "Alright, let's proceed."

Arun and Paul watched as the investigators, Dutton included, conducted the same thorough search of his office as they had of Simon's and of the reimbursement office. Arun provided keys when asked. The only time Arun balked was when they approached the display case containing his family memorabilia. One of the men tried to open the glass top, but it was locked. He looked at Arun and Dutton for assistance.

"Mr. Dutton," Arun said, "these are my personal family items – my father's sash from his duty as an aide Prince Sihanouk, his medals, his two ceremonial pistols, a letter from the Prince himself, and so forth. I trust you will not need to take these."

"Can you assure us, Mr. Chamroeun, that there is not any paperwork hidden in there?"

"I give you my word."

Dutton thought a moment. "I'm sorry, Mr. Chamroeun, but this is a fraud investigation, and you are part of it. By definition, that means I cannot rely on your word. We will not need to take any of your personal memorabilia, but I do need you to open the case, so we can make sure that nothing else is there."

Clearly shaken – this *civil servant* had just told him that his word was not worth anything – Arun got the key and opened the case. Before the inspectors could get to it, though, he held up his hand. "Just wait," he said, then carefully gathered up the family memorabilia himself, one item at a time, and placed all of them on his desk, where another investigator was unloading files from the drawers. The men then checked the case for any hidden paperwork, and found none.

"Perhaps next time, Mr. Dutton, you will know what the word of a gentleman means," Arun said.

"I'm just doing my job, sir. But I am afraid the world does not work that way anymore."

Arun gave a small smile, and then turned to sit back at his desk, just as the investigator there was removing one of the second sets of cost reports from his bottom desk drawer and placing it in a cardboard box.

39

Carrie Pankow had not been easy to find. Charlotte didn't know where she had moved to, whether she had married, or even whether she was willing to see her. But after calling some past friends of hers that Gregory provided, searching through phone books for listings, and more, she finally located her. Carrie really had not moved that far away geographically, just to Philadelphia. From a cultural point of view, however, Philadelphia might as well have been a world away from the small-town atmosphere that so much of the rest of Pennsylvania seemed to emote, Pittsburgh being the only possible exception.

Now with the married name of Halloran and working as a loan officer in a downtown bank, Carrie had apparently successfully rebuilt her life. Charlotte found her address, in a middle-class suburb, and her phone number, but when she called, Carrie begged off. That was a part of her life that was closed and she no longer wanted to deal with. Charlotte politely thanked her and hung up.

But Charlotte couldn't let it go. There was a murderer out there, and Carrie might hold some keys as to why Scott was killed. Charlotte decided to approach her where Carrie wouldn't be able to hang up. She went to her place of work.

The Manufacturers & Farmers Bank of Pennsylvania has branches throughout the state, and several in Philadelphia. Charlotte walked into one in the downtown area, on Market Street across from the Reading Market Terminal. The hustle and bustle of the city, including both the cars and the pedestrian traffic, were to her liking. Philadelphia was a classic East Coast city, like New York or Boston, but with its own identity and charms, from the cheese steak vendor in the market to the cab drivers who sometimes could not find the location they had just moments before promised to take you to. The people, as in any big city, were busy, but friendly.

Charlotte walked through the glass doors of the bank and scoured the desks where the loan officers sat, looking for one who matched her image of Carrie. She found her quick enough. A thin, pretty brown-haired woman in her early 20's wearing a brown, pin-striped business suit was talking with a customer at her desk. Charlotte walked over and read the nameplate, which confirmed that she was indeed "Carrie Halloran." She sat down nearby and waited for the customer to finish his business. When he did, she walked over and extended her hand.

The smile immediately left Carrie's face after Charlotte introduced herself.

"I thought I made my feelings clear, Miss Westbrook. Yes, I knew Scott, but that was a long time ago. I do not want to revisit that part of my life. And what's more, I have to be honest with you and tell you that I think it is really improper for you to approach me at my place of business."

"Mrs. Halloran," – Charlotte thought it smart to use the "Mrs." right off, given Carrie's past history. "I do apologize for coming here, but it is essential that we talk. There is a murderer of three students out there, and Scott, as you know, was his first victim. Your knowledge of Scott may be the key to finding this man. I just can't let you keep what you know secret. And, when you really think about it, would you want to, considering that there may still be more murders ahead?"

Carrie didn't say anything for awhile, as if absorbing what Charlotte had to say. Then she sighed. "Had lunch yet?" she said.

Charlotte shook her head.

"Fine," Carrie said, gathering up her coat. "You can take me out to lunch."

"Alright," said Charlotte, a bit taken aback.

"If what you say is at stake is at stake, I suppose I have a moral obligation to help you, so I will. But you're going to pay for it with a good lunch." She smiled after saying it, letting Charlotte know that she was only half serious.

Charlotte laughed. She liked Carrie's vivacity. "Okay, you're on."

"Then follow me." They went out into the street, where Carrie hailed a cab. "Ralph's," she said to the cab driver, then turned to Charlotte. "Great little old-fashioned Italian place on the South Side in the Italian Market area. It's like something out of 'The Godfather.'"

Ralph's did indeed seem like it was direct from the 1940s. Inside what seemed to be an old brownstone on a largely residential street – only the "Ralph's Ristorante" sign identified it as an eating establishment – Charlotte and Carrie walked in to find customers sitting at small tables set on a black and white checkered tile floor. An original tin ceiling was above, and one waiter, an old man dressed in a black vest and apron, tended the tables. A ceiling fan whirred and turned slowly overhead.

"I hope you brought cash," Carrie said, "because they don't take credit cards."

Charlotte hadn't expected this – what restaurant today didn't accept credit cards? – but she always took a couple of hundred dollars in cash with her when she traveled. "Not a problem."

The maitre'd took them on a sturdy but old wooden staircase upstairs, where they found another dining room, somewhat smaller than the one below, with a bar at the far end. He showed them to a table, gave them each a menu and placed a wine list in front of them.

"Alright, Miss Westbrook, I understand you are trying to do the right thing. You want to catch a murderer. Well, who can blame you for that? But this is difficult for me, you understand, because, well…I ran into some trouble back in high school with Scott. And my husband" – she paused – "he doesn't know about it. And I don't want him to know."

Charlotte nodded. "I think I can make this easier for you, Carrie, if you don't mind our using first names. I already know a good part of this, about the pregnancy, the pressure from Scott's parents, and Scott himself, that you wanted to keep the baby, and that this eventually caused you to leave town."

Carrie looked down at her plate, then nodded. "Who told you?"

"Gregory Betorin."

"Hah! Well, I guess he must be a little hard up. He and Helen have their children. But his parents cut him off."

"That's about it. Can't say I approve of his parents' actions."

"No, but Charlotte, you know, Wilkes Barre is like that. A lot of old Central European stock, very old values." A look of anger flashed across her face. "And a lot of good old hypocrisy, too. Both Scott's father and my own showed that. I still find it hard to forgive him."

"Your dad?"

"And my mom too. Richard Karakas did put the pressure on Scott to get me to" – she lowered her voice, which now quavered a bit, so powerful was the memory – "terminate my pregnancy. But Scott's heart really wasn't in it. Not that I had any false illusions that he really loved me. I knew he didn't. Yes, that was my mistake," she said, getting reflective for a moment. "That was my mistake, alright. I *so* wanted to get out of where I grew up."

She looked Charlotte right in the eye. "Ambition can make a person do strange things, Charlotte. Like force your son to talk a girl into getting an abortion. Or force a girl to see pregnancy as her ticket to a better life."

Charlotte put her hand on Carrie's wrist. "That's all over now."

"Yes, well, on most days it is. But the memory of that child. ... Anyway, my father is really a kindly old soul. Worked as a manager of the local supermarket there. Maybe not the greatest job, but you know, he came home and loved to spend time with us kids. In retrospect, he was the kind of father every woman would want her husband to be. Isn't that ironic? *That's* what I thought I had to get away from. But he was not the type to stand up to a Richard Karakas.

"One evening, my parents tell me to stay upstairs in my room, something they had not done since middle school. They had company coming over, they said. At 8 p.m. sharp, the doorbell rings. I'm listening at the top of the stairs. I recognized the voice of Scott's father right away.

"Let me back up a little here, Charlotte. I forgot to mention that my parents knew about my pregnancy. They didn't like it, they were disappointed in me, I guess I was a little disappointed in me, too. But the idea of getting rid of the baby just never came up at the family dinner table. We were strict Catholics, and that was simply beyond the pale. Certainly I thought of it, and Scott had tried to get me to think about it, but truth was, I was conflicted. What my parents really expected, I don't know. Maybe they hoped Scott would do the right thing and marry me. And maybe that's what they thought Richard Karakas' visit was about.

"But it turned out to be anything but. After some initial small talk, I heard them move to the kitchen table, where my mom brought out coffee. Then Richard Karakas got right to the point. This pregnancy was a noose around both Scott's neck and my own, he said to them, getting in the way of our future. An abortion was the only way out.

"I couldn't see my parents' features, but they must have been horrified at the suggestion. My mother asked if there weren't other possibilities, such as marriage. And then I heard something I will never forget." Carrie bit her lip, fighting back tears.

"What?" asked Charlotte.

"I heard Richard Karakas laugh. Not a loud, boisterous laugh, but a kind of hushed laugh, as if you say, 'You must be joking.' That just froze the marrow in my bones, Charlotte. Like I wasn't good enough for his son, and there was no way he was going to have me join his family. I give my mom credit here, though. She asked him straight out just what he meant. I don't think she expected the answer she got, though. He was so blunt.

"'If you think for one second that your daughter is the kind of girl Scott is going to marry, Mrs. Pankow, you're sadly mistaken,' he said. 'Scott has a very bright future in front of him and he will marry the right girl from a good family. He's not going to let a roll in the hay with your daughter change that.'

"I heard my father tell him that we *were* a good family and that any man would be lucky to have me as his wife. Thank you, dad. My mother asked if Scott's feelings had been considered, was Richard even aware of how his son felt.

"'Scott doesn't want the baby, either,' he said. 'He may not fully realize it yet, with your daughter filling his head with a future for them together. But he doesn't want it. And to the degree he doesn't want it, it's my job to step in.'

"Then he got to the bottom line, real quick. He was a very powerful man in town, head of an investment banking firm. He could make men, and he could break them. And I had two brothers behind me who needed college educations. If my parents went along with this and forced me to have an abortion, those college educations would be paid for. What's more, Scott's dad would see to it that my dad rose up in management, maybe becoming a district manager in charge of several stores. He had that kind of influence, he said, adding he knew the head of my dad's supermarket chain very well.

"But if my dad didn't go along, well, then they could forget about sending my brothers to college. And he could forget about his career, too, because he would ruin them. He'd be out of a job, they'd lose their house, he'd fix it so no one in town, or even other towns, would hire him for any decent job."

Charlotte could feel the tears welling up in her own eyes as she listened to Carrie's story. She had sensed some of this when she met the Karakases, but nothing this raw.

"'What kind of man are you to threaten us like this?' my mother asked him."

"'One that wants what is best for his son,' was what Scott's father said. He left the house then, gave them a few days to think it over. But really, what choice did they have but to pressure me, even if that meant acting against their own principles and religious beliefs?

"I said that I still blame my parents earlier, Charlotte, but I don't really, not when I think about it. Sure, some might say that they should have stuck to their guns anyway, that God would take care of them. But c'mon, they had my two brothers, they had a house, and they also had me. When they did finally talk to me a few days later, I could have gone through with the pregnancy anyway, but I really didn't want to anymore. I had ruined so many lives and I didn't want to ruin anymore. So I agreed to have it. My parents understood, but I think, to this day, that memory has disappointed them not only in me, but in themselves. Maybe they were hoping, in some way, that I would disobey them and have the child, do what we were taught in church, but I wouldn't. I love my family, Charlotte, I realize that even more now, so I did what I thought was right. And I think today I would make the same choice."

"How did Scott react?"

"Relieved. He told me he was sorry, made some noise about how he respected my decision and would have gone along with whatever I had decided. But we both knew that was a crock. I don't need to tell you that that was the end of any relationship that Scott and I had.

"When it was all over, my father was offered that promotion to district manager. It would have meant a lot more money. But he told them to stick the job you know where. And he turned down any money from Richard Karakas for my brothers' education. My mom said he once asked Richard Karakas how he could live with himself. I never heard what the answer was.

"This all happened about six years ago," Carrie said, wiping her eyes, "but it might as well have been an eternity. I left Wilkes-Barre after high school, couldn't wait to get away. I don't know who knew what happened, but I felt like everyone knew, you know? So I moved here, took some computer classes, made some connections, then got this job here three years ago. The bonus," and now she smiled through her tears, "was that I met my husband on the job."

"That's great," said Charlotte. She felt for Carrie like she hadn't felt for anyone in a long time. "What's his name?"

"Brian, Brian Halloran, same as mine." She held up her hand with the wedding ring. "See, I got a good man anyway. And we are going to have children one day. But he doesn't know what happened."

"Will you tell him?"

"Probably, one day. Maybe I should have told him sooner, but I was so afraid, so afraid. And I didn't want to lose him."

"For what it's worth, Carrie, he sounds like a good man. I think he'll be okay with it. And something else. I think he's got a pretty classy wife, too. And that's coming from someone from 'the other side of the tracks.'"

Carrie's eyes lit up in appreciation as she smiled at Charlotte. "So what happens now?"

"Now," said Charlotte, "now I think I may have some motivation for why the murderer did what he did, but I don't know who the murderer is. I have some ideas about how to find out, though."

40

About a week later, an excited James Stadler knocked on the door to Lewis' spacious corner office. Lewis, studying a report, was deep in thought at his desk, which backed two large glass walls overlooking Independence Ave. SW in downtown Washington, giving him a view of the city as the spring buds turned to green, now that May was here. He looked up, startled.

"Sorry, Lewis, didn't mean to disturb you," Stadler said, "but we've got conclusive evidence of fraud in several of those second sets of books that Carla found and our investigators took from Chamroeun's office."

Lewis smiled. "I can't say I'm surprised. How much improper reimbursement do the reports say James Buchanan has been sticking the citizens of this great country for?"

"On the order of $17 million over a three-year period. It's all right there, in black and white. Why these institutions so often keep a second set of books like this is beyond me. And why Chamroeun kept in his office, instead of, say, at home, where it would be harder to find, I don't understand."

"Maybe, deep inside, he wanted to be caught. I sometimes think many of them do."

"Then why not just voluntarily disclose? We have a program for that, and the university would pay a lot less in fines that way. Now we are ready to throw the book at them. We have definite evidence of upcoding and unbundling from our claims audits and now we have these cost reports showing all kinds inflated charges on capital expense, and we also have an eyewitness who saw doctors not supervising residents properly. If they had voluntarily disclosed, this could have been a lot less painful than it's going to be. Especially if, as you say, his conscience was bothering him and he wanted to get caught anyway."

"Yes, James, I agree. But we see this happen again and again." He shook his head. "Well, it's not our job to be psychiatrists. It is our job to protect the taxpayers' dollars. Are we ready to file charges?"

"Within a matter of days. It's just a question of the documents. But are we going to give them a chance to settle first?"

Lewis nodded vigorously. "Certainly. I'd like to avoid a trial, if we can. And now that we've got them dead to rights, we should be able to get a pretty promising settlement, I would say on the order of more than $50 million, if you add in the triple fines the law allows."

"What about Carla?"

"She will get what is rightfully due her, no more, no less," Lewis said. "Now, James, if you will excuse me, I need to inform the Inspector General."

"She should be pleased."

"One would think," said Lewis, as he headed out his office door.

Charlotte received the news of the false cost reports with a studious look. "You know what this means?" she asked Lewis.

"You mean, aside from the fact that we've got the university where we can squeeze them in settlement negotiations?"

"Yes. Good work on that, by the way."

Lewis grimaced. She said it almost as an afterthought. And he knew why. She was still wrapped up in the murders. Any other time, she would have been thrilled to hear this news. It would certainly have meant getting out the laser gun and firing it at the wall. But here she seemed almost pensive. He sighed, audibly.

"What is it, Lewis?"

"Do you feel bad for them, Charlotte, for Chamroeun in particular?"

Charlotte stood up from her desk and walked to the couch, sitting down next to her old friend. Lewis was surprised to see her eyes were moist.

"I do feel bad for him. I've become aware recently of a lot of otherwise good people having their lives decided for them. It's tragic, really. We make our choices in life and we have to live with them. In this case, Arun seems to have gotten caught up in something that became bigger than he ever wanted. And I fear that may have led him to make some wrong choices. Especially in light of these cost reports."

Lewis noticed how she used Chamroeun's first name when talking about him. This empathy for people who were criminals was something new, especially if he understood correctly what Charlotte was driving at. "Meaning that he also may be the murderer?"

Charlotte nodded.

"My God, Charlotte, if he is the murderer, he has killed three people! Why would he even deserve your sympathy?"

"You're right, of course. And don't worry, my friend. We will see this through to its logical conclusion. And I will not waver in our case. In fact, to that end, I need to notify Detective Petrelli. He'll want to bring Arun down for questioning."

"There really is no evidence directly linking him to the murders."

"No, and I hope he isn't the one. But we do know that Scott Karakas was a blackmailer and that, through his father, he learned how to play hardball, perhaps reluctantly in his case. There's a good chance he was using the same techniques here that worked for him earlier in his life. But we lack the person he was blackmailing. Most likely, though, it was someone involved in the fraud case."

"But that doesn't mean it was Arun. He's not the only person involved. It could have been one of the doctors, a faculty member. It could have been Simon Proctor."

"That's right. Those are all possibilities. Although I don't know just what Mr. Proctor could do for Scott."

"Maybe lend him his latest issue of *Intimate Couples*?"

They both laughed. "All I am saying is that Arun is now a reasonable suspect. What Scott Karakas may have been using blackmail to get, if he was using blackmail, could have been anything from his tuition to his grades. And maybe that was enough for Arun to kill him. Maybe giving in to blackmail was just beyond the pale for him."

"But Medicare fraud was acceptable?"

Charlotte shrugged. "Maybe. Maybe Arun believed what he was doing was justified, in some way."

"Then how about the other two murders? Why would he kill them?"

Charlotte shook her head. "I don't know. I don't claim to know at this point. But I have an agreement with Detective Petrelli, so I am going to let him do what he does. Maybe he will find something out."

"So we're done with our part of investigating the murders?" Lewis asked, a little too hopefully.

"Not on your life, Lewis. And don't tell me you didn't get into it a couple of weeks ago when you visited the reimbursement office and Simon Proctor."

"It does have some interest for me. It just makes me a bit nervous that we are doing this kind of work, that's all. You know what Mack said, and then there's Secretary Balcolm."

"Haven't heard a word from the Secretary."

"Because he doesn't know you're still looking into it. If he finds out…"

"Lewis," Charlotte said, taking out the laser gun. "You worry too much." She didn't fire it this time, just looked at the barrel, blew some dust off the top, and put it back in her desk, then looked up at Lewis and smiled.

41

Arun returned to his office the next day and stood in the doorway. He looked around the impressive office in its corner location, the expensive furniture, the original art he had hung on the walls, and finally the display case where he kept the family mementos of which he was so proud. Then he choked back a sob.

Somewhere his father was more than disappointed, he knew. He could picture him, sometimes in uniform and sometimes in his civilian clothes, but either way looking down at him, almost in contempt. "My son," he could hear him say, "My son, how could you make such choices? How could you do this to the family name?"

And now things had taken a turn for the worse, something Arun had not thought possible. He had expected OIG to find the second set of books when they reviewed the material they had taken from his office. And he had expected that at some point he would be named in an indictment, along with Simon Proctor and the James Buchanan University Hospital itself, for various forms of Medicare fraud. *Alright, I am technically guilty,* he told himself, but the greater good was served. Doubts had begun to fray that strongly held stance, but he held firm to it. To do otherwise would be to admit that he was nothing more than a thief, and of the public's money, to make it worse. *I am not a thief.*

But just today, perhaps the most humiliating development of all. He had spent the morning at district police headquarters, where he was told by Detective Petrelli that he was a suspect in the killings of the three students. Detective Petrelli's theory, which Arun told him was absurd, was that Scott Karakas had somehow found out about the Medicare fraud and Arun's involvement in it, and that Scott had then blackmailed Arun in order to get some benefit, just what Detective Petrelli didn't know, but he assured Arun, in the rather tense meeting, that he would be looking through Scott Karakas' financial records, grade reports and anything else, and if he found that the university had done something like waived tuition or given him an "A" when he didn't deserve one, that could very well lead to his arrest.

My arrest. A Chamroeun in jail. Arun sighed and walked over to the display case where his mementos were kept. He looked at them, one by one. There were more than his father's mementos in there. There were also his own achievements. His MBA. His letter of thanks from President Bill Clinton for his work in helping to fight disease in the Sudan. His medals for leading his soccer team to victory when he was a college student.

Of course, his achievements were nothing compared to *le Vieux Soldat's*. His father's achievements were always a source of continuing pride to him. He looked at some of his father's medals from when he had served under Prince Sihanouk. His ceremonial sword, and a letter from the Prince, extolling him for his years of service, as were his ceremonial pistols, each with filigree engravings on the handles.

Arun smiled gently at his father's achievements. The man had put service before everything else, except perhaps his family. Somehow, the Old Soldier had been able to balance his extraordinary duties with life as a husband and father. It had been a rare occasion when he missed a family dinner, or a weekend outing with Arun, and now Arun found that he missed him terribly. His father's final days had been filled with pain, as he was forced to give in to a blood disorder that wracked his body. And this thought brought back to Arun a memory he had tried his best to suppress over the years.

At the very end, *le Vieux Soldat* had lost whatever dignity he had possessed and cried and screamed from the blood disorder that would eventually take his life. Arun could barely stand to visit him, this new version of his father being so distant from the man he knew and loved so well. The dark-haired man with the sharp mind and crisp military bearing had given way to a shriveled remnant of what he had once been. As Chamroeun Reit lay in his hospital bed, hooked up to IVs and other medical devices, down to less than two-thirds of his former weight and his thinning hair now white, Arun could not help but wonder where his father had gone. And then there was that one encounter.

"I am sorry," his father had whimpered, crying. "Arun, you must forgive me. What I did, I did for the Khmer people."

"Of course, father," Arun had said on that dark evening 12 years before. "Everything you did was for the people."

Then a moment of calm passed his father's face, and for few seconds he seemed almost his old self. "Not everything. Not everything. I thought I could help our people by making a bargain with the devil. But I fooled only myself. Do not ever become a victim in a trap like that, Arun. Not ever."

"Father, what are you referring to? I think this must be the disease talking."

Chamroun Reit shook his head and the words came out, haltingly at first, then, as if relieved to finally utter them, quickly. "No. I made a foolish choice. After the Prince lost power, I thought that maybe I could still make a difference by working with the Khmer Rouge. I had hoped that by cooperating with them, I could help mitigate their excesses. But it did not turn out that way. It did not turn out that way."

Tears began to flow down his face as the Old Soldier continued. "I knew I would not be able to curb all their abuses, so I turned my head to some, convinced I had to be there to prevent greater abuses. But after a few months....I found that I was having little effect at all and that, in fact, I had turned my head from what was really going on: mass murders, deportations... *the killing fields.*"

"But you never directly did any of these things yourself!" Arun protested.

"No." Chamroeun Reit gave a small smile. "At least I managed to spare myself that indignity. But it does not excuse everything."

"What else could you have done, father?"

"I could not have been part of that regime, and blackened my own name and the family's. That is why we left Cambodia, Arun. That is why we moved to the United States. I had ruined all that I was and I could no longer live with myself."

When Chamroun Reit finally breathed his last, Arun too felt at peace, knowing his father's suffering was over, and, though he was loath to admit it, his own agony at watching his father deteriorate. In later years, he rarely dwelt on his father's final words, choosing instead to spend his time memorializing the achievements of his life.

Arun's mother, always a loving presence in the house, carried on, but the Old Soldier had been such a dominant presence that she seemed to visually shrink before Arun's eyes. Had she known of her husband's turning a blind eye to Khmer Rouge abuses? She must have, but she and Arun never discussed it, perhaps because doing so would take away the honorable image they had of *le Vieux Soldat.*

While his father had been the dominant presence in his life, Arun also loved his mother deeply. She was the one who provided kindness where his father had been stern. She made the household run smoothly when he was away. And she provided the nurturing to his father's providing the example. When she died from cancer just one year later and was laid to rest next to her husband, Arun had felt the loss not only of his mother, but of his father again, because in some way, he could still feel his father's presence in his mother's actions and words. Together, they had informed his life.

But his mother's death was 11 years ago, and now Arun knew that he too had made a mess of things. He had disgraced the family honor and dishonored his parents. He had made the exact mistake his father had: rationalizing the greater good. It seemed so transparent now. *I committed a crime to save my job and convinced myself that it was for the good of the community.* The fact that his actions had, in fact, kept the university hospital operating, was not the point. If he didn't like the Medicare rules, if he had felt they were unfair, he should have fought them through legitimate means. If he had been dismissed from his position because the rules didn't change, at least he could have held his head high, knowing he had done all he could. But instead, he realized, he had committed a crime.

And now he was being investigated for the murders. If he was found guilty of these, Arun knew, he could not bear it. The disgrace to his family, let alone the prospect of the indignity of prison, or a death sentence, would be too much. Even the *investigation* into whether he was the murderer – something that was not yet public but which he was sure would leak to the press – would be an embarrassment from which he would never recover, even if another suspect was found.

Arun walked over to his desk and removed a key from the top drawer, then walked back to the display case and opened it. He looked again at the mementos, then picked up his father's sword. As a child, he had loved this sword. It was a throwback to an earlier era, when men fought wars with such weapons, and he loved to picture Chamroeun Reit astride a horse, sword at his side, galloping across the Cambodian plains. The fact that the Old Solider usually rode in a car made no difference.

Arun put the sword down and picked up one of the ceremonial pistols. Beautiful craftsmanship, he marveled, as he turned the firearm over in his hands, then studied the filigree. There, on the handle, was etched the Chamroeun family crest. He loved the crest, with its two tigers facing the original family mansion, long since gone, lost to fire.

Opening the pistol, Arun saw that all six chambers were loaded. Both pistols were always loaded, he knew. His father had carried them that way, despite their ceremonial nature. A firearm is still a firearm, *le Vieux Soldat* had said, and one day you may need one.

Today was such a day. Arun pressed the barrel of the pistol under his chin and squeezed the trigger. He never heard the sound of the chemical explosion that sent the bullet through his jaw and up through his brain, emerging near the top of his head, leaving his body and bits of skull fragment among the family mementos.

42

Marjorie was having the time of her life. Vienna had turned out to be the perfect choice for her and Peter to get away. It had everything: great culture, beautiful architecture, history, terrific food, safe streets, friendly people and, not the least, romance. She felt, now that May was here and the end of their month abroad was approaching, that this was just the opportunity she and Peter had needed to rekindle the romantic spark in their marriage.

Not that it had needed much rekindling until the past few months. Peter, under the strain of teaching and working with residents and students at the university hospital, then the fraud investigation and the effect it was having on everyone there, and finally the shock and scare of the murders, had become somewhat withdrawn in the weeks before they left. Marriages go through periods, she knew, and she was perfectly happy to work this one through with him.

Before they left for their month in Austria, they discussed it. She wanted to help, and asked him why he seemed so changed.

"It's the pressure at work from everything," he said, as they talked one night in bed. "I know I have been less attentive than usual. I'm sorry, Marjorie. I hope you will forgive me." He leaned over and gave her a kiss.

"Everyone seems on edge at the university," she agreed. "Lyle, Jennifer, Arun… But who wouldn't be, given the conditions?"

Peter nodded. "Who wouldn't be," he repeated. He leaned over and put his arms around her. "That's why I thought of Vienna."

The idea thrilled her. That was where they had had met, and they both loved the city. "Let's do it," she said.

Peter seemed a bit like his old self for a few days after that, especially after he announced their vacation plans at Nick Rosen's funeral. Up until that moment, he had seemed particularly withdrawn. And at that moment an insight hit Marjorie: When someone is a doctor, in the business of saving lives, funerals must be a particularly sad time. And when the death was unnecessary, even more so. That would explain not only Peter's increased distraction at the funeral – since the murders began, actually – but Arun's, Lyle's and Jennifer's, as well.

The past month in Vienna seemed to turn that all around. If anything, Peter was more romantic than ever. They made love almost every other night, sometimes every night. That hadn't been the case since they were newlyweds, she remembered. *He must have needed to get away so bad.* She noticed a greater lightness in his walk, the way he moved, his very presence. But she also caught herself wondering if that refreshed mood and all that came with it did not seem a bit, well, manic, as if from someone who desperately wanted to have a good time and was forcing himself to. She put those thoughts aside, happy to have this time alone in their favorite city with the man she loved.

This evening they were dining once again at the hotel they were staying at, the famous Hotel Sacher, where both the service and the ambiance were so elegant. Peter ordered the duck, while she ordered veal. As with all Viennese dining, the dishes arrived beautifully prepared. Marjorie savored the flavor from the food as she planned to cut into her first piece. Peter, she noticed, seemed a bit put off.

"Is something wrong with your food?" she asked.

"No, not at all. It looks fine," he said, cutting through the crisp skin and putting a bit in his mouth. "Yes, as always, absolutely delicious." He put down his knife and fork and looked at Marjorie. He seemed flush and was perspiring. His hands were shaking.

"Marj, we have to talk."

She could see this was serious. Was this what was behind his somewhat exaggerated lightness, she wondered. She reached out and held his hand.

"Darling. Whatever it is, tell me. I had no idea…"

Peter leaned forward so his face was just a few inches from his wife's, so no one else in the restaurant could hear him.

"Marj, I cannot keep this secret any longer. I pray you will forgive me and understand. I've done something terrible, Marj, three things, really. I'm the murderer, Marj. I killed all three of them."

43

Something struck Charlotte as wrong as she read Eileen Ashburton's *Post* story about Arun's suicide. Not factually wrong – it was clear what happened, and she found herself sad about the loss of the man she had developed a liking and respect for, whatever fraud he may have committed or condoned. What struck her as wrong was the speculation that Arun was the murderer of the three students, or was in some way connected.

Three days had passed since Arun's death, and all the grisly details had come out, from the janitor who found the body and became violently ill, adding his vomit to the skull fragments, to the police investigation, the background stories on Arun and his family, and, finally, speculation, apparently fed by Detective Petrelli and the police in general, that Arun had killed himself because of the strain of knowing he was the killer.

The theory went like this: Arun was behind a great deal, if not all, of the Medicare fraud at James Buchanan, although why a man with such an honorable past would decide to commit fraud was still an open question. At some point, the three students, who were friends and spoke with each other, found out about it. Again, how that would have happened was just not clear. And Arun found out they knew about it. Still not clear on how that happened. So he killed them to protect his crimes, but then could not live with his guilt and killed himself.

"There's a certain logic to it," Petrelli told Charlotte during a phone call the day before. "We don't, of course, have absolute proof that Chamroeun was the killer, and we will continue our investigation, but frankly, Charlotte, we don't have any more leads. If the murders stop here, we may never know. But Chamroeun is a good bet, I think. Too bad he didn't leave a note confessing before he blew his brains out."

Charlotte grimaced at the *film noir* expression. Petrelli must be deep into Raymond Chandler novels. "What was he like when you brought him in for questioning?"

"Depressed. I wouldn't say uncooperative. He answered the questions, denied he had anything to do with the murders. There was almost a look on his face at one point like, well, he couldn't believe things had reached the stage they were at. We didn't have enough to charge him with, so we released him but told him to stay in the area. He seemed a bit insulted by the whole thing, I think. It was kind of sad to see a man of his stature brought down."

"I imagine it was a lot for him to bear."

"Hey, but he was guilty of Medicare fraud, right? You guys found the set of double books in his desk drawer."

Petrelli was right. She and Lewis had planned to file charges against the university hospital next week. They would still file charges, but Arun's death would probably push it back by a week or more. A settlement involving a hefty fine well into the tens of millions of dollars, as well as a mandatory compliance plan to prevent the same kind of fraud from happening again, were the most likely results.

But now she sat at her desk, almost depressed her. Suicide is such a final, desperate act. And despite his fraud, she continued not to think of Arun as a bad man. Most likely, as she had seen in several cases, he was a good man who made bad choices. He most likely felt financial pressure at the university hospital, or just wanted to increase profits, and took the steps he did.

What didn't quite make sense to her was that he was the murderer. She couldn't totally discount the possibility, but it didn't strike her as being in character. There is a moral difference, let alone a legal one, between financial misdoings and taking the lives of three young people. Of course, she remembered her discussion with Penelope about how desperation can make people do things they wouldn't ordinarily do, shattering their ego structure. But she just could not bring herself to see Arun reaching that point.

What's more, she found it hard to believe that the pressure of the fraud investigation would have driven Arun to kill. His biography, now all over the local papers, showed that he had handled fraud investigations at other institutions before he ever joined James Buchanan. This did not mean, of course, that Arun himself had committed the fraud at those other institutions. It is just a fact of life in American health care these days that if you are in charge of a medical institution, at some point you will run into compliance issues that may lead to fraud investigations. In fact, in two of the three previous investigations in which Arun had been involved, the government had dropped the charges against the hospitals. And in the third, the hospital received a small fine, $25,000, which was really more of a nuisance payment by the hospital to be done with the entire matter. It did not confer guilt, nor did the hospital admit any.

So Arun was no stranger to compliance issues and, given that James Buchanan University Hospital was larger than the other hospitals at which he had worked, he had a larger compliance staff, led by the capable Paul Holden. It was unlikely, then, Charlotte thought, that the stress of the government investigation led to his suicide. What might have done so, however, was his knowledge that, perhaps unlike the other times, in this investigation he was personally guilty.

On the other hand, Petrelli's theory that one of the students may have had knowledge of the fraud and Arun's involvement in it rang true. She had not yet shared this with Petrelli, but Scott, after all, was someone who she now knew had used blackmail before. It was quite possible he had gone to Arun and confronted him about the fraud, then blackmailed him in return for some as-yet-unknown favors.

The police were already checking the school's tuition records to see if Scott had received any special financial arrangements this past year, although given Scott's family wealth, she thought it unlikely they would find anything. They were also checking Scott's bank account, as well as those of Dana Brentano and Nick Rosen, to see if any of them had received any unexpected large sums of cash. And, finally, they were planning to check Scott's grade reports, although Charlotte knew they would most likely turn up little that would be incriminating. Even if Scott had received straight A's, he did that often enough on his own. He had used blackmail only for the rare B. There may have been some other benefit Scott could have blackmailed Arun for, but she was finding it difficult to come up with one. Other than money and grades, what else would a college student blackmail a school administrator for?

So that would most likely leave no proof that Arun was the killer. Just the police department's belief. But the police had already been wrong once before in this case, with tragic consequences for Nick Rosen.

What this all meant, she realized, was this: Detective Petrelli could not be counted on to find the killer on his own. She and Lewis would need to redouble their efforts.

44

Marjorie could barely hear the door of the Hotel Sacher close behind her, so quickly did she run out into the street. She didn't know which way to go, or even where she wanted to go. It didn't matter. She turned left and headed down Karntner Strasse, the broad, cobblestone-paved pedestrian mall that connected the Karlsplatz, where the Hotel Sacher and the State Opera House were, to Stephansplatz, the heart of the old city. Shoppers and tourists milled by her in the remaining daylight.

She kept asking herself if she had heard what she believed she had heard, or was it just some insane surreal dream. Half an hour ago, deeply in love anew with her husband, they had settled down for a wonderful dinner. A few moments ago, she had bolted out of the restaurant, having learned the man she loved and been married to for 12 years was a ...a what? *A serial killer.*

She would have thought it a sick joke, desperately wanted it to be a sick joke, but saw on Peter's face when he told her that it was no joke at all.

"But...but, why?" she asked him, after absorbing what he had said.

"I was being blackmailed. I had no choice. He was going to ruin our lives, Marj. And it never would have stopped. I would not have been able to get a job anywhere, my reputation would have been destroyed. Believe me, I didn't want to do it." He looked at her and she could see the desperation in his eyes.

"Who was blackmailing you, Scott Karakas?"

Peter nodded. "For over a year now. It was unbearable. And then, with the girl ..."

Marjorie tried to get her senses together. Maybe there was a rational explanation and a logical way out of this. Maybe Peter was defending himself when he killed Scott Karakas. She wanted to help her husband and she knew she needed to stay calm to do so. Her thoughts were a blur as her mind raced. *Why are you telling me this now?*

"Alright, let's slow down. Start at the beginning. Scott Karakas was blackmailing you. Over what?"

Peter nodded, took a drink of water. "I wanted to tell you, Marj, but I couldn't. God, I wanted to. But I didn't want to lose you. You're all I have left. And I wanted to protect you. Because once you knew this, if you didn't turn me in – which I am taking a chance here because I believe that you won't – you become an accomplice, at least to the cover-up, whatever they say about wives not having to testify against their husbands."

My God, he's right. I now know who the murderer is. And it's my husband. She struggled to hold herself together.

"What was Scott Karakas blackmailing you over?"

"Improper supervision of residents."

"What?!"

"It may sound like a small thing to someone who has not worked at a university hospital or who doesn't know how the government works, Marj, but believe me, careers have been broken over this and other kinds of fraud, lives shot, families split apart, reputations ruined. OIG has destroyed the lives of good doctors, good doctors, over this. And university hospitals have paid millions of dollars in fines."

"But that's no reason to kill someone!"

Peter shook his head. "You have to understand, Marj, I didn't kill him the first time he blackmailed me, which was last semester. Scott was, well, I learned very quickly just what a monster he was. He has a reputation on campus – still does, even though he's dead – as a great student, popular student. And the funny thing is, he *was* fairly bright. But he had to finish near the top of his class. Wouldn't accept anything less. Said his father wouldn't accept it, and he would do whatever was necessary to get the grades he needed. So one day last year, he walked into my office and asked me to change what would have been a B on an exam to an A. Said it would have lowered his semester grade to a B+. I refused, of course. I told him a B was a perfectly respectable exam grade, but that he was a bright student and could probably get an A the next semester if he tried a little harder.

"Then he hit me with the bazooka. 'You're not so perfect yourself, Dr. Kenyon,' he said. 'You don't follow all the rules and your actions may cost this university big money.' He said he knew that I had left the building on several occasions while supervising residents to tend to any number of other chores I had to do. In two cases I didn't come back. But Marj, I wouldn't have done that unless I knew the residents involved were perfectly capable of carrying on, on their own. And they were."

"But it was still against the rules."

"Against the rules by which Medicare reimburses the hospital."

"So why not just put down in your notes that you left the building?"

Peter gave a weak smile. "You don't understand. It's not the lack of notes saying I left the building. It's leaving the building itself. Medicare takes it on itself to determine what degree of supervision a resident requires. What is 'supervision' anyway? Does it mean you have to be looking over each resident's shoulder during every step of every operation? Or does it mean that the staff doctors must make sure, through observation primarily, that their residents know what they are doing? That means making individual judgments, Marj, and I believed those residents that I left 'unsupervised' in the OR knew what they were doing. That was *my* supervision judgment. In any event, Medicare doesn't care about it in terms of teaching surgery or patient safety. They just don't want to reimburse doctors for time when they weren't 'supervising,' as Medicare defines it."

Marjorie held up her hand. She didn't want to get into the details of Medicare fraud. Not now.

"Okay, so what happened then?"

"Well, he just held this over my head. Said I would be ruined, excluded from Medicare, that I would take the university hospital and all my colleagues down with me. I ... I couldn't let that happen. Do you know what Medicare exclusion means, Marj? It means, in effect, that no other health care institution can ever hire you while the exclusion is in effect, and that's for a minimum of five years! I might as well have become a construction worker.

"So I gave him the A. I hated to do it, but what choice did I have? Snotty rich kid, I figured that would be it and it would be over. You should have seen him smirk when I gave in. There was something of a bully about him, something I hadn't seen before when he kissed up to me in class and was putting on what I now realized was his 'charm' act. And that would have been the end of it. He would have graduated later this year and it would have been over.

"But this past semester, he came at me again. It turned out that getting me to give him an "A" was just a test. He wanted to see how far he could push me. So he ratcheted it up. He wanted me to use my influence at Johns Hopkins Hospital to get him a residency there after he graduated. 'You know I've got you, doctor, so just give me what I want.' It was bad enough, and his taunts just made it worse. I tried to tell myself that he was in his final year and then I would be done with him."

"Did you do it?"

"Not at first. I didn't even know if I could. Yes, I was on staff at Johns Hopkins for several years and I had contacts. It was possible I could. But this was a lot more than getting an "A." He wanted to be a resident at what a recent poll named as the best hospital in the country, a position he apparently was afraid to try out for on his own. Said it would please his father greatly if it happened. So, I…Marj, what could I do? I made some phone calls and he got in."

"I can see why you were upset," Marj said, "but to kill him…"

"There's more, Marj. There's more. Okay? Just wait a second."

Peter took a drink of water. His face was flushed, his eyes desperate. He's acting like a guilty man desperately trying to convince someone of his innocence, Marjorie thought, realizing at the same instant that, of course, that was exactly what was going on.

"It didn't end there," Peter continued. "I was still able to convince myself that once Scott moved on to Johns Hopkins Hospital, I would be done with him, and then all this would be over. But then he came at me a third time with something that made me realize he could – and probably would – hold this over me the rest of my life, make financial demands, whatever. And I just couldn't live with that.

"He wanted me to get his girlfriend a residency at Johns Hopkins too."

"Dana Brentano?" Marj asked, remembering that she was the second student killed … *by the man sitting across the table from her, her husband.*

Peter nodded. "It was no longer enough that I perform for him. Now he wanted me to perform for his girlfriend. And she was not nearly the student that Scott was. She would never have gotten a residency at Johns Hopkins on her own.

"How was I supposed to do this? It was one thing when I pulled a few strings and got Scott in. But it was going to look very odd, and not very professional, for me to call *again* a few weeks later and get another student in, especially when administrators there saw her grades. And how about Scott? Was he going to start having me help out all his friends? And how long would this go on? If he was expanding his demands to include his girlfriend, he was capable and willing to hold this over me, to blackmail me, for whatever he wanted anytime into the future, even years from now. Who knows what for? Career advancement, a reference, money, whatever. And I would have to do it.

"And, worse, I started wondering if Dana knew about the blackmail, and about my mistakes on supervision. After all, she would probably have asked him why in the world Dr. Kenyon would help her get a residency that her medical school performance did not merit. And if he had told her, who else he might have told?"

"So you decided to kill her, too?" Marjorie asked, horrified.

"No! I didn't decide to kill anyone except, except for Scott Karakas. But I've explained that, explained why I had to. Marj, there was no other way. We would never have been rid of him.

"This was not easy for me. I never pictured myself doing anything like this." He paused for a second, then lowered his voice and sounded almost reflective. "But then, when I decided there was no other choice, I had to get practical. It's funny how the human mind works, Marj. Once you decide on something, even something you would never have considered before, you turn to the practical implications. How to do it. In this case, how to do it and not get caught."

Marjorie felt herself gulp.

"I knew that as a doctor, I had knowledge of the human body as well as access to substances that others do not. I tried to think of a way I could do this and have it look like Scott died of natural causes, like a heart attack. And I knew that succinylcholine would do the trick, and we kept a supply at the hospital, which I had access to. I could have bought some at the drug store, but that would have seemed odd, since I'm a doctor and it's easily available at the university hospital anyway. It's the kind of substance where no one would think to look for it in the body unless they were predisposed to do so. There are no obvious outward signs of it having been used. So I just waited until his next private meeting with me. You know, if he had stopped blackmailing me right then and there, had no more private meetings with me, maybe I would never have gone through with it, he and his friends would still be alive. But, of course, he didn't.

"So I was ready for him. Our next meeting was in one of the labs. I knew what he wanted to talk with me about. Wanted to see how I was progressing on getting Dana her residency. I told him it would not be easy, especially since I had already got him in. But he didn't want to hear about it, didn't want to know about my problems. He just told me I would have a lot more to worry about if I did not get Dana in. And he was right. After all, he not only had me on improper supervision, now I was guilty of changing student's grades."

"But wait. Didn't he really trap himself at this point? After all, he was blackmailing you. If he exposed you for cheating Medicare, you could expose him for blackmail. You could have told him that, maybe he would have stopped."

Peter shook his head. "He wouldn't. Apparently he had used this before in other classes, with other teachers, from what he told me. I don't think he thought he could fail. And even if I did expose him as a blackmailer, my life

– and yours, too, Marj – would have already been ruined, so what good would it have done me?"

As if my life isn't ruined now, Marjorie thought. And yours too.

"And sure enough, he came in, cocky as ever, telling me to make sure I got Dana her residency. I went along with it. Then he started making small talk, like he would do sometimes, almost as if he was toying with me and wanted to keep up the torment. I waited. I had a syringe with the succinylcholine in my lab coat pocket. He finally turned his back to me and faced the lab sink, playing with the water faucet as he talked. I took the needle out of my pocket, grabbed him from behind in a headlock and stuck him with it in the neck. And I won't deny it, Marj, in a way it felt good, if only for that instant. That would be the last time he would blackmail me! I know it was wrong, but I would be lying if I said I didn't think he had it coming."

"He had it coming?! Peter, you murdered him. Yes, he was a blackmailer. But what you did was not justified. I mean, c'mon, you have to know that."

Peter nodded. "I do know it, and I did then, too. I was just explaining how I felt at that exact moment." He paused again, then looked her right in the eye, almost pleading for help. "Marj, my nerves, they're shot. I haven't been the same ever since, or with what came after."

Marjorie felt nauseous. Her husband, at least the man she thought was her husband, was not really her husband at all. At least not the man she thought she had married and lived with all these years. There was someone else inside, some stranger in a dark place in his soul who had come out and done these terrible things.

Peter continued. "So I just moved his body over to a corner of the room and left it there, like he had a heart attack. I cleaned up and that was it. I suppose it would have been smarter for me to hide it somewhere, maybe it would be days before he was seen to be missing, but I guess I panicked. I certainly didn't expect that Dana Brentano would be the one to find his body, but really, it didn't matter at that point."

"And then you killed Dana because you were afraid she knew about the blackmail and about what Scott had on you?"

"No. Well, yes and no. I did not plan to kill anyone else at all. I was worried that Dana Brentano knew that Scott had come to me to help her get the residency she wanted, but I wasn't sure she knew. I just figured I would wait and see what she did. I took a chance here, Marj, I did, because if she knew about the blackmail, she might well have turned me in to the police. But in the first few days afterwards, at least, she didn't. Whether she would have later, I don't know."

"But you did kill her."

"With a gun, which I got for self-defense, and almost by accident. Well, not quite, I could see it was her."

He's starting to talk crazy now, trying to rationalize his actions, Marjorie thought. After he killed Scott, he must have lost it a little bit.

"When did you buy the gun?" she asked, trying to calm him down.

"I was so paranoid after the Scott thing," Peter said, apparently, Marjorie realized, unable to call the "thing" what it was – *murder.* "I didn't know what was going to happen. When we went to bed at night, Marj, I would lie awake, afraid that at any time the police would come barging in. Anytime there was noise outside, I jumped. I told myself that this was just because of the Scott situation, that it would pass. But I couldn't be sure. So I got myself a gun, paid for it, license and all. It wasn't hard, given I'm a well-respected member of the community. Said I wanted it for home protection, but in truth, I began carrying it around in my coat for my own protection. You see, I don't know if I could have handled jail. I still don't. And if they came for me, I don't know what I would have done with it, but I wanted some options. Including taking my own life so I wouldn't go to jail.

"Anyway, it was a struggle just to get through each day. That evening, I was walking across the park near the hospital. I was just walking, really, to clear my head, as if that was possible. But the walks did seem to help. It was a nice night, peaceful, some students around, but not too many. Anyway, I was walking near the hospital, when I see Dana there. That's odd, I thought. Why is she here? There are no other students around. That's a pretty strange coincidence. But what if it's not a coincidence? What if she knows I killed Scott and she's going to confront me with it? What if she's already told the police and she sees me now, and she's going to run and get them? She might already know about the blackmail. So what was she doing, saving it up to nail me with the murder too? I didn't know, this all didn't make sense, probably doesn't make sense now, but all these thoughts were jumping through my head, and at the same time, I knew I had to prevent anyone from finding out that I had killed Scott. I had to protect myself.

"So, just to feel better – I would do this sometimes – I reached in my coat pocket and put my hand on the gun handle. It made me feel more secure.

"But then, then she sees me and she starts walking toward me. God, what was I going to do? She knew, she had to know. Why else was she there that night? She must have been following me. And now, what was she going to do, turn me in, blackmail me herself? Then she called out my name. But I was *not* going to jail. I took out the gun and fired. I don't really remember if I aimed at her or not. I don't actually remember shooting her. But I got her right in the head. I honestly don't think she knew what was coming."

Marjorie was crying now. Some of the other patrons at the restaurant were looking over. One of the waiters they had come to know, Charles, came by.

"Is everything alright? Is the food prepared to your liking?"

Marjorie couldn't reply, but Peter looked up at the waiter in his best calm, professional voice and said, "The food, as always, is fabulous, Charles. We were just going over a little family history here. One of my wife's parents is very ill and we fear the worst."

"I am so sorry. Please forgive the intrusion." Charles walked away.

"Marj, I am sorry to upset you so."

"You, you've become ill, Peter. Very ill. You must turn yourself in and get professional help."

"No!" He said it with such force that more patrons looked over. Then he leaned over to Marjorie. "I thought I could make you understand, that you would help me. Don't you see I had no choice?"

"No, I don't see that, Peter. You certainly had a choice with Dana. You didn't know why she was walking over to see you. You just panicked and took another human life. And you didn't have to kill Scott, either. No matter what he did, no matter what happened to you, we would have got through it together."

Peter thought for a second. "Maybe you're right. But medicine, helping people, teaching it to students, that's everything to me."

Like you helped Scott and Dana.

"And what about the third murder?"

Peter sighed. "Nicholas Rosen. That's the one I really feel bad about, because he was already being blamed by the police for what I did."

He's differentiating which murders were acceptable? And he's deciding innocence?

"It's especially troubling because, as I say, he was my alibi for a while. The police thought he had killed both Scott and Dana. I didn't know him well, but everything about him said he was a nice guy. Decent, but not a great, student. Why he was friends Scott, I don't know. Maybe he didn't know about this other stuff. But then again, he was close to them. The three of them were thick as thieves. They went out together, they could be seen talking on the quad. And since I figured that Scott had told Dana about the blackmail, there was a good chance he had told Nick too."

"So you planned to kill him also?"

Peter shook his head. "No, I mean, c'mon Marge, I couldn't kill every person Scott knew. Scott was a popular person, even though he didn't deserve to be. I had to draw the line somewhere."

Unbelievable to hear him talk this way.

"Anyway, if Nick was convicted of the killings, I would have been off the hook."

"You would have been willing to let an innocent man go to jail for you."

"I considered letting that happen, but came to the conclusion that it wouldn't be moral. My conscience wouldn't let me. Having to picture him spending year after year in a jail cell, where who knows what might happen to him, no one who is innocent deserves that. So I had another idea. If he was found to have committed suicide while he was the prime suspect, chances were the police would have figured he killed himself to prevent going to jail. It would have been all over for me, and so I decided to do it."

"It wasn't moral to send him to jail, but you were okay killing him."

"Marj, at this point, I had already killed two people. What more could they do to me? And it's a funny thing about killing someone, Marj. It's like anything else, although you won't like to hear this. It gets a little easier each time."

Marjorie felt her entire body freeze. Where was her beloved Peter, the man she had married? How she wanted him here, to help her and hold her through this! But all she saw now was the crazed man who looked like her husband, but wasn't.

"Did you think Nicholas would agree with your logic? Maybe he would have preferred to live, even if it meant going to jail. You justified the entire thing based on your needs."

"Maybe so, Marj," Peter said, getting angry, "but given the situation I was in, I think that was understandable."

"Peter, you are sitting here arguing about this with me like you are arguing about politics or some university policy, but you killed three people!"

Peter grew quiet at this, then spoke softly. "I know, I know. Maybe I do need professional help. But where would I get it? Any good professional psychiatrist would feel obligated to try and talk me into turning myself in, and I just can't do that. Won't do that."

"What good did you think it would be to tell me? What did you think I was going to say?"

"I don't know. But you are my wife, Marj. For better or for worse. That's what we promised each other. We've had a good marriage, Marj, and I do love you. And I know you love me too. I just had to tell someone. It was too big a secret to keep this long." He paused. "You're not going to turn me in, are you?"

Marj froze. She really didn't know what she should do, or what she would do. Yes, they had made marriage vows to support each other for better or worse, and these were sacred to her. But did that include murder, in fact, three murders? Funny, she thought, but *I've never worried about Peter the way some wives worry about their husbands.* There had never been a doubt in her mind that he was anything but faithful, or that he might drink or gamble to excess. And he had been good to her. *The only problem is that it turns out he's a serial killer.* What was going to happen now? She didn't know. Could this just continue? Was it possible that she could help him get away with this, that the crime would remain unsolved? Could she live with a man like this? Should she stay with him a short while, then get a divorce?

More importantly, and she hated to admit this to herself about a man she had felt so safe with all their married life, but a bit of doubt about her own safety had begun to creep into her thoughts. What would he do if she didn't answer his question by saying, "No, Peter, you're my husband, of course I won't turn you in." Would he, would it be possible that he might kill her? Part of her said that no, this would never happen. But another part knew that what had prompted him to kill both Dana and Nick was the fear that they knew about the improper medical supervision and the resulting blackmail, and he had killed them so he would not be a suspect. Was a man like that willing to live the rest of his life with someone else who knew the truth? Especially if she left him one day? The truth was, she knew that there was no way she could stay with him long term, not anymore. He's a murderer. And any remaining respect she had for him would be lost if he did not turn himself in. But just now, she had her own safety to think about.

"No, Peter, of course I will not turn you in."

She watched his body relax as she said this.

"Thank you, Marj," he said. "Listen, once this is over, we can rebuild our life together. I was thinking that after some brief time back in the States, we might move here, to Vienna, and just start fresh."

"Peter, I said I was not going to turn you in, and I won't. But I do think you should turn yourself in."

"I told you that's out of the question."

"You need to reconsider it. Look at how things have been for you these past weeks. Can you go on like this? You'll have a nervous breakdown. And if you do turn yourself in, you can contact an attorney first, do it on your own terms. Maybe they can cite a mental breakdown in your case and you can even avoid jail."

"And what about my reputation, my career? What will Lyle and Jennifer and Arun think about me?"

She had to get him back to reality. "Peter, c'mon, we're way past those concerns. You're not going to have peace of mind until you do the right thing. And you know now that I will support you all the way."

Peter shook his head. "I was thinking about this. Do you know how many unsolved murders occur every day in the United States? In the world? The murderers never get caught. Sure, some of them are criminal types who think nothing of it. But others are domestic disputes, business killings, whatever. Those perpetrators probably go through months of anguish, just like I am, but one day it's over. They put it behind them and move on. There have been books and movies about this very thing."

"And you think you can do that?"

"I don't know, but it's better than the alternative."

"And what if the police arrest someone else, like they were going to do with Nick Rosen, and that person gets convicted and sent to jail for your crimes?"

Peter didn't respond at first, then said, "I think that at this point, I've done so much to stay out of jail, committed murder, Marj, that it's pretty clear I would let that person take the rap. I hope that doesn't happen, especially if it's someone I know, like Lyle, but I am determined to stay out of jail. And more that that, Marj, all this happened because of the goddamned U.S. government and the OIG, with its overzealous investigations. None of this would have happened if the rules had allowed me to exercise proper medical judgment without second guessing. They should send Charlotte Westbrook to jail for ruining doctors' lives and driving them to this point, not me."

45

Lewis was back on the case. Not one of the Medicare fraud cases he preferred, but back on the murders. And, of course, at Charlotte's urging. She was convinced that Arun was not the killer and did not want to see the man's name besmirched any more than it already had been. The *Post* and other media were already full of speculation linking the late university hospital administrator to the murders of the three students, and Lewis wasn't sure they were wrong. But Charlotte had a feeling about Arun, a feeling that Lewis didn't understand. But he had learned over the years to respect her feelings.

So now he was studying something he had never really expected to study: chemicals that could be used to kill. In this particular case, succinylcholine, the substance used to kill Scott Karakas and Nicholas Rosen. Fascinating substance, he thought, as he read more about it. Commonly used in hospitals, especially before anesthesia, as a muscle relaxant. Doctors like it because it is both quick acting and has the shortest duration time. Usually given intravenously, although it can be injected. One danger with the drug, though, is that it can relax a muscle to the point of paralysis, which can cause respiratory distress, cardiac arrest, or both. And if it is given intentionally, as a murder or suicide device, at larger than normal doses, it can act very quickly. If the subject it is being administered to someone who is conscious, it can also cause what the book Lewis was reading called "psychological distress." No telling if Scott

Karakas or Nick Rosen experienced this, Lewis realized, feeling some horror at what they must have went through if they had. And it was in ample supply not only at medical institutions, particularly hospitals, but also at drug stores.

But to use it as a weapon, that would take someone who was familiar with the drug and how to administer it. The question at James Buchanan was, how would Lewis find out which of the many doctors and nurses who had used succinylcholine with patients had also done so to kill two people?

He was in the James Buchanan University Hospital library now, sitting at one of computer terminals, students around him at other terminals or at tables, all deep into their work. On the screen in front of Lewis was the university hospital's pharmaceutical registry, basically a log showing which doctors and others signed for the drugs and other medical substances they took from the university hospital's supply. That way the hospital could keep track of what was used and know how much and when to re-order.

Lewis scrolled down the pages dated the week before the murder. There were names he recognized and many he did not. And he certainly did not recognize the names of many of the items that were checked out, except for one: aspirin. But he knew what he was looking for: succinylcholine, who had checked it out and when.

And he found it. Sure enough, the week before the first killing, Dr. Lyle Steadman had taken one vial of it. And he was the only person on staff to have done so.

He went back a week further. Dr. Peter Kenyon had taken a vial, and so had two other doctors. There was nothing to be made of this. Without evidence of why they had taken out a vial, there was no reason to suspect any of them of improper conduct. Each doctor could be interviewed as to why, of course, and the cases they were working on examined to see if the substance indeed had been used, but even that wouldn't tell much. A doctor might use the chemical for legitimate reasons that would justify his or her taking it out, and then still use whatever was left over in the bottle to commit murder. Only if a doctor withdrew a vial and had no patients needing it at all might there be legitimate questions raised, but even then there might be a good medical explanation. It might be used as part of a research project, for instance. Lewis was wondering just what good this search might do him.

He went back a few more weeks, now used to seeing the name of the drug and the names of the personnel. Dr. Jennifer Capaldi made her first appearance in the registry for the drug, and there was another one for Dr. Kenyon. Then another doctor, then Dr. Steadman again, then Dr. Kenyon, another Dr. Kenyon, a nurse, then Dr. Kenyon.

Dr. Kenyon, Lewis noticed, took out more of the drug than almost anyone listed in the registry. In fact, over the six-week period preceding the first murder, he had checked out six vials, whereas the most anyone else had checked out vials was twice. Had his cases justified taking out such a quantity? Maybe, but given that it was his understanding that an entire vial was usually not used each time, that seemed hard to believe. Unless the vial was thrown out each time it was opened, regardless of how much was left in the bottle. But even so, Lewis thought, six times was a lot in relation to what the other doctors took out.

He made a mental note to check Dr. Kenyon's case file, with the help of someone who knew how to read medical documentation, to determine just what cases he had been working on that required so much of the drug.

Of course, Lewis thought, if succinylcholine is available at drug stores and Dr. Kenyon wanted to hide the fact that he was taking so much, why would he bother taking it out of the hospital pharmacy? But, as if to answer his own question, a number of reasons occurred to him: maybe Dr. Kenyon thought he could get away with it better if he used the hospital supply, maybe he thought it might look odd for a doctor to buy it at a pharmacy when the pharmacist would most likely know it was free at the hospital. Maybe Dr. Kenyon even thought he was saving money by not going to the pharmacy.

The easiest way to find out, of course, would be to ask the good doctor. But Lewis remembered that the Kenyons were out of the country, in Vienna on vacation. That also raised suspicions. Still, doctors were entitled to take vacations. It might mean nothing.

46

T hen there was the question of the gun.

It was one of the first items that came up in Petrelli's meeting with Charlotte and Lewis in Charlotte's office. Charlotte had thought it a good idea for the three of them to get together and compare notes. She also wanted to push Petrelli to consider possibilities other than Arun being the murderer.

"I'm not saying the man isn't good at his job, but he does seem to go for the easy answers a bit too often," she told Lewis prior to Petrelli's arrival.

"And you are basing this on how many years in police work compared to his?" Lewis asked.

Charlotte dismissed the point with a wave of her hand. "Let's look at his track record here, Lewis. First he jumps to conclusions on Nicholas Rosen, making his life a miserable hell. Only Mr. Rosen's murder gets him off the scent. I will say that Petrelli has a conscience. At least he had the good grace to feel guilty about it afterwards."

"I thought that the two of you were hitting it off now, that you liked him."

"I don't *dislike* him. But I think his work is a little less thorough than it needs to be. And this planting of items in the press that 'Sources tied to the police department say that Chamroeun Arun may well have been the murderer,' just rubs me the wrong way, especially since there is no real proof that it was Arun."

"But you yourself have no proof that it *wasn't* Arun. And you clearly liked the man. Aren't you letting your personal feelings inform your judgment here?"

Charlotte shrugged. "In my opinion that I don't think Arun was the murderer, yes, I am letting my own perception of the man influence my thought. But that is not my point. I am saying that Petrelli has the burden of proof here, and before he starts letting it be known that Arun was the likely killer, he had better have some evidence to back it up. And I don't see any. The right thing to do would simply to say that the case is still open, which, in my view, it certainly is, as what you found about the succinylcholine and Dr. Peter Kenyon's use of it indicates."

Shortly thereafter Petrelli arrived, wearing a light black raincoat over his sports jacket. He looked around Charlotte's office. "First time I've been here," he said to her and Lewis. "Nicer than mine."

Charlotte smiled thinly. Compared to the comments about her surroundings that she would sometimes receive from senior private practice attorneys, who frequently had much more spacious offices, she would usually have been pleased to hear that someone actually liked her own. But she had more important things on her mind now.

"Have a seat, detective," she said, motioning to a chair in front of her desk. Lewis moved from the couch, where he had been sitting, to a second chair near the desk.

"I take it we are here to bring some closure to this entire case and our work together on it," Petrelli said. "I have to admit, Charlotte, I was a bit reluctant when you first approached me, but it seems to have worked out—"

"That's why I asked you here, Al," Charlotte said, leaning forward in her chair. "As far as I can tell, we don't know that Arun was the murderer. In fact, Lewis and I have some reason to suspect that the killer may still be at large."

Petrelli seemed a bit flustered. "I realize that we have no ironclad proof that it was Chamroeun, but it is unlikely that we will find it."

Lewis showed Petrelli the notes he had taken from the university hospital registry. "Didn't your department think to do this?" he asked.

Slightly taken aback, Petrelli said, "In fact, we did have some officers check the registry, but all they found was a bunch of doctors who took succinylcholine out. They interviewed most of them, but there was always a legitimate reason. That includes Dr. Kenyon, I believe."

"Any doctor can come up with a legitimate reason. But did they note the pattern to Dr. Kenyon's signing of the drug out?"

"Well, no, I can't say that they did," Petrelli said, somewhat sheepishly, Lewis thought. "That was a mistake, they should have. But by itself it does not mean that it was Kenyon and not Chamroeun who committed the murders. Chamroeun was guilty of another crime, as you well know, Charlotte," he said, turning his attention back to her. "Medicare fraud."

"Indeed he was," Charlotte said. "But that does not mean he was a murderer as well."

"Look, we should have caught the pattern in the succinylcholine, I will give you that. But I don't see what else we can do. We checked area gun shops, trying to see if we could get a lead on who may have purchased the gun that was used to kill Dana Brentano. We checked every shop in a 50-mile radius around D.C. That includes the home areas of every doctor and staff member who works at James Buchanan. The result? Nothing. No one employed at James

Buchanan purchased any gun, let alone the one that was used to kill Miss Brentano."

Charlotte nodded. "Okay, very good. But—"

"You know, Charlotte, I have appreciated your help on the case so far, but the fact that you are now criticizing my police work does not sit especially well with me. You are an amateur at this side of law enforcement, after all."

Charlotte nodded. "Yes, detective, admittedly, I am. But sometimes even amateurs may find something, as Lewis did with the university hospital pharmacy. Just bear with me a few moments longer, alright?"

Petrelli grunted his assent. Since they had made a point with Dr. Kenyon's pattern of signing out the drug used to commit the murders, what else could he do?

"If we continue with the thread of thought that it might have been Peter Kenyon who was the killer, then a key would be finding out if he in particular purchased a gun recently, would it not?"

"Certainly, but as I told you, we already checked every—"

"—gun shop in a 50-mile radius of D.C., I know. But if we focus in on a particular suspect, detective, wouldn't it be wise to check gun shops outside of the 50-mile radius, particularly in areas the suspect might be familiar with?"

Petrelli nodded. "Yes, that would make sense. But it would have to be limited to places he would visit by car, as he could never get a firearm on a plane today." He paused, thoughtful for a second. "I suppose that could be the case." He looked up at Charlotte. "Do you know of such a place?"

Charlotte looked at Lewis.

"Dr. Kenyon is from Richmond, Virginia," Lewis said. "He grew up there. And he still has family and friends there, because we are told that he visits fairly often."

"I would say a check of gun shops in the Richmond area, at least, is in order, wouldn't you, detective, as well as any other areas that you find he may have frequented?" Charlotte asked.

Petrelli nodded, seeming somewhat chastised. "I am not convinced, but you have a point. And we do want to be thorough."

"You certainly wouldn't want the real murderer still at large," Lewis said.

"Of course, there is one more thing," Charlotte said. "By itself, it wouldn't mean much. After all, lots of doctors take vacations. Another doctor from James Buchanan is in Ireland right now. However, that doctor did not withdraw a great deal of succinylcholine from the university hospital pharmacy. Dr. Kenyon, we know, did. And he's been in Vienna for the past month."

47

C harlotte spent the next few days on the road, visiting both Dana's and Nick's parents, friends and other acquaintances. Her experience in Pennsylvania with Scott's parents, Gregory Betorin and Carrie Pankow had proved so illuminating that she couldn't help but think that visits to the hometowns of the other two victims might also tell her something.

Unfortunately, they didn't. Dana's elderly parents, Roger and Barbara, who lived in Delaware, were not much help. Dana found Roger to be especially quiet, especially for someone who used to sell real estate for a living. His daughter's death had apparently taken a lot out of him. And Dana's mom was apparently turning to religion for solace. She told Charlotte that she was going to church regularly now.

"We didn't go much before," she said. "Maybe if we had ..."

"Stop it, Barbara," her husband said. "That had nothing to do with ... Dana's death."

The two just sat there after he uttered the words. Charlotte realized these two people would never again be the same.

"I am so sorry. It must be a blessing, though, that you still have two sons, both doing quite well."

"Yes, yes, they are," Barbara said, and went on at some length – too long, Charlotte thought – to talk about her sons' achievements, as her husband nodded.

Charlotte explained to them that she was working with the police to investigate the murder and was wondering if there were any friends of Dana's she might visit, or any personal effects she might look at. Dana's mother gave her the name of one old boyfriend and some of her girlfriends. As for Dana's things, they were still in her rented apartment near the university campus.

"We weren't in a hurry to get down there," her mother said.

"And I had made sure the rent was paid through the semester end," said Dana's father, "so we have some time to go down there and clean out the room later. Besides, her roommate, Cecilia, is still there. But feel free to go over if you think it might make a difference."

Nicholas Rosen's parents lived in an apartment in Brooklyn, New York. Charlotte thought she had seen all the suffering she could with the other parents, but she was wrong. The Rosens' lives were over. Nick was their only child, so, unlike the Karakas and the Brentanos, they had no other children to live for. Nick's father, Morris, seemed shriveled and defeated, more so than one would expect for a man in his 60s. A former New York City civil servant in the city's transportation office, he took early retirement some years ago and had spent most of his days reading the newspaper, watching television and talking about his son to anyone willing to listen. There would be no more of those conversations. Nick's mother, Sheila, was about the same age as her husband. She would lean her head against his shoulders, her hands wrapped around his arms, as Charlotte talked to them. Like Dana's parents, they passed on the names of friends. They didn't have any girlfriends' names to pass on because, as far as they knew, Nick had not had any in high school and he didn't tell them much about his social life at college.

"He probably felt we would pepper him with questions," his father said, "and you know, he was probably right. We would have."

Nick's mother showed him her son's room, where all his personal effects from college had been moved, and left Charlotte alone to study them. Charlotte didn't know where to begin, but opened his dresser drawers, looked at the various knickknacks and boxes on his desk, went through some of the still unpacked boxes from college, and looked in his closet. She didn't expect to find anything, and she didn't. She thanked Nick's parents and then left, feeling somewhat guilty at her relief at leaving the Rosen apartment. But the sense of grief had been overwhelming.

The next day she visited Dana's apartment off campus, and introduced herself to Dana's roommate, Cecilia, an average-looking girl with shoulder-length brown hair and glasses with brown frames that were too small for her face. Cecilia asked for identification and, after seeing it, said that, yes, Dana's parents had called to say that Charlotte might be stopping by, but she had to leave for class. She was in law school and could not afford to miss anything. Charlotte nodded. She remembered law school very well.

"Would you mind if I stayed and looked around while you were gone? I could lock up for you."

Cecilia hesitated. "I suppose it's alright. I did see your ID. Just turn the lock on the inside of the door before you leave and the door will automatically lock behind you." She showed Charlotte where Dana's bedroom was.

"I'm going to miss her. She was a good roommate," Cecilia said, choking up a little. "Her parents said that, since the rent is paid up, I could just stay here without a new roommate for the rest of the semester, which was nice. But," she added, looking at Dana's things inside the room, "I do wish they would come and pick up her stuff. To be honest, given that Dana is dead, it's kind of creepy to have everything here."

Cecilia left and Charlotte stepped into Dana's room, going through the same routine as she had in Nick's room. Only this time, since nothing had been packed to ship, everything was exactly the way Dana had last used it. Charlotte opened some desk drawers, looked in the closet, even glanced at a magazine Dana must have been reading and had left on the bed. She walked over to her dresser and admired a wood and glass jewelry box resting on top. Now that is pretty, she thought. She opened the top and, for a second, froze. She reached into the box and took something out, holding it up to study, with just one question on her mind.

What would Dana Brentano be doing with a pair of handcuffs?

48

Scott Karakas walked through the quad toward the university hospital, going over just what he would say. It was about 4:00 p.m., with mid-November daylight still available, and he knew Dr. Kenyon's schedule well enough to know that he would find him in his office.

This was the kind of meeting Scott hated. But he had done it before, more than once, and he knew that the key to a successful outcome was for Dr. Kenyon to believe that Scott relished these confrontations. That was part of the polish, part of the fear factor that worked. It had worked back in high school the first time he had used it, with Del Phinney, and it had worked several times since. The key, he reminded himself, was to be confident, almost brazen, with a touch of arrogance; as well as fearless and, most importantly, to appear to be enjoying himself so much that the person he was talking to would fear that he might just do what he was threatening.

This time was different, though. The last meeting had been to help himself. This time he was doing it for someone else's benefit. But since the person was Dana, well, he thought, it's worth it.

Just the thought of Dana took his mind off what he was about to do and back to their many times together. The relationship had begun like so many of the others he had had over the years. Girls always seemed to been drawn to him, he knew that even back in middle school and, as the years went by, he had learned how to build on it through his smile, charm, and saying just the right thing so they would think that, underneath it all, maybe he cared a little, that all their efforts with him were not just about the physical. But the truth was, in the overwhelming number of relationships, he hadn't really cared. To Scott, the sexual side of the relationship was what it was all about. It gave him not only a physical thrill, but peace of mind, peace that he craved, peace from the pressure of having to achieve, achieve at all costs, to continue to meet his father's expectations. It was the best escape he knew. There was nothing else like it.

When he first met Dana, she seemed like so many of the other girls he had known. She was pretty and sweet and would do anything to please him. She loved holding onto his arm as they walked through the campus and acting the girlfriend. And he liked the cache this gave him with the other guys on campus, several of whom, he knew, also had their eyes on Dana. And their trysts together, which had started as rather routine sex, soon became more adventurous, as they pushed the limits and began doing it not just in their rooms, but at the hospital itself, in different rooms, the lab, patient beds. On his rating scale of sexual partners, Dana was moving up the ladder.

Another factor began entering into the picture, however, one that caused Scott some disquiet. He found that he was starting to care about Dana, that he wanted to spend time with her, not just having sex, but simply being together. He wouldn't say he had fallen in love with her exactly, but he found himself more at peace when he was with her, even when they hung out with Nick or other friends, than when he was by himself. The funny thing was, as he got to know her better, the sex seemed to get better too. This was new for Scott. Was it because they had developed a real relationship? Scott thought that might be part of it, but there was something else, too. Perhaps the relationship was changing Dana, allowing her to open up in ways she had never done before, because she was getting more passionate with each encounter, as if she were letting go of inhibitions that she had long held her back.

Scott entered the hospital and headed up the stairs to Dr. Kenyon's office. He fought back the twinge of nervousness he always felt at such times. "Confident, arrogant and fearless, just enough to scare the shit out of him," he reminded himself.

Peter was at his desk, head down in some papers, when Scott lightly tapped his knuckles on the open door. Peter looked up with an open smile that quickly faded when he saw who it was.

"Got a moment for me, Dr. Kenyon?" Scott asked.

"What do you want, Mr. Karakas?" Peter replied, with a clear look of disdain. "I believe I took care of your last request. There is nothing left for me to do."

Scott grinned and sauntered into the small, cramped office. "Don't sell yourself short, Peter," he said. "There's always something new around the corner."

Peter scowled at Scott's use of his first name. "I've done all I can for you, Karakas. You're going to be a resident at Johns Hopkins. You should be ashamed of yourself, and I should be, too. You've forced me to act against my principles, and I can't say I think much of either of us. Now why don't you say what you came to say and then get out?"

"That's your whole problem, Peter. You're too principled. Did you ever think how much easier life would be if you just let them go a little?"

"Get on it with it. What is it you want now?"

Scott stopped smiling, looking Peter dead in the eye. "I want you to make sure that Dana Brentano also gets a residency at Johns Hopkins next year."

Peter stared at him, as if to say he could not believe Scott's nerve. "You must be joking. I will do no such thing."

"C'mon, Peter, you know what I'm going to say. Don't make me go through the whole thing all over again."

"Dana Brentano? Just because she's your girlfriend? What's next, you'll start collecting fees from all your friends so you can come to me and get them into Johns Hopkins too? Besides, I don't have that much clout over there. I was able to get one person in, okay. But it's going to look a little odd to them if I call back with another request, especially considering that Dana is essentially a B student. Forget it, it's not going to happen."

"Like I said, you don't want to be saying that, *Doctor* Kenyon." Scott had turned menacing, his false smile gone. "Although just what kind of doctor you'll be or where you'll be working – or even *if* you'll be working – after it gets out that you've been ripping the taxpayers off over the past few years ... Well, that's your choice."

"A man has his limits, Karakas. I'm no exception."

Scott shrugged. "Alright then, Doctor. I must say, I respect your principles." He turned and headed out the door. Peter watched him leave, then got up from his chair and walk down the hallway. He knew what he had to do. *Damn it*, he thought, I have no choice.

"Scott, wait, come back," he said. "Maybe we can talk about it."

Scott grinned. Once again, he had him. Like a mouse in a trap. But as Scott closed the office door behind them, he saw the anguish in Peter's face and, just for an instant, felt bad about what he was doing. He wiped those thoughts away quickly. He knew what his Dad would have done, and felt compelled to do the same. Wasn't that the Karakas motto? Get ahead, by fair means if possible. But if not, by whatever means necessary. And do it smart.

Dana was waiting back in her apartment. She heard the doorbell and opened the door. Scott was there, jubilant.

"The machinery is in place. It's just a matter of time," he said, grabbing her in his arms and lifting her off the ground, kicking the door shut behind him, and spinning her around.

"Are you sure?" she asked. "I was a little concerned about how Dr. Kenyon would react. Were there any problems?"

"It may take some time. After all, he did just get me in, so he'll have to find a way to get you into Johns Hopkins too, without it looking too suspicious. But he'll fine a way. I made sure he will." Scott grinned. "You don't have to worry about a thing. He was like a scared little rabbit."

Dana loved it. Here was Scott, the man who could do anything, and now she had gotten his to do this for her. And all because of how their relationship had evolved in the past few weeks. She watched as Scott took off his shirt, revealing the well-honed torso she loved. She began to take her ownclothes off as well, and they were both down to nothing in no time at all. Cecilia was staying at her boyfriend's that evening, so they had the whole apartment to themselves.

"Get on the bed," Dana commanded.

Scott obeyed. His excitement was at fever pitch, both from his renewed conquest of Peter and being with Dana, and he was already erect. Dana quickly jumped on top of him, kissing his face and neck. Then she began the new routine they had both found themselves enjoying, much to their surprise. Dana grabbed the handcuffs that she had set on her nightstand and fastened Scott's hands above him to the metal railing of her bed. Then she straddled him. Scott felt himself entering her. She was in charge and he loved it. He could let go, let go of all the responsibility and pressure and just put himself under her control. It was the greatest peace he ever new. And for Dana, the power was an aphrodisiac beyond compare. Here she was in charge, and in charge of someone who everyone else thought of as a take-charge guy. No one was going to tell her what to do with her life, what kind of career to have, what kind of boyfriends to see, how she should behave with those boyfriends. Now, she was the one who was in control.

Then she did again what she had done for the first time a few nights ago, when she had first ventured the idea of Scott seeking an A for her from Dr. Kenyon. As they were thrusting back and forth, she put her hands around Scott's throat and began to gently restrict his air flow.

"Are you going to do whatever I ask from now on?" Dana asked. "Even if it means going back and doing more of what you did today?"

"Yes, yes, you know I will. I will do anything for you, Dana. Anything."

Dana smiled. Her conquest of him was complete.

Scott lay on the bed with Dana on top of him, delirious in half-conscious pleasure.

An hour later, Scott and Dana met Nick at the Improper Fraction. Nick was waiting for them in one of the booths.

"You two certainly look happy," Nick said.

Dana wrapped her hands around Scott's arm and leaned her head against him. "Scott takes good care of me."

Scott just grinned. Nick smiled back. He wished he had Scott's way with girls and that he had a girl as sweet as Dana. He sensed that Dana caught his mood because she put her hand on his sympathetically.

"How did your evening go with that girl you went out with the other night?"

Nick shook his head. "There's nothing there. Like all the others, a disaster."

"Nick, this is the fourth girl you've said this about," Scott said. "Do you think that maybe you're bringing some pessimism to these things that are turning them off?"

Nick shrugged. "Listen, I will find somebody. I'm just a little choosy, that's all."

"Whoever gets you, Nick, will be a lucky girl," Dana said. "I'd go out with you, but I've got Scott."

"Yeah, right," said Nick. Dana had said this to him before, but he knew it was only because it would never happen. He liked the attention, anyway. "I don't think Scott would appreciate that very much."

"I don't know, Nick," Scott said. "There are some other girls I've seen that have caught me eye ..."

"Careful, sweetheart," Dana said, giving him a warning look and clutching his arm just a little tighter.

"Guess I'd better behave," Scott said to Nick, as all three of them laughed. "Anyway, onward and upward. I was just thinking. Do you realize that next year we'll be practicing medicine?"

"That's right," said Dana. "We'll be residents. No more classes. Hard to believe. After all, we've been in school for more than 20 years."

"If you count kindergarten," Nick put in.

The three friends laughed. "I propose a toast," Scott said, raising his beer mug. "To an illustrious future for the three doctors we will shortly become."

"I'll drink to that," said Dana.

Nick watched as the three glasses clink together, then downed his beer.

49

Marjorie woke early. The early May dim morning light streaming through the hotel window told her it was probably around 5 a.m. She had been waking early every morning since Peter's confession earlier that week. Oddly enough, the confession seemed to have done Peter good, while at the same time making Marjorie a nervous wreck. Peter sometimes slept the whole night through now, whereas before his confession to her, Marjorie was aware of him getting up several times. She had thought perhaps it was the change in locale or the hotel bed. Now, she knew better.

It is an unfortunate fact of married live that many men unload their problems on their wives before they go sleep, or in the middle of the night. The result invariably is that the husbands sleep better, but the wives have problems sleeping. Now, even when confessing a murder, the effect was still the same: Peter was sleeping more soundly, and Marjorie was the one waking up.

And with good reason. She no longer knew the man she was sleeping next to. He was still Peter Kenyon, her husband of many years, the man she had shared intimacies and history with. But he was also now a stranger, a man who was no longer himself, who had seemingly cracked under pressure, to do horrible things and murder three people. And now he wanted their lives to go on like normal. Was that even possible? Could she do that? Would time diminish what he had done and, even if their marriage was never quite the same, allow it to continue? Did she even want to continue the marriage and live her live with a confessed murderer? What would that say about her?

And, although she didn't want to admit it to herself, other thoughts had begun crossing her mind. Peter still loved her, she was sure, but his current calmness must be only a fraction of an inch thick, masking a sea of anxiety and panic. She asked herself the question she didn't want to ask, but which kept coming to the forefront of her mind: Could Peter kill her? Would he kill her, given his track record and his desperation? She wanted to believe that he wouldn't, that the three killings he had committed were unique situations, but the truth was, she wasn't sure.

And another thought kept her awake. Should she turn her husband in? After all, here was a three-time murderer that half the eastern seaboard of the United States was now looking for. Yet her marriage vows, their years together, the fact that, despite it all, she still loved him, were stopping her from doing so. She thought about it, thought that Peter had become sick and needed help. Maybe if she turned him in it would actually be the most loving thing she could do. On the other hand, given the public mood and the press back home, not to mention the murders themselves, they might just lock Peter away for life or execute him. Those were thoughts she didn't want to dwell on. The choices she faced were bewildering, as she wrestled among questions about his well-being, her own safety, justice and more. But one question overrode all: *What is my duty as his wife?*

Peter himself was outwardly almost cheerful, as if his confession and the murders themselves had never happened. Each day he asked what museums or sights they should see, seemingly not taking notice of his wife's nervousness and obvious lack of comfort. So they had spent the past few days as they had before the confession, sightseeing. They visited one of the houses Mozart had lived in, went to the Albertina and other museums, and simply walked Vienna's streets. It would be so easy, Marjorie thought, to simply make believe they were just another couple on vacation and that the confession had never happened.

Except that it had.

The farce even continued to the point of his making love with her last night. It had been a week, but it might as well have been a century. The man who cuddled up next to her with his usual intimacies was no longer the same man, at least not in her mind. She shuddered when she realized that he had already been a murderer during the many previous times they had made love.

But now she knew. And when he approached her last night, she had let him go through with the act. But she had found it impossible to respond, even to hold him.

"What do you want to do today?" Peter asked, awake now and looking at the clock. "If we have a quick breakfast, we can get to the military museum. They have the actual bloody tunic there that Archduke Franz Ferdinand was assassinated in, you know, that started the First World War."

"No, that's ... let's do something else," Marjorie suggested, although nothing really came to mind. She just wanted all this to be over.

"How about the Hofburg? Aside from seeing the palace itself, you know I've always wanted to see the Lipizzaner horses. They put on a show there twice a day. Beautiful animals."

"Okay, that sounds better."

"It's a deal, then. Ready for some breakfast?" The bonhomie was so strained that Marjorie wondered how Peter could even keep it up. But then she realized: It was all that was holding him together. The alternative for him was worse. But she found it just too difficult to begin the day as if they were a normal couple.

"Why don't you go down first and I'll catch up with you later? I still have to straighten myself up."

"You look great, Marj."

"No, I'm not happy with my hair. You go down, Peter. I'll join you in about 15 minutes."

Peter shrugged. "Okay. I'll pick up an *International Herald Tribune* and read it."

Marjorie headed into the bathroom. She could hear Peter moving about the room, then heard the door to the hotel room close. She listened to his footsteps as he walked down the hall toward the elevator bank. Alone at last, she came out of the bathroom and sat on the bed, just trying to relax and collect her thoughts during one of the few times in the past few days when she was able to be herself and not on guard.

She was sitting there about five minutes when there was a knock on the door. She looked through the door's spyhole to see four people, three men and one woman, standing in the hallway. One of the men was wearing what appeared to be an Austrian uniform of some kind.

She opened the door slightly.

"Mrs. Kenyon?" asked the man in the Austrian uniform. He was a short, thin man of about 50, with thinning blonde hair combed straight back on his head. He stood ramrod straight and had the bearing of someone on official business. "I am Chief Inspector Klaus Tyroler of the Austrian Federal Police. May we have a few moments of your time?"

Marjorie showed them in. The other two men were quite different in appearance. One was short and middle-aged, with silver hair and a mustache, and glasses held around his neck by a chain. The other was large, heavyset, and in an ill-fitting sports jacket. But it was the face of the tall, thin, angular woman that caught Marjorie's eye. She knew her from somewhere.

"Mrs. Kenyon, allow me to introduce Inspector General Charlotte Westbrook of the U.S. Department of Health and Human Services; Chief Counsel Lewis Sullivan of her office; and Detective Alphonse Petrelli, Jr. of the District of Columbia police force."

Marjorie took a step back. It was all over. They were here, and there could be only one reason. They had come to arrest Peter.

"I … I've seen both your photos before, in the newspaper," she said to Charlotte and Petrelli.

"Mrs. Kenyon, what we have to say may be difficult for you to hear …" Charlotte began, but Petrelli interrupted.

"Is your husband here, ma'am?"

"No, no, he's downstairs having breakfast. I'm supposed to go down and meet him any time now."

The two police officers exchanged looks and breathed what seemed to be sighs of relief.

"Alright, that will give us some time," Petrelli said. "Mrs. Kenyon, do you have any idea why we are here?"

Marjorie walked over and sat down on a chair in the room. She said nothing, which to her visitors, said a lot.

"I think maybe you do, ma'am," Petrelli continued, "and I appreciate the difficult spot you are in, but I must tell you the truth: We are here to arrest your husband for the murders of Scott Karakas, Dana Brentano and Nicholas Rosen. We also have a warrant from the Austrian government to search this hotel room and seize anything that might relate to the crimes."

"What makes you think my husband would do such a thing?" she asked. "He's a very prominent member of the medical community."

Petrelli and Tyroler began searching the room. Charlotte sat next to Marjorie.

"I know this must be terribly difficult for you," Charlotte said. "I can only imagine what your life has been like."

Marjorie turned and glared at Charlotte. "You … and you too," she said, looking at Lewis. "You're responsible for all this. Going after good doctors, good men and women who are trying to save lives. Second-guessing their medical decisions. You drove Peter to this! He was a good man before you started investigating the hospital, Miss Westbrook, a good man."

Lewis opened his mouth, probably to retort. Charlotte held up her hand to stop him.

"Whatever you think of me, Mrs. Kenyon, I want you to know that we are here to help you. You clearly know something, and if you know that your husband is the murderer, I can only imagine what you are going through. Let us help you."

"You don't know that he was the one who did it," Marjorie said. "That's why you're here. To question him and hope that he says something incriminating. Otherwise you just would have had him extradited."

"Here's what we know," Lewis said. "Two of the victims were killed with succinylcholine, and your husband checked out larger quantities of that drug than any other doctor from the university hospital pharmacy, more than he usually signed out, and he did it a few weeks before the first killing. The second victim, Miss Brentano, was killed with a gun. The police checked all the gun shops in the D.C. area to see if your husband had recently purchased one, Mrs. Kenyon, and apparently he had not."

"Alright, then."

"But then," Lewis continued, "We thought to check the gunshops near his hometown. Richmond, Virginia, isn't it? And they found the shop where he purchased the gun, a Smith & Wesson Model 10, the same make that fired the bullets that killed Dana Brentano."

"Which doesn't mean he killed her. There are probably thousands of those guns in existence."

"Which is why we searched your house and his office while you've been gone. We found the gun, the very one that the police department's ballistics test showed to be the murder weapon, in his nightstand drawer. As for extraditing him, you are correct, we could have done so, but given the unusual involvement of the Inspector General and myself in working with the police department in this case…"

"You wanted to be here personally for the kill," Marjorie said.

"We wanted to speak with him directly, and convinced the police department to go along with our wishes, which they did, given we were fairly instrumental in preventing a deceased innocent man whom I believe you knew – Chamroeun Arun, the former James Buchanan chief administrator – from being blamed for the murders. I had already seen one decent man brought down by Medicare fraud, and I wanted to make sure for myself that we were right this time, even though the evidence left little doubt.

Marjorie gasped. *Arun was dead?* She was stunned at the thought, but it was too much to handle just then. Her mind was on a more immediate concern: Why not just tell them that what they want to know now, that Peter had confessed to her? But that would be betraying her husband, and she could not bring herself to do it.

She continued watching as the rest of the room, including her own possessions, were searched, which took another 15 minutes.

Petrelli looked at Chief Inspector Tyroler, then at Charlotte and Lewis. "Nothing here," he said. "Not that we expected to find anything."

"Mrs. Kenyon," Charlotte said, turning to Marjorie. "How long can this go on? Your life must be a living nightmare."

Marjorie said nothing. Charlotte, Lewis, Petrelli and Tyroler all looked at each other.

"Perhaps we should go down and see Dr. Kenyon in the dining room," Tyroler said. "And bring Mrs. Kenyon with us."

A thought crossed Petrelli's mind: It was possible that Peter might cause some kind of disturbance in a public place like the dining room, perhaps even threaten another guest. Tyroler apparently had the same thought.

"We should try and get him out of the dining room and into a less public place," Tyroler said, "so we can talk to him without disruption." He turned to Marjorie. "Perhaps you can help us there, Mrs. Kenyon?"

The door to the room opened before Marjorie could reply. Peter was in the doorway, a look of shock upon his face. He took in the scene for a second, then bolted down the hall toward the stairwell.

50

Peter burst through the revolving door of the Hotel Sacher's main entrance and into the sunlight. They were on to him and he had to get away. But what to do and where to go? He put his mind to work: Short term, he needed to elude them. Long term, he would have to find a way to leave the country and go elsewhere. He realized now that he couldn't go with Marjorie. If only to protect her, he would have to leave her behind. His mind leaped from subject to subject. He had been shocked to see Charlotte Westbrook in his room. What was an HHS Inspector General doing in Vienna?

He hurried across the street toward the State Opera House, near the Hofburg. He could lose them in the city, he was sure. And maybe going ahead with his plans to see the Hofburg and the Lipizzaners was the perfect place. Since Marjorie knew that he might go there, it was the last place she would lead them.

Or would she? Had Marjorie talked? Had she turned him in? *Did she betray me?* He didn't know, but if she had, then it was all over. The idea of spending the rest of his days in prison filled him with horror. Better they execute me. But not without a fight. *I'm a good man*, he told himself, *a good man.* I was forced into this because of blackmail, and the only reason they were able to blackmail me was because of the government and that wretched Westbrook woman.

He decided to trust that Marjorie would not turn him in. The massive State Opera House was before him, beautiful in its cream-colored walls and blue roof. Pedestrians were already milling about the square. He ran alongside the building and around a corner, which he knew would take him to the Hofburg.

Charlotte, Lewis, Petrelli and Tyroler, holding Marjorie by the arm, met in the hotel lobby. Petrelli was somewhat out of breath, having just raced down five floors. Tyroler radioed for additional men, now that Peter had apparently escaped.

"If he does not have something to hide, Mrs. Kenyon, then why run away?"

"That does not mean he is guilty, Chief Inspector," Marjorie shot back. "I realize this is Austria and you have your own laws. But in America a man is innocent until proven guilty."

Charlotte silenced Tyroler with a look that said, let me talk to her. "You're right, Marjorie," she said, trying to bond with her. "He *is* innocent until proven guilty. But let's not fool ourselves. We found the murder weapon in your house. He took out large quantities of the drug used to kill two of the victims. And now he has run away from us. He certainly seems like he has something to hide."

Marjorie was dealing with what seemed like a million conflicting emotions and thoughts racing through her head. *What to do?*

"Marjorie," Charlotte continued. "Where might Peter have gone? Even without a gun, he might still be a danger to other people, tourists, pedestrians. Who knows what a man in his condition will do? You don't want more people killed, do you?"

Marjorie shook her head. That was the last thing she wanted.

"What happened to Arun?" she asked.

"The police suspected him of the murders that Dr. Kenyon committed, Marjorie, and he killed himself. Shot himself in the head."

Marjorie felt herself getting sick. Arun dead by his own hand? And because they suspected him of the murders that her husband had committed? *This could not continue.*

"Marjorie," Charlotte continued, "Peter might even be a danger to himself."

"I don't know where he is!" Marjorie said. "We were talking this morning about going to the military museum, but then changed our minds and were thinking about the Hofburg and the Lipizzaners. But Peter probably won't go to either place. Because he is probably wondering," she said, choking back a sob, "if I turned him in."

"Then your husband confessed to you that he killed the three students?" Petrelli asked.

"I have said no such thing!" Marjorie said. "And I won't say anything more about that until we have an attorney."

"Alright, Marjorie," Charlotte said, "but at least help us find him now. Where do you think he might be?"

Marjorie paused. She didn't want to take that next step and help them capture her husband. But part of her did. Peter could not go on like this. The situation could not continue. What if he gets panicky and hurts someone else … or himself, like poor Arun? I cannot be the cause of that. I have the knowledge to stop him now, before this gets any worse.

"Alright," she said. "My guess is he went to see the horses at the Hofburg. But I could be wrong. He is going to guess that I did *not* tell you."

Tyroler frowned. Vienna was a big city. "Madam, I am going to guess that you are correct, so we are going to the Hofburg. But you also mentioned the military museum, so I will radio to have some men search there, as well. And if he went somewhere else, it will take longer to find him, but we will. I am going to issue – what is it you Americans call it on your television police shows, an 'all-points bulletin'? – for him. Let us hope that this does not end in tragedy, for anyone, including your husband."

Peter could be shot by the police, Marjorie realized. He could get killed. And she would have literally signed his death warrant herself.

"You'd better take me with you," she said. "If there is a problem with him, I may be able to talk him out of it."

Tyroler nodded. "Yes, I think that is a good idea."

The centuries-old Hofburg Palace, the home of the Hapsburg emperors, occupies several blocks in the heart of old Vienna. Charlotte, Lewis, Petrelli, Tyroler and Marjorie now walked onto the Hofburg grounds. More than just one building, the Hofburg is comprised of several, with some groups of buildings containing cobblestone courtyards. Not all the buildings are open to the public. But those that are show how the royal family lived, including sets of china, crystal and silver they used for various occasions, some of the original furniture, paintings and more. The building that contained the ring where the Lipizzaners performed bordered a courtyard. Red flags hung from above announced it as the home of the world-famous horses.

"Chief Inspector, should we have the building emptied, to protect people?" Lewis asked. Scores of tourists visited the Lipizzaners during their daily shows.

Tyroler paused. "I have been giving that question serious thought on the way over here, and I think not. There is a risk of casualty to innocents, yes, and that must be avoided at all costs. But there is also a risk of casualty to innocents if Dr. Kenyon gets away from us again. Given his likely state of mind, he might hurt someone elsewhere in the city, or even try to take hostages."

He looked at Marjorie. "Does he have any weapons with him? A gun? A knife? Anything?"

Marjorie shook her head. "Not that I know of."

"Let us hope not, but we should also prepare for the worst." Turning to the others, he described the building. "I could empty the building. There are several exits and while I could place men at each one, there is the possibility he could still somehow get out. Or he could hide somewhere once he is made aware. No, I think the best chance we have is to approach him unawares and simply take him into custody. The chances of this approach succeeding increase if his attention is on the horses." He paused. "*And* if he sees Mrs. Kenyon approach him first. After all, they were due to come here today."

They want to use me as bait, Marjorie thought. But what choice did she have? There were lives at stake. Let's get Peter where he and everyone else will be safe. Then they would get an attorney and pursue whatever legal avenues were available to them. But no one else will be hurt.

"What is it you want me to do?" she asked.

Inside the building, the ring where the horses perform can be reached by two centuries-old steep and narrow circular stone staircases, each on opposite sides of the building. There are two visitor galleries that line the ring, one midway up the staircases, and the other near the top. Each spiral staircase makes several complete circles before reaching either gallery. Aside from the walls, only a metal handrail, doubtless added in recent years as the place became a tourist attraction, helps provide balance to those who climb. Along the way up one encounters recesses, each about the size of a human being, that had been cut into the stone walls, where uniformed guards must have stood watch in the days when the Hapsburgs ruled.

Tyroler suggested they begin with the uppermost gallery as there would be less chance of being seen by Dr. Kenyon. If they began on the lower gallery, there was a good chance that Dr. Kenyon, if he was on the upper gallery, might see them as he watched the horses below. But if he was on the lower gallery, it was unlikely he would be looking up. The man does seem to know his work, Charlotte thought.

Tyroler, Charlotte and Marjorie took the stair on the right side, while Lewis and Petrelli climbed the stair on the left. A few tourists were also climbing, and one or two passed them going down. They passed the entrance to the first visitors' gallery, and Charlotte looked out. It was much larger than she had expected, and far more crowded. Spectators filled up the seats along the approximately three-foot-high stone-carved railing that bordered the gallery edge. Others were standing, either in sections along the railing where there were no chairs, or behind those already sitting, and looking down at the horses. A wood-planked walkway behind the seats allowed visitors to walk the full length of each rectangular gallery, which approximated the shape of the oval ring below. In the ring, she caught a glimpse of colorfully uniformed riders on beautiful white horses on a dirt floor, with the horses being directed to walk sideways, or stand on their hind legs. Above she saw the other gallery, perhaps somewhat less crowded than this one. Tourists were taking pictures of the horses below.

When both parties emerged at the upper gallery, three on one side of the gallery and two on the other, Tyroler and Petrelli signaled each other from their opposite vantage points to slowly move forward. Charlotte, moving forward with Marjorie and Tyroler, scanned the crowd in front of her, trying to see if Peter was there. She could see Petrelli and Lewis doing the same on the other side.

Then Marjorie froze.

Ahead of them, not more than five feet away, Peter stood, his side to them, as he leaned on the stone railing and watched the Lipizzaners going through their paces below. There were four horses, each with a uniformed rider on its back, circling the ring, their legs lifting high as they walked, their white flowing manes and tail adding to each horse's sheer majesty.

Tyroler put his hand on Marjorie's shoulder and his finger to his lips. Not yet, he cautioned. He signaled to Petrelli and Lewis to come around from their side of the gallery. He, Charlotte and Marjorie then leaned back against the building wall, waiting as Petrelli and Lewis made the journey to just the other side of Peter, where he cautioned them to stop.

"Now," he whispered to Marjorie. "I want you to walk up to him and put him at ease, just as if you had met him late."

"But he remembers seeing me with you."

Tyroler shook his head. "Your husband is living a dual reality, Mrs. Kenyon. He wants to believe that life can go on as normal. When he sees you, and thinks you are alone, he will be reassured. I have seen this before. Once he is reassured, we will approach him from behind, handcuff him, and take him into custody."

Marjorie nodded. It seemed reasonable and, more importantly, it would leave Peter unharmed. She took a step toward her husband, when suddenly a visitor next to her began a series of seemingly uncontrollable coughs. Peter turned to help her and, still not seeing Marjorie, touched the woman's arm.

"Do you speak English?" he asked. The woman nodded. "I am a doctor, and you might be having an allergic reaction to the dust in here. I suggest you go down—"

Peter stopped mid-sentence when he saw Marjorie.

"Darling, what are you doing here? I'm so glad you made it."

Marjorie walked forward to Peter and touched his arm, but it was too late. With his eyes now facing away from the horses, he saw the others.

"What? Marge, you came here with them?"

"Peter Kenyon, I am placing you under arrest by the Austrian Federal Police, operating in coordination with the police force of the District of Columbia, for murder," said Tyroler. "You will please come along quietly for questioning."

"No!" Peter yelled taking several rapid steps back. Some of the tourists nearby who had heard and seen this encounter began heading for the doors, pushing and shoving those in their way. Others watched.

"Achtung!" Tyroler shouted in German to the crowd, "Everyone please proceed quietly down the stairs. The situation is under control."

Spectators began moving out of both galleries, but it would take some time, given the crowds and the narrowness of the staircases. Below, the Lipizzaners and their riders had ceased their performances, but stayed in the ring, watching the scene above.

"Why are you telling them to leave? I'm not going to hurt anyone," Peter said.

"If that is the case, why not just come along quietly?" Tyroler replied, holding out his hand.

"You're not going to take me. You're not." He saw Petrelli. "You have to understand. There were extenuating circumstances. She," he said, pointing to Westbrook, "drove me to this!"

"Peter, please, it's all over," Marjorie said. "Let's get through this, then find a lawyer. I will stand beside you, I promise."

"Like you did when you led them here?"

"I did it for you, Peter, for us." She took a step closer, but Peter quickly stepped back, hitting the three-foot stone railing. Too quickly, because his momentum carried his torso over the railing and, trying to maintain his balance, he fell over it to the ring below as Marjorie and the other gasped. There was the sudden noise of a commotion below, and they could hear the sounds of horses neighing and riders trying to get the horses under control. Peter had landed in the ring, right in front of one of the Lipizzaners, startling it and forcing it to rear up on its hind legs. Peter apparently could not get up, but was struggling to move. As the rider tried to get the horse under control, it lashed out with its hooves, kicking Peter in the head.

"No! Peter!" Marjorie screamed. She ran down the stairs, pushing through the remaining visitors, the others close behind her. Tyroler got them onto the dirt floor of the ring, where the riders now had the horses under control. Marjorie ran over to Peter and called his name, but there was no response.

Tyroler bent down and examined him, then listened to his heart and checked for a pulse. He looked at Marjorie.

"I am most sorry, Mrs. Kenyon."

As Marjorie wept over Peter's body, Tyroler looked at the others.

"None of this was necessary," he said. "He could have come along quietly."

"I am afraid, Chief Inspector," Charlotte said, "that Dr. Kenyon felt otherwise."

51

"I've been waiting for your visit, my dear," Penelope said with a broad smile as she ushered Charlotte into her office. "But I suppose with all the press attention and plaudits you've been getting, it's been difficult to find time."

Charlotte settled into her usual spot on the couch while Penelope did the same in her chair. As usual, the psychiatrist was wearing an odd collection of clothes: denim vest over formal blouse, men's pants and boots. Her hair was hanging long today, but her eyes still loomed large through her oversize glasses, her lips this time a bright shade of pink.

Charlotte could only nod her head. Since the return from Vienna a week ago, she had been feted by the press, with articles dissecting how she and Lewis had "cracked" the case and how they did it despite opposition from within their own Administration and from Congress. Even the district police, due to Petrelli's presence in Vienna, got some good coverage, although one insightful article by Eileen Ashburton in the *Post* wondered where the police would have gone with the case, given their belief that Arun was the killer, had Charlotte not been involved. Activities that Charlotte had been criticized for before, such as the use of her laser gun, were now "colorful" sides of her "exciting and resourceful personality." Profiles of her and her father began to appear, with several noting how she was stepping out from his shadow. Television news magazines were planning profiles of her.

HHS Secretary Balcom, meanwhile, had seemingly overnight turned from Charlotte's critic to her number-one supporter, with encouragement from the White House, no doubt. The chairman of the Senate Appropriations Committee declared her "a jewel in an otherwise ho-hum Administration." Charlotte liked to think that Mack was sincere when he said that.

"Most likely our budget is secure for the next few years," Lewis told her. Despite the favorable publicity that he, too, was receiving, he seemed to take solace in returning to what was familiar and comfortable – his ceaseless efforts to crack down on Medicare fraud. And knowing that one of the results of their involvement in solving the murders was that the OIG budget would be left alone – or perhaps even increased – was reward enough for him. But Charlotte was also pleased to see that Lewis, although he would never admit it, was perhaps a little more impressed with himself and his own involvement in the case. And there was one especially touching moment that she would never forget. On the flight back from Vienna, Lewis, sitting next to her, had touched her arm. He seemed somewhat hesitant before he spoke, as if unsure of himself.

"I just want to say one thing, Charlotte," he finally said, somewhat haltingly, and she was surprised to see moisture in his eyes. "Well done, well done."

Charlotte felt her own eyes moisten just thinking about that moment. When the two returned to the OIG offices, Stadler, the other attorneys and employees greeted them with a celebratory party, complete with champagne and a cake that read, "The game is afoot!" with a picture of Charlotte in a Sherlock Holmes-style deerstalker hat and pipe, and Lewis beside her as Dr. Watson. "I think the attorneys here have finally accepted you," Lewis said to her, then added, "most of them, anyway."

But through all this, troubling questions remained on Charlotte's mind. This was the first chance she had had to turn to Penelope for answers, and maybe for some therapy herself.

"Where to start?" Charlotte asked, as she sipped some chamomile tea. "Peter and Marjorie Kenyon. Both so tragic, each in a unique way. I am really not that troubled by Dr. Kenyon's almost-last words that I, or OIG, am ultimately responsible for the murders he committed. That's nonsense. He was, in fact, breaking the law, as was the university, and we were right to investigate and now to prosecute. That is our job and, as Lewis is constantly reminding me, we are safeguarding the public's money. Still ...." Charlotte seemed troubled.

"You believe he was a good man and a good doctor before all this happened."

"I do. And by all accounts, he was. But is the government to blame when it undertakes a legitimate investigation and someone cracks?"

"Of course not, Charlotte. And let's not forget that what really made Dr. Kenyon lose his path was not your investigation, much as he might have hated it, but the blackmail Scott Karakas put him under. But you know what, my dear? Even that was no excuse to commit murder. The fact is that many, many people live far more desperate lives or wind up in far more trouble than Dr. Kenyon did, and they do not go out and commit murder. It is important to remember that. Nothing that happened to Dr. Kenyon justified his taking of three lives."

Charlotte nodded.

"But," Charlotte said, "it also does not take away the ring of truth from some of the things he said, about trusting doctors to make correct decisions, how the government second-guesses them, and so forth. The government says it doesn't do those things, Penelope, and I really try not to, but the fact is that we do. Like it or not, we are taking some control of the medical process. And is that really the government's business? And there are dozens of other examples."

Penelope nodded. "The rights of society, as represented by the government, versus the rights of the individual. Or, looked at another way, the rights of individuals to make informed decisions about what they do versus the government interfering with those rights. It's one of the central conflicts of the age, my dear, and there is no way we are going to solve it anytime soon."

"It does make me a little more sensitive to what and how we investigate, though," Charlotte said.

"Which should make you a better Inspector General."

"I hope so." She shook her head. "Some aspects of the case remain so bizarre. I still haven't totally figured out, for instance, what role the handcuffs I found in Dana Brentano's room played in this, or if they were involved at all. Was Scott Karakas such an abuser that he would handcuff Dana when they had sex? And did she enjoy that kind of sadomasochism?"

"Charlotte, this may come as a shock to you, but I believe you have that backwards. It's not only men who like to take control, including in sexual situations. Everything you have told me about that pair of handcuffs, combined with the results of Mr. Karakas' autopsy and the nature of his last blackmail request to Peter Kenyon, tells me that it was Dana Brentano who was dominant in that regard, not Mr. Karakas."

"You're saying that she used the handcuffs on him?"

Penelope nodded. "That would be my informed guess."

"But there was nothing in either of their backgrounds to indicate that they were both into, what would you call it, female domination."

"Oh, but there is. Factors that would not necessarily lead to that kind of sexual activity, but in their case, did. Let's look at their backgrounds. On the one hand, you have a young man who has been driven all his life by his father's demands and expectations to do things that he really didn't want to do. You told me how he had blackmailed a high school teacher, and how he had tried to coerce a girl to get an abortion. But you also told me that his father pushed him to make those demands.

"The result was that Scott Karakas may have found that being a bully would get him what he needed, but part of the conflict within him, Charlotte, was that he really didn't like being a bully. Fear of his father, his early successes with that technique and, frankly, some lack of character, left him relying on it. And look at his female relationships. Before Dana, every one sounds like it was just physical, with no emotional involvement. Until Dana came along and, at some point, took charge of the relationship and Scott himself. Can you imagine what a relief that must have been for him, to have someone else take control and make it able for him to just let go?

"Then, let's look at Dana. By all respects, she seemed a bright young woman, very wholesome and almost the all-American girl next door. Yet, from what you have told me and what I've read, her parents didn't want her becoming a doctor, didn't even want to send her to medical school, because they were a generation older than most parents and felt that being a doctor was no career for a woman. Meanwhile, they had high ambitions for her brothers. Her future, her ambitions, were in the hands of others. Can you imagine how she felt, with her future out of her own control, and in the hands of parents who were so old they were even behind the generation most of her friends' parents belonged to? The unfairness of it!

"And to make it worse, like so many young women, the boyfriends she sought out were like her father, in her case stern but loving types, and, as with her father, she found herself constantly wanting to win their approval and not always getting it.

"Then along comes Scott, who at first seems to fit the pattern of her past boyfriends. He takes charge immediately and, as usual, the relationship begins on an entirely sexual level. But somewhere along the way, something happened, I am not sure what, but Dana must have latched onto something Scott said. Maybe he was opening up to her a little and telling her about how he hated some the things he had done to get his way and wished he didn't have to 'take charge' all the time.

"Somewhere in her psyche, she saw that as an opening, and the nature of the relationship changed, with her probably gradually taking charge more and Scott giving in. It probably began with innocent things, where they would go that night, things like that, but somewhere along the way, began to include how they had sex. She took control. And she found that Scott liked it. And she also found, probably to her surprise, that she liked it too. Here was a man who would follow *her* wishes. As they got bolder, they probably experimented a bit, and I suspect that by this point, Dana was the one choosing the activities. The handcuffs were just one of them. Who knows what else they tried?

"The interesting thing to me, though, is not the sex, but the relationship itself. Because it was only when their positions were reversed – with Dana being dominant and Scott being submissive – that the other parts of the relationship, the feelings of closeness and intimacy, even romance, began to take shape. That was when they really became involved with each other." Penelope stopped and sipped some tea herself. "Who knows? They may have one day gotten married, had not Dr. Kenyon intervened."

"So she asked Scott to blackmail Dr. Kenyon for her?"

"Why not? By that point, she was enjoying having Scott, who everyone else saw as a leader among students, under her control. She wanted to see if she could get him to get her the same benefits that he had gotten for himself."

"And fear of getting caught?"

"The risk for her was small. One, she could have denied that she had ever asked Scott to do any such thing. And the truth of the matter is that we have no proof, and most likely never will, that she, in fact, did. Which is not to say that it isn't true, because I believe that it most likely is. And beyond that, Dana was probably at that point so caught up in her new sensations and feelings that she felt she could do no wrong."

"So the ligature marks on Scott's neck. The police always figured that it was the killer who did it, perhaps in a struggle with Scott."

"A reasonable conclusion. But my guess would be that the hands that made those marks were Dana Brentano's during the heat of sex and control."

This was a lot for Charlotte to take in but, as always, she found Penelope's insights convincing.

"The person we are leaving out of this is Nicholas Rosen."

Penelope nodded. "The classic third wheel, even in murder. In Mr. Rosen, Charlotte, the truth is right before us. It was just as it seemed. He admired Scott, wanted to be Scott, someone he saw as admirable, charming, a leader. And he wanted to have Dana, who he saw as pretty, sweet, probably nurturing, the classic all-American girlfriend. Nicholas Rosen himself, as far as I can tell, had no secrets along the nature of those kept by Scott and Dana. He just happened to be their friend when it all went down. I suppose one could criticize him for bad judgment and maybe bad character assessment in his perceptions of Scott and Dana, but, in fairness to him, everyone who knew those two had the same assessment. The sad thing is, of course, that if Nicholas, genuinely broken up by their deaths, had got what he thought he wanted, he would not have been happy. He would never have done any of the things that Scott did, nor would he truly have been happy with Dana as his girlfriend."

"So he was killed for nothing."

"They were all killed for nothing, in the sense that none of the murders was justified. But in Nicholas' case, especially so. Because if Dr. Kenyon killed him out of fear that Scott had told Nicholas about the blackmail and Dr. Kenyon's breaking of the Medicare rules, his fear was probably misplaced. There is no evidence that Nicholas knew anything. Certainly if he had, he would have told Detective Petrelli rather than go to jail himself.

"Again, as with so many things Scott and Dana were involved with, the issue of control was paramount. Scott and Dana were playing their control games with each other, but Nicholas was not part of that. They already had him under their control, what with the way he was hanging on to them as friends and role models. So there was no need for them to tell him more. In fact, by intentionally not telling him, they were making choices for him, in effect exerting control in that way.

"More than anyone in this entire sad story, Charlotte, Nicholas Rosen's death was the most unfortunate. He was the classic wrong person in the wrong place at the wrong time, with the wrong people as friends."

"He wasn't the only one caught up in events beyond his control," Charlotte said. "There was Arun. I haven't told anyone about this, Penelope, although I think Lewis suspects, but I have some guilt about what happened to him."

"Yes. It was unfortunate that he got caught up in the murder investigation. His suicide was most tragic. But he was, it seems, deeply involved in the university hospital fraud."

"I would say more than involved. I would say he directed it," Charlotte said.

"Then why your guilt?"

Charlotte gave a half smile. "Why indeed? That's what I keep asking myself. Here's the thing, Penelope, that gets at the core of it all: Arun would not have killed himself were it not for the combination of the weight of the fraud investigation – knowing he was already found out, because we had found the second set of books by that time – and becoming a suspect in the murder investigation. I can't say for sure, but my gut tells me, since I got to know the man somewhat, that he might have been able to handle either one of those alone, but together they proved devastating."

"But he *was* guilty of actually directing the fraud."

"Yes, but he was also a man who had a deep personal code of honor and a proud family history. This is the thing. It's where society has put us today, all of us, me included. We put people in positions where they are forced to choose between personal integrity and government rules. Poor Arun. I imagine he was under incredible financial pressure to produce certain amounts of revenue and profits. But with the cutbacks we – not me personally, but the government – put in place on Medicare reimbursement, the university hospital was not getting what it needed to support itself. So what was he to do? Go bankrupt and tell all the students to go home?"

"So he stole," Penelope said. "And yes, from what you tell me, his family history played a great deal in his life. He must have had a tremendous internal struggle over what the right course of action was, probably involving a great deal of rationalization. In the end, it all caught up to him. He must have felt great shame. Then the murder investigation, which proved groundless..."

"And I'm put in charge of investigating men like that, men who are squeezed so tight by the government that they find themselves in a situation where they are forced to either steal or go out of business."

"Charlotte, you can't put the responsibility for all that on your shoulders."

"No?" asked Charlotte, a tear streaming down her cheek. "I suppose not."

"The truth is, we think we are in control, but when we are carrying out the policies of others, or when we have to live by those polices, we are not. You're not, and Arun wasn't. Few of us truly have control of our lives anymore, at least not to the degree people did, say, 50 or 60 years ago." She paused, studying Charlotte's face. "But it is you I am worried about right now, my dear. I can see that, despite all the plaudits you're getting, you are troubled."

"I just wish…I know this sounds little-girlish, Penelope," she said, "but if I can't tell you, who can I tell? You talk about control, and I've always taken a certain amount of pride in being in control of my own life. But now, in my early 40s, I think that maybe I have been fooling myself. I have no one significant in my life, Penelope, no one. And I think it's something I've done to myself. I didn't want to let anything or anyone get in the way of my career. And I've been very successful, haven't I?" she asked with a bitter laugh. "Except that I'm miserable."

"I know, Charlotte, I've seen it in you all along. The question I want you to ask yourself is this: Despite all your plans and ambitions, all your goals and achievements, are you really in control of your life? Is your life what you want it to be?"

The prosecution of James Buchanan University Hospital began officially the next month. After several depositions from key players, including Simon Proctor and Brenda Morehouse, a voluntary settlement was reached, saving the government the costs of prosecution and the university its defense costs and bad publicity. The university would repay Medicare $42.7 million, and also pay fines totaling about $5.3 million. In addition, it agreed to enter into a corporate integrity agreement with the government, part of which involved regular inspection by government auditors of its cost reports.

Paul Holden, the university hospital's compliance officer, was credited with saving the university from far higher penalties and helping individual doctors, such as Lyle Steadman, avoid Medicare exclusion. Dr. Steadman, it turned out, had also skirted the direct supervision rules. He paid $36,000 in fines, complaining the entire way, but he was able to continue to practice medicine. He eventually left for another hospital.

Dr. Jennifer Capaldi, who was found not to have done anything wrong, but who was sympathetic to the university and its plight, surprised everyone and gave up the direct practice of medicine to take over as chief administrator a few months after Arun's suicide. Apparently her loyalty to Arun's memory was such that she wanted responsibility for cleaning up the hospital's practices. No one was sure just what occurred in her first meeting with Wilmotte, but she was seen leaving the building rather grim-faced.

Simon Proctor managed to avoid any financial penalties when James Buchanan settled the case, but he left the university anyway, if only out of embarrassment. Not one to have close friends, it was reported by Eileen Ashburton in a "Where are they now?" piece that ran in the *Post* a few months after the settlement, that he took a job in the San Francisco Bay Area. There was no word on whether he kept his office door locked.

Carla Calloway collected over $8 million from the settlement, but not without her attorney having to file suit against the government to get it. Once the settlement between OIG and the university hospital was reached, the government began to quibble with her about just how much of its successful prosecution was due to what she had told them, and how much the government had found out on its own. The more of the case that the government could say it found out without her help, the less it would have to pay her. In the end, she got most of what she wanted. She did not find her continued work at the hospital particularly wanted, however. Despite no official retaliation moves against her, the social ostracism took its mental toll. Eventually, she and her husband sold their house and moved to Florida.

Marjorie Kenyon returned to Washington after Peter's death to see to his funeral, but didn't stay in the area long. She resigned her position at her architectural firm and relocated to Seattle, where she had family, eventually starting her own small boutique architectural firm. After a shaky start, she began getting clients and by all reports was doing well.

Gregory Betorin's parents, after reading of the case and Scott's history, had a rapprochement with their son and embraced both Helen and their grandchildren. They supported Gregory financially as he found his way back to law school. He also got together with Carrie Pankow for lunch one day and renewed their friendship. The publicity from the case served as a starting point for Carrie to tell her husband about her past. Her husband, Carrie found out, was interested only in her and their future, and his main concern was the strain she had put herself under by keeping her past wrapped up inside herself for so long.

Richard and Amy Karakas continued with their lives as best they could. They still had their other children. But they went out less often and, when they did, those who saw them and spoke with them said that Richard was not quite the same, that a certain confidence was gone from his personality. Amy just seemed angry.

At the *Washington Post*, Eileen settled back into her health care beat, her foray into crime reporting over. Mike was pleased, both with the growth in Eileen's abilities – he planned to give her another big story soon – and in the kick in the ass that her reporting had delivered to the reporters on the police desk, who were now constantly looking for ways to show their worth.

Detective Alphonse Petrelli Jr. drove up the New Jersey Turnpike. The case was over, he knew, but there was one more stop he had to make. It had been an exhausting and frustrating case, perhaps the most difficult in his long career with the D.C. police. And, while he had learned a great deal that would prove useful to him in future cases, in many ways this case had been among the least satisfying.

He had been wrong so often. First with Nicholas Rosen, then with Chamroeun Arun. Both of them were now dead and he couldn't help but blame himself a little for each death. Less so with Nick, since he was murdered, but he blamed himself for his pursuit of the young man, making Nick's last few days miserable when all Nick wanted was to grieve for his lost friends. More so with Arun, since it was shortly after his arrest that Arun had taken his own life. Sure, he told himself repeatedly, Arun was under pressure from a lot of other quarters. But the suspicion that he committed murder combined with the fraud investigation had pushed him over the edge. Which one was more the catalyst for his final act, Petrelli would never know.

Petrelli consoled himself with the fact that in police work, you pursue the evidence where it leads and, by this standard, he had been correct in his pursuit of both Nick and Arun. Any good police officer would have done the same. But did I have to be so relentless, he asked himself. Wasn't pressure on me from the mayor's office and the media also a factor?

He also had to deal with the fact that he would not have been able to solve the case without Charlotte, and while his work alongside her had left him with considerable respect for her abilities, he also resented the fact that her help was needed at all. The press had noted his contribution, as well as that of Chief Inspector Tyroler and the Austrian Federal Police, but most of the attention had gone to Charlotte. And he couldn't really disagree. She was the one who had linked the fraud with the murders, she had discovered the motives behind the blackmail, and Lewis had discovered how Kenyon had taken out extra amounts of succinylcholine, leading him to suggest that they search gun shops in Dr. Kenyon's hometown to see if he had purchased a firearm there.

Damn it, he told himself. He had spent his time chasing two innocent men.

Arun's body, according to his wishes, had been cremated, with the ashes sent back to Cambodia to be placed in the family crypt, alongside those of his parents. Petrelli had inquired about making a donation, and sent a check to an organization representing the victims of the Khmer Rouge.

Now, as he pulled into Brooklyn, he thought about Nick's parents. He had sent them a personal letter expressing his condolences over the death of their son, but they had never responded. Did they blame him for his pursuit of Nick as the killer? He would never know. Certainly he blamed himself.

He got out of the car at the small Jewish cemetery and followed the directions until he reached Nick's monument. There, with freshly tended grass, was Nick's final resting place. The monument, after giving Nick's name and dates of living, said "So much promise ... so much loss."

Petrelli bowed his head, then, as is the custom, took a stone from the ground and placed it on Nick's tombstone.

Charlotte and Mack left the Georgetown restaurant and began what had become their usual stroll down M Street. They had begun seeing more of each other in the weeks since her return from Vienna and the resolution of the murder case. Charlotte found an ease and comfort in her old friend's company, and she sensed that he did in hers. Despite their relative positions in government, as a man and a woman, they connected.

"I suppose I had better get used to you as a celebrity," Mack said. Three people at the restaurant, usually frequented by patrons who were respectful of other diners' privacy, had stopped at their table to compliment

Charlotte on a job well done. A nod in Mack's direction showed that two of them had recognized him, but it was clearly Charlotte who was the center of their attention.

"It won't last," Charlotte said. "This is my 15 minutes of fame. In no time at all, everyone's attention will move on to the next news story."

They kept walking, Charlotte's arm tucked inside Mack's, viewing the displays in the windows, watching the other people strolling, and, they both knew, heading their way to get what neither one of them needed, an ice cream cone. Another two blocks and they would be at Gibson's, their favorite.

"I've been enjoying our time together," Charlotte said, breaking the silence. She still found herself to be not the high-powered HHS Inspector General in Mack's presence, but simply a woman in the company of a man she … what? She wasn't sure, but she wanted to find out.

"I have too," said Mack. "I always enjoy being with you."

What was he saying? That he was wrestling with the same feelings? She had to know. She stopped, turned toward him, and put her arms around him.

Mack laughed in surprise. "What are you doing?"

"I'm taking control," Charlotte said.

"Of my life?"

"No," Charlotte replied, drawing his face to hers, then beginning a kiss that she fully intended to represent more than friendship. "Of mine."

About the author

Robert Sperber has spent more than a decade reporting and writing on health care, including fraud and abuse against Medicare, for publications reaching the nation's hospitals, physicians and others. He lives in the Washington D.C. metropolitan area with his wife, two daughters and two cats.

www.ingramcontent.com/pod-product-compliance
Lightning Source LLC
Chambersburg PA
CBHW032225010726
47494CB00002B/352